Praise for *Night Navigation*:

"The strength of this story pulls Howard's readers along, unable to turn away from a fierce mother and son who are determined to negotiate the future."

—*New York Times Book Review*

"What makes this novel shine is the writer's seemingly effortless ability to bring to the page living, breathing characters, each deeply flawed but trying . . . The story unfolds easily, though it is anything but an easy story. Yet in the abundance of evident pathology there is never a cheap shot: There's no attempt at tear-jerking, no poor-me-look-what-I've-been-through attitude underlying Howard's spare prose, which makes the telling all the more powerful."

—*Chronogram Magazine*

"Harrowing . . . Howard's strength, besides lapidary language, is the ability to build scenes around quotidian activities . . . Stark scenarios will be cathartic for readers who have dealt with them first hand, and profoundly cautionary for those who haven't."

—*Kirkus* (starred review)

"Howard's gripping tale lays bare the marrow of familial love—its messy desperation and its stubborn, enduring beauty."

—Maud Casey, author of *The Man Who Walked Away*

"Ginnah Howard navigates the precarious lives of her people with searing compassion and devastating honesty, opening our hearts to the dark wonder of shared grief and the flickering hope of forgiveness."

—Melanie Rae Thon, author of *The Voice of the River*

Rope & Bone

A Novel in Stories

Rope & Bone is Book 1 of a trilogy. Book 2, *Night Navigation* (Houghton Mifflin Harcourt 2009), focuses on Del and her son, Mark Merrick. Book 3, *Doing Time Outside* (Standing Stone Books 2013), turns back toward the Morlettis: Carla and her daughter and son, Tess and Rudy. Each of the novels is written to stand alone.

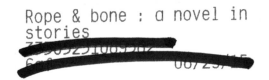
Ginnah Howard
Rope & Bone
A Novel in Stories

Rope & Bone: A Novel in Stories © 2014 Ginnah Howard
www.GinnahHoward.com

This book is a work of fiction. The names, characters, and incidents portrayed in the book are the product of the author's imagination and should not be construed as a factual account of real lives and events.

Published by

Illume Writers & Artists

PO Box 86, Gilbertsville, NY 13776

Printed in the United States of America

Author's mailing address:
Ginnah Howard, P.O. Box 149, Gilbertsville, New York 13776

ISBN-13: 978-1500338947

Design by Jane Higgins
Cover by Ginnah Howard
Author photo by Rose Mackiewicz

Some of the stories in this novel appeared originally in the following magazines:

Tell Them in Changes; *Winter* in Permafrost; *Rescue* in Portland Review; *And We Sell Apples* and *Message* in Water~Stone Review; *Amends* in Ballyhoo Stories; *Circling* in Square Lake; *Castanets* in A Room of One's Own; *Rope & Bone* in Out of the Catskills and Beyond and Glens Falls Review; *ROADWORK* in Blueline; *Potato* in Natural Bridge; *True Romance* in Eleven Eleven Journal.

In Memory of My Grandmother
Amy V. Stalnaker

Rope & Bone: A Novel in Stories

Prologue: Two Women – 1984

Epilogue

1

Women and Men:

Rope and Bone.
Sunday and Saturday.
That and This.

He said, "It was our finest hour."
She wept.

Speaking in tongues
untranslatable,
they move in experimental space suits,
uneasy in the other's gravity.
(To say nothing of the difficulty of dancing.)

To be continued …

PROLOGUE

Two Women – 1984

Del Merrick knew something was wrong, but she didn't know what. A pulling to the left, a dragging. She felt it just as she turned onto Chicken Farm Road. She punched the off button on the radio and listened: a dull thumping, left front. Then she knew what it was even though she'd never had one and miles either way to any kind of help. Damnation.

She eased the car onto the shoulder. Just before it nosed over the embankment to tip into the brook below, she stopped. If someone took the corner wide … it'd be all over.

Should she put the emergency brake on? She knew there was a rule: Before jacking up your car, *set* the parking brake. Before jacking up your car, *do not set* the parking brake. Richard Larson always said, If you understand the concept, there's not that much to memorize. But she had no idea how *this* connected to *that* with what result. She shrugged, pulled up hard on the lever and got out. Dank. The bleak smell of November.

It sure was a flat. She surveyed the proof of her extrapolation: the front left wheel pushed into the flattened rubber, cushioned by a thick matting of sodden leaves. Though each year she'd watched at least one lanky car lover in her remedial English class do his demonstration speech on How to Change a Tire, actually getting down on her knees and pulling the damned thing off was a different matter. Instead of all the art and reading courses, she should have taken one in auto mechanics. She pulled her coat tight against the chill and glanced down the line of bare maples. Only the rush of dark water below for company. No gloves. She pushed her cold hands deep into her pockets.

Charlie Stokes, the man who brought her wood, lived off on a side road quite a ways back. Up ahead a mile or so lived a woman who sometimes roared by the cabin on the back of a huge motorcycle, wrapped around the body of a Hell's Angels sort of person. A Sophia Loren woman—maybe ten years younger than she was, with a daughter on her way to looking just like her mother. Margetti, Moretti? Maybe the man was her husband and he'd offer to change the tire or maybe she could use their phone to call Todd's garage. Still she disliked the thought of the groveling she'd have to do, the subtle male condescension: You never changed a tire before? Richard would say, Come on, Del, it's mostly common sense. 3:30. Dark soon. Well, give it a go; maybe it would come to her.

She tried to picture Terry Benson, the kid who demonstrated last year. First, get out the jack and your spare. God, she hoped her spare was all right. The last time it saw the light was when the Subaru salesman explained where everything was, over 100,000 miles ago. How come it looks so small? she'd asked. These compact cars just have a temporary tire to get to the gas station where you can have your flat fixed. But what if it's the middle of the night or there are only serveyourself jiffy-stops around? His look was kind.

She hoped it had air in it. She raised the trunk door, still listening for the sound of a speeding vehicle from the rear. Below the tattered carpet and heavy cardboard flooring, there it was, looking incongruously new and tidy, fastened in compactly with the jack. *Temporary Use Only* embossed on its clean black side. She pushed on it. It felt fat with air. She was grateful: Permanent seemed like far too much to ask at this point.

The spare tire and the shiny blue jack, folded in its open center, were held stationary by a long peg and a large wing nut. Del gripped the nut, the metal icy on her fingers. It did not give a hair. She tried again; then jammed her numbed hand into her pocket and concentrated on not crying. She walked away from the car a few feet and looked down into the darkening brook. Do not give up.

She tried again in the other direction. Nothing. Lifting the edge of her coat, she gripped the nut through the wool lining and turned counterclockwise with all her strength. Some man, in some factory, six years ago had given this nut one last turn for good measure and now she was standing on the side of a cold, deserted country road unable to get the tire out of the trunk, let alone change it.

Do not ever, in some moment hungry for the affection that the telling of such humiliating tales brings, unfold this as an ironic little anecdote to Richard. She got back in the car, turned on the engine and the heater, and spread her fingers over the lukewarm air. Something to free the jack. She looked in the glove compartment: one of her older son's broken drum sticks and a cupful of laundromat quarters. She got out and looked under the seats: a Mountain Dew bottle and wads of M&M wrappers, her younger son's contribution. And a can of dog food.

She walked back to the open trunk and banged the nut's left wing with the top of the can. It moved. She rammed again, unscrewed the nut and dropped it into her pocket. The jack and the protective lining, she placed on the ground by the flat. Pulling the little tire from its cavity, and beneath it, the—what did Terry call it?—the lug wrench, she carried the spare forward to lean against the front fender.

Her fingers curled for warmth, Del moved back a few steps and contemplated the tire, waiting for further instructions. The lug wrench. She slipped the flat end under the edge of the cap, twisted a little, did the same in a few more places, and the hubcap popped off and rolled to the edge of the road.

Then it came to her—a critical piece of advice: Loosen the lug nuts before you start to jack it up. She put the wrench on one of the bottom nuts, squared her feet, and pulled up. Absolutely nothing happened. She repeated the same approach with the other four nuts, each time giving a cry at what she hoped was the right moment. It was as though the nuts and the wheel were one.

She set the wrench neatly parallel to the jack. She retrieved the hubcap and leaned it against the spare. She tied her white scarf to her raised trunk and stood on the edge of the road, looking back toward Charlie Stokes's and then down the other way, toward the … motorcycle mama. Then she set off at an almost jog, her hands jammed in her pockets, her head into the wind.

Carla Morletti could not remember when she was supposed to turn the numbers upside down, when she was supposed to reduce them to the lowest common denominator. She read the problem again: *You have $53.97 for groceries this week. You have four people to feed three meals each day.* "Good luck," Carla said to the ceiling. *On average, how much do you have to spend for each person per meal?*

53.97; not 54 dollars. Clearly the person who made up this question needed help, or as her counselor would say was "carrying around a lot of free-floating hostility." God knows, she herself detested the 7s and the 9s.

Her final G.E.D exam, or as she liked to call it, the GD E, was only three days away; it was time to stop making jokes, time to stop imagining she had the pale little person who made up the test across from her in a counseling session. It was time to get what got turned upside down straight, and the 9s memorized once and for all.

Okay, there are seven days in the week and three meals a day. She wrote *21 meals* on her paper. There are four people. She crossed off the word *meals* and wrote down *4 x 21= 84.* $53.97 for 84 meals? Probably the test writer had the kind of father who said, Sit there until your plate's empty. Does the 53.97 go into the 84 or the 84 into the 53.97? Does it matter? She gambled on the meals into the money, consulted her multiplication flash cards, and remembered her counselor's You can do it, Carla.

"God," she said, looking heavenward, "what am I supposed to do with the 21 that's left over?" A banging came from the front. Maybe someone who knows when it's okay to round off.

The two women looked at each other through the glass. Both wary.

"Oh, it's you," Carla said as she opened the door, "the lady who lives in the log cabin without plumbing or electricity." Not a Jehovah's Witness. Not someone from social services.

"Sorry to bother you at dinner time," Del said, still breathless from the fast walk.

Carla stepped back and motioned Del inside. "For a minute, I thought you were God."

Del hesitated. The woman must be on something.

Carla opened the door further. "Come on in by the stove. I've always wondered about you, how you wash all that long hair without indoor plumbing for one thing. We call you Mystery Lady 2. What we really wonder is why you or the first lady ..."

"Sally—the woman I'm renting the cabin from …"

"… would want to go out in your yard to pump your water, use kerosene lamps? We used to think the lady—the woman you're renting from—might be one of the sixties radicals. You know: living there off the grid because she was undercover, but when you, a respectable school teacher, moved in, we figured we were wrong about that."

Del followed the woman back through the dark hallway into the warm kitchen.

"Oh," Del said, stopping in the doorway, surprised by a hair curler that floated in the air a few feet over the sink, two pink plastic prongs stabbed through the bristles and wire. Her scalp winced with the memory. A few inches above the curler hovered a carved bird—a swallow, its dark, burnished wings banked for a dive. Then she saw they were fastened to long strings attached to the beam. She gave the delicate branched tail of the bird a small push; she couldn't resist. The swallow's shadow glided across the back wall.

"How lovely," Del said, reaching up again to run her finger along the gleaming wing.

"Yeah," the woman said and then switched her finger back and forth, indicating the two objects floating above her head. "This and that. Something I've been thinking about."

Del waited for more words that would give some clue as to what on earth she meant, but instead the woman smiled and said, "I'm Carla. Carla Morletti."

"Del Merrick."

"I know who you are. Your son Aaron was in Rudy's class until Rudy got left back. Rudy said Aaron's gone to stay with his cousins in Massachusetts."

"Yes," Del said. "He thought he'd like a bigger high school." A flutter of questions darted through Del's mind: curler, swallow, this and that? But something about this woman, this Carla Morletti, said 'end of subject.' And she didn't want to talk about Aaron either.

An old beagle was dozing in a rocking chair. The dog gave Del a sleepy look. She held her hands to the stove. "I got a flat about a mile back and I can't get the lug nuts off. I wondered if there was someone here strong enough to get them started?"

"You have to jump on it," Carla said.

"What?"

"You have to jump on the wrench. All your weight will get them loose enough to turn."

"Maybe I should call the garage. If I could just use your phone."

"Temporarily out of service…" Carla said.

Del looked around the room hoping to see some evidence of a large hairy male who would step forth to rescue her. She was surprised by its order, unlike the jumble in the front yard. She was ready to grovel a little. It was getting dark. The car was practically in the road.

"Steve, that's my husband, isn't here," Carla said, as if reading Del's thoughts. She shrugged. "Temporarily out of the house … due to a fight."

Carla pulled her coat on. "It's better with two," she said.

Del cocked her head.

"To change the tire. Just let me tell my daughter I'm going. Rudy's not here or we'd drag him along, exploit his muscle."

"Tess," she called up the stairs. "Tess, answer me." The house was still. "Just a second. Have to find that kid."

Del could hear her moving from room to room saying, "Tess, this isn't funny. I'm going to help the woman who lives in the cabin change a flat. Tess, do you hear me?"

Del looked more closely at the kitchen. Fastened to the refrigerator, a child's drawing: red and black ghosts floating over rooftops and bare trees. On the window sill, a large pot of pink geraniums. The smell of oranges. She heard Carla come down the stairs.

"Just going to check the basement," Carla said from the hall. "She's getting even. Wants me to fear for her life."

Del bent to look inside a cardboard box that sat at the edge of the big kitchen table. She tipped the box to the light. A child's diorama. A fantasy kingdom. Drawn on the back wall with crayons, a brown and green forest. Glued in the foreground, a pink construction paper castle, a moat filled with blue-black water.

Carla returned. "Her bike's gone," she said. "Mad at me because I yelled at her when she kept pestering."

"This is wonderful," Del said. "See the unicorn just behind the trees."

Carla leaned down. "Look," she said, "the windows to the castle open and close." When she straightened, Del saw Carla's eyes had filled with tears.

"She wouldn't go to school today. She hates school. I couldn't get her on the bus. All day long she's been here working on this, bouncing around. I'm trying to study. I've got a big test Saturday. And she keeps saying to me, See this, Mamo. Look at this, Mamo. All day I say, Oh, that's nice, but I'm not really looking. Finally I say, 'Tess, couldn't you just vanish for a while?' Carla looked up at the clock. "That must have been two hours ago. You didn't see a kid on a bike? Ten. Looks a lot like me. A big mouth."

"No, I didn't see anyone."

"Quick let's go change your tire. You got a spare, a flashlight?"

Del nodded.

"After that maybe you could drive me around the back roads to look for Tess."

Del thought of the temporary tire. But what if we have to go looking for a missing child who makes beautiful unicorns? she might have asked the salesman. "Sure," she said to Carla.

"We'll have to walk to where you're parked. My car's ... temporarily indisposed due to an unknown cause."

Del thought of the dented Maverick pulled onto the front yard with the hood up. "Why do the men who assemble cars tighten everything so much you have to be Hercules to get anything off?"

Carla laughed. "Maybe it's just the moving down the road that does it."

Del leaned toward Carla and squinted.

Carla looked down at her papers. Then she turned to Del and touched her arm. "Say, I'll bet you understand about rounding off."

"Rounding off?"

"Never mind," said Carla. "Let's go do the tire. Find Tess. And then maybe you'll know about feeding a family of four on $53.97."

Del shook her head like she had water in her ear.

"Tess is wily. My guess: once she feels her revenge is as heavy as my neglect, she'll come flying through that door. Got to leave her a note," Carla said. On a piece of yellow paper, Carla wrote in large purple letters: *Back soon. I love you. Mamo XXX.* She set the paper on top of the fantasy kingdom. Then she checked the stove and opened the back door, urging Del to go ahead. "Guard the place, Lola," Carla told the sleeping dog as she pulled the door to.

They stood on the porch looking out into the darkness.

"Chicken Farm Road," Carla said. "Not in your wildest, right? Oh, I could tell you stories. Me, drawing hearts on my notebooks, writing Mrs. So-and-So over and over from different angles. Chicken Farm Road was not the address I had in mind."

Del leaned toward Carla's voice. "Funny, I never thought about the marriage part. I daydreamed about having a hope chest and then that I was expecting. Always wearing a flowing maternity top, covered with little violets."

"You're kidding?" Carla took a few steps forward and looked up at the sky. "No moon, no stars. Better use your flashlight."

Del moved to Carla's side. "Like I said, I've got one, but it's in the car. It wasn't dark when I left."

Carla laughed. "My story exactly." She reached out a hand to steer Del to the right. "Best to avoid Tess's tiger pit."

They moved slowly toward the road, pulled into their clothes against the cold.

Carla stopped. "Okay, I can tell by the ruts we've come to the gravel. We can manage from here. Let me give her just one good shout." She turned and called: "Tess." The word bounded back at them from the dark, but beyond that, there was only the wind, the rustle of a few last leaves breaking the stillness of the November night.

Part I
Wildest Dreams
1946-1984

2

He can do anything:
Come down the steepest place
from the top,
pull an engine,
take her there;
but he has a hard time balancing
with one hand on his jugular
and the other over his balls
while walking on diverging wires.

She's an X-cheerleader
with the possibilities of becoming
a Harpy
or Ma Joad
depending ...

To be continued ...

1
Tell Them – 1963

My FATHER'S HANDS WERE HUGE. His left knuckles gashed as a kid when he rode his bike too close to a moving train. When his fingers were fisted around a glass, the scarred joints bulged from his grip like blind eyes. No matter where I sat at the table, I always saw the white slash of his hand as he drank.

Once when I was trying to draw pictures of American presidents for a seventh grade project, my father lifted a bar of ivory soap from the sink, and with his army knife, using a quarter for George Washington's image, he carved a perfect profile. I watched this magic, hypnotized by the flashing of his knuckles and the emerging face. For the rest of the evening he sat beside me at that kitchen table, guiding my fingers when the nose of Lincoln, the ponytail of Jefferson, took a wrong turn.

This is my only good memory of my father, the only time I wasn't wary. Mostly we all feared him. Especially my mother and my little brother, T.J. My other brother, Bobby, and I inched around him a little less. Sometimes that granted us a margin of grudging respect. But only sometimes.

My father was a sergeant in the army. Off and on he was stationed in places like Korea and Germany; then we would have stretches of peace. My mother would work and she wouldn't drink, but as soon as he was home again, we felt his presence every minute whether he was in the house or not.

On the evenings he came home without a bottle under his arm, he'd eat dinner without saying much. We would try to get it right: Bobby and T.J. wouldn't fight; my mother would say, Tony, don't you want some corn? I'd start the dishes without being nagged. After he ate, he would go out to the garage. Sometimes he'd stand and look down into the engine. Sometimes he'd lean in the big doorway and look up and down the street. He'd watch the birds. Sometimes T.J. would go out and try to talk to him. Can I help you, Dad? Sometimes my father would say yes or no. Sometimes he wouldn't say anything.

On the evenings when he had a bottle, we would know even before we saw him. A difference in the slam of the car door, the way he turned the knob. If I was at the table doing my homework and tried to fold up my books, he'd insist I stay. He'd call my brothers from wherever they were playing and give them orders: Take out the trash. Then he'd pour himself a drink, oily yellow—the color of cat eyes. Sit down, he'd say to my mother. I want to finish getting dinner, she'd say. Let Carla get off her behind and do something for a change. He would pour her a drink.

Then it would begin: You're getting to be a real fatty, T.J. Kids will start calling you fat boy soon. T.J.'s face would burn red. Then he'd duck his head and eat. Or he'd start on my mother. What is this? he'd say, holding up a spoonful of something we were having and pushing it to her nose. By now both of their faces would have that look: the loosened lips, the eyes flat and staring.

T.J. and my mother would spend most of the dinner, eyes down, but Bobby and I wouldn't do this. Bobby would go somewhere else in his head. He'd look at his car magazine, imagine himself making the inside turn, the accelerator pressed to the floor. I'd watch my father's hand raise and lower, and if he looked at me, I would look at him back.

On those nights, without seeming to hurry, I'd try to get the dishes done and my brothers upstairs. If we could get out of the kitchen before the bottle was half-empty, the chances were good that none of us would get into it with him, that T.J. wouldn't get smacked, that we could be in bed with the doors closed before he hit our mother.

One night when I was thirteen, I lay in bed listening to them in the kitchen below. Usually I tried not to hear; usually I pushed the pillow against my ears and said over and over, Make them stop, make them stop, until I fell asleep. But this night I listened. I could not hear words, just snarls, furniture scraping, a cry cut off. I got up out of bed and crept down the stairs. I hid in the dark hallway, just beyond the arc of light. My father stood over my mother. Her arms covered her head. He pulled her hands away, held them up to surrender. Little bleating sounds came from her clinched body. I wanted to scream at her, Fight back.

My father turned so I looked right into his eyes, but he didn't see me in the darkness. I barely breathed. Then my father grabbed the front of my mother's dress and pulled her up out of the chair. Bent over her, he whispered in a strangled voice, You slut. He was huge, his face falling apart; my mother looked so small, a blue flowered doll he lifted in the air.

When he put his fingers around my mother's throat, I backed down the hall and out the screen door. We lived in a stucco duplex up on a hill. The Lucianos' lights were on. It's an emergency, I said. I have to call the police. You must come, I said to the man who answered the phone. My father is killing my mother.

Bobby and T.J. and I watched from the upstairs window. Finally the police car pulled up. Two policemen got out. We heard them stomp across the porch. They banged on the door. We held on to each other. The kitchen became quiet. They knocked again. We heard our father say something, our mother plead. Then we heard her come through the house. We got a call, the policeman said. Is there a problem? She said, Nothing is wrong. Are you sure there's no problem? Yes, she said. Would you like us to come in to check things out? No, she said. I wanted to scream down the stairs, Liar, tell them what he does. The police went back to their car. We watched their taillights move away down the street.

I slept. Then I woke up in the dark. I knew he was in my room. I saw a flash of white and smelled the whiskey. I didn't move. He sat in the chair. I heard him swallow. Finally he backed into the dark hall. I got up and closed the door, loud enough to tell him, I know what you're doing.

The next morning after my father had gone, I said to my mother, He comes into my room nights. He sits by my bed. I'm afraid.

My mother turned back to the sink. She squeezed green liquid into the dish pan. She lifted the glasses and pushed them down into the soapy water. She did not look at me and she did not speak.

2
Hope Chest –1946

ONCE THEY GET DOWN to her grandmother's basement, Del's mother wraps a white rag around all the pink curlers, so the Toni permanent goo won't get on the dress she's making for her. Then she sets the timer for forty-five minutes so the curls don't get too tight.

"All right, step into this carefully." By the time her mother gets all the buttons buttoned, Del itches all over.

"Now don't wiggle," her mother says, "or I might end up sticking you with a pin. I've got to finish this dress tonight so we can put it in your suitcase. Your father's going to think you look stunning."

Her father? Mostly she thinks of him by his name: J.V. Lowe. Her mother never says anything bad about J.V. Lowe, but somehow Del can't really think of him as her father since she hardly knows who he is.

Though she does know for sure her mother's exaggerating with that word "stunning," but truly she loves the dress: pink stripes with a full skirt and twenty pearl buttons all down the front. She hopes she'll at least look a little bit pretty because she hates the way she looks in the picture on her mother's dresser. Her front teeth are too big and her glasses are crooked on her face and the way her mother pin curls her hair makes it stick out all funny. And she's wearing a stupid Brownie sweater which she also hates. Every time she looks at that picture she wants to cry. Clearly her mother thinks that's how she really *does* look because for Christmas Del wanted a pair of patent leather shoes with little bows on them and instead her mother gave her brown oxfords with yellow crepe soles. The ugliest shoes she's ever seen, but she had to say thank you anyway.

"All right raise your arms so I can pinch it in just a little on the sides. I suppose I'm going to still be taking tucks in your wedding dress when you grow up."

"Don't be talking marriage to that child already," Grandmother Nadiker says over by her Maytag where she's busy putting the roomers' sheets through the wringer. "She's only seven years old."

"And eleven months," Del says. She does want to get married for sure and go on a honeymoon. And have a hope chest with embroidered dresser scarves. Grandmother Nadiker has already promised she'll make her some of those when she gets a little older and some pillow cases too.

But what Del really can't figure out is why any of the women in her family married the men they did. Her mother married J.V. Lowe who was fifteen years older and who she ended up saying goodbye to when Del was three and who'd already been married one time before that and one time after and who Del hasn't seen since she was four. This partly because he lives far away in a place called Savannah. Though he did send her all fourteen things she'd put on her Christmas list last year. The best one being a birthstone ring, blue for babies born in September.

But even though she doesn't really know J.V. Lowe, tomorrow she's going to go all by herself from Charleston, West Virginia to Georgia on a bus to visit him and his new wife for one whole week. He told her mother he's going to take Del crabbing, whatever that is, and dancing. Her mother once said that J.V. Lowe was a wonderful dancer, and that's why now she's busy making Del this pink dress. But the thing is even if she does look pretty, Del isn't sure she wants to go visit this person who she might not even recognize when he picks her up at the Greyhound station in Savannah even though she's seen a picture of him and he does look nice with black curly hair and a friendly smile.

"Tell me again about the bus and everything," Del says after her mother slips the dress down off her shoulders and has her step out of it.

Her mother removes the straight pins from between her lips and takes a sip of her Coke. Del watches the little stream of smoke drift up from her mother's Herbert Tarrington. There is always a sweating bottle of Coca Cola and a cigarette burning in an ashtray when her mother sits whirring away on her featherweight Singer sewing machine, the needle going up and down so fast that Del wonders how her mother manages not to sew her fingers up.

"We'll finish packing your suitcase tomorrow evening when I get home from the clinic. Then you're going to have a good scrub bath after dinner. Instead of going to bed at eight, I'm hoping you'll stay awake, so when you get on the bus at eleven, you'll be able to sleep. The fourteen hour trip will go faster that way. Just before we take the taxi to the bus station, I'll give you your seasick pill."

Her mother takes another drink of Coke and places the edge of the pink dress under what's called the presser foot.

"Tell the part about the bus driver," Del says.

Her mother laughs. "Okay, one more time, then I have to finish this. Your father has already talked with the bus drivers who do the run from Charleston to Savannah, so they're all set to keep an eye on you. I'll introduce you to the one who goes as far as Winton-Salem when I put you on the bus and then he'll introduce you to the next driver who's taking the bus the rest of the way."

"How come he knows the bus drivers?" Though Del isn't quite ready to say my father, her mother says she's got to stop calling him J.V. Lowe.

"Like I already told you, your father does the books for Greyhound, so he knows all the bus drivers. He's even arranged it so you're going to get a free two-way ticket."

"What do you mean 'does the books'?" Her mother's already explained this to her, but she wants to see if her mother will keep being patient because this will show if she's also a little nervous about Del going alone such a long way. After all she's only going into third grade and she absolutely knows Jackie Louise Nolen's mother would never let her do such a thing. Jackie Louise isn't even allowed to walk downtown by herself or go through the colored section.

Her mother smiles. "Adele, you know what doing the books means. You're just trying me. Okay, now scoot over there with your book and read until I do this last adjustment on your dress, so I can put it on you one more time. Then we'll take the curlers out and wash your hair. Maybe you should go put on your sweater; it's chilly here in the basement."

Del doesn't think the basement is at all chilly. She loves every single corner in her Grandmother Nadiker's tall brick house that her grandmother bought with the ten thousand dollars the government gave her after her son, Del's Uncle Harold, got shot down in his plane. She and her mother and her grandmother live on the third floor, and her grandmother's four roomers live on the second: three secretary ladies and one kind of old man named Mr. Riley whose room always smells of cigars and going to the toilet number one even though her grandmother does all kinds of things to air it out. All the roomers work at the state capitol building which is only a few blocks away.

But Del guesses the basement is her absolute favorite place in the whole house because there are always magical things going on there. Grandmother Nadiker weaves rag rugs on a big loom out of balls of cloth which she lets Del wind up. Sometimes Del holds the thin paper patterns in place while her mother pins them on the silky material so she can cut them out and then put the pieces together like a puzzle to make beautiful evening dresses.

In fact her mother has all different kinds of wonderful clothes. When her mother goes to work at the clinic, she wears a stiff white uniform with white stockings and white shoes she polishes whenever she gets even one smudge on them. On her head she wears a starched white cap that has a special black velvet ribbon around the middle. Special, because this is the cap that all nurses wear who got their RNs from Charleston General Hospital.

Even when her mother has to leave the house for emergencies in the middle of the night like when there was a polio epidemic and she had to apply something called Kenny packs or when she had to go help with people who'd been burned in a big fire downtown, she puts on her uniform. When it's very cold she sometimes wears a wonderful dark blue cloak that's made out of heavy wool and has a maroon strip at the top. Del isn't allowed to put on the cloak because then it would drag on the floor and get all dusty.

But she is allowed to try on some of her mother's party clothes. One of her favorite outfits is a black full circle skirt with an aqua one-shoulder top that has a little ruffle called a peplum. Her mother lets her put on the skirt and swirl around so fast it makes her dizzy. These beautiful clothes are for when her mother goes out on dates with Joe who owns the huge, gigantic Rock Lake swimming pool made in an old quarry in Nitro, but which has been closed this summer because you can catch polio going in the water.

"Del, instead of standing there daydreaming, how about helping me with the inventory," Grandmother Nadiker says.

Along the whole back wall of the basement are shelves that hold canning jars of food her grandmother's put up: tomatoes and pickles and mincemeat and sauerkraut and applesauce. All the jars are sealed with a rubber ring and clamped down, so they don't get poisoned.

"All right," her grandmother says. "I've done as far as the green beans down on the third shelf. Start counting there. And don't let your mind drift off like you did last time."

Del touches each cold jar as she counts in her head because that helps her stay concentrated. When she gets to the end of the next shelf where the rhubarb starts, she calls out 36 and her grandmother writes that on her inventory list.

Several times a summer Grandmother Nadiker goes out and leans on the fence while she and their neighbor, Grandma Egbert, compare how many of each thing they've put up. It's a secret contest.

Grandma Egbert has a big garden in the field way in back of the row houses and almost every warm day she puts on her green sun-suit and sets her hoe and shovel on her shoulder to go there to weed and harvest. Sometimes Del helps her. Grandpa Egbert sits in the shady corner of the porch in a chair. He doesn't ever move or speak. Del knows this because she once sat on her grandmother's front steps and watched him for a long, long time. Someone brings him out in the morning and someone takes him in at night. Del's never seen who does this, but for as long as she can remember she's seen his bony, bald head and his pale ears, still as they can be, sticking up over the back of a rocker. Maybe this is why her grandmother's always telling her she better look before she leaps. It would not be fun to be married to someone who never laughs at your jokes.

"No thank you," her mother tells the colored man who offers to take the suitcase into the bus station when the taxi driver sets it on the curb. Instead she picks up the heavy bag with both hands and half carries, half drags it. Del sees that the bus station is in a part of Charleston where her Aunt Velma told her and her cousin, Lois Carol, who's twelve, to never walk on their own.

"You go first," her mother tells Del when they get to the entrance.

Del pushes on the big glass door, but it's so heavy it won't go in. Last year at the Diamond Department Store she got stuck in a door just like this one.

Her mother has to set the suitcase down so she can help. She takes Del by the shoulders and the two of them step into the huge bright room. "Now stay right here and don't move an inch. There's no time for you to go to the bathroom again. Remember since there aren't any toilets on the bus, you are not to buy any Coca Colas with your money."

At the mention of the money, Del touches the gold clasp of her new red pocketbook that has a shoulder strap her mother insists she wear so it goes across her chest for fear she'll lose it. She's going to put it the right way as soon as she can. Besides her money, five whole dollars, she has Juicy Fruit gum, cherry Life Savers, a little package of Kleenex, and an Archie comic book folded up. Plus one extra *Mother Sill's Seasick Pill.*

There are all sorts of people everywhere, several of them stretched out and sleeping on the long benches, but there are very few children because they're supposed to be home in bed.

Once her mother gets through the door with the big bag, she gives Del a little push. "Quick, help me find the gate that says Savannah. It's time for the bus."

For a minute they stand in the middle of the echoing room with the high ceiling. Her mother, who always knows everything, has a lost look on her face.

"There it is." Del points to Gate 10.

"Oh dear, they've almost finished boarding. Hurry." Her mother begins to carry and drag the suitcase in that direction.

Going through the gate door are a few raggedy, tired-looking people who don't seem friendly. Right then is when Del decides she does not want to go to Savannah. She does not want to spend one whole week with J.V. Lowe and his new wife. She wants to go back to her grandmother's house now and listen to her brown radio.

She takes hold of her mother's pocketbook strap and forces her to halt.

"I don't want to go," she says. She squints up her eyes. She is not going to start crying like a big baby right here in front of all these people she's never seen before in her whole life. "I don't want to go dancing and crabbing."

Up ahead the man who's been taking tickets at Gate 10 turns away and starts to close the door.

"Mr. Richards," her mother calls. "Please wait. I'm Ginny Lowe."

Right there in front of all these people, her mother stoops down and puts both her arms around her. "Del, of course you're frightened to go off to a strange place and spend time with your father. But I think it's important for you to get to know him. In a few days after you get there, I'm going to call you on the telephone. If you decide you want to come home, well, I'll ask your father to put you on the bus to come back that very day." Her mother stands up and motions to the driver who comes and picks up the suitcase.

She smiles at him. "Just give us one more minute."

She presses a hand on either side of Del's cheeks and turns her face up. "I'm going to put you on the bus now and see that you're all settled. I want you to be brave. I believe this will be a big girl adventure you're going to always remember. And when you come back home, I want you to sit beside me while I make your new school clothes, so you can tell me all about it."

She takes Del's hand and leads her out to the roar of the engines and the smell of exhaust. She helps her go up the high steps into the now almost dark bus, a sea of stranger faces going back and back. The faces watch her as Del passes down the long aisle.

There are only a few seats left. Her mother chooses the one next to a colored lady in a black dress with a white lace collar and a black hat who's sitting by the window near the back of the bus.

"Is it all right if my little girl sits with you? She's going all the way to Savannah and the bus driver knows to help her out if she needs anything?"

"Why certainly," the woman says. "I'm getting off in Beckley, only a few stops along." Turning to Del, she says, "Maybe you'll be lucky enough then to have the whole seat to yourself so you can curl up and go to sleep. Would you rather sit by the window so you can see more?"

"Why that'd be lovely," her mother says.

The woman steps into the aisle and Del scrambles onto the seat that prickles the backs of her legs. Her mother quickly leans in and checks to make sure she still has the piece of paper with her name and address and telephone number pinned to her blouse under her Sunday school coat.

"What if I start feeling sick?" Del says.

"Then you are to walk up and tell the driver and he will pull to the side of the road and get off with you so you aren't sick on the bus." Her mother leans over further, presses her cheeks again and kisses the top of her head.

"So grown up to go all that way on your own," the lady says, sitting back down.

Soon Del's mother is standing outside where she can see her. The bus starts to go backwards. Her mother waves and waves and waves until finally the bus turns onto the street.

"So you're going all the way to Savannah," the lady says.

"Yes," Del tells her. And then she makes herself say it right out loud. "I'm going to see my father because my mother thinks I ought to get to know him."

"Well, that's nice."

Del presses her forehead to the cold window and watches the bus speed along the Kanawha River. Well, she doesn't know if it'll be nice or not. After all what does her mother really know about fathers? Her own died of a burst appendix when she and her twin sister were a few years old. When Grandmother Nadiker had to ride in from the country on her horse to get supplies, she had to leave the two little girls in the care of a big sheep dog named Blue who grabbed them by their underpants whenever they started to do something dangerous like heading for the river. Quite a few years later, her grandmother married Mr. Nadiker and they had Uncle Chuckie and Uncle Harold and then Mr. Nadiker also died of a ruptured appendix during the Great Depression before Del was born. Her mother said she'd never gotten along with Mr. Nadiker. So, in a way, her mother never really had a father either and she seems to be all right now that she's grown up.

For a long time Del watches the houses and trees and streets flash by. Places she's never seen before. When the bus crosses a railroad track, it has to first stop and open the doors. The lady says that's the law.

After a while when it doesn't look so new out the window and she feels like she won't miss anything, Del pulls her dress under her so the seat doesn't scratch so much. She pushes down on her new permanent which her mother says will be prettier once it gets washed a few more times. Then she pulls the pocketbook strap over her head before she turns the clasp to look again at what's inside. She takes out the Juicy Fruit. Just as she unwraps the foil, she remembers she needs to be polite, "Would you care for a piece of gum," she says.

"No, thank you." The lady smiles. "Already I'm getting drowsy and I'm afraid I might swallow it if I go to sleep."

Del laughs. She likes that word "drowsy." She's glad the woman doesn't tell about her dentures like Grandmother Nadiker does when she's offered gum. Soon the woman does go to sleep, and Del's glad about that too because she doesn't want to make conversation like grownups sometimes feel they need to do with children. She just wants to be quiet and watch everything go by out there in the dark.

She rests her arms on the cold metal that runs along the bottom of the window as the bus passes slowly through small towns with only one row of houses, their porches up close to the road. One grocery store and one filling station. One white church, sometimes without even a steeple or stained glass windows.

Del knows these are mountain towns and that sometimes the people are so poor they live in the hollows and they don't go to the hospital to have their babies. She knows this because her mother had been what is called a public health nurse. She helped these women have babies right in their own bedrooms. Her mother said they spread papers down on the floor and delivered the baby there because they didn't want to mess up their beds. In a way it seems a little like how Jesus was born, only Mary and Joseph used straw.

After the bus drops the lady off in Beckley, Del does have the seat all to herself. The bus is very quiet and dark. Some people snore just like Mr. Riley, but she doesn't feel sleepy at all. Carefully she folds her coat up under her so she can sit up a little higher.

In a town with the beautiful name of Bluefield, a woman in the same kind of uniform as the driver gets on the bus with a tall stack of white pillows on her shoulder. "Only 25 cents to rent one of these all the way to Charlotte," she says. "Any soldiers on the bus, you can have one to use free, compliments of the Greyhound Bus Line."

The soldiers laugh and make some remarks Del can't understand, but the lady doesn't pay any attention to them and just keeps on moving through the bus giving out pillows. Del opens her pocketbook and digs out a quarter from the little change purse. She raises her hand to show she wants to rent one also.

"My, my," the lady says, "are you traveling all alone?"

Del nods and takes the pillow.

"How far are you going?"

Del tells her Savannah, Georgia, but somehow this woman just seems nosey, so she doesn't tell her anything more since it isn't any of her business.

At first Del can't decide how she wants to do the pillow. Finally, she settles on puffing it up against the arm rest by the aisle, then she spreads her coat on the seat. She pushes her head into the pillow's starchy smell and stretches her legs out. She wants to stick her thumb in her mouth, but she knows never to do that in public.

For a long time she just watches the sky and lets herself move with the slow rolling along of the bus, swaying with it as it goes around the mountain curves. Except for the sound of wheels on the road, the bus is silent. This part of the trip is what she likes best, that everyone in the world is asleep but her. A slice of moon appears and disappears and appears again through the branches of trees. Never has she seen so many stars sparkling—sparkling like a diamond crown.

3
Win – 1965

WALKING ACROSS THE HOT ASPHALT of the truck depot in Ogden, Utah, with Vicky limping along in spike heels beside me, our situation finally hit me in the head—a head still sore from where my father ripped out four big wire curlers. Carla, I said to myself, you better watch out from here on in. At fifteen, what we saw as a grand escape from a bad giant and a wicked stepmother turned out to be the opening episode of one of those dramas that, even after all these years, still keeps closing with to-be-continued music.

The minute we sat down at the lunch counter, Vicky, my best friend since third grade, said to the tired looking waitress with *Rosalee* embroidered on her heart, "Which way to the little girls' room, please?"

This of course cleared up any fuzziness in Rosalee's suspicions: two runaways had just sat down at her station. I can still see the row of drivers on the opposite loop of the counter giving us weary once-overs, then returning to their food. They wanted no trouble. I noticed Vicky had shoved our envelope of *Millionaire Cash Quiz* entries under my pocketbook for safekeeping. Our fat envelope containing almost one thousand completed quiz tickets. We were holding off sending them in until the end of the month, and until we found someone twenty-one we trusted to front for us without wanting a bunch of our fifty thousand one-month winnings, and even a good chance, our Million Dollar Grand Prize. We figured who else could have saved a thousand tickets? Who else would have been willing to collect from everybody in the neighborhood who smoked Winstons, Camels, or Salems and pick through the trash cans along the boardwalk? Plus keeping a constant eye on the gutters.

We'd even gotten thirteen more tickets since Newark. Collecting quiz entries was like being on a perpetual treasure hunt. To say nothing of the benefits to our education, an education which up until that point had been lacking in forward drive. Questions like, *What is the world's longest river? What classic film ends with the epitaph "It was beauty killed the beast"?* Words like *classic* and *epitaph* had kept us busy hauling out big books at the library when we weren't going through somebody's trash. Prior to this we were barely interested in what was the capital of New Jersey. Now that we were both dropouts, we figured this outside source of knowledge was even more valuable. Especially for Vic—reading *True Romance* while she was getting her hair teased was about as far as she'd ever gotten in print. Me, I'd always fled into any good stories I could lay my hands on: Mike Hammer taking no lip or that poor guy Ethan who ends up stuck in a kitchen listening to those two women—definitely he would have been better hitting the road like Vicky and me. Now there was a story I couldn't put down and probably a lot closer to the truth about romance.

While Vicky was dolling up in the ladies, I ordered a bowl of chicken soup—the most mature thing I could think of. My first effort to throw some confusion back into Rosalee's mind with the thought that maybe at least one of us had some sense and this might delay a call to the sheriff's patrol. Working my way through a trucker's portion, I began to figure how Vicky and me could get ourselves transported from Utah to California without getting molested or turned over to the juvenile authorities.

Me being in charge, just like at home, started when Vicky showed up at the Greyhound bus station—the first leg of our journey—wearing for her runaway outfit a see-through blouse with a push-up turquoise bra underneath.

"Vicky," I said, before we bought the tickets, "you need to change into something less noticeable." Even at fifteen I was a wonder at understatement. I didn't see my father calling the police—good riddance to a stick in his craw—but I knew Vicky's stepmom was going to be plenty pissed about the one hundred.

Vicky's only response to my suggestion was to push out her lower lip.

My inclination was to smack her, but beneath the make-me puss, I remembered all our mingled tears. Plus she had the money, having stolen it from her stepmother's purse, and she had the cousin in Monterey who said she'd give us a bed.

I felt a little easier when Vicky pulled a baggy sweater over her bouffant and removed a few layers of decoration. But then the ticket man informed us we only had enough money to get as far as Utah. Fortunately a hippie on the bus gave us the steer on hitching with a trucker, an owner-operator going straight on through, the delivery of a load of steel the main thing on his mind.

When Vicky returned from the bathroom, she scooped up the treasured envelope. "Praise the lord and pass the ammunition, I actually forgot where I put this," she said.

And pass the ammunition? I did not ask. Vicky was an army brat like me, even had a brother in Nam at the time, and she was big on military lingo. She slid onto the stool and lost herself in the dessert section of the menu. I bit my tongue on the suggestion that she order something grown-up. I had to peel my own eyes off the pie à la modes.

Rosalee rotated into our zone just as Vicky lit up a Winston and I saw the woman flinch.

"A hot fudge sundae, please," Vicky said, "with maybe an extra squirt of whipped cream." This offered up with her best Sister-Mary-Martha smile.

I could see by the set of Rosalee's lips she was about to take Vicky on. For a minute she settled in above us. Then she spoke, "We got a great burger-fry special, with a little tomato and lettuce on the side or there's the chicken soup like your friend had. Keep your strength up."

Vicky blinked at the unaccustomed maternal concern. I held my breath. Then she returned to her study of the menu, chewing away at the edges of a peeling nail. "Okay. I'll take a grilled cheese and the sundae. With the extra squirt."

While Vicky alternated between the sandwich and the mound of cream, I began to survey the lay of the lot. I remember it had the feel of an airport. Beyond the gritty glass there must have been several hundred semis parked on the steamy blacktop. Even inside beneath the icy hum of the air conditioning, there was the smell of exhaust, the roar of engines. From the center of all that noise, a tower rose into the haze, and off to one side, rows of bright orange pumps beneath a sky of metal. Out the other window, a string of pay phones, all of them occupied. At the sight of the phones, I felt another jab of guilt. I knew my mother would be worrying. I should've left her a note, but I guess I was punishing her for letting my father take a whack at us whenever. Then I started checking out the truckers. How best to connect with a trustworthy driver who was going our way?

As if she was in my head, Vicky said, "How about that guy by the first pump, the one in the yellow shirt?"

"Why him?" I said, turning his way.

"Because he's gorgeous. Nice muscles. And he's got good taste in clothes."

I said, "Vicky, are these the qualities most necessary for our safe conduct?"

She gave me a sour look and began working her way through the fudge section. I imagined my spoon making one quick dive into all that warm chocolate, but I saw Rosalee had us in her periphery.

"I was thinking I wanted someone no taller than me," I told Vicky. "Someone who weighs about a hundred pounds less than my father."

With that Vicky extended a loaded spoon of fudgy ice cream my way, "Sorry," she said, "I forgot."

"Well, I didn't forget." And with that I pulled from beneath my sweatshirt the wire curler hanging on a string around my neck. "My good luck charm," I said. "My mean-men reminder."

"Sort of like going steady with your past, huh," Vicky said. "I was wondering about the bulge in your esophagus."

Esophagus. One of our new words from a Body Parts quiz ticket.

I saw that Vic was scraping the last of the goo from the sides of the dish so I turned over the check. $6.75. Beneath the amount, Rosalee had drawn one of those yucky smiley faces, only instead of wearing a smile, the mouth was twisted into a sort of sideways question mark, giving the face a what-the-hell's-going-on stare. If not a sign of full support, I felt at least she was not about to redneck.

"How much money is left?" I asked, pushing the check over for Vic to see.

Vicky began to root around in her big bag, piling a few of the things she'd dared to bring along on the edge of the counter in order to get to the money at the bottom: a wad of dayglow underwear, her blow dryer and curling iron, silver nail polish, a St. Christopher statue and her rosary. Then she counted out the bills and change in the protective darkness of the bag's flaps. I glanced around to see if the underwear had fired the engines of any of the truckers across the way. It had not. They were still fueling up on home fries and talking diesel prices and weighing stations, but I did see Rosalee peering around the coffee urns.

"Twenty dollars and change," Vicky said. Then she counted out the money for the food. Plus a dollar. "For the tip," she told me with finality.

I started to protest since this was all the money we had, with still a long way to go, but then I felt some of the burden of supervision lift. Vicky was right; Rosalee deserved it. Instead of paying the check right away, we continued to hang in the protective cool of the counter. No point hitting the asphalt until we had a plan.

How to find a good hitch and how to get that driver to risk taking on a couple of fifteen-year-old girls running away from home with no very clear plans for their future or even the next day? Vicky and I debated this, trying to come up with a good story.

> Our parents are divorced and our dad has custody
> and he won't let us see our mother, but now she's
> sick so we had to run away.

"No," Vicky said, "sounds too much like Little Red Riding Hood."
And besides we looked nothing like sisters—me, dark and Italian; Vicky, a Mick with orangy hair and freckles.

> We're on our way to private school and someone
> has stolen our luggage and we don't want to worry
> our guardian who we live with because our
> mothers and fathers, who were good friends,
> were killed in a Fourth of July car accident
> a few years ago.

"Sounds like a bad soap," I said.

Finally we came up with this plan: We would pretend we were using the phones and we'd eavesdrop on small men who were talking to their wives and kids. We would then approach the most likely of these and tell him the truth. I had a father who whacked me around, and Vicky's father had run off and abandoned her to the care of a stepmother who couldn't stand the sight of her. That Vicky had a grown cousin in Monterey with a job and a place to live who said she'd put us up for a while until we could manage on our own.

It was then I noticed if Rosalee bent her ear any further our way, she'd knock over the Danish. Vicky noticed too. We stopped mid-sentence and turned toward the leaning woman expectantly. She didn't blink, just bent even closer and fixed us with her calm authority. "Carla, Victoria," she said, "let me look him over before you commit."

We paid the check and pushed out into a blast of heat and roar. We decided if we split up, we could eavesdrop on twice as many drivers. Vicky headed for the first row of phones and I walked down to the far side. It seemed to me you could right off divide the drivers into two groups: cowboys and regulars. I immediately eliminated all the cowboys and any large regulars. Also anybody who gave me the eye. Down at the end, I saw a Possible: a short guy in a sweatshirt and dungarees. A baseball cap. I thought I'd walk by, see if I could check his eyes, catch a little conversation. Just then Vicky appeared, waving her arms for me to follow her, pronto. I did. As we went around the corner, she pulled me into an empty stall and pointed to the faded pant legs and large Champion sneakers visible below the divider next to us.

She mimed I should listen hard to our next door neighbor and then began to go through the motions of making a phone call so anyone going by wouldn't wonder what we were up to. Two fifteen-year-old girls at a truck depot under any conditions was already pretty weird, though certainly afternoon was a better time than later. The guy on the bus who'd steered us to a truck hitch warned us not to be hanging out in the evening since we might be taken for a couple of hookers.

The feet in the next stall indicated a larger than average male looming up beside us. I was about to tell Vicky the guy she was stalking had already failed the size test when I found myself drawn to his sound. I rested my ear against the partition and listened hard. Mostly his side of the conversation consisted of deep laughs and occasional warm "uh-huh's." When I heard him say "then where did you throw the ball?" I decided he must be listening to a kid's blow-by-blow of some game. When he finally said, "I love you, Charlie," I knew it must be his son. When the man said that, I moved him over into the Possible column. And when I heard him say, "See you soon," I took hold of Vic's arm and motioned her to get ready for our first approach.

As he passed our stall and started toward the depot, Vic and I watched his every move. He wasn't so tall. He had a big head of regular brown hair. His nose was too big and his eyebrows were too bushy and his ears were too sticking-out for handsome, but he walked straight and his hands had an easy swing to them.

"Possible, possible," I said to Vic and the two of us made a beeline in his direction. Just as we were about close enough for us to call out, he made a turn around the side of the building. We speeded up, but when we got to where he'd veered off, he was nowhere in sight.

There were four doors down that side, but none of them were marked in any way.

"You try the last two and I'll start checking here," Vicky said, laying her hand on the first knob.

I grabbed Vicky's hand to keep her from barging in on the Possible in the shower or on the can which was definitely not the best way to introduce ourselves. Vicky reached with her other hand.

"Don't you remember the horrible things that happened to that girl who started opening doors?"

"What girl?" she said, removing her hand as though she'd touched something hot. Vicky was not one to look before she jumped, but she could be stopped right on the brink if you could throw a right word at her and *horrible* was one of them. You know the kind of person who loves to get terrified, who goes to see scary movies and during the now-it's-on-the-first-step … now-it's-on-the-second … grips your arm so hard she leaves bruises, walks home petrified in the dark sure there's something lurking behind every car, has nightmares, and then calls you up the next day begging you to go see it again.

"What girl?" she repeated and came over close to me with her eyes huge, ready for gore.

"You know—Alice—from that quiz ticket on Children's Literature, the one whose neck got all stretched out, and then got all tiny."

"Oh her," Vicky said placing her hand back on the knob. "That wasn't because she opened doors. It was from something she ate."

"I think it was both," I said. "Just come over here for a second. I've got a great idea." The only idea I had was trying to slow Vicky down. "Let's just sit over there on the bank under that big bush, have a cigarette, and wait for at least fifteen minutes. If he comes out, we can approach him in a way that shows how mature we are for our age. If he doesn't come out by then, we can decide what to do next. Maybe go back and see what Rosalee thinks." I took out our pack of Winstons and started easing her toward the only patch of grass, the only shrub in that entire blacktop paradise.

Just as we got settled, I saw a man coming straight toward us across the lot—a regular looking guy in a gray sweatshirt and a dark baseball hat. Maybe the guy I'd seen talking on the phone earlier. Vicky and I leaned a little toward each other.

The man stopped far enough away for comfort, but close enough for conversation. He smiled in an okay way. "I hear you girls are looking for ride to the coast. I'm leaving with a load for Oakland in a few minutes. Maybe I can help you out."

"How'd you know we were looking for a ride?" Vicky blurted. I wished she'd been a bit more polite, but I sure was wondering the same thing.

"I overheard you talking in the restaurant. Naturally I was wondering why you were hanging in a place like this."

I was checking him out real good by this time. "Why would you want to take on the possibility of so much trouble?"

"Yeah?" Vicky said.

"I've had my hard times on the road. And not that long ago either," he told us.

"How old are you?" I said. I knew me and Vic were being a little brassy.

"Twenty-seven. How old are you two?"

"Fifteen," Vicky told him.

"Fifteen. Holy moly, I would've said you were seventeen, eighteen. Running away from home, huh?"

"Yeah," Vicky said.

There was silence for what was beginning to feel like a long time. "Fifteen," he finally said. "That could be a lot of trouble. This your first time out on your own?"

There was something about that question I didn't like. Vicky must have felt the same because she didn't pipe right up.

The man glanced back across the lot. "Look, I'm willing to give you a hitch to Oakland. Pretty much going straight on through with both of you prepared to scoot up into the bunk if I got to stop for a weigh. But no matter what, I got to get moving."

"How far is Oakland from Monterey?" Vicky said.

"'Bout two hundred miles." I could see he was ready to turn and go.

"Carla and me have got to huddle for a minute," Vicky said. "And then if we decide to go with you, we've got to make a trip to the powder room. Could we meet you in the restaurant in five minutes?" Hooray for Vicky. I was wondering how we were going to get this guy in for Rosalee's inspection.

For the first time the guy shifted into a clear, readable expression: irritation. "You see that blue truck over by the first set of pumps, the one with the steel pipes on the flat bed? You girls meet me in ten minutes if you want to go." He looked at his watch. "I'm out of here at exactly 4:30. If you do decide to go, I'll pick you up over there by the dumpster." He pointed to the road back onto the highway.

It struck me that if we got picked up there, a good chance nobody'd see us even get into the truck. And no way we were going to get him looked over by Rosalee before 4:30. He turned and started away. There was something about how he kept his arms tight to his sides I didn't like.

Back over his shoulder, he said, "And I want you to sign a little statement saying you're coming with me of your own free will. Don't want one of you yipping up with some wacky charge along the way." And quicker than quick he was out of range.

"Ain't going to win Most Congenial in the Mr. America contest,"

Vicky said, struggling back into her spikes. "Oh, Carla, how could I have been so dumb to wear these stupid shoes?" she grabbed my arm to stabilize. "Quick, let's get to the bathroom. Can't think straight till I pee. My teeth are about to levitate."

Our Eastern Beliefs ticket.

We started toward the main entrance to the depot as fast as we could go in Vicky's condition. The big clock said 4:23. Seven minutes to come to a decision. As we spun past the big glass doors that went from the entry room into the restaurant, I tried to see back through to Rosalee's loop. I couldn't catch sight of her or even be sure I was checking the right section. But I had to go too bad myself to miss a trip to the lav.

Vicky and I both tore into adjacent booths, and as soon as we hit the seats, she began talking. "Carla, what do you think?" she called underneath. "Should we go with Mr. Uncongenial or what?"

"I don't have a totally yes-feeling about this guy. What about the other man? He looks more okay."

"But we don't even know what happened to him. Or if he'd even give us a ride if we found him. Or if he's even going our way."

"There's just something about this guy ..."

"Oh, Carla ..."

"And I don't like where he's picking us up. Like he doesn't want anyone to see us getting on."

"I was thinking that was good. I figure step-witch has the police out looking for me by now. Probably got an all states bulletin going. Maybe figuring out something from the bus driver who dropped us here. We need to get trucking. I do *not* want to get hoisted back to that hell-home."

"And what if he was to try something, our signed statement would make it pretty hard for us to threaten to call the cops as any kind of deterrent."

"Deterrent?"

A frowsy looking woman by the sinks turned to look at us as we emerged from the stalls.

"Yikes," Vicky said, "4:27. No time to rendezvous with Rosalee." Vicky took my arm and propelled me into the same little section of the revolving doors with her. "Carla, I think we should just go with this sure thing. If he tries anything funny, the two of us put together are way bigger than he is."

Back in the scorch of the sun, I felt even more reluctant to just leap into such uncertainty. "I don't know, Vic."

Vicky was kind of pulling me along. "Come on, Carla. I *cannot* go back to living with that woman. I just can't. And you know you can't be in the same house with your father anymore. Imagine after this if the police bring you waltzing into the living room."

Vicky guided me up onto the curb by the dumpster, right where the guy had pointed. The clock said 4:29 and I saw the blue truck with the steel pipes starting to move out.

"All right. All right," I said. "But I want my *no* recorded." Just then I heard a shrill whistle, the kind made when someone knows how to get their two fingers in their mouth and lets the air go through just right. "My mother," I said with wonder and started searching the lot. I swear to god I was sure it was my mother. Only my mother could whistle like that. Really I expected to look across that black asphalt and see her standing there with her feet set apart and her fingers to her mouth, a mouth just like mine.

Vicky put her arm around my shoulder and turned me in the direction of the depot. There, standing at the corner, her fingers still up to her lips and waving a white towel with her other hand: Rosalee. And standing beside her the man I heard talking to his son Charlie on the phone.

Rosalee was motioning us to quick come on.

Right then I saw the blue truck was starting to make the curve toward the exit road. The roar was so loud, the truck coming on so fast, I grabbed Vicky's arm and pushed her in back of the dumpster. I shook my head *no, no.* Then, at what felt like the last minute, the truck curved away, the windy heat of it sucking at us and finally leaving me and Vicky caught in the stink of exhaust.

"That takes care of that," Vicky said.

Rosalee was still waving us on. Vicky and I headed across the lot as fast as we could. Vicky tried stepping out of her shoes, but the tar was too hot. At last we made it to where Rosalee and the man stood, clearly involved in some sort of negotiations—Rosalee's arms going and the man's folded tight across his chest.

When we stepped up on the curb, Rosalee took hold of my elbow with one hand and Vicky's arm with the other. "Charles Murray, here they are. Carla …"

"Carla DeLuca," I said.

"And Victoria …"

"Vicky O'Mara. Pleased to meet you."

"Mr. Murray and I are discussing the possibility of him helping you out, getting you closer to your cousin in Monterey. Mr. Murray and I are long-time acquaintances. I've already talked to his wife, Mary, and she and I agree it would be good for you to go on with him to Elko, Nevada. Get to their house about 10 p.m. Mary will help you figure what's best for you to do from there."

All the while Mr. Murray's arms remained wrapped around his body.

"But," Rosalee said, "Mr. Murray is still considering. After all he could bring a lot of trouble on himself agreeing to give rides to girls as young as you."

Rosalee turned toward Mr. Murray. "Perfectly understandable. No question you'd be taking a risk. But I say, What if it was your daughter, Catherine, wouldn't you want …"

Mr. Murray raised his hand. It was clear to all of us, even Vicky, that Rosalee was waging a major campaign.

He turned to both of us. "Why are you two running away?"

"Charles, …" Rosalee said.

But again Mr. Murray motioned her to stop. He looked at both of us. Not mean, just give-it-to-me-straight. Vicky explained about her father running off, her stepmother, even about stealing the money, but saying as soon as she got a job she was going to pay it back. I managed to tell about my father without mentioning the curlers he ripped off my head.

Mr. Murray walked away for a few minutes, his hands in his pockets. Finally he came back to us. "I know I'd want someone to help my daughter out if she was stuck somewhere."

Stuck somewhere. Yep, that was me and Vicky.

He nodded at Rosalee. "Carla, Victoria, are you all set?"

We both nodded *yes*. "Thank you," we said. We didn't need to consult. The thought of a shower, stretching myself out flat, sounded so good I could almost feel my toes pushing down the length of cool sheets. If you ever rode for days sitting up on a bus, you know what I mean.

"I'm over there. The green truck with the reefer. The long gray refrigerator car. There at the end of that first row. I need to get along since my kids are staying up until I get home and they've got school tomorrow."

Rosalee hugged me, then Vicky. "Write me here, c/o of Rosalee Sullivan, when you get to your cousin's."

The three of us started across the lot.

"Mr. Murray, don't judge me by these shoes," Vicky said. "I know better now."

Mr. Murray laughed. "You will drop her a card when you get safely to where you're going?"

We nodded. Safely to where we're going. Did I ever feel like I got to that place?

Mr. Murray opened the passenger door. "One of you will need to get onto the bunk up behind the seats. Just slide the panels back. Better not to have the two of you up front. My son's ridden up there so I think you can manage."

Vicky stepped forward and he gave her a hand up. At which point she took off her shoes and jammed them down in her big purse. Finally we were all settled in.

"What was the blue truck all about?" he said.

"We were thinking of getting a ride to Oakland with that driver," I told him.

He laughed. "Without Rosalee Sullivan's stamp of approval? You can get a good night's sleep at Elko and in the morning you can talk to my wife, Mary; get the bus schedule to your cousin's."

Behind us up in the bunk Vicky had twisted around on her stomach and propped herself up on her elbows so she could look out above the two seats, see the road and not miss anything.

"Oh, I'll bet these are your kids," Vicky said. "Could I slip them down just long enough to show Carla?"

"Sure," he told her, already beginning to prepare for takeoff. "Those are this year's school pictures."

Vicky extended the first photo out so we all could see it.

"That's Charlie," Mr. Murray told us. "He's thirteen. Getting to be a good shortstop." That same straight ahead look as his father's. The same clear eyes. "And that's my daughter, Catherine. She's sixteen. She's had kind of rough year. But she seems happier now."

Catherine. The girl staring back at me had a look I've often seen in my own mirror. Head a little to the side, a sad there-must-be-a-better-way-to-do-this face. Both kids backed by that cartoon blue sky with the sweet wisps of clouds that school photographers always use. I thought of my brothers, Bobby and T.J. Wondered how they were managing against my father without me. Same kind of pictures my mother had stuck around the edge of her dresser. Same sky. Same Disney clouds. Everybody happy; now smile. Yeah, right. I decided I'd definitely call my mother from Elko, let her know I was okay.

The truck began to move out, started to slowly change gears as it curved onto the ramp. "Going to get pretty noisy," Mr. Murray said. "You'll get bounced around some. You aren't riding on good suspension like me."

We swung out onto the highway. A good breeze moving through the truck. Bouncing along at seventy. Over my shoulder I saw Vicky poking around in her bag.

"Mr. Murray," Vicky spoke loud over the rattle and roar and leaned out as far as she dared to throw her voice into our ears. "Carla and I may be about to come into a ton of money. One day soon you might be able to tell the story of how you and your family and Rosalee Sullivan rescued these two lost girls who went on to fortune and fame." Vicky took a gulp of air and dashed on. "I figure we only have eleven tickets to go to fill our goal of one thousand. Then we're going to send them in for the One Hundred Thousand Dollar Monthly Win and that makes us eligible for the Million Dollar Grand Prize."

Mr. Murray smiled, and though he kept his eyes carefully on the road, he had his ear cocked Vicky's way and he was listening good.

"Let's get busy and knock off the last eleven tickets. Sort of like when me and my brother played the alphabet game when my dado was moving from one army base to another. Only the answers are in *here*." Vicky made a tilted half-circle in the air above us, kind of gathering the three of us together, and being careful not to pitch herself right into the front seat.

"Ready for the first question?"

"Ready," we said, and both leaned a little more her way.

"'What Zodiac sign is represented by a scorpion?' Oh, this is a tricky one 'cause it's so easy. Carla, remember how we always used to mess these up? We figured nothing so obvious could be right. We said, 'Hey, what do those Quiz Guys think we are anyway?'"

"Vicky," I said.

"Okay, ready?"

Mr. Murray and I started laughing.

"All right, people, let's get serious. 1. Aquarius 2. Pisces …"

Heading into that real blue sky, the three of us riding high above the road, Vicky dangling like some dizzy angel over me and that good father—sure, even at fifteen, I knew it was never going to be Ever-After—but right then I was happy. Happy clear through.

4
Do What I Want – 1955

ANGEL EYES, *try to think that love's not around, but it's uncomfortably near ...*

The gym was dark, but filled with the buzz that follows a big win. The team drifted out from the locker room. Del saw Lee Merrick come through the door, his dark brush cut still wet from the shower, the pale blue of his shirt luminous in the light from the exit sign. She was glad she'd worn her pink cashmere sweater, glad to be dancing with Jeff Holbrook, the best dancer in the class, low dips to *Angel Eyes.*

Lee leaned against the stage. Soon he was ringed by senior girls: Jeananne and Trudy, Mary Lyster and Lily DeMarko. *I've hungered for your touch a long lonely time* ... Next Dizzy Engels stood before her. She had to say *yes.* Then Trem Thompson, his hands sweaty, the oily smell of his hair tonic. She must dance with all the boys who asked. *Sh-boom, sh-boom ... If you do what I want you to, Baby, we'd be so fine.* But the chances were good when the last dance came, she'd get what she'd been wishing for all week.

It was a small high school, the lab school for the adjoining teacher's college, only sixty to a class and many of the boys off to Ivy League colleges next fall. Small enough so everybody knew everybody and often Lee was at the center of that, rising up—tall, taller than all the rest. His cheeks ruddy, his dark eyes lit by some joke. People were drawn to Lee: the cafeteria ladies whose aprons he untied on his way to the cooler; Joe, the custodian he philosophized with down in the boiler room. The teachers even let him sneak dogs into class, sit them up at a desk wearing Trem's horn-rimmed glasses. Trem would be the valedictorian, but it was Lee who was the star of the basketball team, president of the senior class, sportswriter for the *Gold & Blue*. And always the friend of the less popular, always making sure everyone was invited to the parties at Trudy's.

As the last dance neared, she managed to free herself to be in the right spot. *Too real is this feeling of make believe, too real when I feel what my heart can't conceal.* She watched him move across the gym and when he reached her, she placed her hand on his shoulder and rested her head on his chest. His warm fingers on her back, he leaned into her. She could not breathe.

Trem Thompson caught up with her by the lockers, "Lee said to tell you we're going to walk."

She nodded, stifling her desire to shout. Part of her second wish coming true. Usually after basketball dances, a bunch of them walked home, but it was always a last-minute thing. Her, waiting to be invited, the only girl who lived in that direction.

Half the girls in the school were in love with Lee Merrick. They even asked *him* to dance. Del never approached him. She avoided his stairs when he had hall patrol. But each night she laid out her dark straight skirts, soft sweaters, the polished Capezio flats and each morning she got up early to wash and brush-dry her short ashy hair, making it feather up evenly above her ears. Mostly Del dated boys home from college and when she must go out with one of the boys from the high school because there was no gracious way to say no, she did not let him kiss her. The way she stood in the hall, where she sat in the cafeteria, when she went to the library, all of it was staged to show her indifference to Lee Merrick. She was only a junior, the newest girl in that small high school, a transfer from a tough junior high in a neighborhood where she and her mother lived in an apartment right on the line between okay and slum. Maybe the only one who didn't live in a house, the only one who had a part-time job, and she was pretty sure the only one whose parents were divorced. But she is the one Lee takes to the prom.

While Trem fidgeted, afraid Lee and the rest would take off without them, she pulled on her new winter coat, a beautiful dark plaid with a hood and a wooly wine-colored lining. She'd had it on lay-away for weeks at the store where she worked as a stock girl Thursday nights and Saturdays, deducting a little each time from what she gave her mother until she had enough.

They were just setting out when she and Trem turned the corner: Lee and Van Tran, Dulce, the Fits twins, all of them wearing the names Lee had given them. He called her Dello. Early on had slid her name together—Del Lowe became Dello. From then on, they all called her that.

They crossed over to Lake, the street that ran along the edge of the park, their breath cold in the November night. She walked beside Trem. Lee and Van Tran just ahead talking about the Celtics, with the rest of them moving backwards. Dulce, who Lee sometimes called Sweets, had stolen one of the twin's hats and he was dodging about trying to throw it to anybody in the open. Here and there along the edge, a street light caught them. Del was always the only girl and she felt that everybody but her vied for Lee's attention: jostling each other off the sidewalk into the piles of leaves. The string of corny moron jokes—What do you do to keep a moron in suspense? I'll tell you tomorrow. Ha ha ha. Knowingly stupid stuff, but powered by such peals of glee. These boys seemed to have much more fun than girls, girls with their talk, talk, talk at slumber parties, with always the undercurrent of nastiness: slam books and virginity tests.

All along the park Del laughed a lot, but never said much. That night everyone was pretty quiet, the feeling of snow coming on, Christmas break in sight. Then people began to drop off toward their streets. Trem used to tag along, but the last few games he'd given that up. Finally only Lee and Del were left.

"Let's take the short cut," Lee said, his fingers resting on her shoulder, as he guided her along. They cut across the edge of the woods. Several times she had to take hold of his arm; it was so dark. No houses for a long stretch. She never went this way when she walked home alone. In fact after dark, always walked down the middle of the road on the side streets.

Lee began to sing, "*Red sails in the sunset ...*" She joined in, "*... way out on the sea. Oh, carry my loved one home safely to me.*" This was the best part—the walking and singing with Lee. "*Tell me why the stars do shine. Tell me why the ivy twines.*" They reached New

Scotland, the amber glow of the street lights. Directly across the way, set far back, The Lakewood Home for Children. Dark trees lined the entry road, their branches pressed into the starry night. A large gray stone building on one side of the drive, a two-story house with a long porch on the other. A light in an upstairs room.

"My parents," Lee said. "My father will be just getting back from looking in at all the cottages. Making sure everything's battened down. My mother will be checking the clock."

Lee's father was the director of the children's home, a place for kids whose parents were dead or just couldn't take care of them. Sometimes Lee talked about what he called life-in-the-orphanage, the trickiness of having your father sitting in judgment. Sometimes he's dead wrong, he told her. It's complicated living in an institution where you're a kid, but not really one of *them*. Treat *them* like *us*, even though they aren't. His mother gave him and his brother her I-expect-you-to-set-a-good-example talks; gave him the silent shame-on-you whenever his behavior dipped below gold star.

"My parents don't want me to have anything to do with Bill anymore."

"Why?"

Bill was one of the Home boys. Older than they were. Nineteen. A couple of times he'd come along to things.

"You can't mention this to anybody. Not even your mother."

"I won't." Bill had a strange high laugh and looked at her funny. He made her nervous.

"He's being accused of statutory rape."

"What's that?"

"One of the girls at the Home. She's only thirteen."

"And did he do that?"

"I'm going to go visit him in jail. No matter what my parents say." His voice floated in the cold darkness above her. "You know sometimes I actually envy the Home kids. I hate all this don't-forget-to-say-thank-you crap."

To Del, Lee's father and mother always seemed like the perfect parents: a tall, handsome couple who came to all his games; a father who never shouted directives from the stands like Trem's did. A family who went on camping trips and played dominoes after dinner.

Her own upbringing was so different, so unconventional. At night when her mother came back to their tiny apartment from her job as Director of Religious Education at the big church across the street, a job she left nursing for because she was such a great organizer, the two of them made hot dogs and beans, hamburger casseroles, while they discussed the problems of the world. Parental directives were few and succinct, so liberal that sometimes Del actually wanted her mother to place a few restrictions in her way. She could never remember a time when her mother said something she did was *bad*. When Lee talked about his family, she didn't tell him how different her life was; she just listened and nodded her head.

They crossed the street. This was the point of decision. She lived about a mile further. Was Lee going to walk her the rest of the way or would he stop and wait with her until the bus came along? She held her breath and prayed.

Lee reached over and pulled her hood up. "Want to walk?" he said. She nodded. He looped his arm across her shoulders and they started off. Lee opened his mouth and gave forth with his best baritone, "*Angel eyes, that old devil sent.*" He squeezed her shoulder and she sang too. "*They glow unbearably bright.*" But she was careful not to let him hear the joy that blossomed in her throat.

Hard winter came on and they'd all been skating in Washington Park and soon after everybody else had dropped off, Lee halted, pulled her arm to stop her right there in the middle of the alley. "Let me show you something interesting," he said. "But wait. Here, hold my skates for a minute while I tie my shoe." And while he bent down he said, "What's the future you really want? You know, if you could make your dream come true?"

She started to say she hadn't decided, but what was his dream, when he interrupted, "No, first tell me what *you* want."

She actually felt nervous about doing such a thing. Then she started to tell him about becoming a commercial artist, what she'd done her career term paper on: to go to art school in New York, to get an apartment in the Village.

"Really," he said, "Is that your real dream?"

And that stopped her. "Well actually, that's not what I want most," she said, looking straight ahead into the dark. She took a breath and came right out with it, "I don't want a big career at all. What I want is to live in a regular family." She looked at Lee sideways.

He nodded and tightened his grip on her shoulder. "Right," he said.

"I've always wished I had brothers and sisters." Every time she hesitated, he jiggled her a little to go on. "My father left when I was three and I've only seen him two times since. I hardly know him." She hesitated.

"Even though you haven't seen him much, maybe he knows you better than you think."

"No. For Christmas he sent me an ugly, a hideous, ring, with a big a curly gold leaf. Not something I would ever wear."

She didn't tell the rest of it: that without her father knowing, her mother contacted the store and exchanged the ring for a set of stainless silverware. She didn't say that sometimes after these walks, she takes the chest, with its dark purple lining, from her closet to look at the gleaming rows, that she thinks of this as the beginning of her hope chest. Sort of.

"What about Garvey? We always wondered what happened to him?"

Garvey, her mother's second husband. Del never called him stepfather. "He and my mother separated last spring. We don't know what happened to him." She did not say, And I don't want to know.

"Well, he was a pretty talented guy."

"He was weird," she said.

Last year, right after she transferred to The Blaine School, Lee, the whole crew, had seen Garvey when the art teacher invited him to show slides of his work to all the art classes. Garvey was a strange looking man, with a pointed chin and teeth that clicked. He was even taller than Lee, but so thin and white you felt you could see right through him.

She was eleven when her mother married him and she had wanted to like him. He had given her a white rabbit with pink ears. She had wanted to be able to call him Dad and for them to be a family, but in fact he repelled her. He turned out to be a liar, especially about money. He even forged her mother's name on some finance company loans. Not something she wanted to tell Lee.

"So what else do you want?" Lee said, leading her around a big truck.

She took another breath and said it, "I want to live on a farm and have four or five children." Then she hesitated, feeling that maybe she'd said too much. It wasn't that she'd never told anyone this. She talked to her mother all the time, told her most anything, but never a boy that she liked. Maybe none had ever asked.

"Yeah, and what else?" Lee said, steering her along across the streets as though this all made good sense to him.

So she just kept talking without even really seeing where they were. "A lot of girls dream about themselves in a white wedding gown, but ..." she stopped not sure she wanted to actually say this.

"What?" he said.

"What I always picture is me wearing a blue-flowered maternity top. Me, expecting a baby."

When he didn't react, she rushed on. Him, moving along in the darkness beside her, listening. She told him about once staying at a friend's grandmother's farm when she was a kid, about waking up in the early morning, going out to feed the cows and eating hot biscuits for breakfast and how she liked the smell of manure steaming up in the fields, how after that she'd always wanted to live on a farm. "Something about the sun in the cold morning room ..."

And right there, in the middle of a sentence, he took hold of her shoulders and turned her around. Laughing, he said, "Look."

She had gone right by her apartment building.

Then he said, "Look in your hand." And she looked down and saw she was still carrying his skates. "Here's the interesting thing," he said. "Just get people talking about themselves and they'll end up doing most anything you want."

Right up through the winter it was the same. Del continued to be the only girl and she swung back and forth between embarrassment and being thrilled by the boys' audacity. But sometimes it wasn't all singing and jokes. When she asked Lee what happened to Bill, he told her he didn't want to talk about it. In fact, sometimes Lee didn't say a word for blocks, cupping his fingers over her shoulder, marching her along in rhythm with him. And once after what felt to her like miles of nothing, he turned, only a block from her street and said, "That isn't *me*." Then left her standing there, mute and afraid. From then on, though she always hoped he was going to walk her all the way, she was never sure.

Then one night, the first time it was warm—one of those winter thaws—he led her to the big swings at the end of the playground. While their swinging shifted them back and forth from darkness to the light from the street, he talked. "Weird things happen," he said. For the first time the sound of his voice made her as uneasy as his silence and she wanted him to stop, for them to pump high into the night sky. But he kept on going. "Four years ago when I was four-teen," his words came steady and slow, "one summer night after my parents went out, I broke into a cabinet in my father's office where he kept his stash of silver dollars. These silver dollars were a big deal."

He looked at her and then went on. "Whenever my brother or I did something that showed we were developing good habits, my father rewarded us with a silver dollar: perfect attendance, if we got all E's in the conduct column, if we saved half of our allowance for a month."

He gave a weird laugh that didn't sound like him. "Robert got sil-ver dollars up the wazoo, but at the last minute, I'd always end up doing something that made it necessary to withhold the prize. Then, always a little psychology talk followed on how it's important to earn something. You know."

Actually she didn't know. Her mother had never practiced any kind of reward system. But she just nodded her head like she did.

Then he said, "My fingers started itching, actually itching, to get hold of those dollars." He held his hands toward her like maybe she'd understand if she looked hard enough. The playground light shadowed his face. She was cold and ready to go home. "So ..." he said, leaning toward her, "one evening, after my parents went out, I slipped into my father's office. Took the extra key he kept hidden in a can in the garage." Again Lee gave that laugh. "I know everybody's hiding places."

Several lights went off in the house across the way. The seesaws loomed up. Always there, out the corner of her eye, as if they were something else. She wanted to say, My mother will be wondering. But by now Lee knew that wasn't so.

"I didn't let anybody see me go in." Only Lee's voice in the dark, steady and low, the creak of the swing when he turned her way. "The box—one of those metal tool boxes—was behind some files. Locked with a little silver lock. 'Course I knew where he kept that key too." Again he laughed like this was a funny story. "Had some trouble getting the lock open. You know why?"

Of course she didn't know why. And didn't want to either. Lee was being creepy. She shook her head. "Because I was wearing my mother's garden gloves. Okay, so I get the thing opened. Every one of the top compartments is practically running over with silver dollars."

It wasn't the story itself; it was the way he was telling it. Between each part he'd stop to look at her. Like did she get it so far? She began to listen for the place she could say, Let's start walking, I'm getting cold.

He said he took a few from each section. He didn't even count them, just wrapped them tight in a piece of paper so they wouldn't make any noise and stuffed them into his pocket. "I felt such a rush … happy," he said, his voice loud then.

Beneath the sounds of his words, she heard the creak of the chain as Lee twisted the swing slowly around and around. Her chin was rigid, her teeth ready to chatter. She wanted that to be the end of the story, but it wasn't. He said when he went to put the box back on the shelf, he saw that the top section lifted up. "Guess what was in the bottom," he told her.

She did not want to guess. He waited. "I don't know," she finally said.

"A gun. A revolver."

She imagined herself standing up and starting off toward home. From then on his voice came to her as though the air was water. He said he'd wanted to touch it, to take it out and hold it in his hands, but he was afraid. He buried the wad of coins in the woods in back of the cottages. For days he waited, sure any minute his father would confront him. The spit dried up in his mouth and he kept thinking his parents would hear the clicking each time he spoke. Finally he knew what he had to do. The end of the week he dug up the money.

He put it back in the box.

"Then do you know what I did?" He reached across like he was going to take hold of her swing, but she pushed back a little as if she was about to make that first lift into the sky. "Do you?" he said again.

"No," was all she could say.

"I took the gun out and held it up to my head. I said, If it's got bullets in it, that'll be my reward." She stopped breathing. His swing was almost touching hers. "I pulled the trigger. Nothing happened. I put the gun back in the box. Then I went out and practiced lay-ups."

He had stopped turning and she could tell he was looking right at her, even though she could not see his eyes. "Well?" he said.

All she said was, "Lee." How could this be true, that someone who had almost everything would do that?

Then he said it again, "Well?" He waited.

Finally she said what she was thinking, "Did you really do that with the gun?"

There was a whir of wind, the whirl of Lee's body as the swing unwound. He rose and started off across the playground. "No," he said, "I didn't."

After a while, heading into spring, in the dark hall of her apartment building or now and then in his father's car, Lee kissed her, not just the joking around kisses of before when they had stood for hours on the front stoop swinging their bodies in the cold, him asking her, if she wanted to feel his knees to see how they were shivering, if she wanted to feel the split cartilage of his cold nose. Maybe it was April, and he was more serious and when he started to unbutton her blouse, she silently stopped his hand. She was afraid of what he might think of her if she allowed this. She was afraid. For a brief time when Del was in ninth grade, she dated an older boy from the Catholic high school and he lay down on top of her in his car, moving his body and sweating, and afterwards she felt sticky and vowed not to allow that anymore. Then it would happen again. But Lee was not like that boy and most of the college guys who tried over and over. Whenever she pushed *his* hand away, he stopped. She hoped he understood that this was what she had to do.

More and more no matter how good she felt the time had been, when she turned to walk up the stairs to the apartment, her body felt heavy. She'd walk by her mother's room. She'd lie down on her bed in the dark with her coat still on and often later she'd get up and sit at the desk and write a letter to Lee. She'd ask him about the distance she felt between them. She'd try to explain why his saying or doing this or that, or not saying or doing this or that, made her feel sad. She would cry while she wrote. Then she would put the letter in an envelope, write his name and address on it and lock it in her shoe-skate box with dozens of similar letters and push it back under her bed.

Winter ended and the spring days flashed by with a speed that alarmed her. June—most of her friends graduated. Lee, tall and dignified in his dark blue cap and gown, delivered the class president's farewell, urging them all to head into their futures with a spirit of adventure. The next day Lee and his cousin set out on a cross-country trip that would last the rest of the summer and then off to a college hundreds of miles away. No postcards. No goodbyes.

In September Del headed into her senior year with a dull ache in the back of her eyes. One of her teachers warned them in an opening lecture not to waste the best years of their lives. Her first days back registered as a series of empty spaces like a child's discarded punchout book: Lee's long body did not lean against the ice cream cooler, his blue oxford cloth shirt open at the neck, his gray chinos slightly pouched at the knees. In the dark of the gym his hand did not rest on her waist. After games the November night along the edge of the park was still. Instead of taking notes she started hundreds of letters: *Dear Lee, How are you liking college? Dear Lee, Just a note to see what … Dear Lee, The old gang is certainly …* The rest of the paper filled up with dark flowers, vines, staring eyes. *Excuse me while I disappear, angel eyes, angel eyes.* In the mornings she slept until the last possible moment; then she pulled on whatever her hand grabbed from the closet. Some days she stayed home and wrote her own excuses. She did not rinse her hair in lemon juice to make it shine.

5
True Romance – 1966

First thing that morning, Miss Murgy, a tall witch of a woman, cornered both of us like she did every day. "Girls …" with that she clinked a teaspoon on a shot glass, "do I have your attention?"

"Yes, m'am," Vicky said.

6 a.m., six days a week, Miss Murgy, the spoon on the shot glass, clink, clink. I am not making that up. If it wasn't for Vicky's willingness to m'am her—all her yes-Sister years at parochial school—we would've lost that job cleaning the Monterey à la Go-Go our first day. And let me assure you à la anything it was not.

"I expect you to have all the cleaning done right before the painters get here: Lysol both bathrooms, scrub the ashtrays, disinfect the top of the bar …."

Same list every morning, only difference was that this time at ten o'clock we were to help painters cover everything up before they got started. Then hallelujah, because the bar would be closed, we had two days off in a row for the first time since we arrived. I planned to crawl into bed and not get up again.

Witch-woman switched on the lights in the go-go cage. When they didn't blink, she said to Vicky, "Find the defective bulb and don't wear those shoes when you do it. Break your neck and think you can sue me."

Murgy never looked my way. She knew if she saw my face, she'd have to fire my ass and where else was she going to get such cheap labor. We figured she paid us about fifty cents an hour—just enough for us to chip in on Vicky's cousin Theresa's rent and to stock up on Winstons, peanut butter, and Kotex . Believe me, Lysoling the john after an evening's use by the à la Go-Go clientele was the least of it. Vicky and I spent some time at first trying to figure out how someone like Miss Murgy could be the owner of a place like the Go-Go. Vicky was sure she was a lapsed nun.

Just before Murgy went off to her job in some government office, she issued her final order, "While you assist the painters, I expect you to conduct yourselves as young ladies."

Young, yes; but ladies was definitely a stretch. Since the painters were probably a couple of winos Murgy commandeered off the street corner, I figured we'd have no trouble on that one. Even with a new paint job, no matter how much Windex and Lysol, how much of last night's attempt to drown the misery we hauled out to the alley, there was no disguising à la Go-Go's true nature: a biker bar where both the customers and the furnishings were dented and chipped and beyond hope.

Except for Vicky up in the cage testing bulbs, we finished by 9:15. That gave me enough time to curl up for some solitary shut-eye in the biggest booth. There was only a twin bed in the spare room at Theresa's, so Vicky and I had to lie head to feet. The first thing I saw at the crack of dawn every morning was Vic's chipped toenails. One good thing at least: Vicky did not kick in her sleep.

I had just crawled into the booth when the go-go lights started blinking. Vicky had found the bad bulb. I knew this meant she was going to do what she did every morning when we finished early: practice. But maybe not, if I appeared to be sleeping. Then I might not have to listen to the Supremes screaming *Stop! in the name of love* for the hundredth time. One reason Vicky didn't hate this job as much as I did was that she saw it as a step toward her dream of becoming a Go-Go Girl.

"Carla," Vicky called. Too late once again. "Here are two quarters. Press B8 twice when I tell you I'm ready?"

"B8? I thought it was B7."

"No, I'm starting on a new song." She tied her shirt up midriff-style, pulled her jeans down a little, and stuck out her hip. She centered herself in the cage and glanced over her shoulder into the big mirror that covered the wall behind the bar, pyramids of bottles and big jars of pickles and sausage blinking in and out below her. "Ready," she said.

"Vic," I finally had to ask, "why would you want to be up there getting ogled by a bunch of drunks?"

"Oh, Carla, stop being so grouchy. Don't you have any dreams?"

My dreams at sixteen? Hard to say, but being in a cage wearing a leather miniskirt and knee-high boots and wiggling around was not one of my fantasies. But she was right about the constant bad mood. Three months ago, when we first arrived, after our big escape from Jersey, I actually believed a new life was about to open up. That's what I told my mother when I called to reassure her I was safe. Her less than enthusiastic response might have clued me in.

"Yeah, dreams," Vicky said again. "I think we're lucky to be working here at the à la Go-Go. Better than the Five and Dime. Now hurry up and press B8 please."

Just as I was about to hit the button, there was a loud banging at the service entrance. While Vicky quick made her way down the steps from the cage, I went to the back door. "Who is it?"

"Painters," a voice called.

I unlocked and swung the heavy door back. The man held one end of a long ladder. Straight ahead dark eyes. Maybe a head taller than me. A nice mouth. But it wasn't just that he was good-looking. "Morning," he said. I must have said something. Definitely I stepped aside because next thing I remember he and another guy were bringing that ladder into the bar. But here's what I do know: some current of heat hit me. I am telling you this without any romantic touch-up. Zap ... Zap. I'm sure he felt it too.

They set down the ladder. "Steve. Steve Morletti," he said, "and this is Richie Rollins."

"Carla DeLuca. And this is Vicky. Vicky O'Mara." Vicky dropped a little curtsy. My first time actually introducing somebody else.

Then the four of us got busy. With Steve Morletti directing us, Vicky and I upended the stools onto the bar. We shoved all the tables into the middle and stacked the chairs on top. Steve and Richie brought in scaffolding to do the ceiling first. Richie dropped a lot of quarters in the jukebox and he played many times a kind of music I'd never heard. "*Kind of Blue* by Miles Davis," he told us.

Steve overheard Vicky telling Richie about our Million Dollar

Cash Prize entry, the thousand tickets we'd had Theresa send in for us. Very quietly, he told me, "You know, kiddo, those contests are pretty much all con. One chance in a zillion anything coming your way on that." In a way I already knew this, but then I knew it for sure. Maybe I'd tell Vicky what he said, but probably not.

Finally around 11:00, we began to help them cover everything. Steve Morletti on one end of the big cloths, me on the other, a sort of reverse of my brother and me folding the sheets. Just as we were putting the last cloth over the Go-Go cage, Steve Morletti said to me, "How old are you, Carla?"

"Going on nineteen," I said, without a flicker. I am a practiced liar. All those lies necessary to protect myself and my brothers all those years. "How old are you?"

"Twenty-five," he said, "and in the middle of a divorce." With that he gave me a hand down. "That's about it. Nothing to do now but paint. So what are you going to do with your two days off?"

Vicky had told them how excited we were to be getting that much time all at once. "I'm going to sleep. This getting up at 5:30 every morning is nasty."

In a way I hated to leave the bar, but really there was nothing more for us to do. Steve was already climbing up to the second level of the scaffolding, one of those men who's quick and sure. One of those bodies you can't help but watch. Each part a pleasure to see.

We waved goodbye. "Nice to meet you," Vicky called and we headed for the back. Just as I was about to close the door, Steve Morletti stepped to the edge of the platform and cupped his hand to the side of his mouth, "Waxing crescent tonight. Get yourself down to the beach. Step into the sea. It'll wake you up."

I didn't know what to say to that, so I shut the door on all that energy. Waxing crescent? Uh-oh, I thought.

It was pouring rain. Vicky covered her bouffant with her jacket. "Hunky guys," she said.

"Hummm." I didn't say anything to Vicky about that zap-zap between Steve Morletti and me. Telling her would have made it ordinary. Instead I turned my face up to the raining sky and ran.

Wet through by the time we got back to Theresa's, we put on dry T-shirts and crawled under the covers. We often did this on rainy days when we got back from work. "Cover my feet up," Vicky commanded.

I tucked her toes in and listened to the rain on the tin roof. Twenty-five. In a way that was only six years older than me because really I was a lot more nineteen than sixteen. Out on my own in the world while other girls my age were sitting in school, taking notes about things that meant nothing to them and never would.

When I woke up, Vicky was propped at the other end of the bed with a big stack of romance magazines piled beside her. She'd found a box of them under the bed when we first arrived. "Want half a PB and J?" she said, extending the sandwich toward me.

What I wanted was the cold half of a grapefruit, already neatly cut away from the rind, each triangle pried loose from its little divider. Pink grapefruit. My mother's morning gift to me when times were good. But I knew that Theresa's refrigerator most likely contained nothing beyond a near-empty carton of milk about to go sour and maybe an ancient box of Velveeta cheese, dried to hard orange along all its edges.

I sat up and took the sandwich. "Thanks," I said, "but tomorrow we've got to buy some fruit. Scurvy prevention."

"Scurvy?"

"Our Four Food Groups Prize Ticket. Your gums ever bleed?"

"Carla, doesn't it seem to you we would've heard something about our prize money by now?"

"Hmmm." I didn't have the heart to tell her what Steve Morletti said.

By now Vicky's nose was buried back in the magazine. The bright yellow banner with the words TRUE ROMANCE was the only sunshine in this room, I'll say that: picture of a girl with dimples and perfect teeth smiling out. Story titles printed inches from her glowing face: *Our Shameful Baby, The Day Before Our Wedding He Married My Best Friend.*

"Vicky, how can you read that junk?"

She didn't answer me. I leaned over the edge of the bed and felt around in the box for the only real book it contained. Instead of crap like *He Seduced Me With His Soul,* this book's cover grabbed you with:

A tender and bawdy fable of some gaily disreputable
avoiders of work, drunks, fancy ladies, benign bums
and social-outcast philosophers.

Benign bums. Social outcast philosophers. Sounded like a lot of the patrons of à la Go-Go. Whoever came up with these words? A good talker, for sure. I opened to the first page. *Cannery Row in Monterey ...* shit, this story takes place here ... *is a poem, a stink ... chipped pavement and weedy lots ... honky-tonks.* I don't know about the poem part, but the stink, the glare ... sounded a lot like Theresa's neighborhood. I read on. Kind of like the guy who told about Ethan, but more packed in, well ...like sardines. The opposite of Mike Hammer. I read the first page again. No question I'd have to haul out the dictionary if I wanted to get every word, but it sounded good even without that. Yeah, a poem.

Vicky took hold of my foot and shook it. "Listen to this, Carla, these stories are not all mushy romance. This is from a complete suspense novelette, *I Invited Danger.*"

"Please," I said. "I'm reading something real."

"No, listen. I've got an idea how we can make some money." Then she glared at me over the top of the perfect girl on the cover, a girl whose eyes said she'd never even had a nightmare, much less a father who came into her bedroom and stared at her in the dark.

"I'm listening." Sometimes it was best to humor Vicky.

"Okay, here's how the person writing this builds up the suspense. In shaky red letters before the story even starts, kind of like an ad ..." Vicky turned the magazine and pointed to the red column, then she read from the side like kindergarten teachers do, her finger bouncing over the words: "'I'm in trouble, the man said. I need help. I opened the door a little wider to ask him to enter, then I froze. What would happen if my husband came home and found us together?'"

"See, Carla, you'd have to go on and read the story. You know you would."

"Not me. I'd say what kind of dumb bunny would marry a guy who'd be jealous because you let a man in to use the phone."

"Oh, Carla, you're just giving me a hard time—you know by the title *I Invited Danger* that the man is not coming in to use the phone."

"Well then, she shouldn't have opened the door in the first place."

"Forget all that. Here's my idea. Read this." She handed me the magazine.

True Romance is a women's magazine written by the readers. We look for true stories that involve real people and real emotions. Stories can range from 2,000 to 10,000 words. Currently we pay two cents a word.

"Two cents times 10,000. The two of us working on it together—we could probably knock off a story a week."

"And what fabulous true story might you begin with?" I said.

"*We Hitched a Ride With Danger.* How a trucker tried to rape us and how we fought him off. We've got all the details we need to make it real. Mr. Uncongenial. What a semi looks like inside, the sounds. We could even use Rosalee as a model for the waitress who warns the girls not to hitch with that man, but they don't listen."

"And what about the rape part?"

"Oh, we can make up all that stuff. Plus you can throw in a few real things from your experiences with Babylove Stewart."

"That was just playing around. Me, taking advantage of him. Now, I want to read *you* something. You think we could ever knock off something like this?" I held the book to the fading light.

"Cannery Row's inhabitants are as the man once said, 'whores, pimps, gamblers, and sons of bitches,' by which he meant everybody. Had the man looked through another peephole he might have said, 'Saints and angels and martyrs and holy men,' and he would have meant the same thing."

It was dark. The rain had stopped. No wind. There was no one on this stretch of beach, only some green lights in the distance. The ocean was quiet. We pulled off our shoes. Vicky took my hand and we walked into the waves. It pulled at the sand beneath our feet. Above us, a sliver of moon high in the blue-black night.

"Waxing crescent," I said.

"What's waxing mean?"

"Coming or going. I mean to find out."

6
His Arms – 1963

W HEN DEL ROUNDED THE CORNER onto West 71st, she noticed a strange troupe in front of her mother's building. The dog-woman, her orange head bent far forward, listening to a tall man who appeared to be dancing with one of her Dobermans. When the man turned, Del felt a jolt— something familiar about the way he moved. Now he seemed to be dancing with both dogs. She imagined the four of them joining hands, paws, and lifting into a Chagall sky.

For weeks on her way to and from her graduate classes, Del had passed this unusual woman, well over six feet with her piles of dyed red hair, striding along on her high platform heels, her short black sheath exposing an amazing stretch of white legs and flanked on either side by two male Dobermans, all three of them equally emaciated.

But this was the first time she'd seen this rather scruffy-looking man. And there was something off about the way these two concentrated on each other's faces, the largeness of their mouths as they spoke. She felt that double urge: fascination and the need to look away. As she neared the group, she saw she would have to circle around them to get up the stairs. She was wary of passing too close to the dogs. Then she heard a familiar voice. She knew who it was. "Lee? Lee Merrick?"

"Dello." He lifted the dogs' paws from his chest and turned toward her.

It was Lee, his dark eyes, his Roman nose with its split cartilage, but he didn't quite look like himself. That boy she had loved in high school —star of the basketball team, at the center of everything—Big Man on Campus.

"Lee, I didn't know you were in New York." Of course she didn't know; she had not seen him since high school, had not heard from him since her junior year in college. He was heavier now. Older.

"Just got out of the army. I'm doing temp typing for Manpower. Staying at the Y."

The rosy flush was gone. Though he couldn't be more than twenty-four. He even had some gray hair over his ears. He needed a haircut. His brown corduroy jacket needed to be cleaned.

"Dello, this is Ursula Radovich. Del Lowe."

Dello as in jello. How long ago that was. "Yes, I've often passed you out walking your dogs." The woman watched her face with an unsettling intensity and then she nodded—this Ursula Radasomething. Del would have liked to hear her voice.

"Nicholas and Boris," Lee said, bowing to the two dogs who were still sizing her up, the hair on their backs slightly raised. "I was just talking to Miss Radovich about walking Boris and Nicholas, about me taking them for runs in the park."

Del noticed that Lee's words were slow and deliberate, his face turned toward the woman who nodded again, waved her hand at Lee and moved off toward the hotel, both dogs snugged to her body. Del looked back and forth between the woman and Lee. Let him volunteer information; she wasn't going to pump.

"How'd you know I was here?"

"The old woman who lived downstairs from your mother's apartment on Lancaster. She saw me poking about the mailboxes. She said you were living in New York with your mother, that you were going to school to become a teacher."

"Miss Loomis." Surely he hadn't come to New York just to see her. He certainly wasn't knocking himself out to charm her now. She began to dig in her bag for her keys. "Come on upstairs." She pushed her fingers down past all the stuff on top. "If I can ever unearth my keys. My mother will be glad to see you." He smiled, but didn't say anything. She was beginning to feel breathless from tossing him possibilities that never got returned. "I'm staying with my mother while I finish my master's." He nodded. Between not being able to find the damned keys and Lee's refusal to small talk ... What did he expect? She hadn't seen him for five or six years. And really what she remembered most about loving Lee in high school, those times he walked her home … was how unhappy, how confused she felt.

Well, here she and Lee were years later and once again she didn't know what he was up to. She dropped her bag on the steps and began to unpack some of its contents to have more room to search. "Are you serious about the dogs?"

"I am," he said.

She leaned toward him expecting him to elaborate. But no. This conversation was like dancing with someone you can't follow; he kept not being where she thought he'd go next. Lee pulled a package of Luckies from his pocket and extended it toward her. She shook her head. She smoked, but not on the street. She watched him light up, his fingers rough and slightly yellow. Funny, but she actually felt shocked to see him with a cigarette in his mouth. She was the only person she remembered being a smoker in high school and that only at home, an occasional one of her mother's Tarringtons.

He reached his hand toward her bag. "May I?" he asked. And before she could answer, he poked his fingers down into the little front pocket and fished out her keys.

"Good lord." She moved around him to start up the steps. "Come have some coffee and tell us what you've been up to." She was not going to give any false signals of great interest.

Lee bent his head back and looked up at her with his dark, dark eyes. She saw again the triangular mole just under his chin and a pale scar below his lip she'd never seen before. She motioned for him to follow, but he didn't move. "How about walking up to the diner on the corner?" he said.

"Well … I have a paper due…"

"Up to you." His eyes no longer searched her face.

She saw it was up to her. Lee had never been one to press. Those nights after games when she'd pushed his fingers away from the buttons on her blouse, he stopped, but always followed by a kind of non-goodbye—Lee, heading down the apartment stairs, the click of the heavy door below, her standing in the dim light of the hall, alone and sad. She could say no, she really had to work on her paper and he would head on out and that would be the last she'd see of him. She didn't know how she felt about Lee's sudden reappearance, but she knew it didn't feel right for him to just turn and go. Still considering how ragged he looked…Not only had she often felt unhappy with him, but there had been times when he had frightened her, when his strange behavior had been scary.

Del looked up the five stories to her mother's living room window, her waiting paper, a cup of tea. It seemed clear what the sensible thing to do was. She turned and went back down the steps.

For the first time Lee laughed. "Dello, Dello," he said. Then he cupped his fingers around her shoulder like he used to on those dark walks home, and as he turned her toward the corner, he said low into her hair, "Am I glad to see you."

All through college she had dated a wonderful boy, Nathan Berman, a med student going on to become a pediatrician. And from the moment you met him you knew that was just what he should be, his freckled face smiling, his slightly protruding ears inspiring trust. He liked people. From the start, she liked him. Lee had been the only boy she ever cared about until then. But Nathan was different; he made her laugh. Though she and Nathan always stopped short of taking off their clothes, of that final act, she loved to kiss him, to lie on his bed, pressing her nose into the heat of his neck, his comfortable body. Her mother had cautioned her to wait; it's a beautiful experience, best shared in marriage. Anyway she didn't seem to be ready for anything more and Nathan didn't press either. A relief from those high school years of fending off the sweaty advances of college boys in the backseats of cars, popular boys who she felt nothing for, wet kisses that left the skin around her mouth chapped for days.

But from time to time she felt restless with Nathan's continual goodness, the ever-calm of his hazel eyes, felt an urge to be difficult that she'd never noticed in herself before. During one of these restless times, she found a letter from Fort Huachuca, Arizona in her sorority mailbox.

October 9, 1959

Hello, Dello Dear, Yes, here I am, a payroll clerk for the US Army, a member of the Remington Raiders: we never backspace!

I have been thinking of you.

Thinking of you warmly. The military life has little to recommend it other than keeping me in constant touch with a feeling of longing. So if you are not engaged and you feel so inclined, it would be a pleasure, a sweet pleasure, to hear from you.

What are you reading these days? What are you thinking about? Do you still wear white night gowns with little rosebuds? Do not be frightened. I cannot eat you up from way out here in the desert. Lee

All that year, every few weeks or so, they wrote. She told him of her excitement over her Russian history course—the thrill of hours of tracking through primary sources in a dusty corner of the stacks to refute some hypothesis posed by her handsome, brooding professor who seemed ill-matched with his thick, unattractive wife and their house full of little children, and she told him what a wonderful person Nathan was, how these letters actually eased her need to pick away at their relationship. She did not mention that sometimes on lazy Sunday afternoons, she found herself staring up at Nathan's ceiling thinking about Lee, the long stretch of his arm lifting out of the rolled cuff of his sleeve.

Whenever she returned from class to find a letter, she would prolong her pleasure by first making herself a cup of tea and taking it carefully to her room where she would sprawl on her bed and slowly read and reread. Each letter was a surprise. Though they were always voluminous and horny, the contents varied. Sometimes they were full of Lee's enthusiasm over what he was reading: William James, Gunter Grass, J. P. Donleavy. Sometimes they were witty recountings of a recent episode incited by what he called The Demon Drink and the consequence of being busted to E2. His stories of his descent were usually followed by ironic descriptions of his present program of reform—reading outlines and tennis matches and early morning runs. Often he told her of his long walks in the desert—the lizards and strange flowering plants. The desert, a place of extremes, he said, that's why he felt such connection to the land around the base. Everything less distorted in desert time.

But then at the end of that year they stopped writing. She couldn't remember who had let the last letter go unanswered. Nathan was doing an internship at Children's Hospital in Boston. She was writing him and going down for weekends and she or Lee simply lost the rush of energy, the need to compose themselves in print.

The diner was almost empty, the only waitress read a magazine at the end of the counter; Bennie, one of the neighborhood characters, talked softly to himself at a distant stool. Just coffee, they told the woman as she started toward them with menus, *WANDA* stenciled in capitals on her chest. Lee put his old jacket on the hook above the booth and sat across from her. He began to look more like himself, that boy backed by the starry night above New Scotland Ave. "I'm thinking walking dogs in the park beats sitting in an office," he said. He told her he'd already approached five or six people out being pulled along by their pets. He would only consider large dogs for his clientele. He'd gotten addresses, phone numbers, promised to send them references.

"New Yorkers gave you their addresses on the street?"

"Dogs like me," he said and laughed. "Maybe you could be my assistant."

"I wouldn't have thought you'd pick a place like New York to settle in," she said.

He turned both of his hands face up and shrugged. "I wanted to see you."

"Oh." That was all she was ready to say.

"And I want to write."

"Write?"

"Stories. Right now I'm working on a something about Bill Robinson."

"Bill Robinson?"

"Bill Robinson, from the Home. You remember. He made you nervous."

Was the orphanage, The Lakewood Home for Children, that Lee's father directed, even still there? "Whatever happened to Bill Robinson? The rape charge? You never answered me. We were walking along the park and I said, What happened? and you didn't say anything." This was making her nervous too. Getting close to the dark of those walks home, the playground swings off in the shadows.

"That's what I'm writing about—me and Bill and Roberta Gatling."

"Roberta Gatling?"

"The girl."

"You and Bill Robinson and the girl? You were part of that?"

"I'll give it to you when I get to the end. See what you think."

Over the third cup of coffee while he arranged the crushed cigarette ends around the edges of the ashtray, he told her some of what he'd never mentioned in his letters, summed up college: Rampage. Suspensions. His parents distraught—what had they done wrong? His feelings of guilt. He did not frame any of this in bravura. He'd just made a mess of it. He'd joined the army, hoping for something. Because he couldn't come up with anything better. And then somewhere in the endless middle, he'd started writing. First the letters to her: Hello Dello Dear, and then on to other things. He looked up and smiled. "So, here I am in New York. Starting over."

"Do you remember the time you tricked me into carrying your ice skates for miles?"

Lee laughed. "Are you still pissed about that?"

"'Here, hold my skates while I tie my shoe,'" you said. And then you asked me to tell you all about my dreams for the future, prodded me on until you got me to admit that my real dream wasn't to go to art school and live in the Village, that what I really wanted was to have three or four children. I poured out my vulnerable little heart for blocks—so caught up in telling you my fantasies that …"

"You walked right by your apartment house."

She felt the heat rise in her face. What had made her cry that night so many years ago … well now it was anger…Pissed. Damn right she was pissed. "And do you know what you said?"

"Yes."

"'Get people talking about themselves …'"

"And they'll do what you want."

"I'd think you'd be too ashamed to repeat that." Her voice was so loud several people at the counter looked their way.

Lee took hold of her hand. "Just because I tricked you into carrying my skates doesn't mean I wasn't listening … doing two things at once." He turned her hand and lifted her finger. "You told me about a ring your father gave you that was so ugly it made you cry. My father once gave me a set of folders for collecting stamps—the last thing in this world I'd ever want to do, so I had some idea how that felt."

Was he conning her once again? Her hand didn't feel easy in his. She wanted it back. Still not one to beg, he doubled her fingers into a soft fist and let go.

Lee rose and headed for the men's room, stopping first to say something to the waitress, to give her a sheet from a small notebook he took from his pocket.

On his way back to the booth, Lee once again stopped to talk to Wanda who handed him a paper. He settled himself once again across from her and slid the folded placemat over so she could read it. "The names of people who come here who have dogs who might be looking for a walker. Wanda's going to give them my name, help me maybe line up a few more customers.

"Here's what surprised me," he said, going right on with the conversation as though there'd been no break. "I was surprised to hear you were going to be a teacher." She didn't offer any comment. See how he liked stepping off into air. "Last you told me, you wanted to move to a farm to have that big family. Mist steaming up off the grass."

"Well … I'm still surprised you even heard it."

"Anyway," he said, "you weren't that keen on school. Always reading novels inside your desk in the back of the room. Or drawing. What changed your mind?" He fished two Tarringtons out of her pack, lit it for her. Then lit one for himself. Settled back against the cushions.

She almost said, What is it you want me to carry this time? Instead she began to talk. How had she ended up going to grad school to get her certification to become a teacher? Just out of college she had gotten a job in Boston writing replies to stockholders about errors in their dividend checks. All day long she sat at a desk in the middle of a hundred other desks with women dictating into Dictaphones. She shuffled the files around in her basket. Some days the tedium was so immense she fell asleep leaning on her hand, her pen resting on a yellow pad, stalled in the middle of a word.

"Working was not what I expected," she said. Then she confessed something she'd never mentioned to anyone, "My final day there I had so much old, I mean *old*, correspondence piled up in my basket, I couldn't leave it behind. Too damning. So I stuffed it all in a big file, my personal effects, I said, and took it back to my apartment and dumped it all down the incinerator."

He laughed. "Bad," he said. "Very unprofessional. But what about Nathan?"

Nathan Berman. She told him that was over. She'd ruined that. He waited, but she found she didn't feel like saying any more.

He nodded and leaned toward her. "When I got to the place I was crossing off the days, got short, as they say in the army. I started wondering what you were up to. Some days I'd say, No, she's bound to be married to wonderful Nathan by now. Probably has a couple of kids. But then I'd think, No, she didn't marry Nathan. He wasn't for her." He moved a little closer and squinted, as though he were doing some kind of diagnosis. "You didn't love Nathan," he said.

She looked across the table at Lee. "I don't know what happened, why I made the turn to here." Lee waited. So she went on, "When I was a kid, I loved to read books about English orphans. I'd hide down in my grandmother's basement under my mother's sewing table. I'd read and cry. Later, old novels by Gene Stratton Porter—*Girl of the Limberlost*. She had to cross the swamp and kids made fun of her muddy shoes. But then when I was just going on thirteen, I read the most wonderful book of all. That's what I told my mother when I finished it: This is the best book I will ever read. You know what that book was?"

He looked at her, his eyes intent, his chin resting on his two hands, one fisted around the other, the sleeves of his blue shirt rolled back to his elbows. She was about to tell him how she'd been imprinted on Rhett Butler like a baby duck. Frankly, my dear, I don't give a damn. But right at the edge of that she halted, looked into those dark eyes across the table and what her mouth said instead was, "Did you hold that gun up to your head and pull the trigger?"

"Yes," he said.

Lee swung on his jacket, opened the heavy door and they stepped out into the lights of 71st street. He rested his hand on her shoulder. Only September, but how quickly the darkness dropped down and that first clear smell of fall coming, summer gone. Neither of them said much on their way back down her quiet street. No Ursula now or any other dog-walkers. The hotel doorman, smoking beneath the big awning, the lobby bright behind him, the only sign of life. That, and the lights inside the brownstone apartments stretching to West Side Highway and the river. Del saw from halfway down the block the glow of her mother's living room.

Her mother had come to New York to run the outreach programs in a big west side church: the nursery school, the evening English classes, the after-school activities for kids wavering on the edge. Then Del had decided to move to the city to get her master's, to get certified to teach art. In graduate school she might fall in love and marry. She borrowed the money for tuition and moved in with her mother. They slept on narrow bunk beds in the tiny bedroom, squeezed into the fifth floor walk-up. They often reassured each other: It's only until the end of school, just one year.

At the bottom of the stoop, Del tipped her book bag toward the hotel lights to once again search for her keys. Lee supported the bag from the bottom so she could dive in with both hands.

"Next couple of days after work, I want to make the acquaintance of a few more potential dogs. Like I said, maybe you could be my assistant on the days you don't have classes. You think your mother would be willing to give me a reference, maybe accept a few phone calls to attest to my trustworthiness with canines?"

"I think so. You can ask her yourself. She's home." She found the key and started up the steps. Then she saw he had again remained on the sidewalk, his hand resting on the stone ball of the railing. "You aren't coming up?" She lilted her voice and managed a smile, but once more she felt that jar of surprise, that sudden drop from what she'd assumed.

He waved. "I'll be in touch," he said and started across the street. Then, just as she went to close the door, she heard his voice from somewhere up the block, "Dello, check the sky."

She searched across the way and then stretched out to scan the expanse above the river. Nothing. Cautiously she took a few steps down. Still seeing nothing, she turned in irritation to go upstairs. And there it was, bulging above their building—the moon—an immense orange, squashed along one side.

October. Only a month ago she could never have imagined that she would be beside Lee Merrick, five dogs leading the way. At the corner of 72nd and Central Park West, Del leaned into the thick warmth of Bernie's big furry body. This great Bernese Mountain dog was her favorite, with his general mutt matter-of-factness.

"Stay," Lee said to his three charges: Boris, Nicholas, and Manny, the Masher, a little Boston bull, his bulgy eyes perpetually anxious. Manny, Lee's one exception to only taking on large dogs.

Del laughed once again at their entourage: Lee, shawled in a red blanket her mother had given them, the thermos of cocoa, his box of dog biscuits and other canine paraphernalia humping beneath; her, layered in old sweaters and flannel that Lee had found at the Salvation Army for the cold fall mornings—and five hairy beasts, their joint breaths forming frosty balloons above them.

"Go," Lee said as the sign flashed *Walk* and all five dogs moved out, Del running a little to keep up with Ragu, the Great Dane. "Here," Lee said, passing her his leashes while he picked up the *Times* and three hot pretzels.

"Look." Del pointed to the clumps of sumac gone red, the lemon yellow ash shimmering beyond. They halted for a minute just to take it in. "That's all happened in less than a week." She'd been tunneled in since last Thursday: concrete and asphalt, the subway, classrooms and the stacks at the library. "People who don't come to the park would hardly know fall's going on." She shifted the dogs' leashes to rest her right arm.

"That's why we've got to get out of the city as soon as we can," Lee said.

We? Lee had talked several times of moving upstate, going into business with his rampage-buddy from his freshman year in college. Spray painting barns. His friend owned a landscaping business and had the sprayer, ladders, the beginning things he'd need. He couldn't see working for somebody, he said, and the painting would be seasonal, leave him time to write. Didn't he want to go back to college? Wouldn't it be good to get his degree? What for? he said. He could read on his own. Lee's parents had both graduated from college. Her mother hadn't. Going to college had been her mother's plan for her ever since she could remember.

Halfway across the park they came to the big open field where Lee ran the dogs most days, a place away from cross streets and baby carriages. The early morning cover had lifted and the Indian summer sun suddenly made Del feel she might pass out in the sauna of steamy Salvation Army wool. She peeled down to an undershirt, then held all the dogs while Lee set up camp—spread the blanket and tethered each dog to his appointed tree or shrub. She stretched out on her stomach, using their piles of shed clothes to pillow her chest and pulled the record book from Lee's bag to make out the dog-walking bills—her job while he ran the dogs.

Lee crouched and reached across her to pull the pretzels from the folds of the paper. She looked up into the blue cloth of his shirt, the tiny stitches around the pocket, and smelled the heat of him. He saw her and reached down to stroke her shaggy head. Using Ursula's dog clippers, they had cut each other's hair last week. "Good groom," he said.

She pushed up against his warm hand. For most of their time together since Lee arrived in New York, they had talked. Floated around the city on words. She had told Lee of her last relationship with a man she worked with in Boston, her pretended orgasms, about the terrible diaphragm, her fears that perhaps she was frigid. He had listened and nodded and when she had finished, it felt like something heavy had lifted.

Often after the dogs had their runs, she and Lee would sit, back to back, each forming a rest for the other and he would read to her what he was working on, his deep voice vibrating through to her chest. But he never kissed her, never held her close. It was as though he was waiting for something.

Lee smelled one of the pretzels and set it aside. She laughed. He looked at her and then laughed too. He had the habit of always smelling his food before he started, whether it be a hamburger or a pickle. When she had asked him why he did this, he had been surprised, like he assumed sniffing was common practice, and then he'd thought about it and said because he liked to smell things.

He passed her a pretzel. "Still warm," he said and tore the last one into five pieces, while the dogs watched expectantly. Each day Lee alternated the order in the same pattern. "Manny, you're first." Manny got ready.

"But why bother feeding a different dog first each day?" she said.

He stopped to consider. "Maybe some habit from sports. Or some mental game to fill the void."

"It reminds me of the first time I ever saw you. Do you remember when that was?'

He was busy licking the salt off his pretzel. Again she laughed.

"Now don't ask me why I do *this*." He extended his long pink tongue to move slug-like around the inner loop of dough.

"Stop," she said and covered her eyes, in an attitude of mock repulsion. At the same time surprised by the pulse of sexual heat.

"Do you remember or not?" she said again, working on her breathing.

"I know it was sometime right after school started, my senior year. 1955. You had this fuzzy pink sweater you used to wear." He looked at her breasts, his eyes warm. "That sweater was a favorite fantasy in the locker room." He smiled, his eyes now turned back into memory.

"Oh," she said. "I'll give you a hint. You were down on the outside basketball court coaching a bunch of junior high kids." He shook his head. "Don't you remember?"

He squinted his eyes closed, thinking hard. "Nope. Blank chamber. Probably another case of wet brain. Cells sacrificed to boiler makers." This was his only allusion to his drinking since that first afternoon at the diner. As far as she knew, he'd done no drinking since he'd started seeing her. He reached over and ran his hand down her spine. She shivered. "But hey, I do remember that sweater. You in that sweater. Only partial brain damage. There's still hope." Lee rose to unfasten Manny.

Del yawned, stretched in the heat of the sun. Once again Lee looked at her, but she found it hard to return his stare. She turned away, slid down on her belly, the cushion of sweaters, like a hand on her breasts. "After the bills, I may have to take a nap," she said.

Lee reached over and circled her eye with the tip of his finger. Manny whined. "You look tired," he said.

"I was up doing lesson plans."

"What're you going to lessen?" Lee squeezed the nape of her neck.

"Three point perspective."

"Your idea? Or something the regular teacher's pushing?"

"He's working his way through the usual."

Lee bent his body as though lifting a heavy burden. "Too bad you can't tap into the class from a different angle. Find the thing that's wanting to get out."

"You think that'd work with ninth graders?"

"Fourteen. Fifteen. The time of the perpetual hard-on. What's actually going on in there—the fight they had last night, the girl they caught in the hall … The medium for that."

Each week she did mini-lessons at a junior high in Harlem. Then next semester she would actually do fifteen weeks of student teaching in that same school, under the same teacher. Just the thought of it tightened her stomach.

"You'll do fine," Lee told her. "Just barrel on through; that's what most of them are up to." Del watched him trotting around the field, the loose lift of his arms. He saw her watching and smiled.

She opened his record book. Soon Lee returned and untied Boris and Nicholas for their runs. As he passed, he once again tousled her hair. Again that shiver.

In a while Lee came back across the field, the two Dobermans panting on either side of him. Boris sniffed at her on his way by. Lee glanced at the pile of bills she had ready to go. "Slowly, slowly I'm getting a little money together," he said. "This *for now* plan is working out okay. You know—*okay* because it's not forever."

"Yes," she said, even though she didn't quite know. What was Lee planning? And what part did she have in that plan?

Lee was on the far side of the field now, Bernie, a dark shaggy form backed by the thinning bushes. Fall and winter and spring and summer and then she'd be done with the master's, permanently certified to teach secondary art. For now or forever? Mostly she was working on making herself get up in front of the class, learning to do the drawing demonstrations without turning her back, and things with Lee seemed to be going okay one day to the next.

She stuck the finished bills in envelopes, wrote the dog's name neatly in the corner of each one. Just a few more to go and then maybe she could nap. Lee seemed to need less sleep than she did.

The dogs kept him busy much of the day. Usually he spent the evening writing alone in his room at the Y, sometimes late into the night. His first story about Bill Robinson and Lee and several other Home boys waiting in line outside the cellar door to go in to Roberta Gatling, stretched out on a damp blanket in a dark corner that smelled of mildew and mice. A story that made her cry. This going on at the same time she and Lee were singing *Red Sails in the Sunset* when they took the short cuts home after high school basketball games.

And he wrote a piece on his grandmother, Lena, who made him special cookie men with tri-colored buttons, who laughed when he jiggled the loose flesh of her underarm. Lena. His father as a small boy coming home from school day after day and when Lena did not open the door, fearing she'd finally done what she so often threatened—stuck her head in their gas oven.

She folded the rest of bills into envelopes and pulled half of the blanket under the low branches of a box elder. If she could just sleep for even ten minutes, she knew this stupor from the heat and late night would lift. She closed her eyes. In the distance, Lee's laugh. She snuggled down, still felt that warm pressure between her legs, the swell in her breasts against her arms, the memory of Lee's long pink tongue.

She woke to the feel of Lee's body against her, his breath on her neck, the blanket pulled over them. The air cool now, the bright of the sun no longer pulsing through her lids. Still sunk in that languor of half-sleep, she returned the pressure of his knees, the bottoms of her feet stretched against his toes. His warm hand slid along her ribs. Then he took hold of her hand and placed her fingers on her zipper. His body became completely still. She knew he was saying, Up to you. Up to her, but the languor, the sweet pressure between her legs was gone. What she felt now was a hard, cold bump, a root or a rock, poking her in the side. Her eyes still shut, holding onto that darkness, knowing there was no hope if she were to open them, she unzipped her pants. She felt Lee against her, undoing his belt. Without too much awkwardness, she managed to get her pants and underwear below her knees and from there to hook them with a foot to push the whole wad off. At least she didn't have to attempt the unlacing of shoes, but removing her socks, long gray things, with holey heels and red bands around the tops, well, that was impossible without sitting up. Her legs, unshaven all week, prickled. Lee slid his arm under her neck and turned her toward him. He pulled her in close, ran his fingers through her hair.

"Not the best of conditions," he said. "Better times are coming."

She rubbed her cheek against his smooth chest, in answer, rested her hand on his hip, his chinos only down a little, just the front undone. She tried to relax.

"Almost time for the after-work joggers," he said. And then laughing, he rolled her onto her back and himself on top of her. As though by reflex she spread her legs. She felt his zipper press into her thigh. "Better times, I promise you," he said as she felt him go inside her.

She raised her hips, tried to feel his rhythm. She wanted to give him pleasure. The ground was hard and cold beneath her. He pushed into her, into her, raising himself on his elbows. Within minutes she felt his whole body tighten, then loosen, become heavy. She held him, moved her hands along the goose flesh of his sides. But she did not pretend.

He lifted himself off. He reached down and found her underwear and pants beneath the blanket and pulled them up and handed them to her. "The joggers have arrived," he said.

For the first time she opened her eyes. All five dogs were stretched out sleeping. With Lee holding the covers she managed to wiggle into her clothes, and when she did, Lee pulled her against him again, nuzzled his head into her shoulder. "Takes a while," he said. "It'll get better. You'll see."

Lying on their backs, they watched the sky through the branches, watched yellow leaves spiral down. He raised her hand and slowly traced a circle on her palm.

"Looks like you may have been lurched," Wanda said, filling Del's coffee cup for at least the third time.

Del looked up from the stack of student drawings and shrugged. Her fourth week of student teaching and she felt overwhelmed, a knot tightening at the base of her neck, a knot that never let go.

"Could be," she said, in a light tone she did not feel. She pushed the money for the bill across the table, wanting to have no more commiseration. *Lurched*? Another one of Wanda's expressions that Lee would have tucked away in his little notebook. Wanda, another one of Lee's acquisitions, their waitress, the woman who had waited on them that first afternoon at the diner, who now, whenever business was slow enough, was drawn to stand by their table and chat, to tell Lee of her life, her daily pains. "I wouldn't let him do me that way," Wanda said, gathering the money and giving the table a perfunctory swipe with a sour towel.

Though Lee was already an hour late, she found herself wanting to speak in his defense: how he was usually so punctual, how she didn't feel he was *doing* her any way. She would wait another fifteen minutes and then go on home. It would be too late for *Gold Rush,* the final showing in the Chaplin Festival on East 63rd. Afterwards they might have made love as they had a few times before on the narrow couch in the dark of her mother's living room. *Made love* was surely not how it felt. Lee hurriedly pulling her underwear down, leaving his khakis on. Not surprising, he told her, that under such conditions she couldn't cum. She felt relieved to forego that scramble, that joining which left her feeling isolated. Inadequate.

"Men," the waitress said as she moved away.

Out the window Del saw Lee crossing the street and actually felt the urge to call to Wanda: see, here he is after all. Quickly she gathered up her papers and reached for her coat. If they took a crosstown bus, maybe they could still make the movie. Through the big windows she watched him approach. She leaned toward where he would pass, ready to tap on the glass. Just as he came even with her, she raised her hand; then she pulled back. He looked funny: the slackness around the mouth and jaw; that blurry lack of focus; his whole body, his movements through space, thickened, delayed. Though she had never seen him in this state, she knew what was wrong, remembered that same blurry look of her own father over his Cuba Libres, the lascivious leer of Aunt Bet's husband on holidays.

She knew she must get to him before he entered, before that large, bleary self stepped into the florescence and heat, before the diners turned his way. His army story of overturning an eight-hundred pound pool table moved her forward. She waved to Wanda and stepped out just as Lee opened the door to come in. She took hold of his sleeve to turn him aside.

He shook her off. "Don't," he said and opened the door again. "Got to go see dear old ... waitress." He reached out a hand and leaned against the frame. "Wanda. Got to see what old Wanda's up to."

"Lee," she said. She knew that pleading voice would not help, but there it was. Her whole body was shaking.

He turned his head and looked back at her. A look of dawning, like he was just realizing who she was, and like he didn't much care for what he saw. Then he swung his body around and when the glass door caught him in the shoulder, he thrust it fiercely away and stepped toward her. "Dello, Dello dear."

She saw that all of his energies were now focused on her. Still wasn't that better than him going on into the diner, a possible scene, perhaps the police? He leaned unsteadily toward her. Everything in his face pulled down. His dark eyes examined her, then tightened with suspicion.

She breathed. "Let's go back to the apartment. I'll fix some spaghetti." She started to take his arm, but instead she moved toward the crossing light and hoped he'd follow.

"Spaghetti," he slurred. "Won't that be lovely," the words thick as though his tongue had grown too large for his mouth. But he kept on moving across the street more or less beside her, every now and then jarring against her and then straightening himself with a shake. "Spaghetti with your lovely mother," he said as he slowed for the curb.

Her mother. She did not know if she would rather have her there or not there. Maybe it would have been better to make light of his condition, but she couldn't. She felt relieved to be moving forward, heading them toward safety. Maybe the cold air, the sleet, would help to clear his brain.

Just as they passed the corner drugstore, Lee veered off. "Got to get something," he said, and before she could speak, move, he was inside. For a few seconds she watched him caught in the bright light, the wet shoulders of his brown corduroy jacket, his dark head lifted above the pyramid of colored bottles, bath sponges, the metallic sun that shown on the beach scene display. She saw his mouth open and knew he was calling. She opened the door and went in.

"Got any prophylactics?" he yelled and began to move down the aisle marked *Eye Care* and *Vitamins*. So far she and Lee had used nothing. Lee turned to look at her. "Prophylactics. You know rubbers."

For the first time she felt like laughing. Just then a short man in a white coat with a very shiny head appeared at the end of the aisle. "May I help you, sir?" He did not seem frightened.

"Lee," she said.

Lee turned toward her. Again she had the feeling that for an instant he couldn't quite place who she was. "Ahh, my lovely," he said.

Del looked toward the druggist, his face neutral now. "Lee," she said again.

Lee seemed to lose energy, to deflate. "Never mind," he said. "Never mind." Then he passed carefully by her and out the door.

"Sorry," she said and followed. All the rest of the way down her street, Lee didn't speak. His head was hunched into his coat, in retreat from the icy rain, his hands in his pockets. She saw that the bedroom light in her mother's apartment was on. Ursula's rooms were dark. She imagined Boris and Nicholas watching them moving down the street, not recognizing Lee. He was someone else. Maybe her mother wouldn't come out. She could call in with a jolly voice through the door. Lee and I decided not to go to the movies. Too nasty out there. Spaghetti, coffee and maybe Lee would be more okay. He could sleep it off on the couch. She could make some plausible explanation to her mother. After all this was the first time Lee had done this since he came to New York. As far as she knew.

Lee bumped ahead of her up the five flights. Still silent. Fine. She felt all she was really doing was biding time until the alcohol could pass through his body, until he could eat, sleep, until he could return to himself. Maybe they were through the worst of it. As she opened the door, she saw there was no strip of light coming from the bedroom. She put her finger to her lips.

Lee mimicked her, his finger thrust straight up hard against his nose. "Quiet," he said in a loud voice, knocking into the tall bookcase that separated the living room from the kitchen. "Got to take a piss," he said and did not close the bathroom door behind him. She heard the toilet seat bang and turned to get the coffee going, the spaghetti water on. She heard the steady stream of his urine.

Finally it was quiet. She waited for the toilet to flush. She heard him stumble into the living room. Maybe he would flop down on the sofa and pass out. This would be the best scenario. Instead what she heard was the scrape of the big living room window. In February. In the middle of a sleet storm. Then a loud cry of laughter. She lowered the flame and stepped around the bookcase divider. Lee was leaning out the window, one hand gripping the raised glass, one foot wedged against the baseboard, the rest of him, his whole upper body outside and framed by the top pane. "My god, Lee," she said, starting toward him.

He actually turned so that his eyes peered at her through the glass. Again he laughed, a raw rattle of sound close to a scream. "Get back," he said.

And then her mother was there behind the bookcase, motioning her to go slow, to not indicate her presence.

"Lee," Del said, her voice surprising in its calm. "Come back inside." Again he laughed and raised himself further, leaned out above the street, his knuckles white from the weight. She imagined the whole frame breaking free. "Lee, please. You're scaring me." The phone was on the table by the window. Perhaps someone across the way would call the fire department, the police. "Lee. I …"

He lowered his body. She saw the color return to his hand. He sat on the sill, but still with his other leg hanging in the dark rain. His outer hand holding onto the raised window. She saw his fingers appear along the edges of the glass. "What will you do?" he said.

"Just come back in. Go to sleep for a while."

"I need a cigarette," he said, reaching his hand toward his pocket, and for a second shifting his balance so that the knuckles of his left hand paled again.

"Wait … I'll light you one." Del turned and already her mother was searching in her pocket, then lifting out a cigarette, extending it, with matches, toward her. Del almost dropped them in the exchange. Her hands were trembling, her jaw quivering, so that for a moment she could not bring the match to the tip, but finally she drew in and started slowly across the room.

"Don't touch me," he said. "Put it in my mouth and go on over there."

"Lee."

"Go on," he said.

She moved back, but only to the center of the room. She looked across the way to see if anyone was watching. The windows were all dark. He smoked, holding the cigarette between his lips. She saw his body relax, his foot rest on the floor. He leaned his head back against the frame, his lids began to droop. "Lee, don't you want to come in and stretch out on the couch, cover up with a warm blanket?"

He lifted his head and looked vaguely toward her. Then, he slid, collapsed slowly to the floor.

For a few minutes she and her mother did not move. Then Del reached across Lee and gripped the window. She eased it down and turned the lock until her fingers felt it slide under the catch. She stubbed out the cigarette. Her mother handed her a pillow, a blanket. Again they stood silent for many minutes. Finally she bent and spread the blanket over Lee's wet body. As she pushed a corner of the pillow beneath his head, his eyes opened, widened in fear, then dimmed with recognition. "Marry me," he whispered and then he slept.

7
Winter – 1972

ONE MINUTE RUDY WAS SITTING UP close to me, asking how could Geppetto make a little boy out of a piece of wood, and the next, Steve was pounding up the stairs, yelling, "Carla, get blankets, warm clothes; we're leaving, we won't be back." Then Rudy was crying—a thing he seldom did now that he was a big-boy four. He kept saying, "Why are you mad, Papo, why are you mad?"

Steve had already disappeared, his voice booming from the foot of the stairs, "Jane and Richie are coming too." Then the door banged shut.

It never crossed my mind to say, Stop, wait, no. I just started grabbing stuff and throwing it into paper bags, cursing Steve and my ignorance for not seeing that when I ran away from home at fifteen and hung out on the streets with bikers, I was headed for this turn not too far down the freeway.

That night while I tore around the apartment, Rudy was right behind me every minute, saying, "What are you doing, Mamo?" "Mamo, why are you mad?"

"Be quiet," I told him.

Finally when we were jammed into Richie's Chevy, sitting to the ceiling on top the blankets and bags and pillows, we found out what happened: Steve and Richie had gotten into a fight with a couple of guys in a bar, broken a lot of glass; Richie'd shown a gun and because they were both on probation, it wasn't going to be long before the police would be at our door.

"Where are we going?" I said.

"Up near Klamath Falls."

"Klamath Falls?"

"Oregon. To cut pulp wood. To stay out of sight for a while."

We arrived in the night, slept in the car in front of the mill office. A full moon. Everything white and frozen. Richie ran the engine off and on, but it was an old Chevy, an old heater. Rudy twisted into a little ball between us and sucked his thumb, something he hadn't done since he was a baby.

Steve and Richie got jobs in the morning. Their boss rented us a furnished trailer for almost nothing about fifteen miles up in the mountains. And it turned out it was for almost nothing. A rusted turquoise trailer, with half the windows boarded, squatting in a narrow ravine between two icy mountains a quarter mile from the road. Spruce branches loaded down with snow. Right away I understood those trees. We stood there in the cold looking at that trailer. Rudy clung to my knees. He had not said two words since we left the apartment. He just kept looking in my face and he never let go of some part of me.

We smoked a joint and went inside—two dark holes for rooms in the back with a couple of stained mattresses. In a ten by ten space in front, an old cook stove and a rusty potbelly, a dangerous looking pipe leaning out a hole on the side. Mouse turds and trash. No toilet, no water, no lights. And freezing cold. I wanted to cry. I gave Steve the isn't-there-any-other-way look.

"No," he said, "we got this on credit."

I knew from our inventory in the car he was right. Between the four of us we had three packs of cigarettes, some grass, a few bottles of beer, one jar of instant coffee, a dozen hot dogs, toilet paper, tampons, and eighteen dollars and forty-three cents. Plus I had a couple dozen goof balls, undeclared.

Jane and I started clearing out the junk while Steve and Rich brought in wood. Steve got the pipe a little safer, built a fire. They found a frozen brook not far from the trailer and an outhouse in back. It was a kerosene cook stove and the tank was half-full. Things were looking up. Richie made a sled out of an old square of plywood by fastening a rope through a hole. Jane and Rudy and I broke a place in the ice and filled up a bunch of plastic milk jugs we found in the trash. We hauled those back, with Rudy smiling, finally, and whipping a piece of leftover rope in the snow. His eyes said, Mush, you huskies, but no sounds came from his mouth. "See, this isn't so bad," Jane said to him. He didn't answer.

We heated water in a big old pot and began to clean away some of the filth. Steve cooked hot dogs that we ate with our fingers, licking the warm grease as it ran down our wrists. We stayed stoned and rode on this Family Robinson rush through January. Richie and Steve started bringing in money. Richie met a truck driver who got us pot or anything else we wanted. We found a junk store and bought kerosene lamps, a card table and chairs, a small black and white TV we could run off a battery. Steve put an old antenna up and we crowded around watching shadows swimming through snow. We pulled the battery back and forth to the car for recharging.

Rudy had never been a chatterbox, but at the trailer he wouldn't answer any of us. Even when he played with his little truck, though he moved his lips, no rudnnn rudnnn came out. I knew there was nothing wrong with his hearing because sometimes I'd whisper, Rudolph, and he'd always turn around right away and smile at me funny. I tried to get him to talk: How many fingers? How old are you? Nothing.

It started to get on Steve's nerves. "Leave the kid alone. He'll talk when he feels like it."

When there wasn't anyone around, I tried to coax him. What was the name of that dog that lived next door to us back at the apartment before we came here? I didn't say *home* because we'd lived so many places since Rudy was born, I'm not sure he knew quite what that meant. Not that I knew much more about it because my father was in the army and I must have moved nine times before I got to fourth grade. Anyway it didn't matter how I said it because when I started with the questions, Rudy walked away.

I got scared maybe he was retarded, but then I thought, No, that can't be. Before we left Monterey, he could sing along with all the popular songs, fill in the words when we read stories over again.

February. We got by, figured we could make it till spring, figured we could go back to California by then. But. Jane got pregnant and puke-sick every morning. Steve and Richie had a blow up: I'm tired of you doing this. And I'm fed up with you doing that. Rich and Jane packed and left in the night. I'm sorry, she said as she hugged me goodbye. Jesus, me too. I thought of the days there with only Rudy.

I'd be talking to the walls.

The first week they were gone, Steve stayed in town. "Just till I get paid so I can get a car."

"Take us with you. I'm not staying out here by myself," I screamed after him as he walked out to the road to hitch to the mill the next morning. An angry dog face looked back at me and snarled. It was not the face from five years ago, straight-ahead eyes, alive and surprising; not the mouth that talked about the crescent moon back when we met. Said, Carla, you are one pretty woman. Bet that snarling face was the one Steve's first wife left, packed up one day and said, I never want to see you again. And a few other things.

When he kept walking, I thought, Screw you. I'm taking the kid and leaving this hole. "You'll be sorry," I called to the black leather speck in the distance. My mind filled with getting even, to the sight of him coming home that next Friday night to a dark, cold trailer. No me. No son. I turned to go back and saw Rudy standing in the doorway, his little face pinched, silent tears, four going on forty. Then I cried too, wondered how I got to this place, living in a beat up trailer. Just what my father always used to forecast, that I was going nowhere.

I picked up Rudy, felt his chicken-feather head under my chin. I closed the door tight against the wind. "It's okay, Doodle," I said to him. We sat by the stove. "Papo will come back with a car Friday. Maybe he'll bring you something. How would you like that?" But he didn't answer.

Anyway where would I have gone, hitching with a child in the middle of winter? Not to my mother to hear my father make I-told-you-so sounds. To hear him say, What's the matter with the dummy? I looked around the little kitchen. There was enough food, enough wood. We'd survive.

February and March I slept. I did enough phenobarb to keep me under. Something bad was happening to us, but I was too doped to do anything. Steve blamed me; I blamed him. We barely spoke, fucked in the dark, then rolled away and did not touch. Steve got an old car, one that wouldn't start. Every morning we heard him screaming at it. He sounded like my father. Rudy and I stayed out of his way. When we knew he was finally gone, we hauled in wood, dragged water back from the brook. With a black crayon, I X'd off the days on the calendar hanging by the sink. I washed dishes and watched the inch-by-inch track to spring when I was going to do something for sure. During the day I slept, curled on a mattress in front of the stove. I never read to Rudy anymore. Instead he sat in the crook of my body. He colored and watched junk on TV. The cartoon voices laughed from a distance. When the battery died, he just sat in silence. He never made any sounds, not even when he cried. Curled on that mattress, my body felt thick, wrapped in a cocoon. Always there was the smell of kerosene.

The more sleep I got, the more I needed. Before Steve got home, I tried to be up cooking something at the stove. He came in and glared at me. I stopped getting dressed, stopped combing my hair.

"You should see yourself," he said. "Why don't you get cleaned up and lay off the pills. I can't stand to look at you."

"So don't," I answered. I felt ugly. I didn't care.

Then it happened.

I opened my eyes to darkness. Steve was shaking me hard. "Jesus, Carla, wake up. Something's wrong with Rudy. I think he's poisoned. Maybe your pills."

I heard Steve calling to me down a tunnel, felt him slapping me, heard Rudy's name. I sat up and saw Rudy wrapped in a blanket at the foot of the mattress. His face dead white, his body still. Steve pulled on my pants, put my arms in my coat. "I tried to get him to throw up. Nothing. He's unconscious."

Steve carried Rudy down the long snowy path to the car, kind of pushing me ahead, saying firmly every time I staggered, every time I fell, "Get up, Carla. Keep going. We have to get him to the hospital."

Finally we came to the road. I held Rudy on my lap. The car started. Steve drove the fifteen miles in silence. I sat looking into the strange still face of my child, saying over and over, Please, God, let him be all right. I promise, I promise…

When we got to the emergency room, they rushed him away. Steve told them off to the side what he thought Rudy took. I looked at the floor.

"What happened?" a nurse asked

"I don't know," I said. They knew I had neglected my child, but they didn't accuse me.

Steve and I sat alone in the waiting room. He didn't accuse me either. Once he touched my arm and said, "We'll hear soon."

Finally the doctor came out. "I think he's going to be okay. He's sleeping. We'll know more in the morning."

We stayed with him in his hospital room all night. From the waiting room, I brought in a book I hoped might make Rudy happy, something to take us back to the good times in Monterey. All night we watched his small body, unmoving beneath those white sheets. Now and then Steve leaned over the bed and placed his hand on Rudy's chest to feel him breathing. And though I wanted to stroke his cheek, what right did I have?

I sat there beside Rudy in all that darkness, my arms wrapped around that book, and thought about this: What *had* happened? But all I could remember was Rudy's face above me, rolling my head back and forth and pulling on my hands. Then his fingers in my mouth wiggling my tongue. "Let me sleep," I said. "Just a few more hours, please."

Finally gray light came into the room. Rudy opened his eyes, but for a long time he didn't move. Steve took one of his hands and squeezed a little, a game they used to play. Then he rolled the bed up, put another pillow under his head. All the while Rudy was silent. I wanted to tell him how sorry I was, but I couldn't face him.

After a while Rudy shifted, and opened his eyes. Right then I lifted the book and placed it so the first page was in front of him. "You know who that is, Rudy. That's Geppetto. And that's Jiminy. Remember? But it was as though he didn't hear me.

Steve set the book aside and lifted Rudy into the wheelchair. He pushed him from the window to the door, from the door to the window, over and over. "Oh, Rudy, Rudy," Steve said, tears in his throat.

Those words and the soft squeak of rubber, the slight motion of Rudy's chair were the only sounds for a long time. Then when I thought I could not bear another moment, I heard a whisper, a voice I didn't know.

"Why did he want a little boy?"

Ten days later we packed up the car and moved back to Monterey.

8
Nickel Limit – 1964

Even with chunks of her missing where the silver backing has peeled away, she is enormous. Resting her hands on the wide shelf of her protruding abdomen, Del bends a little to examine her nude reflection in the smoky dresser mirror that had belonged to Lee's grandmother. Two weeks overdue, she looks like she swallowed an immense ball. Her swollen breasts with their great brown nipples and glistening stripes of stretched skin look more like cubist fruit than parts of the body she knows.

3:45. In an hour or so Lee should be starting to gather up his paint stuff. Oh, let him get home at the usual time. She drapes the wet towel over the bedroom door and begins to rub in cocoa butter, a gift from Sue who said it's supposed to help prevent stretch marks. Sue, the wife of the friend who backed Lee's spray-painting business, pressed Del to accept maternity care packages, small things she still had on hand because she said she certainly was *never* going through that again. Del likes Sue, but her blow by blow accounts of her forty hours of labor are not soothing.

Mostly though she feels prepared. She likes her doctor with his wooden leg, the little five-bed hospital in an old house, how dark they keep the nursery. Twelve miles does seem a ways. Still everyone says first babies come slowly, and besides she can picture Lee being up for a delivery in the backseat if need be. They've both read what you need to do.

In fact, it's Lee who convinced her it would be better to have the child naturally if all goes well. They read *Childbirth Without Fear* and she practiced the breathing, with Lee kind of coaching. The main thing is to stay as relaxed as possible since it said much of the pain was really caused by fear: tensed muscles working against the natural delivery. She knows when to breathe long and deep, when to pant, and when to push. At least as much as you can know before really going through it. It's funny she'd never even heard of natural childbirth before Lee told her about it. She was born cesarean and assumed that was how all babies were born. It wasn't until she was ten and began to wonder how come there wasn't a doctor ever mentioned as one of those in attendance around the baby Jesus that she found out otherwise. Even though her mother, a registered nurse, had told her about how babies were made when she was quite young, she'd been pretty hazy on graphing it out anatomically—making it sound more like a gardening project, the planting of seeds. Lee would have even liked a home birth, but Del didn't feel ready for that. The big thing he said was no anesthetic. That was bad for the baby. Unless of course you needed it because something went wrong.

As she smoothes in the last dab of cocoa butter, a small bulge pokes out by her distended navel, then that la cucaracha roll and another mound jabs up beneath her hand. "Hello," she says to this always surprising miracle. A foot? A fist? "Time you made your move, you stubborn kid."

When she speaks, Clyde, their wayward boxer, sprawled on the foot of the bed where he is not supposed to be, raises his head and wags the stump of his tail.

"Not *you*, Clyde," she tells him. Though certainly stubborn applies. Clyde, so dubbed by Lee, appeared at their door months ago, a scrawny, brindled boxer with unclipped ears, and a broken rope around his neck. Already an outlaw. All their inquiries brought forth no owners. Either he'd come too far or, as Del suspects, his former owners were feeling well shed of him. He will not be reformed from his need to fight and has caused them no end of trouble with their neighbors and landlord. Only last week he ripped through the screen in the bedroom window to get out on the roof where he raved away at his number one enemy, a giant black dog.

"To say nothing of the cost for a new screen, Clyde," she tells him, leaning over into his pug face. Hearing her scolding tone, he slinks from the bed and out of her sight—maybe headed in to sniff the meat. Hugging the towel around as much of herself as she can,

Del pads into the kitchen to check on the hamburger. She wants to have the meatloaf well on its way when Lee comes up those stairs. She squeezes the thawing mound. The outer layer is gooey, dead-brown and giving off the spoiled stink of warm blood, but ice-hard at its center. 4:00. And still the war with the terrible support stockings ahead and the meatloaf to get mixed, using the new recipe Lee's mother sent her.

With a shove, the butcher knife splits the frozen center in half. By the time the street lights blink on, she should hear the sound of the holey muffler. She drops the chunks into a bowl and sets it in a few inches of hot water. If the car hasn't backed into the driveway by then, well, she knows what that might mean. Meatloaf and baked potatoes and…There is no not knowing it anymore. She opens the cupboard—a small can of peas, the only choice.

Clyde stands tensed at the top of the stairs, watching the front door. There is no partition that closes off their apartment from the entry, nothing to keep him from bolting out if someone leaves the downstairs door open too long. Plus the lack of privacy. This is why the place is only sixty dollars a month. Clyde gives her a long look. "No, it isn't time yet," she says and steps carefully around him.

She lets herself down into the funny nursing bra, a great hammock of straps and buckles and manages to find her way into the right holes of her underwear, her toes bypassing the places she slit to add in more elastic. Then she rests on the edge of the bed to wrestle on the stockings—support hose so snug one feels mummied inside their opaque rigor. She hurries to stretch the elastic, one inch at a time up her swollen thighs.

She hears Clyde plop down, probably at the head of the stairs. What to do with Clyde when she goes into labor? For a week or two before her October 25th due date, she was ready, setting out her hospital bag full of things her mother made. But October 25th passed and day after day nothing happens. She has stopped even looking for the bloody show every time she goes to the bathroom—which is often indeed. She has settled into a stoic calm.

Her shoes? They are sticking out from beneath the bedspread. She needs to start putting them up after she takes them off, somewhere she can reach them without stooping. With concentration, so she doesn't tip over to perhaps lie kicking on the floor like a fat beetle trying to right itself, she manages to bend down. The drone of the Doyles' TV murmurs through the sagging floor boards. It's a comfort to know there's life below, the scream of a kid, Madge's laugh. Especially when Lee is in a silent time.

She drops her green corduroy maternity dress over her head—this tent of a thing the only clothing that still fits over her strange bulk. She pushes her short ashy hair back into place and leans into the mirror to put on a bit of pale lipstick. Lee has taken to calling her Buddha-Mama from how she looks in the tub, but this hardly bothers her at all. She loves so much about being connected to this demanding swell of life within her. Anyway she knows she'll soon lose the fifty pounds once the baby is born.

She looks out the window and listens. Let it have been a good spraying day at the barns. Lee has become more and more withdrawn these last weeks. A bad sign. He had been okay for months. This would be a terrible time for it to happen—the baby coming, the rent due soon. But how he hates the spraying. His arms and hands always giving off a faint barn-red glow no matter how hard he scrubs. His conversation this past week mostly muttering about the stink of paint, how he never has the time or energy to write. The pressure is on to finish before true winter sets in. Lee will not get the other half of his money until the whole barn is done and approved by the county.

The recipe, *Meatloaf Supreme,* perfectly typed and filed in the shiny wooden box, is in the section headed, *Entrees.* Right between *Basil-Buttered Fish Sticks* and *Jungle Pie.* For her twenty-fourth birthday last month, Lee's mother sent her the box, loaded with easy, economical dishes, many of which Lee grew up on. Since their fifteen-dollar-a-week food budget means tuna, hot dogs, or hamburger has to be central, these entree cards are the only ones smudged with grease. She squeezes the meat; the final frozen hunks give way. Right off she sees she doesn't have several of the main ingredients: the ½-lb. ground pork, the green pepper, and probably most critical for making the meatloaf "supreme," the can of Chef Boyardee sauce. No way Madge Doyle will have any peppers on hand, but since canned spaghetti is a frequent entree on Madge's menus, there's a chance she may be able to borrow some sauce. The whole concept of an entree will make Madge whoop with laughter. Madge, who often says, Hon, you want to know how not to do it, drop in on Clay and me. Really, she and Lee *like* to drop in on the Doyles. Their laid-back ability to live in so much disorder is somehow reassuring. The four of them play marathon games of nickel-limit poker most weekends. None of them has enough money to go anywhere. And drinking isn't part of it either, so she doesn't have that worry.

4:15. Still enough time. She puts the oven on preheat. *350 degrees for 1 hr. (or until done in the middle.)* Clyde follows her down the stairs. He loves to go visiting too, loves to lick the sticky faces of Madge and Clay's kids, Tammy and Kevin. She raps on the door. The noise from the TV is so loud she doubts if Madge could hear a gunshot, let alone the sound of knocking. She and Lee have decided they do not want a TV even if they could afford it. Not only is it not good for children, it's just so mind-numbing, period. She bangs with both fists. More than likely Madge is stretched out on the couch doing a crossword puzzle or reading a thick romance—part of what she calls her "anywhere but here" collection—and Kevin and Tammy will be sitting eating Cocoa Puffs with their noses almost touching the screen. She puts her mouth to the crack and yells, "Madge, it's me, Del." Still no response. She tries the door, but it's locked. Well, it'll have to be meatloaf minus the supreme. Maybe she can just up the onions and salt. As she starts back up the stairs, Clyde rears up against the Doyles' door and begins to bark nonstop.

Through the racket she hears Madge's voice. "Turn that boob-box down, s'il vous plaît." The door opens. Clyde squeezes past.

"Del. Don't tell me you've gone into labor."

"I don't think I'm ever going to have this baby." She steps into the living room which is much less scrambled than usual. "I wonder if you might have some spaghetti sauce for the Meatloaf Supreme."

Madge does whoop. "Now there's an oxymoron if I ever heard one. Maybe you could siphon some off from a can of Spaghetti-O's."

Madge's head is covered with pink foam rollers, placed at odd angles, hanks of her hennaed hair still sticking out here and there. She pats the whole business and gestures toward Tammy who is standing on a chair, a big purple comb sticking out of the pocket of what must be one of Clay's work shirts, *Syracuse Concrete* stamped on the chest.

"I'm going to be a beauty-parlor lady," Tammy says.

Clyde busies himself eating the stray bits of cereal that have dropped on the rug.

"That's right, baby. We're not going to let them Betty-Crocker you. Kevin, turn the TV down." When he doesn't respond, Madge reaches over and lowers the volume. She takes the mirror from Tammy and examines her head. "Tammy's getting me dolled up for our seventh anniversary. Clay's bringing home Chinese. That'll do it, lovey. Thank you." She helps Tammy down from the chair.

"Seventh anniversary," Del says. She has been married for seven months. "I can't imagine."

"Me either," Madge says. "Let me see what I can excavate by way of sauce."

Tammy joins her brother close to the screen. Looking out the corner of his eye, Kevin ups the volume. The slamming of cupboard doors, the banging of things being moved about. Madge sometimes only unpacks the groceries that have to be refrigerated. The rest she leaves sitting in bags on the counter. Eliminating the middle-step she calls it. Likewise, rather than wash the pots after dinner, she puts a little water in them, sets them out on her back stoop, and when she needs one, she opens the door, gives it a quick scrape with a spatula and dumps a can of whatever in.

As scattered as Madge is, Del is still hoping Madge will take care of the baby some so she can sub at the junior high just up the hill or maybe do a little waitressing at the diner across the street. Something close so she can run in to nurse the baby and check on things. True, Madge is not who Del might have chosen as the ideal child-care person, but she isn't a screamer and she always grants Kevin and Tammy a kind of resigned patience. We're all in this together, she often tells them. Anyway Del figures mostly the baby will be sleeping those first few months, and after that they'll be more on their feet to find a better situation.

Madge returns from the kitchen, bearing a bottle of ketchup. "No sauce, but I'll bet that hamburger'll never know the difference. Lee either. Lee around?"

Del's stomach gives an anxious lurch. "What time is it?"

"Humm," Madge says. "No clock. But I'd say it's heading toward five. I was hoping he could stick a mouse trap up in the hole in the ceiling. I can't reach it even on a chair and Clay's phobic when it comes to rodents."

Del takes the ketchup and opens the door. Clyde follows. "Lee should be here in the next half hour." Her voice is too cheery. She has never said much about Lee to Madge. But of course Madge knows. Clay knows. Just as the old woman on the other side of the house must know. All had to have heard Lee's banging arrival home in the middle of the night a few months ago. The smell of burning paper. Home…

By the time she lifts her belly to the top of the stairs, she's panting. She dumps half a cup of ketchup onto the hamburger. The onion's squishy. She peels away the first layer and cuts what is left into pieces. Her eyes tear. Home. Since she finished graduate school at the end of July and came to live with Lee here in their own little apartment, they're doing better. Mostly. So much better than the occasional get-togethers via Greyhound that once required her to hock her typewriter and Lee to sell a pint of blood to pay for the round-trip. Then only a day or sometimes two before he had to turn around and take her back to the bus station in Syracuse, with the added tension of possible car trouble—the oil light coming on or the thermostat shooting up to the danger red zone or worse, and her worrying if they'd make it on time. Critical that she get back for student-teaching by the next morning.

Madge's seventh anniversary. It's true she can't imagine the forever readjustment of one's self to another. The trying to figure out what Lee really wants, what she's done wrong that has caused him to stop talking. Her only-child-self who'd been allowed so much room, who'd seldom bumped up against anything she couldn't sidetrack until now.

Half a cup short on the onions. She dumps in some extra salt and pepper and wipes her eyes. Lee will think she's been crying again.

The marriage had begun in such a rush. The positive pregnancy test at Sanger Clinic in March when she was already six weeks along, the week or so of having that reality sink in, with Lee making jokes about other options—like her bouncing herself down the stairs.

Then the blood tests and license. Lee's farewell to his dog-walking service and preparations to start a barn-painting business upstate, and for a few dithery days, her on the rim of chucking the student teaching and the final graduate courses to go with him. After all, what she always wanted, she reminded her protesting mother, was to stay home and raise a family. But Del, her mother said, You only have four months to go.

The rounded lump of meat in the middle of the pan looks like the real thing. She drizzles a puddle of ketchup onto the top and sets it in the oven along with two wrinkly potatoes. She reaches into the heat and tweaks off one of the eyes she's missed. Even though they've only been married seven months, Lee has already turned the wedding into funny stories for Sue and her husband. Lee has even written a wedding short story that's been accepted in some off-beat magazine in Oregon. But when she really thinks about it, it doesn't make her laugh. The honeymoon. Certainly a detour from the scenes in romantic novels. Running for the train at Grand Central to get off somewhere in Connecticut at the first stop where they could see through the moving window, a huge motel sign blinking just over the hill. At that point in the replay Del always grimaces—their first night of wedded bliss—sunk in the torpor that comes in the early months of pregnancy. She fell asleep soon after Lee entered her body. There is one slender fact she holds on to in the middle of all Lee's ironic re-workings of the marital material: Lee asked her to marry him before her pregnancy was known; no replotting is going to change that.

The silverware drawer is jammed as usual. You have to pull on it from just the right angle or it settles into its crooked offness with more determination. And never too hard or it comes flying out and sends everything crashing to the floor. When it opens, she sees mice have left their droppings once again. She should put out traps too, but the flipping around of the trap in the night, finding their small twisted bodies the next morning, is too awful.

True, maybe she and Lee wouldn't have managed to get married if she hadn't gotten pregnant, but she knows she married him because she wanted to, cannot imagine having married anyone else. And aren't things mostly smoothing out now?

Clyde's nails click on the stairs as he goes down to greet Lee when he does arrive. Amazing how the dog always knows, probably by the change in the fall light, that the old Pontiac will, should, appear at the curb sometime in the next fifteen minutes. If it doesn't get a flat, if the starter hasn't given out altogether. Still, for a car that only cost fifty dollars, it's doing all right.

She hears the Doyle's door open and the sound of Kevin's voice in the entry, then Clyde's friendly growl of response. Madge must have forgotten to lock Kevin back in or he's gotten up on a chair and slid the bolt. Del smoothes the bed and goes to the head of the stairs.

"Kevin," she calls to the five-year-old, "be careful not to let Clyde out the storm door."

Kevin has both hands on the knobs of the inside door and both legs up, swinging it slowly back and forth as he sways his weight. He doesn't answer.

"Kevin," she says again.

He and Clyde look up at her. "What?" he says.

She laughs. "You know what."

He smiles. "Okay," he tells her.

"Thank you. Because we don't want Clyde getting into any more trouble, right?"

She turns into the kitchen to check on the meatloaf. *Supreme* is not how she would describe it, sitting now in a pool of grease. Okay, she isn't much of a cook compared to Lee's mom, but she's getting better at making the fifteen dollars cover what they need, though certainly it doesn't allow for anything exotic. Each grocery day she takes her little red plastic calculator to the market and carefully clicks off each purchase, never again wanting to have to eliminate items because she doesn't have enough money after the cashier rings the groceries up.

Everything is ready for Lee's arrival. She circles to the end of the hall, the space they've turned into the baby's room. She keeps her ears attuned to the noises in the entry. Kevin can't be counted on fully. Only five and already this kid is way ahead of them.

She likes to just stand to the side and look at the baby corner. Her favorite baby things are the undershirts, with the little overlapping shoulder pieces so you can slip them over the baby's head more easily. She refolds the stack of nighties, tucks in each drawstring, and puts them on the top shelf where the soft blankets have been. Only one arrangement is possible—the crib, a loan from Sue, in the corner. Beside it, the little bookcase for the baby clothes, the stacks of diapers, all gifts from her mother. She painted the bookcase white with what was left over from repairing Clyde's damage to the bathroom door. She wishes there was room for some kind of changing table, but at least there's a window and on this she has hung yellow cafe curtains she made from some material Lee's mother sent. She would have liked something more nursery-looking; yes, even with little chickens or Bo-Beeps. Well, maybe not Bo-Beeps, for secretly she's hoping for a boy, a son for Lee. Though of course just a healthy baby, boy or girl, will be fine. Certainly Lee has never said.

There's a scuffle of sound below. The storm door opens and slams. Oh god. "Kevin," she calls. She knows it's not Lee, or Clyde would be leaping and whining with joy. "Kevin," she calls again, starting for the stairs. She looks down just in time to see his little head ducking back into the Doyles' apartment. No dog.

She pulls her jacket from the hook. Clyde's rope leash with the choke collar is not on the nail where it's supposed to be. She makes a quick tour through the rooms, trying to think where she set it down after Clyde's walk. As she passes the refrigerator, she scoops up a few sliced hotdogs buried in the beans from last night's leftovers in one hand while she slides her arm through her sleeve with the other. Should she turn the oven off? And then she hears the terrible screeches of a small creature. Clyde has hold of something.

When she reaches the front porch, she listens for the direction of the cries. Just then the street lights flick on. Where is Lee? She searches the street up ahead by the light of a passing car. Somewhere off to the left now, she hears stuttering growls. She runs, cradling her belly in her hands as she heads across the road. She doesn't scream. If Clyde knows she's panicked, he will only clamp down more fiercely.

Up near the intersection, the taut back legs of Clyde appear just beyond the wheels of a parked semi. She rounds the edge of the truck. Clyde has hold of a kitten, a small wet mess of white fur that yowls and claws as the dog shakes it. Del would have preferred the enemy black dog to this—someone's loved kitten being mangled by her delinquent pet. She makes one last backward glance toward the front of their apartment, willing the Pontiac to be there. No sign of Lee.

Even if she had Clyde's leash, it would have been near impossible to get the kitten away from his clenched grip. Hot water might part two warring dogs, but she knows of no way to make him let go now. But she must try. She tosses away the hotdogs and takes hold of a large branch lying in the gutter, then she straddles Clyde's backend, gripping his rear between her two legs. She raises the limb and brings it down hard on the back of the dog's head. Surprised or momentarily stunned, Clyde drops the wet bundle. Del tightens her legs and latches hold of Clyde's collar with both hands. But either the kitten is too paralyzed with fear or too injured, for it does not scoot off as Del had hoped. Several cars pass. Surely they must see what's happening. All she needs is for someone to lift the kitten to safety. Her knees are weakening. Just as she shifts to ease the ache in her back, a pain in her abdomen seizes her and she feels a gush of warmth down her thighs. "Clyde, if you cause some harm to this baby..."

Then Lee is there. His one hand setting her carefully to the side while he lifts Clyde with the other. "Pick the kitten up in your jacket," he says. "I'm going to put Clyde in the house."

"Lee, I think my water just broke."

Clyde, subdued now, held tight in his arms, Lee looks at her, his face full of concentration. In the last light she sees the small flecks of red paint speckling his neck and chin. He smiles. "At last," he says. "All right. Put the kitten on the floor of the car, by the front seat and wait for me there. We'll take the kitten to the vet. It's right on the way, and head on to the hospital. Maybe Madge can track down an owner."

He starts across the street. "Dr. Sullivan and my bag. And turn off the meatloaf," she calls after him and he nods his head that he's heard. She remembers she fastened the leash to the downstairs railing. He'll see it when he turns on the light.

Beyond the terrible ache in her back, the pain of the contraction has eased. She pulls off her jacket and manages to work it under the torn kitten. The kitten looks up at her and gives a small cry. She carries it to the car and slides in after it. Out the window, Lee's long body moves toward her, her suitcase in one hand and Clyde held firmly on his leash in the other. Why had she worried so? Lee has come home. He was right there when she needed him. Lee settles

Clyde in the back.

"I'm going to put him in the vet's kennel just for tonight. Can't risk any more trouble." The car starts right up. "I finished the barns today. Dr. Sullivan's nurse said she'll get hold of him." He leans across the steering wheel and looks the kitten over. "Hard to tell," he says. "Madge is calling the vet."

Another full contraction takes hold of her.

"Here's a good one," she says. Lee places his hand on her hardened abdomen. Begins to count. She puts her head back onto the seat and closes her eyes, breathes long and deep.

Clyde rests his cold nose on her neck. Somehow Lee will get them there. Above the low rumble of the motor, she begins to form the story they will tell:

On the day you were born …

9
Peripheral Vision – 1966

LEE DID NOT GET OFF the 11:26 from Syracuse that brought him home nights from his job at the circulation desk. The bus pulled away, leaving the space where he should have been, blank.

It was then that Del knew.

The apartment dark behind her, with only the low hum of the humidifier, the sporadic thuds of Mark's fists as he turned in his crib. Del leaned her forehead against the winter glass to search the street once more. She willed him to be there: tall, his corduroy jacket open, no matter how cold, long strides to cross the street, never looking either way. Great peripheral vision, he always said. But he was not there, the road unmarked by his prints. Only the two dark tracks moving off as far as she could see. Only the empty laundromat, a few snowy cars in front of the bar. She listened for the bus to stop further on. Maybe he was sleeping and didn't wake up to pull the cord. Her forehead ached; the cold began to move down the bridge of her nose.

When had she first known this night was coming? When had the rush of morning talk, dinner conversation, run down? Their few words reduced to necessity: We're out of milk. I can take care of Mark until three.

He had been all right in August. Summertime. He was still working afternoons at the sawmill; she was waitressing breakfasts and lunches so they only needed Madge to take care of Mark for an hour in between. They had even been happy in August, she's sure of that. As soon as they ate dinner, they headed out with Mark in the stroller and Clyde on his leash. They walked the loop from their apartment to the edge of town; then up the hill and back the other way. Almost always they caught the changing of the light, that time when the trees, the houses shine. Then the coming on of August dark, the voices on porches, the creak of swings, and always the smell of mowed grass, something sweet, unnamed.

She pressed her cold fingers against her forehead, moved away from the glass. She knew he would not be home until long after last call. She knew in a few hours, when the alcohol rose inside him, he would call her, and she would answer—fear of an accident, the scream of the phone piercing Mark's sleep. Because she must. She slid the closet door open. Mark turned, made snuffling noises, but he didn't wake. In the dark she felt for her plaid skirt, the green sweater. She hung them on the back of the door, ready for school tomorrow.

Yes, he had still been fine in August. They'd been happy. After the walks Lee would put Mark to bed. He was always better at that than she was. While he rocked Mark, she would take a bath, then lie on the bed in her white night gown. Wait. When all was quiet, Lee would lie next to her. Night air would drift over them, float them along on the chafing of crickets, the occasional whir of a passing car.

After Mark's birth, it was always right. As though something in her body had given, eased. She was filled with desire, that thick, languorous longing, her limbs heavy, her skin alive. Yes, it had been all right then. Walking along beside him in the dark, a little breathless, she sometimes felt she might dissolve, melt into the summer night, all overlapped by the air.

12:00. She needed to be as ready as she could be. But that was hard to do when she didn't know what was coming. Only that something was. The kitchen. With just the street lights to guide her, she gathered the student sketchbooks into one stack, the papers she must finish during her free period into another. She slid them into her bag with her gradebook and set them beneath the chair. She pushed the trash basket under the table out of sight and the kitchen matches beneath the dish towels. Though surely he wouldn't do that again. The bathroom. The razor in the bottom of the hamper. And on second thought the toothbrush glass too.

She went into the living room. Lee's typewriter was pushed to the back of the card table. His notes and books, usually lined up and ordered, lay in piles. His maps and outlines, usually tacked along the wall in neat rows, had fallen to the floor behind the table. The wadded pages of the novel he'd been working on were jammed behind his thesaurus. Just leave it, he'd told her. A reminder of what it's all come to. Weeks ago. He hasn't written since. She pried open the folds of one of the crumpled sheets and spread the paper flat with her palms, then tipped the page toward the light from the street:

> *Merrick / Dry Season*
> *206*
> *the man sat in the back of the bus, the don't-fuck-with-me seat, a brown paper bag on his lap, his stained hands tightening on its bulging sides as though*

The rest of the page was blank. She wadded the paper again and placed it back where it had been.

When had it all started to change? In the fall she began her first teaching job: junior high art, the kids often out of control. Lee, working three to eleven at the medical library so he could watch Mark while she was at school.

It was then.

That had been the beginning. Sometimes she'd already dropped exhausted into sleep before Lee even got home. He started writing at night. She'd wake to hear him beyond the closed door, the rhythmic click of the keys, working on this novel. Even when he came to bed at two or three, she would turn and know he was still awake, his body restless and tight. By November he hardly slept at all. He stopped writing. She would hear him go in and out, in and out, walking the loop, even sometimes taking Clyde. By Thanksgiving he had passed into silence. It was as though the sound of them living together had been turned off, all of their rooms dimmed. Her own movements stiffened, her throat and jaw clinched until even her few words came out strained and unclear. Only Mark would not be stilled. He slept less, cried more, banged his highchair fiercely with his spoon.

The last time it happened, Lee had burned a whole stack of the manuscript, thrown it in the garbage can and set it on fire. Little charred pieces of the novel fluttered up for days. The smell of smoke. She had a vision of his typewriter crashing through the window, but it would be too obvious to place it in its case. Instead she skidded the table into a dark corner out of the light. What he did not see, perhaps ...

She checked on Mark, curled on his stomach, his dark hair, so like his father's, twisted in his fingers. The street light cast bars of shadow across his blue sleeper. Clyde lay stretched by his crib, the dog's eyes open and brooding as though he knew too.

What else could she do? She'd thought of going down to the Doyles' when she knew something was coming, of taking Mark and spending the night on their couch, but fear of the scene he might cause when he found them gone kept her frozen in place. He didn't ever move toward her. He wouldn't hurt Mark. She felt sure of that. But beyond this ...

She must sleep. Two hours or three before his call. An hour or more after that before he'd come home, driven by someone he'd se-duced into his web in the bar. How he caught people: Get them to talk about themselves, he said.

Best to stay dressed. She got under the covers on her side. She closed her eyes, but still there was the blinking of the *Coors* sign across the street. Finally she felt herself going down, down to some-where else. Sleep. Heavy and dark.

She woke to the phone ringing, but for a few seconds she couldn't move. Her legs, her arms buried beneath some massive weight. Her mind and body separate. Mark cried.

She found the phone in the dark, her hand lifted the receiver, dense and cold. "Hello," she said, as though this were any call. She could not say anymore. Silence, except for a distant juke box. She worked on breathing, in out slow. She pulled the door closed on Mark's cries. And sat down, with the phone held a little away from her. She waited.

"I don't love you," he said. Only his breathing. Then just a whisper, "Thought you could save me." A low laugh that was not a laugh.

Tears forced themselves from her closed eyes. She curled her head onto her knees. Mark's deadened cries, far off singing.

"Have to kill myself," he told her. "Last option."

"Come home," she said, and then he was gone.

She lifted Mark from his crib, wiped his nose—his body rigid with anger, his sobs, long and shuddering. She walked through the apartment with him: the kitchen, the hall, the living room. "It's all right now," she murmured, her mind numb, her body burdened by the weight of this child. When Mark calmed, she changed him and rocked him to sleep. She lifted him into his bed, then quietly rolled the crib down the hall to the far side of the kitchen, pulling the door shut slowly until she heard the final click. As far from his father's arrival as possible. Clyde lay down by the door. And Del slept too.

She woke to voices outside in the street, a loud radio, the slam of a car door. She turned over, got ready. The downstairs door opened and crashed back against the wall. "My last hope," he screamed.

Her body began to shake. She moved to the edge of the bed.

He came heavily up the stairs.

She worked on calming her hands, her legs. On becoming invisible. She felt him pushing through the dark and heard Clyde whine. She waited.

Finally he sat down on the side of the bed. Only the sound of his breathing. The sour smell of alcohol. Then he began to struggle with his clothes. The unlacing, the unzipping, the unbuttoning. At last he fell back against the pillow. She felt him trembling beside her. If she reached over to touch his face, she knew his cheeks would be wet.

She did not move.

10
Rescue – 1974

I REMEMBER IT WAS RAINING and I didn't have an umbrella and I was standing there on the corner, waiting for Rudy's school bus, thinking, Why don't I have an umbrella? I'm twenty-three years old and I've never owned an umbrella. As far as I could remember my mother never owned one either and did that mean I was going to go through the rest of my life with rain coming down on my head?

So there I was, waiting, and I knew the bus was pretty late, even though I didn't have a watch either. The same exact story as the umbrella. I was waiting there on the corner with December rain, Monterey rain, running down my back, and that got me thinking about backbones as in my father always saying I didn't have one and then thinking about that in the same way as umbrellas and watches. You know: Was there some kind of connection? Rain and more rain and Steve hadn't been home for three days and I was down to my last cigarette and a half and my period was at least six weeks late. Merry Christmas. Happy New Year.

Rudy was the first one off the bus. He was wearing a hat made from a paper bag with the letters E-F-L pasted on the side. His smile disappeared when he didn't see Steve. Steve had been picking him up since he got laid off from his painting job.

"Where's Papo?" he said.

In jail. On the road. Gone to doggie heaven.

"I don't know, but I'll bet we'll hear from him today."

Hello, Carla, I'm in trouble.

"Told me that yesterday," he said, and pushed a wad of wrinkled school papers at me. His hands were covered with purple and red scribbles. I buttoned the papers in on top of my heart, a heart already bearing more than it could bear. How could it possibly take the weight of another child?

"I like your hat," I said. "Don't you want me to stick it inside my coat so it doesn't get soggy?"

"Have to wear it," he told me, going straight through the deepest puddle available. "I'm Santa's helper."

The letters began to curl.

"Then we better hurry." I took his hand and we ran.

When we came up the alley in back of the apartment, Rudy went ahead to check for Steve's Harley. Still gone. Then he started up the stairs at a gallop. All four flights.

"What's your hurry?" I called. "The door's locked. Papo isn't up there."

Before he took off his coat, he looked in all the rooms, even the closets. Then he got up on a chair and pulled a couple of pieces of bread out. He replaced the twist'em around the end of the bag and turned it about twenty times.

"Hello," I said to the back of his head.

He didn't answer. He was busy taking down jars.

I saw that his teacher had printed *Messy* across the top of his penmanship paper, a paper bruised by the weight of his effort, each crooked letter leaned into with such force that you could read it with your fingers on the other side. His teacher did not know about his talent with twist'ems, that no air would ever penetrate to any bread he was protecting.

Rudy spread practically half a jar of marshmallow gloop on top of the peanut butter before I closed the lid.

She did not know that Rudy's father was absent without prior notice. Mrs. Miss Ms. Ludlow, lend me your ear.

"How are the 2s coming?" I said.

He smacked the other piece of bread on top and smooshed it down just a bit. Then he licked the knife. Then he studied the problem: how to cut off the crusts without squishing out the insides. He pried the top off and set it back on the counter. Using both hands he sawed around the edges of that piece, then lifted the crust frame up to inspect various sections of the kitchen with one eye winked shut. Next he maneuvered the knife around the bottom crust, careful not to get into the goo. He placed the top back on and lifted the whole sandwich up out of the bottom crust and set it on his Grateful Dead plate. He drooped the empty crusts over the sandwich, put the lid on the peanut butter, and the jars back on the shelf.

I pulled his chair out for him. "What about the 2s?" I said.

"What about Papo?" he said.

"He must be okay or we would have heard something."

"Heard what?"

Sirens. Shots. The whirring of wings.

"Are you supposed to do a sheet on the 2s for homework?"

He rotated his chin in a motion somewhere between a yes and a no. His father's chin, his father's avoidance of being pinned down. Rudy was a child of few words. And those few words were offered up with care, one at a time, each with its own separate space in the air between us. But mostly he spoke with his eyes, his chin, his shoulders. His silence. And there was not a day that his silence did not remind me of that dark night in Oregon, the stillness of his small white face in my lap. Each day wanting the courage to ask, "Do you forgive me?" But too scared his body's answer wouldn't be Yes.

The phone. My heart did its usual dive into my stomach and Rudy was off his chair and lifting the receiver before my breath kicked back in.

"Papo? Papo, where are you?" he hollered down the receiver as though into a dark hole that held his father.

Let Rudy drop the first line of rescue to Steve, give the first hard tug at his neglect of family and home, I thought, but then I saw Rudy's confusion and he pushed the receiver my way.

"Some lady collecting, with Papo yelling in between," he said.

Even though half of me wanted to say No, I said, "Yes, we'll accept."

"Carla, it's me."

Steve—and spoken in the careful tones of a man walking on a wire.

"Yes," was all I said. Not, where the hell have you been; not, Rudy and I have been worried sick. Not, I think I'm pregnant and oh, dear god what am I going to do if I am? Let him inch along, his body tensed for the fall like I'd been the last three days, waiting for the ring of the phone that I knew, oh yes knew, would be bringing more bad weather.

"Carla, you aren't going to believe this ... Carla, are you there?"

"Yes," I said and then I saw Rudy, big eyed and worried. I pulled him onto my lap. "Talk to your son for a minute and let him know you're all right."

From where we sat in the hall I could count the layers of linoleum in the kitchen, the current piece just beginning to chip and curl along the edge. Apartments. Moving in and hoping tomorrow you'd have the energy to scrape away the bits of rotted something stuck to the dairy section door in the refrigerator, that you'd have the heart to lift out the whole vegetable bin to deal with what was thickening underneath. Apt # 6, Myrtle Ave. How on earth did I land here?

I shifted under the weight of Rudy's tense concentration. He listened and listened and nodded and frowned. "But how did they lift you and your motorcycle into the air?" was all he said. And then after a while, "Okay. But Mamo wants you home right this minute!" He handed me the phone and returned to his chair in the kitchen, but instead of eating his sandwich, he just sat there watching my face through the frame of his crust.

I locked the receiver against my ear and waited, waited for the big story I wasn't going to believe.

"Carla, are you listening?"

"I am," I said.

"I was standing at the counter of the Stop and Go, waiting to buy a pack of Luckies and head on home just like I told you I was going to ..."

If he was once-upon-a-timing as far back as standing at the counter, he couldn't have been calling from jail; they'd never have allowed the sprawl of time necessary for such a slow beginning. And it didn't sound like the way a man in traction would open. Even so my heart upped its volume at his tone of repentance. This was some *new* unbelievable tale and it was going to cost more money that we didn't have and more forgiveness that I didn't have either.

"... when this big dude by the gas pumps sees me through the window and lights up like I'm his long-lost and motions me to meet him outside. And his energy is so strong I actually leave the line without the cigarettes and when I get to his van he hugs me and hands me a cup of something purple which I figure is wine, and Carla, if I was one of those kooks, I'd say I'd been abducted by aliens, because the next thing I know the van blasts off and I see the earth spinning below us in the distance. That's the last I remember and then next thing I know, I'm here."

"Here?"

The muffled sound of voices no doubt through Steve's hand over the phone and then an unmuffled blast of, no question about it, Grace Slick telling me I gotta find somebody to love. And if it hadn't been for Rudy's deep frown of concern, I probably would have slammed down the phone right there. Then Steve was back in my ear.

"I'm on the road between Sparks and Lovelock."

As pissed as I was, I had to laugh. Me, I was one stop beyond that. Rudy put down his crust and began to eat his sandwich.

"Nevada, Carla. I'm in Nevada. That's where I landed."

"Nevada?"

With that Rudy went over and started searching his map of *The United States of America*, the one he'd brought home from school and insisted on fastening to the front of our refrigerator, the one that had the question, *WHERE ARE YOU?* in large letters across the top, a question I found doubly irritating the first thing in the morning on both the days when I knew the answer and on the days when I didn't have a clue.

"Nevada," Steve repeated in a voice with all the energy drained off, a voice that was dragging itself along.

Just as my heart was about to slump into sympathy, I straightened up and got my backbone clamped into place. "And when will we have the pleasure of your return to Monterey, California?" I said.

I saw Rudy was running his finger back and forth between Nevada and California, right to the little red dot we'd added to mark about where we were. "This is us and this is Papo; this is us and this is Papo," he kept whispering in a kind of lullaby beat with the swing of his finger.

"Well, that's just it, Carla, there are complications."

"Complications?" I said, going on with my straight-woman routine.

"My motorcycle's got engine problems. I'm out of money."

"He's being held captive against his will," a distant man's voice said, followed by laughter, female laughter. I was feeling less and less confusion about what my position would be in regards to any request for rescue.

"Carla, it's not like it sounds."

More and more sure of what had to be done about the lateness of my period.

"Carla, I want to come home."

There was a women's clinic next to the Safeway Market that did them. But I couldn't remember the name of it. I pulled the phone book over, trying to think what to look under.

"Carla, I'm going to need your help."

Medical. Clinic. Physician. I figured no way the ad was going to come right out with it.

"Carla, I'm sorry. Bad acid. A bad trip. It was a crazy thing to do."

I knew the J bus went right by there. The appointment would have to be while Rudy was in school. And how long would it take to get that kind of appointment?

"Carla, you know I love you and Rudy. And yes, I know I've got a wacky way of showing it."

No money for bus fare. We'd have to take back all the bottles, go through all the pockets, down behind all the cushions.

"Carla, I need for you to take Manny's truck. I know he won't mind. The keys are in a black box under the seat on the passenger side. That's the only way I can think of to get my bike back there. Rizzo will advance you some money on my next painting job. I get my unemployment check next Monday."

I figured I'd need to take a taxi back. I wondered about the four flights of stairs, who I could get to meet Rudy's bus if necessary.

"You're going to have to figure the best way to get to Route 80 north. Then just stay on that heading toward Reno. I'm at the Lovelock Motel. Room 7."

There it was:

> *Woman-to-Woman Clinic Reasonable Fees*
> *Complete Confidential Gynecological Care*
> *825-0000 for information and appointments.*

"And Carla, fill the radiator before you head out and bring two or three gallons of water in case … Carla?"

I hung up the phone.

Rudy came over and leaned against me. He patted my back.

114

"There, there, Mamo, there, there."

The pregnancy test was positive. I knew it would be. We figured seven weeks.

The woman behind the window must have been about my age. "How are you doing?" she said.

"I'm okay."

"Do you feel like you'd like to talk to one of our counselors now? It's set up so there's plenty of time for that."

"No," I said, "I just want to get it over with." I felt like five more seconds of her caring eyes and I'd dissolve. I couldn't help but notice that tacked along the ledge next to her desk were two little school pictures, above that, a framed photo of her, surrounded by a smiling family.

There were two other people waiting: a pale, puffy girl sitting beside a woman, probably her mother; there was that same something about the eyes, the hunch of the shoulders. Daughters and mothers—like watching one of those trick films that speeds up the time in between, that showed who the girl would be in twenty years after she got flattened and widened and pulled down. She couldn't have been more than sixteen, the age I was when I met Steve, when I got pregnant with Rudy. Sixteen. I didn't even let my mother know I was expecting until after Rudy was born. She was three thousand miles away and besides I knew she'd tell my father. I didn't want to give him all those extra months of satisfaction about how right-on his predictions had been.

I took a seat on the same side as the woman and the girl. That way I wouldn't have to look at them, and they wouldn't have to look at me. The waiting room was small, with nothing extra and painted a sort of no-color beige. Not blue, not pink, not yellow—like they knew you felt lousy and they understood enough not to try to cheer you up. I noticed there were no pictures on the walls—like they couldn't think of any subject that wouldn't rub it in.

The advance from Rizzo was enough to pay the one hundred to the clinic, plus take us through a few weeks of peanut butter and hotdogs until I found a job. I'd just told Rizzo it was a family emergency and he hadn't pressed me. I got the feeling he knew if I was asking, we must be pretty down and he could spare it, so he did. He said Steve was a good worker and he felt confident he'd make it up to him.

Steve. When thoughts of Steve bored through, I plugged them up; Not Now, I told myself, that, and Keep Moving. From the minute I put down the phone on Steve's voice, I'd been on the move. I hoped my anger would keep a fire blazing under me long enough to get done what I needed to do. First I told Rudy Steve was working on a plan to get back home and set him to searching for loose change at the bottom of every jar and pocket and under every piece of furniture to find us enough money for milk and chocolate syrup and cigarettes. While he was busy, I called Rizzo and then the clinic.

During the intake interview on the phone, the woman asked me why I'd decided to terminate my pregnancy. I was ready for that one: I said my husband had abandoned us and that I needed to get a job, that I'd been using something, but that I'd gotten pregnant anyway. (This foamy stuff I had to squirt up inside myself at just the wrong time.) That I already had a seven-year-old and I needed all my strength to take good care of him. All of which was true. I didn't feel it was necessary to get into the gory details—the Lovelock Motel, etc. They'd advised me it was likely I'd be out of there by 1:00, but that I should have alternate plans for Rudy, that the stairs would most likely be okay, but I should have alternate plans for that too. I arranged for my friend Marie to pick Rudy up if she didn't hear from me by 2:30. Her apartment was on the first floor, and I knew we could stay with her for a few days if we had to. What's up? she'd asked. I told her I was looking for a job and there was a chance I'd get tied up a little longer than I expected. I wasn't going to tell her the real reason unless I absolutely had to. She would have cried and carried on. Marie was a good Catholic; plus she and her husband had been trying for a kid for a couple of years with no success.

My hands were sweating and my heart was making itself noticeable. The woman had described in clinical detail what would be involved in the procedure—that's what she called it—"the procedure." She said it would be best if I could bring a relative or friend along for support. No one I knew would have supported what I was doing. Only a few years ago I'd have been slipping down some back alley.

I remember that my mouth was incredibly dry and that got me

thinking about the expression *hard to swallow*. That, and if I was nervous, how was that girl, who was just a kid herself, feeling? I saw the mother squeeze her daughter's knee and then go plowing through her pocketbook to come up with tissues for them both. I got to thinking about what it would have been like to have the kind of life where my mother would have been sitting next to me, passing out Kleenex. Then I started thinking about how if I had had that kind of mother, maybe I wouldn't have had Rudy. And then I started to think about not having Rudy—a kind of flash of pictures started passing through my mind, pictures with holes in them where Rudy had been cut out. And that was a big mistake or a great blast of grace because right then the fire went out.

I didn't know if it was me or the clutch, but every time I tried to ease off to accelerate, everything heaved and shuddered. Rudy kept looking at me, studying me like I was an interesting bug or something.

"Watch the parking lot," I told him. "I'll get it. We won't start out until I've got the feel of it. Remember I haven't driven standard since I was fourteen." Back when Babylove Stewart and I use to whip around up in the field in his father's old Pontiac.

"Papo's counting on us," Rudy said. I saw he had folded the road map down into a small square so that all that showed was the section where we'd traced our way from Monterey to Sparks in purple marker. We were going to ask beyond there.

"Let's just take a little time out while I have a cigarette and you eat some animal crackers." I pressed the brake slowly down; the truck lurched and stalled. I sat there staring out over the blurred expanse of blacktop, feeling at one with the abandoned shopping carts. The rain's steady drumming beat on the roof, but at least the lot was almost empty. That gave me the room to get up enough speed to practice shifting when I'd mastered the brakes, keeping in mind our lack of tread.

I noticed that instead of eating the crackers, Rudy was carefully laying the various animals out on the seat between us and hum-chanting a mix of Jingle Bells and Away in the Manger.

Another Christmas in Monterey. Sweet Jesus, save me.

"What are you up to?" I said.

He didn't answer me. Then I saw that he was looking for pairs. He'd set out an elephant, then he'd carefully sort through the box looking for a match.

"That's a good way to work on the 2s so you don't get behind," I said. After several tries, my handwriting gave up on a note explaining Rudy's absence to Ms. Ludlow. "2 added to 2 gives you how many in all?"

He still didn't respond, just sort of shook his head, one of his too-silly-for-words shakes. He continued lining the animals up in pairs.

"Kind of like Noah's Ark, huh?" I said, and with that he looked at me as though perhaps there was hope for me yet. Caught in his mood of concentration, I studied our immediate surroundings—certainly not the conveyance the Lord would have approved of for a rescue operation. I noticed that the knob on the radio was missing, that the side mirror had a crack right down the middle, that what had been a small wet spot on the ledge behind the seat was verging on becoming a stream.

Manny's truck figured in perfectly with the rest of the caper: The radiator had been down a couple of inches, the two back tires were heading toward bald, and one of the taillights had been out. Marie's husband had run me through a quick review of the H pattern, cautioned against riding the clutch, put in a couple of quarts of oil, added coolant and water, pumped up the tires, changed the back bulb, listened with fascination to the engine. He left us with a shake of the head which I knew meant he'd pray for us, but that the possibility of a successful round trip was a real test of his faith.

Once I realized I was going to let my body carry on with what it was up to; once I realized I was going to accept the baby that appeared to be floating our way, I put Rudy on the phone to Room 7 of The Lovelock Motel with the following instructions: Tell Papo I said we are going to try to rescue him this one last time, and that he better be ready and ever-after grateful which Rudy smooshed down to "Papo, we're coming, but you better be good for goodness sake."

Steve knew nothing about my being pregnant. Even before Lovelock, I was thinking it over, wondering if I had the strength. I knew he'd be happy; Steve loved babies. And why not? He'd feed them, change them, take them to the park, even get up in the night.

When he felt like it. But here you go, Carla, when he didn't. The thing is children are so … so all the time and forever. And I'm not talking about laundry.

The animals were spread out in little paired groups all over the seat and Rudy had turned the box upside down and was patting the bottom so that crumbs were falling like confetti over all the couples.

"You need to eat those before they get any more yucky and then clean up the mess," I told him. "We've got to take a few more practice runs and then we've got to hit the road. We do not want to be trying to find our way in the dark on top of everything else."

"There's only one bear," he said, his eyes all squinted up with concern as he looked down into the box.

"Come on, come on," I said. The reality of me setting out to drive to Nevada with Rudy in a broken-down truck that burned oil and leaked water and god-knows-what else finally hit my nervous system. I turned the ignition and fluttered the accelerator. The bugger actually groaned to a start.

"Put those animals away and prop the pillow up against the dashboard and remember how you have to squinch down if I tell you to.

"He's going to be lonely," Rudy said like he hadn't heard a word.

"All right. All right." I took a full breath and let it go. I knew once I told Rudy, there'd be no more possibility of that final exit. "I'm going to tell you a secret, but you've got to promise you're going to give me your full cooperation for the rest of this adventure."

"What secret?"

"That you're going to be my Rudy on-the-spot co-pilot."

He looked up at me and smiled and began to pick up the crackers. "I promise," he said.

I counted on my fingers. "Sometime in the middle of the summer, about seven and half months from now, you are going to get a baby brother or sister."

He didn't say anything and he didn't look at me. He just kept putting the animals back in the box two by two. I waited and listened to the idle of the engine. After he carefully closed the box, he plumped the couch cushion into place. Then finally he turned and looked at me hard.

"You better not be fooling around," he said.

"Cross my heart," I reassured him. "We are going to have a baby."

I waited and after a few minutes, he turned and looked at me hard again. "Good, but now I want you to tell me how we get a baby."

I reached up and wiped the window with the edge of my sleeve. And one defective defroster. "How do you think we get a baby?"

He looked at me suspiciously. Then he leaned back and looked out the window. His forehead puckered up like he was squeezing his thoughts one by one. Finally he said, "You tell what you think first."

"All right," I said, "but I want to wait until we're on our way in fourth gear, a little more sure of the road. Then I promise we'll figure it out."

"Okay," he said.

I turned on the lights and pushed down on the clutch while I shifted into first. We heaved toward the highway. "This is it," I said. Once again I was going to have to go out there before I got the feel of it. I sped up and swung the truck a bit wide to avoid a cart. The wipers squeak-squeaked, leaving ragged smears right in my best line of vision. I ducked my head to get a better view of the approaching traffic. I glanced at Rudy. He was sitting up straight with his hands folded in his lap. I flicked the right signal and pressed down while shifting into second. There was a terrible grinding of the gears as we leapt onto the highway. Several cars honked. My heart banged and my hands shook and everything on the truck that could vibrate, did. Standard transmission, Life—there were just too many procedures to do simultaneously.

"Sparks, here we come," I shouted and got her up enough to shift into a lunging, scraping third.

11
Cornerstone – 1976

THE GLOB OF OATMEAL Aaron meant for the compost pail over-shoots and hits the side of the kerosene stove.

"What a spaz," Mark says.

"Was that comment necessary?" Del grabs the dishcloth, but just as she bends to go at the mess, Lee takes the cloth from her and tosses it to Aaron.

"Nice catch," he says.

Aaron grins and wipes the blob off just as it's about to drop to the floor.

"Try scraping one thing at a time," Lee tells him. "Be easier that way."

"Yeah, and we'll be here all day before he gets the dishes to me." Mark lets the bowls drop into the dishpan just this side of breaking.

Lee lets it ride. Instead he reaches over and squeezes the back of Mark's neck, then goes out to the shed to haul in enough wood for their weekly bath that evening.

Del sweeps the last of the little piles into the dust pan. Since they have no electricity, there's no way to really suck it up. This is one of the minor disturbances of living in these temporary quarters, their new pole barn, until they get the stone house built. The broom most-ly just lifts the gray grit into the air to settle again and by tomorrow the concrete sloughs off another layer. She hangs the dustpan back on the nail by the door. One thing handy, you want to hang some-thing up, just pound in another nail.

"All right," she says, "I'm off to do rocks."

Aaron gives her a little wave and begins to empty what's left in the oatmeal pot, one spoon at a time. She'd like to show him how if he bangs the pot hard on the edge of the bucket, most of it will plop out, but she doesn't.

Just as she steps outside, she hears Mark hiss, "What a dummy."

For a minute she sits in the doorway to unlace her stone-gathering shoes enough to wiggle her feet in. Her pale legs, a little hairy and spindly-looking, rise up out of steel-toed boots with dirty yellow laces. But unflattering as they are, no question they're much better than her Keds for scrambling around and picking up rocks.

She scoots over to let Lee pass with his load of logs. "I'm going down to the brook now," she says. "In two minutes."

"Yeah, what a day. Look at that sky."

Blue, blue. Not even a wisp of white. What she'd really like would be to just sit here and draw the thorn apple trees or Lee's parents' house far across the way, the cedar shingles against the red glow of the blackberry canes on their hill.

Above the bang of the dishes, Lee's voice, "When everything's put away, come get me." A voice in no hurry. "No fighting's part of the deal."

"Tell *him* that," Mark says.

Not a sound from Aaron. He knows to lay low. Though she can't see him, she knows Mark's chin is angled out just this side of what Lee will let pass.

Lee doesn't take the bait. He's so much better at this than she is. And this is why it was doubly hard when he wasn't with them. She feels her face go into what she's come to think of as her grimace of regret. She's sorry, sorry, sorry. She brings her fingers slowly down over her forehead. Sometimes that helps. It always goes back to when Mark was four. The first time she and Lee separated. Aaron not quite two. That cramped little apartment she'd moved them to in Marwick. What she could afford. How could she have let Mark stand there in the dark in his wet pajamas while she ripped the soaked sheets off his bed? Night after night. Maybe why it feels like he's had her in a hammerlock of guilt ever since.

The clunk of nails hitting the bottom of a can: Lee, gathering his tools. "Aaron, you can open all the windows now," Lee says. Isn't Lee's voice, like hers, always a little more tender with Aaron?

"Dad," mock protest from Mark. Lee has ruffled Mark's hair or jiggled his shoulder, some affectionate gesture Mark's eleven-year-old self is starting to shrug off.

There's the slide and click of each window. The only evidence that Aaron is still there.

What will they do when it gets too chilly to open the windows? Even out in the morning air, the fumes from the kerosene cookstove waft toward her. This is the only part of living in the pole barn without water and electricity that really gets to her. But right after Lee's parents retired back at the family farmhouse across the way, they'd offered them the cookstove that was stored in Lee's grandpa's chicken barn. Plus the fuel's cheap. And every penny counts if they are to build without borrowing and live on her teaching salary alone. Lee keeps saying, Two years. Maybe even less. But still, how sickening the fumes may be in winter with everything closed up tight to keep out the cold.

Lee, right behind her now, gives his final rally. "Then you can both do whatever you want until after lunch when I may need you to help me level the first set of forms." She hops to as well. Puts on her work gloves.

Lee threads by, the can of nails tucked under his arm. "Only a couple thousand rocks more to go," he says.

How she wishes he'd touch her. She watches him walk toward the site, his carpenter belt slung low on his slender hips, his raggedy cut-off shorts. In the distance, the old blue work-truck he bought for two hundred dollars, just beginning to shine as the sun comes over the hemlocks.

Their own private road, nestled between the hill and the brook. Fifteen acres on the edge of the old family farm, a gift from Lee's parents. Your dream-come-true: the smell of manure, mist coming off the grass, Lee reminds her when she feels overwhelmed by the prospect of drilling their own well, lifting all those stones up onto the scaffolding when the walls rise above her head. They still make love once a week or so, but even then, he does not kiss her.

From inside there's a crash of something, but no sound of glass. "You dork," Mark says, just loud enough for her to hear. She starts for the brook. It'll only get worse if she intervenes. Two years at most of them all living together in the one big room. We can make this work,

Lee counseled them during their first dinner in the pole barn a few weeks ago, *if* each of us does our part. They'd had a good year living with Lee's parents while Lee took down the chicken barn, salvaging the beams and boards to build his parents a garage and to use in the stone house. Lee not drinking. Why shouldn't we do even better here on our own? he said.

The path to the brook takes her past the row of pines Lee put in two years ago to block the site from view when they first began to think about building. Them starting over after the second separation when Aaron was in kindergarten, after the years in Wisconsin where she'd gone to teach, to get over, to get away from Lee once and for all. Already the pine trees are several feet above her head and bushing out to touch each other. The field, the road, the old farm house where Lee's parents now live will soon disappear. Tucked in the one sunny spot in front of these trees, six marijuana plants Lee recently repotted. A project he's carefully tended since he started the seeds in coffee cans in February over in the shop he was finishing in his parents' new garage, following to the letter the *How to Grow Your Own Dope* manual they'd gotten through the *Whole Earth Catalog*. Coffee cans he hid here and there all winter whenever his parents might stop by to see how the construction was going.

The plants wink at her dangerously now. No question they are an alien green, distinct from any neighboring vegetation. She's mentioned this several times to Lee. Relax, he said. But risky or not, marijuana seems to be such a good thing. Not like alcohol, clearly so poisonous for Lee. She enjoys it too. Maybe the first time she's ever been so aware of the moment they're in—past and future worries disappear. Plus the pleasure of sex after they've smoked, getting up later to eat something garlicky and hot. Surely marijuana is one of the reasons for their new-found peace.

She hears Aaron scream, one of the things he does when Mark goes too far. Likely Lee has his ear cocked that way as well. Mark knows Lee is tuned in now. There are no further battle sounds. Still she's always afraid Mark in a rage might strike out with something heavy. Mark, who has from birth refused to fold in. He's their barometer, registering the pressure.

Hanging onto the bank, she steps down into what Aaron calls

their brook bathtub, now just a deep basin lined with rocks. This place where on warm June afternoons, the four of them soaped up good and ducked under. Even Coal, Lee's parents' lab, raced from their house across the field to wade in it whenever he heard laughter. But that's over now, the brook likely to be dry until the fall rains when it will be too cold for ducking. Plus the loss of their water supply for dishes and washing up.

She scans the basin for good stones. She and Lee hope to at least have the walls of the house poured before the temperatures get too cold for mixing concrete—even with him working alone once she starts teaching again in the fall. She squats to tip a few of the bigger flat-faced rocks on edge. Beauties. But Lee will have to carry those. In the distance she hears him hammering, singing a song she can't quite catch. She listens for the kids again, but hears nothing.

She got this job of stone-gathering by default. Trundling the loaded wheelbarrow away from the site while Lee dug the trench for the footers, a job that took the whole of last summer, had turned out to be much too heavy for her. The digging itself impossible since she never managed to get the shovel up and out, but rather the clogs of earth and gravel came raining back down on her head. It was then she was given the task of hauling from the brookbed what Lee jokingly called the ten thousand stones to pile at intervals along the four-foot deep trench. At least she hopes he was joking. Unlike Lee, the greatest joy for her is when the manual labor part of the day is done. He says he can still write in his head while cutting wire or sawing boards for the window frames, but she cannot draw while carrying stones.

She bends down. Wedged between the roots of the sycamore what may be the most perfect cornerstone she's ever seen. On this treasure hunt for flat-faced rocks at least four inches deep, cornerstones are the most exciting finds. Her goal is to get five great cornerstones and twenty good face stones each morning. Plus a pile of uglies. Get them all heaved to the top of the bank and over to the site, then she can go sit on her rear in the field to draw while she eats all the wild strawberries in reach.

There's the unmistakable thud, thud of a ball. Mark, shooting baskets. And further down the brook, the crash of rocks. Probably Aaron, building truck bridges. They've passed inspection.

Down on her knees, she shimmies the stone back and forth until it drops out. She runs her hand along its perfect gray sides—as close to a ninety-degree angle as you can get. She hoists the cornerstone onto the bank above her and scrambles out too. Lee, bent over his work table under the big maple that will one day shade the stone house, is pounding stakes into a window frame to hold it solidly in the wall once it hardens.

"Lee," she hollers, struggling toward him, the rock held against her chest. He looks up and smiles. "Wait until you see this beauty," she calls, wanting to extend the rock out, but it's too heavy.

Mark and Aaron, then Lee, empty their gallon jugs of water into the big canner sitting on the hot grill. Lee opens the door on the stove, so they can see the flames. "Our first fire in our Ashley Thermostatic Wood Burning Circulator," he announces.

"Cool," Mark says. "How much wood can you put in?" He squats down and holds his hand toward the flames.

"Careful," she says.

Lee closes the door. "See how this handle locks down—always have be sure to do that."

"Don't let fog-brain do it then or we'll all burn up."

"Mark," she says, but Lee flashes her a look and she says no more. She rests her hands on Aaron's shoulders, but he soon steps away and drops on his knees beside Lee.

Lee squats between the two boys. "It says you can load it right up, with some green wood on top to dampen it down. Supposed to be able to go twelve hours without refueling. 'Course we won't really get to know the stove until it starts to get cold."

She pulls the stool over and sits behind them. Surely Lee will do most of the fire-building just like he's the one to get the kerosene stove going in the morning and the Aladdin lit when they need more light than the kerosene lamps give.

"If you want the stove to run hot, set the lever about here." Lee moves the lever up. Mark reaches over and touches it.

"Right," Lee says. "Aaron, push it all the way down and look in at the damper door."

Aaron pushes down a little.

"More," Mark says. "It's not going to bite you."

Lee reaches both arms out and pulls them in closer so they can both see into the small box. She leans in too.

"Now what happens is that the stove can adjust the temperature—where you've got the lever set—because there's a coil that loosens or contracts to open and close this air vent. The more air, the more fire." He pokes a screwdriver through one of the spaces to show how the round of metal flops up and down. "Basically, that's it." He stands up. "All right, let's unload the rest of the water." Now that the brook is dry, they must haul water from Lee's parents' spring every few days.

"I've got to go first," Mark says. And he's out the door.

They have an outhouse, but Lee encourages Aaron and Mark to go off in the bushes when they just have to pee. They all know that by the time Mark gets back, the bringing-in-water-chore will be almost done. A thing Lee will talk to Mark about again one night while they're shooting baskets or just off somewhere.

Once the canner on the wood stove is full, Lee and Aaron fill the second canner on the back of the kerosene stove and the water reservoir within the stove. Mark appears in time to bring in the last four gallons, all in one trip. A good workout for building muscles, he's told them.

"That'll do it," Lee says. Both boys plop down on their beds. Aaron spins his globe. Just name a country and he'll tell you the capitol, every major mountain range in Russia. Mark pulls his curtains closed. All they can see of him is one foot jiggling against the hem. Mark—always some part of him in motion. Maybe in the night, there may be times when he comes to a complete stop in his sleep, but she's never seen it.

Most of all she loves the kerosene light—all the rough planks, the silver backing of the insulation, the concrete slab, what makes this home temporary, fades in the soft glow. She sees Coal has snuck up on Aaron's bed. A thing he would never do at Lee's parents'.

Aaron points to his father sitting in the big galvanized wash tub, snugged close to the Ashley. There is too much of him to get his legs in. "You look like a half-albino flamingo," he says and laughs at his joke.

Mark mutters something, goes back to his book, tipped down to catch enough light.

Lee's face, neck, his forearms and the parts of his legs between his shorts and work boots are burned a bright pink, the rest of him, ghost-white. One of his long striped legs is up in the air, almost over his head, trying to scrub his dirty toes without getting water all over.

They are still figuring out the best once-a-week bath routine. She gets to go first since she can take the hottest water. Then Mark, then Aaron. With their knees splayed, the three of them can sink under up to their necks.

"Next time we'll know to save some hot to add in," Lee says, giving up on his toes.

She dips her fingers in the bath water. "Brrr," she says. "Want me to wash your feet?" She lays her warm hand on his shoulder. The muscles contract, that flinch of withdrawal. Always the stab of hurt when he does this. She turns, begins to fold the laundry piled on their bed.

Lee boosts himself out of the tub. From the dark corner she watches him, one leg on the chair, then the other, working the towel up his long body, rubbing the soft hair under each arm. Lee's body almost all over smooth. Even his feet. He looks up and sees her watching. She sets the stack of folded towels in the box near the stove.

"Louder, please," Aaron says. Aaron is leaning so far over the edge of his bed, one more inch and he'll be out on his nose.

She wishes Mark would still let the night's reading be in her and Lee's big bed, with her in the middle, each of them snuggled next to her, but ever since they moved into the pole barn, Mark has insisted on this new arrangement—her sitting in the rocking chair, close to him, Aaron in his own bed.

"Keep going. We're getting to a good part," Mark tells her, jiggling her foot which he's tucked under his quilt.

"Hard to see," she tells them. She pulls the kerosene lamp to the corner of the table and lifts the book closer to the light. She should have had Lee light the Aladdin before he walked Coal home. She turns the page:

"'There's no one nigh,' said he, looking over his shoulder, is there?'

'Why do you, a stranger coming into my rooms at this time of night, ask that question? said I.'"

"I know who the guy is," Mark says. He has his pillows piled so that when he needs to see the pictures or to reread a good part, he can reach out and take the book from her hands.

"I know too," Aaron says, from the other side of the room.

"You do not."

She laughs and holds the book away from Mark's reaching fingers. "Well, even if you both know, don't say until we get there."

"More scary voice," Mark says. He cranes his head around the edge of the book. "Aaron, there's a picture. She's not showing the picture."

Laughing, she hands the book to Mark. "We haven't gotten to that side of the page," she says. "You're just prolonging the suspense."

Aaron comes over, dragging his quilt and looks at the picture too.

"Definitely I know who this is." Mark points to the man's grizzly hair, his dark bulk, rushing up the stairs toward Pip.

"Definitely," Aaron says and begins to settle on the bottom of Mark's bed. She waits for the bellow of protest, but instead Mark hands her the book with a smile.

"Go on," he says. "And make it really dramatic."

In the distance they hear a long whistle.

"Dad calling Coal," Aaron says, burying everything but his face in his comforter.

She tucks the covers around Mark's chin and kisses his cheek. Strokes his dark head, takes in the mossy boy-smell of him. At least he still lets her do this. The reading, the tucking in, a way through his barbs to show him how much she loves him. She pulls his curtains and then goes to peek in at Aaron who is curled so far under she can see only the top of his head, his yellow hair sticking out like corn silk, one hand curled around Pooh—Pooh, wearing a mask and a gun holster. Mark and Aaron have turned the whole set of stuffed animals her mother made them into a gang of bandits: Eeyore and Kanga and Piglet and Tigger, even Baby Roo, sporting some bad-men gear. For Christmas they'd asked for Mr. Hook and G.I. Joes to play war and robbery. Their grandparents said it didn't feel okay to give them such violent things, guns. So Mark and Aaron whittled pieces of wood and shot everything in sight. But for her, hearing them play these pretend games of conquest in the big room, long rainy afternoons, without arguing, fills her with hope.

Lee has blown out all the lamps but the one by their bed. He is under the blanket with the *Whole Earth Catalog* opened on his knees. She crawls in beside him and arranges her pillows so she can see too. They've spent many hours like this all winter at his parents, researching what they needed to order: their Aladdin, their Ashley, which Ken Kesey said was "a mighty good little hard-heatin' cheap working stove." Pamphlets on organic gardening, free-range chickens. Even home burial.

Lee turns the big page so she can see better. He points to the diagrams and reads: "'The Hydra-Drill is designed to drill water wells 3 ½ inches in diameter and up to 200 feet deep.'" He copies the address for Deeprock Manufacturing Company. "See, supposedly you can just keep attaching this casing here as you go down."

She nods. Whatever Lee thinks. She knows almost nothing about it. They were so disturbed by the way the man who put in their road ripped out so many trees, did so much more than they'd asked him to do, that they've agreed if they can possibly do it themselves, they will. Plus it'll be much cheaper.

"Three hundred and eighty-five dollars. 'Course a lot of it depends on how far down we have to go. I can just see the pipe hitting a big rock and then making a U-turn to come up behind me." He closes the book and raises up to blow out the lamp. "I'll send for the information tomorrow. Decide when we've had a chance to look it over good." He moves down into the bed, but doesn't stretch himself from corner to corner as he will sometime in the night. "Going to start pouring the footers tomorrow," he says, the voice he uses when he wants her full attention. "We'll all have to help."

"All right."

"I know the Nearings used a hand-operated mixer and I'm going to start that way, but I've got a feeling we're going to have to end up doing it with a gasoline motor."

"That's what I think you should do. We are not the Nearings."

He laughs. "Yeah, either way, it's going to be tense for a while until we get the hang of it. Concrete waits for no man."

She'd played a minor role in helping him and several others pour the slab for the pole barn, so she knows this is true, how tense it can get. "I wish I was better at this kind of thing," she says.

"Oh, we'll do all right." He squeezes her arm.

She would like to press his hand in return, but before she can, he raises up on one elbow. She had been sure all talk was over. Her body braces, a change of routine.

"I got an invitation in the mail today. My twentieth high school reunion in November."

She raises up a little too.

"A letter from Trudy Gotlieb. Trudy Cohen now."

"Do you want to go?" Twenty years since she's seen these people. Walked home with them along the park after games. Nineteen years since she graduated, but it's Lee's class she was close to.

Lee turns over, pulls the covers up. His voice low now. "I don't know," he says. "They want me to give a little class president speech at a fancy dinner. I am definitely not going to do that."

She shifts her body so she can at least give him some of her warmth. He sounds so lonely.

"Maybe we'll go to the party the night before at Trudy's parents," his voice even quieter now. "Smoke a little grass, drop by. See how it goes."

"Now that my mother's back in Albany, we can take the kids and leave them with her," she says. "If you decide you want to go."

They lie there in the dark, the howl of a dog or coyote up in the hills. The sound of Mark's adenoidal breathing. Summer air, grass, mud, just a tinge of kerosene. A lightning bug has come in through the window. They watch its dance of flashing light.

Lee's class reunion. She'd like to go. Stand in Trudy's parents' rec room. Listen to *Angel Eyes* again.

She snuggles down. She knows that once Lee thinks she's asleep or at least settled in, he will get up. She presses her bottom against his, it'll be all right. Warmth, the sunny smell of clean sheets. She closes her eyes.

Hard to know how long she's slept. Lee is sitting in his big Morris chair, the plaid slipcover she made looks black behind his graying bush of hair. He's writing, his grandmother's breadboard across the arms, the lamp turned as low as it will go and still let him see his words on his yellow pad. He taps his pen against his teeth, looks off. She often watches him at night when he thinks she's sleeping. Do Aaron and Mark watch him too? Do they keep their ears cocked to his silence, count the days when his words begin to run down?

Good night, they had told him. Given him their good-night kiss. Him sitting there in that tiny kitchen in Wisconsin reading the news. Her tucking the kids in. *The Wind in the Willows.* One chapter only. She's sure of that. Mole visited Toad at Toad Hall for one cup of tea. But that's all it took for him to fold his paper under the salt shaker. Take his corduroy jacket from the hook by the door. Two months later they got a card: *I'm in Florida, picking oranges. I am all right. I miss you. Dad.*

Keeping him in their periphery at all times, can they keep him here? At eleven and nine, do they already know what she knows: No, no they cannot.

12
And We Sell Apples – 1977

I HEAR THE CAR DOOR SLAM. Steve, about to duck daddy-duty: Just gonna take a run to the Quickway.

"Rudy," I say, "go get in the car. Tell Papo I said *WAIT*."

Rudy turns the TV up. I turn it off. The sound of the muffler. I open the door and scream, "Steve!" as in STOP. I hand Rudy his sweatshirt. "Go. This minute." I tug Tess's sweater over her head. She starts to cry. Rudy puts his hands on his ears and goes behind the table where he knows I can't reach him. Rudy, at ten, still has the reedy body of a boy, but the gonna-make-me thrust of his chin always makes me want to reach out and grab him.

Three years old, big as she is, I sling Tess up on my hip and turn off the light. "Fine," I say. "You stay here all by your lonesome while I go to Aunt Peggy's."

I step outside. The trees, just starting to glow on the hills. Sometimes I love this place; sometimes I don't. I close the door and start for the car. Steve's eyes dead ahead. Dead in his tracks. His best cap, pony tail combed. Premeditated duty-ducking while I'm in the basement trying to figure out why the washer isn't washing. "It's okay, Love," I tell Tess, tucking her head under my chin. "You can play Fire Station at Peggy's."

I slide in. Put Tess between us. "Going somewhere?" I say.

He says, "Carla," as in Spare Me. "What about Rudy?"

"He's just waiting for me to stop screaming before he comes on board."

"Have you stopped screaming?"

"Drop us at Peggy's. Pick us up on your way back from the Quickway with the milk."

Steve grins.

"Why didn't you take your bike?"

"I wouldn't have been able to fit everybody on."

I knew this meant it wouldn't start.

Rudy climbs in back, clutching a big plastic bag.

"What you got?" Steve says, tilting the rearview so he can check him out.

"Something."

We both know it's his blanket. In case. A something he cannot sleep without.

"Ice cream," Tess sings.

"You got any money?" Steve asks us all.

"No," Tess says.

Steve tilts the mirror again to look at Rudy. Rudy, his gonna-make-me double. Rudy stares out the window. We both know he's brought his entire stash—every nickel, dime, and penny he's managed to squirrel away. Rudy, already counting the lifeboats.

You can see why.

Tess yells, "Papo has money."

We know this is true or he wouldn't be heading out. I even know about how much: maybe twenty and change. Enough for a toot at the Eagle. Plus a few joints on his person. Payday tomorrow and plenty of house-painting ahead before the winter layoff, so Hey, doesn't a man have a right?

I look back at our home-sweet-home. Not as ramshackle as it was when we moved in two years ago. Steve has just put on a new roof; my morning glories have made their way up the strings for the first time. Steve's Harley, our lawn ornament. All of it backed by those hills and not a house in sight.

"See how good the gray roof looks," I say. Steve had wanted bright green shingles that made me want to cry. He pulls onto the gravel. The Maverick sounds even more ragged than usual. Chugging along on Chicken Farm Road. Cross my heart: Chicken Farm Road. Could I come up with that on my own?

I lean toward Steve over Tess's head. "You better do something about that muffler or you're going to get stopped."

"Carla," he says, as in Don't Bring Me Down.

"Plus," I say, meaning the car's lack of legality on all fronts.

I open the glove compartment to look for a brush. The smell of pot. Something flips onto the seat. Tess picks it up and begins to zigzag it down my thigh in time with her siren sound—Tess, the Fire Chief. "Let's return that to the station," I say, taking the hash pipe from her. I wave it by Steve's nose. He breathes in. I shove the pipe way to the back and slam the compartment door. "Plus, plus."

"Tess, see why I don't always take your mother out to play?"

"Yes," Tess says.

Steve makes the turn at Grat's Bend. We pass the log cabin, one of our few neighbors. Place has no electric, no inside plumbing. Outhouse in back. A pump for water by the steps. Woman who lives there makes baskets—Sally Somebody. Hippie-type. Probably she calls us Hell's Angels. Very *No Trespassing*. What can you expect? Steve's explanation. Got her marijuana growing practically in her front yard. Only sun available where the power lines run up through the hills. We check her rows of corn to see if we can spot her plants.

"Tucked away sweet as you please," Steve says. "August, harvest in sight."

"Your harvest has been right along," I tell him. Steve keeps going out and trimming off a few leaves every few days, drying them in the oven.

Up ahead, a tall man is walking along the side of the road: ragged shorts, even from the back, looking forlorn. His shoulders. His wild hair. Something.

"It's the guy who's building the stone house back behind the gravel bank." Steve slows. "You know, the one whose wife moved with their kids to that white house across from the Eagle. This summer."

"One of them's in my class," Rudy says. "Aaron Merrick. He's my friend."

All news to me.

Steve pulls up beside the man. "Can I give you a lift?"

He looks our way. His eyes the eyes of the people who tell you they're Jesus. Kind of eyes, you see them coming, you cross over.

"No," he says. That's all. Then his hand sort of brushes the air, shoos us away and he keeps on going.

"You sure?" Steve says, rolling along at the same pace.

"Steve," I hiss, "can't you see he doesn't want ..."

But he keeps right on talking, "I'm Steve Morletti. We just live back over the hill there."

The man shakes his head. Doesn't look at us again.

Steve rolls the window up and takes off slow, not to throw dust. "Poor devil," he says.

"What's wrong with him, Papo?" Rudy whispers, touching his father's shoulder.

Steve speeds up. I watch the man, now just a dark spot moving along the edge of the road.

"I don't know, Rudy."

"He looks crazy."

"Yes, he does."

"Maybe you should take him to the hospital."

"Maybe I should, but he wouldn't want me to."

"How do you know?"

"I know."

Steve comes to Route 8, pumps the brakes for the stop sign. I know he must be up to something. He never stops there. The oil light comes on.

"Plus," I say.

Steve puts his arm over the seat and squeezes the toe of Rudy's sneaker. "How 'bout I stop and get some ice cream at JAKE's for you and Tess, then we drop you at Peggy's for a few hours. A few hours only. Get your mother out to hear a little music."

I feel an instant lift.

"Okay to stay with Aunt Peggy for a little while?" I say to Tess, scooting her onto my lap.

Rudy leans over the seat and looks at Steve and me. "She is not our aunt."

"But she loves you like she is, right?" I say, placing my hand on his cheek.

Rudy thinks about this.

"Yes," Tess says, patting Rudy's hand. "Yes, she does, Rudy."

"Where are you going?" Rudy says.

Steve puts the car in park. The oil light goes off.

"We're going to the Eagle and we will bring you home to sleep in your own bed. And your mother or I will drive carefully."

Rudy pushes back in his seat and rolls the window down. "All right."

"Ice cream," Tess says.

Steve pulls out onto Route 8. "Cherry Garcia," he tells her.

"Light this," Steve says as soon as we get back in the car. I wave to Tess, standing on a chair in Peggy's front window, already wearing the plastic fire hat. I can tell by her lips she has her siren on.

"Wait till we get away from the curb." Peggy's next door neighbor is secretary of the Grange.

When he passes the Civil War monument, I take a toke and pass it to him. "Steve, don't forget what we promised Rudy," I say through my held breath.

"I won't."

I hear the music before we round the corner at the fire house. Fiddles. A harmonica. My heart ups another notch. "What a good idea." I scoot over against Steve and run my hand along the hard muscles of his thigh.

"That's right. 'Be my baby tonight," he sings.

A bunch of people stand smoking by the side door of the Presbyterian church.

Steve pulls up to the curb.

"What are you doing? Why are you parking here?" I can see there are still a few places in the Eagle lot across the street. I take the joint from him and hold it down by the seat.

Steve practically has his nose pressed to the windshield. "Tell me I'm stoned, but is that or isn't that Nooley standing by that church?"

It *is* Nooley. Nooley—who's been among the missing for several months. Since the winter in fact. We called and called. Leave a message, all we got. No one around when we went by.

Steve opens the door and calls, "Nooley, you dog, where you been?"

Nooley comes toward us, looking back over his shoulder a few times. The clutch of people disappears inside.

"What's up?" Steve says, giving him a hug.

I lean out the door. "Nooley," I say. "you are looking … fit as a fiddle." Nooley, always too thin, always in need of a good scrub, is totally made-over: flesh-colored, not the usual dinge, clean shirt, no holes. Hair shiny.

"Hop in," Steve says. "Have a toke. Killer weed this year. Some of Bergen's seed."

Nooley backs up a few inches, like suddenly we're infectious. "I've got something I have to do now," he says and starts to turn.

"You okay, Nooley? You in trouble?" Steve asks.

Nooley steps off a little more.

"I was. I am. Not the kind of trouble you mean. Take it easy," he says and moves toward the church.

Steve hesitates for a second, then starts off after him. Calls out, "Nooley."

"Don't you get it?" I holler. Nooley stops, but I can't hear what he and Steve are saying. I stick the now dead roach in the glove compartment and get out of the car. No odor once I close it up.

Nooley gives me a little wave goodbye and he's gone.

"You are not going to believe this," Steve says.

"Yes, I am."

"Nooley is going to a ..." Steve looks around and lowers his voice as a distinguished looking guy in an expensive suit passes us going into the church. "... a AA meeting."

"I know." The band must be on break. The day the music dies. "Let's go. Just leave the car here."

"Carla, the Moonies have got him. He's not himself. I'm going in there and check it out."

"You're what? Have you lost *your* mind? Maybe I better take *you* to the hospital." I start for the Eagle.

Steve catches up with me. "Listen, Carla, it's an open meeting. A speaker's meeting. Anybody can go. Come on. We'll sit in the back."

I keep on walking. The band is making tuning up sounds now. I am ready to dance. "Think of Nooley. You think Nooley wants you barging in? Barging in high?" Steve makes a quick about face.

"Who knows," he says, "might do us both good."

Us?

I watch his ponytail bob across the church parking lot, his nice back. Watch him disappear behind that door. What the hell. I follow. The minute I open the door, a blast of laughter hits me, booms right up those cold stairs. An AA meeting? I tug my sweater down. Red.

Not distinguished, but I know I look good in this color. I give my-self a look-over, a smell, on the way down. Nothing incriminating. The ho-ho-hos lead me to the room. Mostly guys, maybe a dozen, sitting in rows. Maybe three or four women. No generalizations possible, except most of them are yucking it up. No smile from Nooley. Steve, in the back, hands folded in his lap, on his best behavior. An empty chair beside him. I wish I had a name tag that says *Visitor*. A quick glance—nobody I know. One good thing. A sign on the front table says: *Whom you see here, what they say here, let it stay here.* Fine by me.

I expect the distinguished guy to be the leader, but no, an old, been-through-the-wars, man gets up. He's got one of those skid row noses. "Welcome," he says, beaming me and Steve with an extra gust of heat. "My name is Vic and I'm an alcoholic." Get me out of here. He hands a plastic sheet to a man in the second row. "Conner, would you read the opening?" Double get me out of here. I give Steve a hard jab in his ribs. In case there is any doubt in his mind as to my level of gratitude for getting me into this.

"'Alcoholics Anonymous is a fellowship of men and women who share their experience, strength, and hope ...'"

My hope was that I'd be dancing by now—the broken washing machine, Mamo this, Mamo that, hushed beneath a soft buzz.

"'The only requirement for membership is the desire to stop drinking ...'"

Yes, desire, definitely desire licking along on the edges of that. I give Steve another jab in the ribs. Vic hands a book to a woman sitting on the side. A woman about my age. Late twenties maybe. Pretty. What is she doing here?

"Roberta, could you start us off by reading the First Step? Page 4 in *Daily Reflections*."

A lot of people already have these little gray books open. I've got to tell you one of the parts I hated most about school was the going up and down the rows—lamp is a noun, run is a verb.

"'Step One,'" Roberta says, "'We admitted we were powerless over alcohol ...'"

And no clue how many steps we are going to have to climb. No way to count up and be ready, doze off until it's your turn. Steve jitters beside me. How's he going to fake through that one if the book comes his way? Steve is one of those people who turns his *p*s into *d*s. Road signs on the Thruway, a problem, if I'm not along to navigate. All his brothers. And Rudy sees some of his letters backwards as well. Dyslexia, they call it.

Roberta passes the book to the man next to her. "'Two. Came to believe that a power greater than ourselves ...'"

The God thing. I see the only way I'm going to get through this is to do what I used to call the wile-aways. Tacked here and there on the walls are dog-eared posters: *AA=Attitude Adjustment*. Right next to that: *Live and Let Live*. Another one says: *H.A.L.T: Hungry, Angry, Lonely, Tired*. Couldn't have put it better myself. Everybody closes their books. Evidently they've made it to the top of the stairs. *Change or Die*. Triple get me out of here.

"Now I'd like to introduce our speaker ... Jim," Vic nods to the distinguished looking man. The man stands up and goes behind the long table. He looks out, eye contact with every one of us. I get the anxiety lump. What you'd expect this guy to say is something about why the stock market is a wise investment. Instead he says, of course, "Hello, my name is Jim and I'm an alcoholic." And I'm sorry, but I am not going there. I've got enough sad stories of my own and a washing machine that will no longer agitate, that needs an Attitude Adjustment big time.

I take myself to Elsewhere with one that works every time: A my name is Alice, and my husband's name is Al. We come from Akron and we sell ...

Steve gives me a poke. I've made it all the way to Z and I'm on my second round. Always more challenging: A my name is Athena and my husband's name is ...

"Carla, get in the circle," he says.

No way out of this one. You just wait till I get you home.

"Let's say the Serenity Prayer," Vic says.

I've got Steve on one side and Vic on the other. Both squeezing my hands like they're going down. Finally we're out of there. Steve and I, the first ones up the stairs, and across the parking lot, lickety-split. We are at one on this. Steve lights us both a cigarette and we take that smoke in like it's water and we just crawled into the oasis. We can see Nooley would like to go out another way, but his truck is right behind our car, so he can't hide.

"Don't suppose you'd like to join us at the Eagle," Steve says. "Sounds like a good band."

Nooley shakes his head. "Got to get going," he says. He gets in his truck. It rumbles. He signals. We watch him disappear down the road. No, see you later. No, drop by. Nooley, our friend since way back in California.

"This makes me sad," Steve says. "This breaks my heart."

"Me, too," I say.

We start toward the Eagle. They're playing a blue song. It makes me want to sit down on that beat-up porch and cry. I go to open the door into the bar, but instead I turn to Steve.

"Yeah," he says, "might as well go get the kids. My heart's not in it."

Rudy throws his plastic bag on the backseat and gets in. He looks at us with suspicion. "What's wrong?" he says.

I settle Tess on my lap. She's sound asleep, but will not let me pry the fire hat from her fingers. It cuts into my leg.

"You're early," he says, tapping me on the shoulder.

"Just not a very good band," I say. Rudy shakes his head. Tell him another one.

Steve drives slowly past the Inn, then up Fyler Hill. "You know," he says, "maybe I *will* take the pledge."

I close my eyes. I'm going to have to wring every piece out by hand. Icy water. The jeans. The sweatshirts.

Steve sighs. "Be a good thing for both of us. Yeah, I think I'm going to take the pledge."

It's dark now. The hills have disappeared. No stars.

"Go right home, rip those plants up," I say. "Glug, glug whiskey down the drain."

"Soon," he says. "Soon. Who knows? Maybe even tomorrow."

You believe that, you believe anything.

13
Dear Loved Ones – 1977

Del blinked. So hot, bright, after the dim calm of the lawyer's office. The lawyer's reassurance: *Standard procedure. Entirely reasonable.* Lean on that until the worst was over. She cupped her hand over her eyes and looked up and down the street. Where did she park the car? Sally's car. Leaving the Valiant for Lee—her final noble gesture. For a moment her only memory of Sally's car: what it wasn't—not new, not red. Then she recognized the dog toys in the backseat of the gray car in front of her. The key fit.

Her hands on the steering wheel were so wet she had to keep wiping them on her skirt. Her lawyer attire. Her, *I'm still an attractive woman* outfit—the tasteful black sundress with its well-ordered polka dots. Entirely reasonable. She wasn't going to go beyond the appearance of that. What she could morally claim.

By now Lee would already have gotten her note saying she'd withdrawn even his half of the joint account: four hundred dollars—pitiful amount though it was. Plus she'd said, *and I expect you to finish paying my mother the money she loaned us to build the pole barn since you're still living there.* But tomorrow when Lee got the lawyer's letter—then he'd *really* know the truth. This girl, this girl with braces, him picking blackberries—even using the same goddamned pails that she'd threaded with just the right length cord to hang around her neck so she could use both hands for picking. Revenge. And he'd know she had a right, more than a right. All those years. But this, this ... the eighteen-year-old Presbyterian minister's daughter, Aaron and Mark's 4-H leader for gods sake. A girl whose handwritten recipe for granola was in their recipe box.

She signaled and started to pull out. The blast of a horn. She hadn't even looked. She put the car back in park, wiped her hands, adjusted the mirror. Lee would know as soon as he read *legal separation*. He'd really know when he read *child support*. Entirely reasonable, but beyond what he could pay. He'd know that finally, finally she'd had enough. No more starting over. The triumph of vengeance swelled her throat. And she wasn't done yet.

But she needed to calm down, to keep her eye on the road, or she wouldn't even make it back to Danford. She turned onto 23, longer, but the back way put her up in the hills, the stone house visible below, its half-shingled roof, maybe even Lee up there hammering. She could not bear that. She moved onto the shoulder to let the truck that was tailgating pass. Take her time, quiet down, before getting back to making the new beds with Aaron and Mark.

The road had just been tarred, that thick acrid smell. She rolled the window up. So hot, between her breasts, a line of sweat, seeped into the elastic band of her slip. Loose gravel spattered the car, pinged her nerves. The beds. Another fantasy plan.

How could she have thought she and Lee could be on friendly terms? In those first days after she and the kids moved to town, her relief at having escaped from the tension of the barn must have given her a temporary optimism, and in that mood, she imagined they could see each other, when necessary, for the good of the children. But that first time he came to pick up Aaron and Mark, that illusion ended. There she was making strawberry jam, hulling the ripe fruit, her fingers red with the juice. Hello, stranger, he said, as he stepped into the kitchen. Smiling. Able to smile. Thin and lean, much like he'd been when they'd first met. For the umpteenth time she did the numbers—twenty-two, Jesus, twenty-two years ago. When she saw him resting against the frame of the kitchen door in that summer light, it was like none of it had happened. What she wanted, more than anything, was to cross to where he stood, to be touched again by him. Instead she continued to pinch out the green stems, to slice each berry in half, to drop each section into the metal bowl. She hid the shaking of her hands and spoke to him about the weather, calling, Your father's here, through the house. The next time before he arrived, she went upstairs, concentrated on washing the windows to the rhythm of *never again*.

She braked for the stop at the foot of Fyler Hill. Onango Creek winding below. The thicket of blackberry canes where she'd seen Sara and Lee picking together, her buckets glinting. She'd forgotten she'd have to pass those. Was that how it was going to be—every place she went some goddamned reminder?

Del balanced the two-by-four on the edge of the step. When she bent to place the saw blade on the pencil line, a pain caught her in the small of her back. She saw that Mark was dripping stain all over the sidewalk. She opened her mouth to scream, but then clamped it shut. Aaron sat on the porch, reading a fat book about long-ago kingdoms, on hand to fetch and carry and trying to stay out of the fray. Just seeing him, his glasses crooked, his sneakers untied, calmed her. He looked up, came out of the blur.

"See if you can find a box or something in the garage that I can set this board on." Of course she'd left the sawhorses with Lee. Aaron loped off, making a wide detour around Mark, who had already slung stain at him several times. She sat down on the steps to rest, tried not to look at the mess Mark was making. The boards he'd stained so far, all streaked and uneven.

What in god's name had she been thinking? A family project: Let's make you some simple beds with tops that lift up to put stuff in so your new bedrooms won't be so crowded. The truck delivered the wood. The three of them unloaded the lumber and stacked it in the yard. August. The sun shining, her feeling settled, the kids coming out of their daze, actually laughing together for the first time since their move into town at the end of June. She'd spread out her diagram, with all the dimensions. She'd saw, Mark would stain, and Aaron would help wherever needed. And they'd gotten off to an okay start.

But seeing Lee and Sara along the creek yesterday … So shaken, she could barely ride her bike back to town. What was it Lee told her? Late in the spring, the dark days of a terrible winter giving way to brief hope when he returned to the pole barn after living up on the bluff in the tent. This friendship with Sara, it's over. You know, a relationship uncomplicated by history. And she had believed him. And what did it matter? She left because she could not stand one more day of silence, his withdrawal from her touch. Silence that began in November—right after they returned from Lee's twentieth high school reunion. Was it something about seeing those people again?

A crash in the garage. Mark gave her a what-did-you-expect shrug.

"Aaron, are you all right?"

His muffled voice, "I'm still looking."

"You better go in there before he destroys the place," Mark said.

She should get moving, go help Aaron, but her body was so weighted she couldn't get up. She should never have sat down.

Lee's silence? That was the question she kept coming back to. Singing on New Scotland Ave., then one week later Lee stopped talking, stopped writing, stopped doing much of anything. Silence that soon covered them all. Was it her? That he just couldn't love her, the weight of that? They had not gotten their wood in soon enough so they were burning a lot of green; the pole barn was cold. The meals were especially terrible. Lee, remote; her, throwing out words from time to time; Aaron and Mark's heads bent, anxious to be done. It was hard to get the food down. All trapped in the one room of the pole barn, the air heavy with the weight of Lee. It was hard to breathe. In March Lee moved into a tent under a stand of pines overlooking the valley. His only explanation to the children: He needed to be alone for a while. They went on. They didn't talk of him. When they came home from school, sometimes they would hear the sound of his hammer building trusses for the roof of the stone house. Occasionally they would look out to see him passing along the ridge of the hill. She didn't know if the children tried to visit him. They didn't say and she could not ask.

One day an old friend of Lee's drove up their road, stood talking with Lee by the stone house. Then the friend backed past the barn. He got out and knocked on the window where she was doing the dishes. She slid the window open. Lee needs to go to the hospital, he said. I tried to get him to go with me, but he won't. What do you mean? Look at his eyes, he told her. Then he got in his truck and drove away.

A week later Lee moved back into the pole barn with them. But still the silence, the not touching. Somehow she found the energy to pack up and leave. Picking berries with Sara. Why did it matter? She was never going back anyway. She kicked the board hard. It went skidding down the steps. Mark gave her a long look.

"Where'd you go this morning?" Mark said. The brown stain still dripping onto the walk.

She picked the board up and set it back against the porch. "Please—don't let that get on the concrete. It'd be better to use a rag." She did not add *like I told you.*

"Then I'd get this shit all over my hands."

She was not going to let him provoke her. At least he shifted so the stain fell on the grass.

"You could've at least told me you were going. I needed drum sticks, to get out of this dorky town."

Do not unload it all on him. She'd already done way too much of that. "I had some business I had to take care of." She breathed, slowed down. "You must have been over at the school shooting baskets. I'll borrow Sally's car again next week. You can go with me then."

Later when it all calmed down, she'd tell them about the legal separation. Maybe they could talk about the silence. So far there'd been only what she told them the day she packed up their stuff at the pole barn and moved them to this little house in town: Your father and I cannot live together anymore. You can visit with him whenever the three of you work it out.

Aaron dragged a small beat-up table across the grass, ripped-up clumps of earth trailed behind him. He laid the two-by-four across it, rested the other end on the step. Still not even, but maybe better.

"Thank you," she said and once again placed the saw carefully where she'd measured. Pressing her free hand on the board to steady it, she began to saw, every inch an effort.

Mark stepped in closer. "Did it have something to do with Dad?"

The blade of the saw snagged halfway through. She screamed. Mark and Aaron backed away. She didn't look at them. She yanked the saw, but the blade was stuck. She screamed again, a snarl from deep in her throat through clinched teeth, "Goddammit."

Mark glared at her. "I don't want the dumb bed anyway," he said. "Why can't we just sleep on the floor?"

Her body still bent over the board, she twisted to face him. "Mark, why do you always ..." Then she stopped. She pushed the board until it would balance on the edge of the step, the saw still wedged in the cut, and walked to the sidewalk in front of the house. She realized she was not breathing, her teeth and throat still clamped shut on god-knows-what hateful words.

She turned and moved back to the problem of the saw. She didn't look at Mark. She felt him somewhere behind her. Aaron had retreated to the porch, his book open in his lap. She took a deep breath. What she needed were the sawhorses. Of course Lee would have known how to get a saw through a board without it catching.

Mark had once again started to slap stain on the boards lined up against the other end of the porch. He looked up at her, his mouth tight, his eyes surly. Dark eyes so much like his father's. He was still putting on too much stain; it ran down the board, slopped off onto the grass. She would just suggest again in a quiet way. "Mark ..."

"Don't," he said. He dropped the brush and moved down the side of the house. "Just don't." He yanked open the screen door. "Why do you have to be such a martyr?" he yelled.

"Mark ..."

The door slammed behind him. Aaron looked up at the bang and then returned to his book. She glanced across the street toward the Eagle, the few cars in the parking lot. People at the bar couldn't help but hear her shrieks. Martyr?

She pulled on the heavy garage door. It folded up with a rusty whine. Somewhere in the jumble, something to place the boards on so the saw wouldn't bind. When had Mark started to greet almost every approach with a feint of his own, a who-cares shrug, the sarcastic aside? In utero was often the answer that came back to her when once again she picked her way around Mark's defenses. But of course no surprise that beneath his prickly surface, Mark was often afraid. As a child, and even now at thirteen, he would not go on an escalator or elevator. She remembered their first summer when they camped on the land, while they dug the foundation and before they'd had the pole barn put up, Lee had built Mark and Aaron a wonderful sleeping fort, just down the slope from their tent platform, made of wooden walls with a huge piece of clear plastic stretched like a covered wagon for the roof. So you can look up at the moon and stars and watch the squirrels, he told them. But at the first sign of a summer storm, even heat lightning, she had to quickly go to Mark, slide in beside him on his cot and hold him tight until the night became quiet again.

The old bed springs fell back against the wall. Nothing that would do for sawhorses. She grabbed the rope and pulled the garage door down hard with a bang. The stained boards looked awful, gummy and dull. She took a rag and attempted to even out some of the dark brown streaks.

She turned to Aaron, for a moment tried to breathe in some of his distance. She wanted to say something sarcastic about Mark, something that would draw Aaron to her corner, but he had made it clear at an early age, he did not want to hear it. She passed her hand over one of the new bed frames and realized *it* would do.

"Aaron, help me turn this on its side. I can use it as a kind of sawhorse. It's low, but it'll be better than the steps or the porch.

They eased the frame over. Aaron smiled at her, his teeth still too big for his child's face. Her eyes filled. "Thanks," she said and went to get the half-cut board. No, she could not give way to that. How, how was she going to do this—finish these beds, get the three of them through all the years ahead?

The angle was better; the saw began to move, if not smoothly, at least it didn't bind. It cut more easily if she didn't bear down so hard. As she slid the last board across the frame, Mark drifted into view, a huge T-shirt of his father's, hanging below his cut-offs, leaving only his thin brown calves stretching long to his bony ankles. So vulnerable, the miracle of such awkward grace. Her son. She looked away.

Mark carried one of the just-sawed boards to the steps, then aligned the stain can and rags along the edge of the porch. He pressed the brush against the side of the can to get out the excess and then began to lightly apply the stain to the top of the board and rub it in with a damp rag, just as she had shown him. There was the problem of the stain splatters that were bound to seep into the porch and steps, the possibility that stain would flick onto Mark's T-shirt, his prized shirt on which he had spent hours meticulously copying the calligraphy of two Chinese characters with a permanent marker across the front and the back, and which months later he finally revealed meant *Caution: Musician Working*. So typical of Mark to put something he valued in the way of likely calamity. But so precarious was the balance of each moment, she retreated from making any more suggestions.

"Okay, guys," she said instead, "we're almost ready to take all the parts upstairs, then, kazam, put them together."

"Yeah, right," Mark said, rolling his eyes at Aaron who started laughing too at her obvious attempts to make light of what they all knew would still be many hours of anxious effort. But perhaps lest he seemed too congenial, Mark dampened Aaron's cheer by adding, "What are you laughing at, Goofy? How about getting off your butt and bringing the boards over here."

She straightened, swung her arms to ease the ache between her shoulders. The last board cut. She surveyed Mark's progress: the stain was much more even, only five boards to go.

"Those look good, Mark. How about one of you going over to JAKE's for ice cream?"

"Me," Aaron said.

"Yeah, sure so you can get out of work." Mark set down the brush and looked at his stained hands.

She saw that his T-shirt was still free of any sign of damage. "Why don't you both go? And get us hot fudge sundaes or whatever you want."

Mark and Aaron smiled, and in that lightening of spirit, she ventured floating a suggestion in Mark's direction. "After we eat, why don't you throw on that old blue shirt of your father's before you do any more staining." The mention of Lee, even at the distance of *your father* darkened the moment. She counted out the money to Aaron, while Mark cleaned his hands with thinner.

But before Aaron could get the money into his pocket, Mark took his hand and dumped the change into his own. "Fog-brain might lose it," he said. Aaron didn't even bother to protest.

"You want vanilla ice cream?" Mark asked, knowing that's what she always had.

She watched the two of them go up the block: Mark, a little ahead, with Aaron trailing off to the side, just out of the perimeter of striking distance should Mark let fly.

"Don't forget the nuts," she called and Mark waved his hand in the air to signal he'd heard.

It was not just his wiry hair, his dark eyes, something about the way Mark moved—the slant of his shoulders, the angle of his jaw, his hands—she didn't know, but all of him together, Mark in the distance, always made her see Lee again, as he was in high school, watching him disappear down her street after he'd walked her home.

She could lean up against the tree and bawl, or she could start nailing the tops of the beds together. Of course she would not speak against Lee to them. She almost never referred to him at all. I'll take care of you; you can always count on that, was what she told them the first night they moved to town. And martyr or no, she was sure they believed this just as she believed her own mother who had once said these same words to her.

She leaned the board Mark had finished against the side of the porch and closed the stain can and set it out of the way. Maybe after the ice cream they'd call it quits for the day. Get a fresh start tomorrow. She sat down on the steps to wait.

All their lives Lee had been drawn to the stranger, taken on a glow of excitement from those first conversations of discovery. But this time watching Sara close beside him, her face turned up and listening, Sara, in her blue and gold track shirt, the blackberry canes reaching out, where was she going to put that?

Tomorrow he would open the mail box and there it would be— the letter from the lawyer. Already he must have gotten her note: *Since you never paid your share of the loan from my mother to build the pole barn, I've closed out the account.*

She stood up and looked down the sidewalk. No sign of Aaron and Mark. Let him get the letter from the lawyer with no warning from her. She moved back to the boards for the top of the bed and set the crosspiece that would anchor them together in place. She sank her knee onto the piece to hold it and pounded in the first nail. How she wished she had come up with some cutting answer to his parting words: I'm sorry I've taken the best years of your life. She hit the next nail as hard as she could.

Between the bangs of the hammer she watched Aaron and Mark returning: Mark, well in front, working his way down what was left of his cone; Aaron, balancing on the stone wall that rounded the corner by the fire house, the white cup with her sundae held in his outstretched hand, his untied laces flopping. Then Lee's parents' brown car appeared, floated by the two boys. Why didn't they honk, roll down their window to call? It all happened at once. Their car stopped across the street with the engine still running. She put down the hammer. Mark and Aaron came into the yard. Aaron handed her the white cup, the cherry, the whipped cream oozing down in the heat. Aaron and Mark started to cross the road, smiling. Lee's father put his hand out the window. Stay away. As though they carried with them some dread disease. Mark and Aaron retreated to the yard, stood there close together.

It was then she knew. She set down the cup. She crossed the street knowing. She got in the back seat. Neither of them turned. All three of them looked straight ahead.

Finally Lee's mother said what she already knew, "He killed himself."

Forever she would remember her first thought: You bastard, I knew you would have the last word.

Dear Loved Ones, Forgive me, his final note said.

That night, for many nights, they all slept in the same room. They were afraid of the dark. If only she had not left Lee out there all alone. How could she have left him out there alone?

For days when friends came to comfort them, everything she said was really about this: Lee's death was not my fault.

Her in-laws decided to have no funeral service. Later, after some of the shock was over, the five of them could gather to bury his ashes on the land.

Two days after his death, she received a letter from Lee. *First payment on the barn*, the note said. Nineteen dollars fluttered to the floor. She could not touch it.

One afternoon Lee's mother come up the walk, she sat down on the narrow roll-a-way couch. "Lee's father doesn't think I should tell you this … You know about Sara Miles."

She nodded.

"It's important for you to also know that besides the note he left to all of us, he left a note addressed to Sara. We've given it to her."

He left a note addressed to Sara. His final note was addressed to Sara. She reached across and took hold of Lee's mother's hand. "Thank you. Thank you for telling me," she kept saying.

She was not The One. She was not His Last Hope. She was not to blame.

Mostly after that, she felt nothing. She went about the routine of getting ready to go back to school, for hours forgetting what had happened. Though she read *David Copperfield* to Mark and Aaron each night out in the little hall between their two rooms so they could be quieting down in their own beds, they did not talk about what had happened. Mark and Aaron asked no questions.

Only two weeks after his father's death, she sent Aaron off to scout camp. It had been something he'd wanted so much that winter when the plans were made. When asked, he said he still wanted to go. Wouldn't it be better to fill his day with structure and things he enjoyed? She packed his suitcase, putting in absolutely everything the check list suggested, sewing name tags on all his T-shirts and shorts, even his socks. She sent him letters and several packages filled with his favorite gum, homemade chocolate cookies, another *Dune* book. When she received no response, no phone calls, she thought, Well, maybe that's how he had to do it. But when she picked him up at the bus, he was pale and dingy. He would say nothing more than it had been okay, and when she opened his suitcase to pull out the expected wads of dirty clothes, everything was just as she had packed it, nothing had been used.

One day she saw Aaron writing in the journal his father had given him for Christmas. When he left it tucked under a stuffed panda bear Lee had won for him the day they went to the fair, she did something she would not usually do. She opened it and read what Aaron had written: *I think my father knew he was going to do this thing and because he loved us he sent us away.*

Then Aaron had carefully drawn a line through every word.

This thing. Sometime in the night on August 7th, Lee crossed the field to his parents' house and took the twenty-two used for the woodchucks and returned to the pole barn. The death certificate said, *Immediate Cause: gunshot.* No way any of them can ever cross a line through that.

For months she could not go to the land. She had Sally bring her the Valiant. And when she had to drive down the road on the other side of the wide field that ran up to the pole barn, she looked the other way. She asked another friend to come and remove the chair Lee had been sitting in when he died.

One day when she had to stop at Lee's parents, his mother was busy making blackberry jam. "Lee brought me all these berries. They've been in the freezer. I couldn't stand to see them go to waste. Would you want some when I finish?"

She shook her head. No she did not want any.

One gray afternoon in November she and Mark and Aaron followed Lee's parents up the hill looking down on the roof of the stone house, the roof Lee had shingled only a few weeks before his death. In the hole Lee's father had already dug beneath the only tree on the slope, he placed the box with Lee's ashes. The Presbyterian minister joined them and read a few words from the Bible. Standing there in the cold, her children beside her, the whole time, through all the 44 words, all she could think of was how strange it was that Lee's parents could have asked the young girl's father to be a part of this. When he finished, they all walked back down the hill.

They did not touch and they did not cry.

14
Amends – 1982

T HE KITCHEN I SNUCK OUT of seventeen years ago kept fading to black and white, with this layer of something between me and them. I could hear what they were saying, but their words were muffled, their movements slowed down. It was like I hovered over them all, watching: my brother Bobby, who'd gone from bodywork to DeLuca's Auto Sales, from beer to Tanqueray. I watched him grab all the salami from one side of the cold cuts plate brought over by the Lucianos. At thirty-one he was still Bobby. Bobby the Bad, who at fourteen was already banging against the world, hardening up as fast as he could—stealing tires, cutting school, taking his pick of the boldest chickies in the neighborhood, several who he later married, banging up against them as well. My brother, T.J., still a little chubby, with the same bad haircut—too high on his neck, too close to the scalp over his ears. Careful T.J.—rearranging the cheese and bologna to make Bobby's assault on the platter less damaging. T.J., who very much wanted us to act like a family should, sat with a yellow pad in front of him, his pen ready.

"Let's decide what the gravestone should say," he said. "Carla's going back on the bus tonight. Let's not leave it all on Ma's shoulders."

My mother—at the sink, her back to us, washing dishes—said not a word.

Trying to think of words for his gravestone still seems unreal. I found it hard to believe I was actually there. Before it all started to come down, I would have checked somewhere between unlikely to impossible that my body would be in Newark, sitting in the same chair I always sat in, where I could best deflect his smacking hands.

My only happy memory of my father was when he helped me

draw pictures of the American presidents for a seventh grade project, how he carved the profile of Washington out of a bar of soap

Newark, twenty years later—Bobby and T.J. in their usual places too. My mother, her back to us at the sink.

"Ma," Bobby said, "stop washing the dishes already."

Bobby's tone was so close to *his* tone, it made the back of my neck creep. Obediently, she dried her hands and sat down on the edge of her chair, like a nervous bird with one wing caught. She looked caved in and cracked along the seams, wearing one of those pitiful polyester suits that used to fill me with shame when she'd show up for the annual parent conference. I felt so guilty about that later, I'd try to make it up to her with offers to mop or clean out the fridge.

I hadn't seen her since Tess was born, eight years ago, when she actually came to Danford for a few days to help Steve and me get settled. We went through the motions of calling her a few times a year. Every now and then she'd call us. In either direction it was risking more bad news. I remember one Christmas I had to return to the unwrapping of our presents with the joyful news that lately he'd taken to keeping her up half the night with his harangues: the way she'd ironed his shirts, how she overcooked the green beans.

Way before I left home, I'd said, So why don't you leave him? Get the hell out. Back then she'd twist her ring around her finger and look away. Later, when I'd say it over the phone, there'd be a long pause; then she'd go on about an entirely different subject in, I swear to god, a cheery voice.

I looked at her close for the first time since I arrived. She was only forty-nine, only seventeen years older than me—how troubles can flatten you, what daily worry can do to your mouth. I remember her as being pretty, my pretty mama, when I was little.

"How about In Loving Memory?" T.J. said, and then he actually wrote that down.

In the piles of pictures in my mind, I doubt I could have come up with one *loving* memory. Sometimes things started off okay: the trimming the tree, stuffing the turkey, but by the time they'd reached the halfway mark on the bottle, we always knew we were on our way down and it was just going to get more and more dangerous. From then on you simply tried to find cover until they'd passed out and you could wiggle free to inventory the wreckage. Paydays were bad; holidays were hideous. The changing of the moon, the seasons, a round of bad luck, a stroke of fortune.

When T.J. got no response, he said, "Ma, do you think we should put Tony or his full name? Anthony, or was it Antonio?"

My mother lit up another cigarette. Her last one was still burning down in the ashtray. Bobby and T.J. followed suit. I wanted one, but on general principle, held off. A cloud of smoke hung over the table, like the whole family connected in the same hazy talk balloon.

"Ma?"

"Tony is the only name I ever knew your father to use. That's the way he signed everything. At least what I saw him sign. He never signed much. He was suspicious of signing things."

"Well, how about his birth certificate? What does that say?"

"I don't know if he had a birth certificate."

"Ma, everybody has a birth certificate. What year was he born? We'll need that for the stone too."

My mother shrugged. If someone were to ask me the main thing I remembered about my mother, I'd say "her shrug." That, or acting like she didn't hear us at all.

"Maybe he's got it stashed away," Bobby said, finishing off the last of his drink, and in the same flow of motion pouring himself another. Once again I noticed my mother wasn't drinking. I hadn't seen her with a glass since I got there. I remember as a kid, my father would always say to her, Have a drink, Angela. She'd say, I want to finish mashing the potatoes. Sit down and have a drink, he'd say again. And she would.

"All Ma and I found were his car insurance papers and some notices from the V.A.," T.J. said.

"Check the big locked box in the back of his closet," Bobby announced.

"What box?" T.J. asked him.

"Way in the back beside the chimney."

We all stared at Bobby. Evidently my mother didn't know anything about the box either. A big box in the closet of the man she'd lived with in that duplex for at least twenty years and she didn't know about it. I remember one of her repeated bits of advice, the phrase uttered like some prayer of caution any time one of us was about to take any kind of action: *Don't go looking for trouble*. But of course Bobby knew about the box. He'd been looking for trouble right from the go. He never got in my father's face, but once he hit his teens, he stopped cowering, did pretty much what he wanted and I guess my father signed off, split his discontent between easier prey—my mother and T.J. I was long gone.

"What's in the box, Bobby?" I said.

More than likely he'd had a go at that lock back when. I was surprised by the sound of my voice. Beyond the opening dutiful exchanges and the Steve, Rudy, and Tess are doing okay, I hadn't been part of the conversation much since my arrival the night before, my arrival when the rest of the family was at the funeral. Carla, I hope you can make it to the funeral home. For Ma's sake, if nothing else, T.J. said when he called. The way I feel, I told him, it's better I'm not there. When they got home soon after I arrived, T.J. took me aside to say, I could run you out to the cemetery, Carla. No, I said. I wanted to add how my curse might interfere with his ghost's final departure, how we certainly wouldn't want that.

"Bobby," I said again, "any idea what's in the box?"

Bobby didn't answer. He just stood up. I swear we all looked toward my father's empty chair, then toward the garage, still fearful *he* might catch us out. We followed Bobby up the back stairs to my parents' room, first me, then T.J., then Ma, still looking behind her.

We came to a halt outside the closed door, piled up against each other. Even my mother seemed to hesitate. Bobby turned the knob, then reached back and kind of pulled us all in. Dark. And that smell—though I couldn't give it a name—even as a kid I knew what it meant. Even in the daytime, the dark green shades were always down, the windows closed. I don't remember ever seeing the bed made and every possible surface was weighted down with dark piles. I'd hated going into that room. I learned to quiet my own nightmares, T.J.'s, to con Bobby back into bed, to measure out the cough syrup and get the glasses of water, how to read the silver line of mercury rather than go into that room to rouse my mother. Once my father sent me up to get his lighter. Right on the bedside table, you damned ninny, he said to my reluctance. I remember holding my breath before opening that door and then having this wild urge to rush in and rip down the shades, to open all the windows, to start heaving all the dark piles down in the alley. I must have been fifteen, a few months before I finally got away.

Bobby groped around for a second, looking for the overhead switch. I almost yelled out, Don't—the dread of seeing all of that despair. Yes, finally I had the word for it, the *despair* of my parents' stained lives, caught in the terrible overhead light. But before Bobby found the switch, my mother crossed to the bedside lamp, and with more energy than I'd ever heard from her, said, "Open up the windows, Carla."

I opened every single one as far as they would go, with T.J. pushing ahead of me to raise the shades. Summer twilight and the sounds of birds settling in for the night filled the room. The bed was made, the dark piles gone.

"I don't know about the shades," my mother said.

Bobby smiled at her, an honest-to-goodness smile. "What would the neighbors see, Ma? We're not up to anything illegal here, right, T.J.?"

When T.J. answered with one of Ma's uncertain shrugs, Bobby raised the flat of his hand.

"Whoa, let's stop right here for a second. Are we all agreed we should pull the old man's box out of the closet and break the lock and go through its contents together? I don't want to hear any of that, *Bobby the Bad made me do it* stuff later."

Nervous laughter.

"Well?" Bobby said.

"You honestly never managed to jimmy into this box, Bobby?" I said.

"Nope. Sorry to tarnish my dare-to-do-anything reputation, but even I was never as nuts as that."

"Okay," I said, "Of course I'm in favor of opening up the box."

My mother and T.J. nodded.

"Let's hear it loud and clear," Bobby said.

"Open it," T.J. told him.

"Yes," my mother agreed and then she laughed. I saw that my mother had pulled on the bulky pink sweater I'd sent her one Christmas. I was amazed at how that changed her appearance and ashamed at how much easier it was for me to look at her then.

Bobby opened the closet and we watched him push back through the hangers, heavy with dark clothes I'd never seen my father wear. I was glad it was my brother's job and not mine.

"It's here," Bobby called and we all caught our breath. "Give me a hand, T.J.," Bobby muttered. "The son of a bitch's heavy or maybe it's just catching on the floor boards."

They pushed it out into the dim light—an old army footlocker, dented and scratched, with a large rusted padlock jammed through the steel ring.

"Ma, you and Carla, go on down and clear off the kitchen table. Got to set this up on something so we can get at the lock."

"What about looking around for some keys?" I said. But Bobby just shook his head.

We went down and my brothers followed, heaving and jockeying to make the turn at the narrow landing. My mother spread one of my father's old army overcoats out and Bobby and T.J. rested the box in the middle of that. We all stood and stared at its secret bulk for a minute until my mother turned away to make coffee. Bobby and T.J. went out the door that opened into the garage and came back with a bunch of screwdrivers and picks.

"Where are his bolt cutters?" Bobby said. "They're not hanging where they usually are and they're not in the trunk of the car."

I thought of saying how *he* probably knew what we'd be up to and once again he'd done his damnedest to prevent it.

"Ma, don't you think he might have the key tucked in one of his drawers, maybe in one of those pockets?" T.J. said. "Bobby, maybe we should do a thorough search before we go any further."

Bobby shook his head again and added a little of my father's Irish whiskey to his coffee.

"Sounds like a good plan to me," I said.

We sat and drank coffee, waited for Bobby to respond, watched him continue to pick around delicately up inside the old lock.

"Why not hunt for the keys, Bobby?" I finally asked him. "What else do you know?"

Bobby looked at my mother and then he said, "Because when he got moved downstairs, when they had him pretty much knocked out on morphine, I searched through all his stuff, thinking I might turn up the keys—drawers, pockets, tucked up under the ledges, you name it. You didn't ever see any padlock keys around did you, Ma?"

She shook her head no.

Bobby stopped picking at the lock and again looked at my mother; this time long enough that she had to meet his eyes. And when she did, he said, "Sorry for nosing around, but I knew you'd be afraid to do such a thing, and I figured there might be something important in there we ought to know about before he died. I gave up on the key, but somehow I couldn't quite bring myself to cut the lock. It was like against all odds he might have got off that bed and come up those stairs and found me breaking in." Bobby pushed all the tools off to the side. "We're going to have to come up with some cutters."

"What do you think is in the box?" I said to the rest of them. Each of them got an alert look, but nobody responded. "What do you wish was in the box? What do you wish we'd find down in there after we lifted the lid?" Still nobody spoke, but I could see they were all thinking.

Then my mother gave a hoot of laughter, a laugh I don't think I'd heard from her since we were kids. We'd play Button, Button Who's Got the Button and my mother would get to laughing so hard at Bobby's and my bluffing and T.J.'s stricken expression, like he had hold of something hot, that she'd beg us to quit. Stop, stop, she'd say, holding her sides and sometimes she'd just reach out and pull us all toward her and we'd squeal and wiggle around. That reminded me of other games too—like us hiding all over the house and her whistling her amazing whistle through her fingers to let us know she was coming, ready or not. Those rare times happened less and less, like a slow leak of my mother's energy, around the time we moved back to Newark, when I was starting fourth grade. The year my grandmother died. And even before that such games were only played when my father was stationed overseas.

My mother poured more coffee. T.J. tucked in next to me for protection like in the old days; my mother on the other side of the table where she always sat—within arm's length of my father; Bobby, the most distant, at the foot, closest to the door. We stared at the box, now blocking the head of the table, that empty place where he no longer was.

"Button, button, who's got the button?" I said. I opened both of my hands. "Bobby, what did you hope you'd find when you came on that box?"

"You know, I didn't give that much thought. Mostly it pissed me off that it was locked. But then it kind of steadied me too. You know, Jesus, right to the end he's not going to give an inch."

T.J. leaned forward, his face so earnest I felt that fear I'd always had when he used to go up to bat or when the ball would head straight for him in the outfield. I'd be the only one from the family at his Little League games. Just do your best, I'd tell him. But when he'd miss, and he pretty much always did, he'd look crushed and on the way home he'd say, I'm glad he didn't come; better he wasn't there. Sometimes it was all I could do not to shake him and scream, Don't care so much. Toughen up for Christ's sake.

T.J. spoke softly, looking right at the box. "Sure, I'd like to find something nice. Like maybe some of those goofy cards we used to make in school for Father's Day. You remember that card I made him in fifth grade? Mrs. Ormsbie said it was the most beautiful Father's Day card she ever saw. I know it was the biggest. Made out of a giant sheet of construction paper. Remember it had a strip of paper folded down like a jack-in-the box so that when you opened it, *I love you* was supposed to pop out? But of course by the time I got it home, I'd opened it so many times, the strip had lost its spring. Remember that card, Ma? It was green, bright green."

"I remember the Mother's Day gift you made for me from first or second grade—your hand print in plaster."

My mother's eyes welled up and I wasn't sure what I'd gotten going here. None of us said so, but I was pretty sure that hand print plaque was something Bobby brought home from kindergarten.

"Well, anyway," T.J. said. "Whatever's in it, I'm for getting it out in the open. There's this saying 'Only your secrets can make you sick'."

Some more Al-Anon lingo, I knew. But I wasn't going to touch that line with a ten foot pole. I felt confident we were not going to find any confessional journals in that box.

"Maybe the Lucianos have some cutters," I said. Better to get on with this before the good of my mother's laugh was completely drained away.

"I'll go," T.J. said.

"Thank them again for the cold cuts," my mother called after him.

"Did you ever write him letters?" I said.

"Yes," was all my mother offered.

Both Bobby and I stared at her, surprised I suppose, though I don't know why. We both wanted her to say more.

"Maybe some records of his family," Bobby said. "Where he was born. Maybe his parents immigrated from Italy. I know we're Italian. And not just on your side. The name DeLuca. Just look at us."

My mother twisted her ring. Would she keep on wearing that ring? "I never remember your father mentioning anything about his family. Sisters. Brothers. Nothing. When I first met him, I asked him questions, but right away he said, 'I don't want to talk about it.' The evening we knew he most likely wasn't going to live through the night, I asked him again, 'Don't you want me to get in touch with someone in your family?' He just shook his head no. 'Don't you want a priest?' I said."

"What did he say?"

"He just gave me that terrible look."

I knew exactly the one she meant. So did Bobby.

"Where did you meet him anyway?" I said.

She laughed. "I met him at a church dance. Saint Mary's."

Bobby leaned her way in surprise, "You met him at a *church dance*?"

"Well, sort of. That's what I told your grandmother. In truth, I met him on the corner outside the church dance. He was driving by with a buddy. Home on leave. 1949. I was just a little high school girl."

"And how old was he then?"

"Old enough to know better, he told me. I always thought he was about twenty-five then. I knew he was a lot older than me. He certainly knew more than I did. I didn't know anything. Nothing. It's hard to believe I could have known so little."

"You mean he never even told you how old he was?" I said. "And how long before you got married?"

"A few months after." And then she looked away. "Not too long after that I had you."

Something kept me staring at her even though I knew it was a mean thing to do.

After what felt like a long time, she looked back at me, "Yes, sooner than I should have," she said.

I'd always figured that, but somehow it seemed good to make her say it.

"He wasn't always so hard. He was such a good-looking guy," she said. "Especially in his uniform. Whether you like it or not, you all look like him. Especially you, Carla."

"What about his army records? Maybe they're in the box," Bobby said. "If not, probably we could get some more information from the V.A."

The mention of the V.A. made my mother shrink a little. "He wouldn't go to the hospital, Carla. He said terrible things about the V.A., but finally I had to get somebody to come in. He got so bad. Mrs. Luciano got somebody from Hospice. She said, You've got to have some help. He's got to have something for the pain. Don't be afraid. And they came in the end. I think if he could have, he would've raised up and hit me for bringing strangers into the house. As weak as he was, he did grab me; You better not get a priest, he said. That's why we had it at the funeral home. He told me I was to have him cremated. Burned up, Carla, put in the fire. But I just couldn't do that; I couldn't." She started to cry.

Bobby looked at me like I was supposed to do something; both of us sat frozen in our chairs. After a minute of her sitting there, crying into her hands, Bobby spoke in a gentle voice, "It's all right, Ma. You did it the way you had to do it, and T.J. and me felt that was right. I know Carla does too."

"Of course," I said and went to get her some tissues.

T.J. came in with bolt cutters and turned them over to Bobby. "You okay, Ma?" he said and put his arm around her shoulders. Dear, sweet T.J.

Bobby gestured toward the cutters. "Are you up for this, Ma?"

She wiped her eyes and blew her nose on the wad of toilet paper I'd handed her. "I am," she said. "Yes, I am. And I don't want any of you to be afraid." Again she surprised me with a laugh. "We aren't going to find anything worse than what we already know. And we survived that."

I could feel T.J. sort of hovering—mother-henning us—like he might be going to try to cluck us all into one of those love circles. Now everyone join hands. I was certainly not ready for that.

Instead my mother raised her hands, push-pushed her fingers, a photographer signal that if we didn't get in closer we wouldn't all be in the picture. We all leaned in a little. Then she said, "Well, didn't we?" and we all three shook our heads yes. Yes, we did.

"All right, Bobby, might as well have a go at it," I said, before things got further out of control. We awkwardly pulled back into our places. My mother and I moved out of the way, and Bobby and T.J. approached the box. They pushed it over to get a better grip. Then Bobby stopped and turned my way.

"What?" I said.

"I was just thinking that after bringing up the idea of us telling what we thought might be in the box, you didn't commit yourself on a thing."

T.J. and my mother were also looking at me. "Yeah, Carla, you must have had something in your head to get us going," T.J. said.

"You know, I think it was just that I was buying time, trying to do something with the fear I felt pressing up under my ribs. What do they call it … random dread?"

"Dread of what, Carla?"

"I'm not sure? I guess that's the point."

"Yeah," Bobby said, "but why not take a stab at it?"

"Okay, but this is going to sound pretty negative. But then what else is new, huh? I think I *don't* want to find something nice…What would I do if we opened up this box and found our school cards, Ma's letters, the article from the paper when you got that scouting award? Jesus, then I might have to bring it all up again, start sorting through it."

"Really, Carla. Couldn't you use a little *nice*?" T.J. said.

"Oh, get on with it, Bobby. I'm not sure of anything."

With that Bobby fastened onto the old lock and—ping, ping—the lock dropped into T.J.'s hand. We just stood there.

"You open it, Ma," Bobby said.

But T.J. motioned us all back a little and slowly eased up the lid as though there might be some unknown beast lurking in that darkness. We all leaned over and stared in. Old newspapers stacked an inch or so below the top.

Bobby took one out and looked at the date. "July 1965. Does that mean anything to you, Ma?" Bobby handed the paper to my mother. "Why don't you spread it out on the counter to see if you can find something that he might have wanted to keep a record of, something about one of us or about him. How old were you, Carla, in 1965?"

"I know that exactly," I said. "July of '65 was when Vicky and me ran away. I was fifteen. Good lord, fifteen. Seventeen years ago."

"I must have been thirteen," T.J. said, "and Bobby, you were fourteen."

Bobby laughed. "Look under the arrests section. I was in and out of jail along about that time. It'll say 'name withheld because of age.'"

My mother was busy running her finger up and down the columns while Bobby slowly lifted out another few layers. Below a few inches, he came upon wads of paper. He picked one up and squeezed. Then he picked up another and did the same. "What the hell?"

He pawed down through the wads, squeezing here and there. He laughed again. "All right. Each of us is going to reach in and take out one wad and then wait until everybody has one before you squeeze it."

Each of us felt around for a second before making our selection. It was like those grab bag things we used to do in school at Christmas when the teacher wanted to make sure that nobody got left out and that nobody got anything better than anyone else— which of course pretty much meant everyone got something lousy like a box of crayons or a cheesy coloring book or an icky plastic top that wouldn't spin.

We all stepped back from the box, squeezing.

"I haven't got a clue. Not a clue," I said.

"Me either," T.J. said.

"Clueless," Bobby said. "Ma?'

"Not a single idea," she answered.

"Okay, go," Bobby told us.

Slowly we began to unwrap. Deep inside the wad, nestled within at least three sheets of paper—a bird … a carved bird. My fingers uncovered its wings. Rage tightened in my chest. My arm drew back to smash that fragile creature against the wall. Only the sudden fear on my mother's face stopped me. I pushed the bird away from me as though it was on fire.

Bobby and T.J. and my mother held their birds up. Turned them this way and that. I made myself look. Each bird was completely different from the other three, the largest, about four inches from the tip of one wing to the other, the smallest, maybe two. And here's the thing—all four birds were in flight.

My mother squeezed my shoulder; then she cleared away the coffee cups. Bobby set the whiskey bottle back in the cupboard and they began to draw wad after wad from the box. I saw that the date on the one of the newspapers was as recent as 1981. Each time one of them reached a center, they held up the bird they'd uncovered for the others to examine. They didn't say much and they did not extend any of them toward me. They seemed to know that I would not, for the life of me, could not, touch them.

Every round of three birds, T.J. would hold each one, sometimes swoop or glide it through the air, depending on what the tilt of its wings seemed to suggest. My mother worked at spreading each set out carefully before they started on another group. I found myself looking at those ordered rows with that mix of fascination and dread. The birds had three things in common: all of them were in flight, all of them were things of beauty, and set deep in each flying body was the slight curve of a wire loop, raised just enough to slip a thread or tiny hook through.

I was surprised to see that even though none of the birds had its distinguishing colors, my mother knew most of the names—a chickadee, a nut hatch; a junco, maybe; a mourning dove, no question; a cardinal or perhaps a blue jay. She even went out to the garage and got a much-used bird book she said was my father's. From the pictures Bobby identified a killdeer, a finch, a swallow, a grosbeak.

Though I had no desire to touch them, I knew I could not leave. "Forget the bus," I said. "I'll call Steve and go in the morning."

Later I tried to get my mind to go into the mystery of my father and the birds. My father and those fragile creations. Like putting the birds on one side and my father on the other and trying to get the scale to balance. How could *this* possibly go with *that?* But that night—the night of the birds—something in me, in us all—knew better than to try to give it a name.

The birds were carved out of many different kinds of wood. T.J. was the expert on woods. He had been a model-builder. Bobby always said it was the glue, but I always thought it was his way of dealing...

"What kind of wood do you think this one is, T.J?" my mother said.

Maybe cherry. Smell it—black walnut. White pine. Rosewood. Already there were at least twenty, tipped in flight across the table, a regular bird sanctuary. Beneath the wads, there were stacks of graph paper, with precise drawings of wings carefully ruled, little numbers noting the angles, the lengths and widths. Clearly it was the wings that mattered most.

Finally Bobby came to the bottom. At this point he had moved the box to straddle the two sinks to make more room. We studied the delicate birds spread out before us. Each of them glowed with a soft sheen. Rubbed and rubbed with some sort of low gloss oil, T.J. explained. We could have said beautiful, unbelievable, perfect, fragile. But we didn't.

All of a sudden T.J. hopped up. "I know what we need," he said. He clattered up the back stairs and returned with several spools of dark and light thread. Without a word, Bobby pushed those off to the side and went out to the garage. He returned with a roll of fishing line and a packet of thumbtacks. He retrieved his drink and replenished it. Then he took out a knife. First he lifted a bird and studied it, as if he was judging what layer of space it should inhabit; then he cut a length of line, threaded it through the loop and tied it tight. T.J. stepped from a chair onto the long counter and Bobby handed him the first bird—a pale dove. Using my shoulder, my mother climbed to the top of the step stool and Bobby handed her the line of the next bird. When she raised her hand to fasten it above the sink, I took hold of her waistband, just to ground her and anticipate any wobble.

There was no plan. Bobby determined the lengths. T.J. and my mother got their own rhythm, picked their own spots. I anchored.

Before long, birds were floating in the air above us. Bobby opened the windows and doors all through the downstairs. He lit a bunch of candles and set them around the kitchen, then switched off the lights. Going from bird to bird, Bobby gave each one a gentle push. The birds' winged-silhouettes moved across the walls.

No, they did not soar, but they did turn and turn and turn back again. Along with them, our four shadows, our hands reaching up. And this is what finally came to me: here we all were—homing in, searching for a safe place for the night.

15
Underwear – 1982

Eᴅ Dᴜɢᴀɴ'ꜱ ꜰᴇᴇᴛ were too small. Del's first impression. The minute Pete, her carpenter friend who'd helped finish the stone house after Lee's death, showed up at her door with this Ed Dugan, his diminutive feet disturbed her. Thought you wouldn't mind me bringing Ed by to see how you did the stone walls, Pete said. But right off she did mind. If she'd been drawing this man, his feet would have been the main idea—his black cloth slippers with the little straps across the in-step would've been what jumped off the paper. How unlike feet in work boots Dugan's feet were.

Sitting around the table having a couple of beers after he and Pete had inspected her walls, somehow Ed Dugan got to telling stories about his life, the kind of life that's interesting to hear about, but you're oh so glad you didn't wake up one morning in the middle of. About being a heroin addict in the '60s. About shoplifting books. How he used to "boost" underwear—steal exotic lingerie to give to his wife. How his wife died from an overdose a few years after they split up. How, after the police notified him of her death, he had a hard time finding his four-year-old son who'd been living with her. Del felt sad for the child and wondered how his son came out of it, but she didn't much like Ed Dugan.

Del was in love with a married man. Two or three times a month he'd call, and she'd put down the phone and get in her car. In between she would think about that man, Richard, Richard Larson—of following his red lights along the snowy back roads till they stopped at the edge of a field, how in that white stillness his warm hands took off her clothes.

***

But the next time Del met Ed Dugan, she was lonely. She hadn't heard from Richard in several months. She was telling herself to get on with her life. She had a few drawings in a small show in Boston— a series of hands doing things. Pete and his girlfriend said stay at our place. After the show they went to a park where there was a good reggae band. The sun was shining. They all went off to share a joint, and this Ed Dugan showed up wearing Timberline work boots, the laces still bright with newness. "Want a ride back to Pete's?" Ed Dugan said.

She got in Ed's van. He took her by a house he and Pete were renovating—replacing the porch, all the rotting sills, the roof. "Paid for by a federal grant. Nice old couple struggling to stay on in the city."

"How'd you match all that Victorian trim?"

"A little experimenting with a scroll saw."

Twilight caught in all the scallops and curls. "Nice work," she said. And it was.

"Right work. We bid low and give them a solid job."

Maybe she'd been wrong about this man. They had to go around Pete's block a few times before Ed found a parking spot. "Well, thanks for the ride."

"Check the moon," Ed said "A perfect half." And he took a joint from behind the visor. "Want to celebrate the best of all moons?"

"All right," she said. She wanted to celebrate something. On about the third toke, she started telling him her troubles. Ed Dugan listened. He was sympathetic.

Then he told her this: When he was a little boy, and his mother came home late, she got him out of bed and made him stand in the bright lights downstairs. She asked him his name and when he said it, she mimicked him in a high nasal voice: Little Eddie Dugan. Little Eddie Dugan. When he told Del the story and his voice went up high; it was like he was his mother, and she was little Eddie Dugan looking up into her cruel eyes. Ed used the word "pain" a lot and in a way Del had never heard it used before—*emotional* pain. Mostly her mother had taught her to go from the negative incident to doing something about it, without much in between.

When Ed walked her to Pete's door, she said, "You want to spend the night?" She had never done this before—slept with someone she didn't plan to ever see again.

Later she tried to find the moon through the skylights, but it was gone.

The next day when Ed Dugan took her to the airport, he said, "Maybe I'll be passing through your territory this winter. If I do, I'll give you a call."

"All right," she said. When she turned to wave goodbye, she noticed he was wearing penny loafers, each foot giving off a copper shine.

The thought that maybe she would see Richard Larson, that they could slip away to hold each other and laugh, had buoyed her through the heaviness of those days, but then even that had stopped. He didn't call. She never saw his truck around town.

Whenever Del tried to talk to her son Mark, tried to figure out what was going on with him, tried to get him to go for counseling, he left the room and slammed the door behind him. His senior year, but he refused to go to school. She'd find him sitting with his knees touching the TV set, watching soap operas and game shows when she got home from work. The only way she could get said what she needed to was when she had him in the car and she was going fast enough for him not to follow through on his threat to jump out. Her other son Aaron avoided any real contact as well. I'm okay. Don't worry, all she could get out of him when clearly he was not and she should. Besides all that, there was her mother. It had started last Christmas. They'd been sitting and drinking tea in her mother's Albany apartment. When her mother looked away, the hand holding her cup tipped and began to pour the tea on the rug. Del jumped up, alarmed.

"What?" her mother said, looking back again so that her hand righted itself.

"Atrophy of the brain. Like hundreds of little strokes," the neurologist said. Progressive, no treatment, he told them.

And now her mother had just come to live in a little apartment in Danford. As soon as Del got her settled in, her mother, always the great problem-solver, laid out the plan: I want to remain on my own as long as I can. When I can't manage any longer, I'd like to come and live with you. Of course, Del said. But when my mind goes, when I can no longer do anything, I want you to take me to a nursing home. Then she insisted Del drive her to the Marwick Nursing Home where her mother made all the arrangements. While I still can, her mother said. No resuscitation. No artificial feeding or hydration, no respirator. Write it out, Del. Then let me put a mark since my fingers will no longer do my name. You sign as a witness, she told the nurse. Don't cry, Del, her mother said all the way home. It'll be a few years yet.

Each morning before she went to school, Del stopped to help her mother get set up for the day. Each evening she drove back again to get her dinner, to help her get ready for bed. Getting stoned in the car on the way made it possible for her to walk in smiling. Each week her mother came up with new solutions to that week's losses. Since I can't button any more, buy me five pairs of those sweat suits, the ones with elastic waists. My fingers won't push these little things to turn off the lights, get me lamps with pull-chains. When she retired, Del's mother had planned to reread all the books she'd loved: *The Hobbit* and *Wind in the Willows* and *Grapes of Wrath*. All of Dickens. All of the *Ring Trilogy*. But she could no longer read. By the time I get to the end of the paragraph, I've lost what happened at the beginning. But she could understand perfectly when read to. The brain is a wondrous thing. So every evening Del read her a chapter or two.

When Del said to her mother, "Where did we leave off yesterday?"

Her mother said, without hesitation, "Rose of Sharon was down by the railroad tracks with the old man that was dying." But she could not, absolutely could not, understand how to change her thermostat. Del had spent the last half-hour with her mother's hand in hers to guide her fingers, saying, "If you push this little tab toward where I've marked it in blue, the room will cool down. If you push it toward the red line, it will get warmer." Over and over she showed her, but finally her mother slapped the wall and they had to it give up. She helped her mother get dressed for bed, her little mother who seemed to be getting smaller by the day.

"Funny, you have to tuck me in," her mother said.

Del squeezed her mother's thin hand. "You've been such a good mother, you deserve all the tucking in you need." She pulled the chain on the light. In darkness lit only by the night bulb's orange glow, she could stop smiling.

When Del stepped out onto the apartment porch, it was snowing. For a minute she just stood on the steps and watched the slow fall of big flakes, watched and remembered: Christmas, only three weeks away. Maybe this year it would feel more okay; maybe Aaron and Mark wouldn't feel their father's absence so much. Five years.

The sidewalk and street were already covered. The house across the way was edged in blue lights. She stepped off the porch and let her head fall back to catch a few flakes on her tongue. Let it be an easy winter. Let her mother have at least one more good year.

She tiptoed to the car, trying to leave the white carpet unmarked and slid into the dark cave of the front seat. The snow cleared with one swish of the wipers, but the rest of the car was entombed. She fumbled around for something to brush off the snow. No scraper. Then she saw that something was written on her back window, five carefully etched letters she tried to read in reverse: E L G A E. Richard. Richard and his lovely arms. Smiling Richard was waiting for her at the Eagle.

A few years ago Richard sometimes showed up after a drawing class she was taking in Marwick. She'd come down from the studio, her board under her arm, hoping. And sometimes when she opened the car door, there was a note in the steering wheel: a line of poetry "O penny, brown penny, brown penny, I'm looped in the loops of your hair" or an X or a heart, once a rose. Then she knew he'd be waiting downstairs at Spencer's, sitting at the bar, grinning, and later she'd follow him to Danford along the back roads.

She searched through the glove compartment and found a funny wire brush of Mark's. She wished she'd taken a bath. He might even be gone by now. She reminded herself to call Mark and Aaron to say she'd be a while. Meeting Richard at the Eagle was risky. A small town. People knew his wife, Ellen, his children, Andrew and Lisa. But probably as soon as he saw her, they'd leave.

She pulled into the Eagle parking lot and drove through to the rear. She didn't see Richard's car or his truck. She took a few deep breaths and turned the mirror down, but she saw almost nothing, only her eyes, rayed with laugh lines. With age. No cars she recognized. Quiet for a Saturday night. She went in the back, past the big roll of canvas fire hose that hung on the wall. Mert Bennet sat at one of the booths. Mert Bennet always sat at one of the booths.

Richard wasn't in the bar so she stepped into the big room. There were two men playing pool. One was young and looked a little like a Taylor boy grown up and the other was an older man she'd never seen before, a little beat looking, with a felt hat pulled down over his eyes, black Converse high tops. No Richard. She turned to leave when the older man looked up and laughed. She recognized the laugh. She winced and then covered her disappointment with a smile. He stopped laughing. He looked so different without the beard, without the long hair.

"Ed?" she said. "Ed Dugan? I didn't recognize you without …"

"Just passing through," he said, "so I gave your house a call. Your son told me where you were."

"Oh," she said. Then everything happened fast. They had a few beers, went out to his van and smoked, toured Danford. Population 500.

He said, "I'm heading up to Ithaca to stay with a friend, to do some writing, but I thought I'd visit with you for a few days."

She said, "Well, I … I'm not sure how my sons will …" She followed him to her house in her car. He hadn't needed any directions. For a minute she just sat with her hands on the steering wheel, with Ed waiting by the walk, trying to think what she was going to say to Mark and Aaron. Ed Dugan, the first man she'd ever brought home. All the lights were on and even from outside, Del could hear the music blasting.

"Black Flag," Ed said.

She opened the front door. Mark was sitting at his drum set; Aaron had the oven open. The smell of brownies filled the room. Sam nosed Ed's shoes. She had to shout over the stereo.

"Mark and Aaron, this is Ed Dugan. He's a friend of Pete's." Mark and Aaron liked Pete, trusted him.

Ed crossed and shook Mark's hand. "Nice drums," he said. "Zildjian cymbals." Then he turned to Aaron, took his hand. "Brownies. Unadulterated, I assume."

Aaron laughed. So far so good. She lowered the volume.

The chess board was set up on the coffee table. Ed sat down there. "Who's the chess player?" Ed said.

"Me," Aaron said. "I learned from my Dad."

"Maybe we could have a game."

"Sure," Aaron said.

Ed put his hat back on. "Wait. I've got something in the car, you might be interested in, Mark." He returned with a black case. He opened it and took out a guitar.

She hoped Mark and Aaron wouldn't think Ed Dugan was trying too hard.

"Cool," Mark said, coming around to sit on the couch to get a better look.

"Fender, 1954. It was pretty beat-up, but I think I've got it back to a good sound." Ed played a few chords.

"Nice," Mark said. Ed handed it to him.

Wait a little before she told them the other part about Ed Dugan, how he'd be visiting for a day or two. Aaron cut the brownies and she poured them all glasses of milk. Aaron and Ed played a game of chess. Mark and Ed jammed a little. Mark played one of his tape mixes that he'd put together on different tracks—him doing the bass line, layered over him playing drums. And of course Ed befriended Sam.

But about eleven o'clock when she said, "Ed's on his way to Ithaca, but he's going to stay here for a day or two," everything slowed down. She couldn't quite read Mark and Aaron's expressions—they vanished too quickly.

The next morning Ed Dugan made crêpes. Del and Ed read the *Sunday Times* all morning. When Aaron passed through with a copy of *One Flew Over the Cuckoo's Nest* under his arm, Ed said, "I once met Kesey in a bar in Portland."

"Did you?" Aaron said, his legs all they could see as he disappeared back up to the loft.

Mark did not come out to play his drums.

"Want some lunch?" she called through his closed door.

No answer.

"I thought Mark might like to know I helped do the sound at Woodstock."

But Del didn't think he would. Well, after all Dugan was only going to be there for another day or so. For dinner he made tostadas. And though Mark and Aaron didn't say much when they came to the table, she saw they couldn't resist the aromas and had abandoned their protest when she'd called cheerily, "Dinner's ready."

And didn't she bend over backwards to accommodate them sometimes? A couple of days of jarring of their space—was that too much to ask? And what a pleasure to sit down to meals made by someone else. That night, in the darkness of her bedroom with the light from a little lamp Ed attached to the book, they started to read *Ulysses* out loud, something she'd always wanted to do, though she did feel uncomfortable about how noisy her old iron bed was and right above Mark's room.

In the morning when she stepped out the door, even Mark was dressed and ready to go after missing school most of the week before. Ed already had the ladder up to start cleaning out the gutters, Sam beneath him, wagging his tail.

"We meant to get that done in the fall, but things have been so, well, with my mother, I just …"

"Hey, it'll only take me a few minutes and then I have the rest of the day to write."

"Thank you," she said.

Mark and Aaron were already in the car.

Ed gave them all a little wave as she backed down the driveway.

"When's this guy leaving?" Mark said.

"Probably tomorrow or the next day."

"Probably?" Aaron said.

The first thing she saw when she got home from work was the shelves Ed had built above the refrigerator.

"Well, you mentioned you wished you had some place to put things."

"How'd you do it?" she said. "They're just what we needed." And all of it constructed from salvaged boards from the beds she'd made for Mark and Aaron when they'd been living in town. Ed started passing her plates and glasses to arrange on the first shelf.

"Plenty more scrap lumber down in the barn to build you a cabinet underneath, with a silverware drawer, a section for pots and pans, maybe a bin for the potatoes."

"What about your plans to go on to write in Ithaca?"

"Only take me a day or so. There's a beautiful thick plank I can finish off for a good counter."

The last of the big planks from the chicken barn Lee had taken down.

"Well ... if you're sure it won't delay you too much. Cabinets, more space to work, that would be great."

In the evenings Aaron and Mark remained in their rooms. Ed went on cooking and fixing things as though all was well. The cabinets were a real plus. He'd even divided the silverware drawer into little compartments, left one long section for the big carving knives.

On Thursday when the three of them headed out for the car, Ed was busy shoveling the walk. "Have a great day," he said.

Mark and Aaron said nothing. She imagined herself standing by Ed's van, the snowy wind blowing, her waving goodbye, Well, it sure has been nice, she'd say. Hope the writing goes well.

The next day when he was still there, she took him to meet her mother.

"*Grapes of Wrath*," Ed said. "I spent a few months in Monterey. Even met some of the old guys Steinbeck based his characters on."

"*Cannery Row*," her mother said. "That's another one of my favorites. You must tell me all about it."

When they got home, she didn't say anything about Ithaca. That next afternoon when she got back from school, Ed said, "I took your mother a little box lunch."

"Ed, what a kind thing to do."

"Not at all," he said. "I like your mother."

Four or five days after Ed Dugan arrived, he walked in the house with a big bag and said, "Guess what? I just got a job painting a church ceiling, forty feet up on a scaffold." And he pulled out a pair of white painter's pants, the ones with the big pockets.

"Oh," she said. It didn't seem friendly to say, What about Ithaca? Instead, she asked, "How long will that take?"

"About two weeks."

Aaron and Mark looked at her funny and went to their rooms.

The next night Ed worked overtime. With Ed not around was a good time to talk. What to say?

"You know it looks to me like Ed is planning on staying for a while," she said. "At least a few more weeks."

Aaron looked up from his book. "You talk like you have no control in the situation."

"I knew it," Mark said and got up from the table.

"Mark," she called to her son's retreating back. "Please stay and at least ..." and the slamming of a door finished the sentence.

"One or two days," Aaron said and returned to his book.

"Well, I mean, he already has the job, I can't say, 'What about Ithaca?'"

"Why not?" Aaron asked, turning the page.

The next week her mother said, "Del, you don't look happy. Don't you want Ed there?"

"I don't know," she told her.

When she got home, she said to Ed, "How's the ceiling coming?"

"Looks great," he answered. "Now we're doing the walls."

One night, after Ed Dugan had been around a few weeks, he was lying on the bed. She felt him watching her undress.

"Why do you wear white panties?" he said.

The question surprised her. She had never liked the word *panties*. She slipped her nightgown over her head and turned to pull back the covers. By then she had a reply. "I like them." She re-answered this question in her head all week long.

Friday, when he came in the door after work, he handed her a package.

"Open it," he said.

She was making spaghetti. "What is it?" she asked and lowered the heat under the sauce.

"You'll see." He put his hands on her shoulders and sat her down at the table.

She pulled off the wrapping, lifted the lid, and pushed back the tissue paper. It was red.

Mark came into the kitchen. He stepped around the chair to get into the refrigerator. "Hey, a present. What'd you get?"

Mark lifted up one sheer red corner a little.

She did not look at her son. She did not look at Ed. "Oh," she said.

"Whoa," Mark said. "Whoa," he said again as he went in his room.

"They're pretty wild," she said to Ed. From what she could see, it was a pair of red rayon bikini underwear, with a black lace flower that appeared to be stitched right where you'd guess. "Well, thank you." she said, smiling politely. "Though I can't quite imagine …" She closed the box and returned to the sauce.

Ed gave her a strange look, the face of someone new. He took the box and stomped upstairs.

At dinner Ed was silent. She was cheery.

"Have mom show you her present," Mark said to Aaron.

"Lighten up, Mark," she told him.

"What present?" Aaron asked.

"If you'll excuse me," Ed said. He took the paper and went back upstairs.

"What's his problem?" Mark asked.

Later when she finished the dishes, she went up, a tightness inside. She knew she should get it straight. The lights were out. She pulled off her jeans and reached in the closet for her gown.

"Put them on," Ed's voice whispered from the bed.

"Oh, Ed, I …"

The darkness was heavy. Some edge in his command frightened her. Ed rose up and gripped her arm. Hard. He handed her the box and let go.

Obediently she pulled off the rest of her clothes, slipped the silkiness up her legs, over her hips. He led her to the bed. She was someone else; she was inside a stranger's body.

"Open your eyes," he said and she did.

She had never felt so aroused. A man she'd never seen before rose and fell on top of her body. She hated him.

"Do you want eggs?" he said the next morning.

One day led to another. She taught negative space and complementary colors. She went to her mother's before school, again on the way home, and then back to help her get ready for bed. Sometimes her whole face felt numb from mirroring her mother's brave smile.

"Please tell Ed how much I appreciate him putting on those grips so I have something to hold onto when I step out of the shower," her mother said.

She told her mother she appreciated Ed's help too: taking her mother to the dentist, the shoveling of walks, the shopping for groceries.

Del did not tell her she had dreams of pushing herself through gluey fog, inch by inch, of waking exhausted. How Aaron and Mark had withdrawn. How Aaron read at the table and Mark had stopped coming to meals altogether. How she heard him fixing food after she and Ed went to bed.

All right, fine, as long as everyone was civil. Let her get through this thing with her mother. She had no energy for anything more.

One dark February morning she stopped at her mother's on her way to school. The minute she pushed open the door, she knew something was wrong. No lights and no sound.

"Mother," she cried as she went back to her bedroom.

She turned on the overhead light. Her mother sat on the edge of the bed, her hands gripping the quilt on either side, her eyes frightened. Del took hold of her shoulders and looked into her face. She felt her relax.

"What?" Del said. "What happened?"

"It's time I come to live with you," her mother said. "I can't do it anymore."

Her night light had gone out. She didn't know where she was in that darkness. She sat on the edge of the bed all night, not knowing which way was up, which way was down.

Mark would have to give up his room, move into the loft with Aaron. There was no other way. That day Ed helped her move her mother to live with them when he got home from work. By then he was subbing in a high school in Marwick. A woman from up the road came in to look after Del's mother while Del was at school. Ed put side rails on her mother's bed. He drove her to Binghamton for an eye exam.

"I couldn't manage without you," Del told him

Del never saw Richard in town, never even saw his truck parked at the hardware or the grocery or the Eagle. She heard that he and his wife had separated.

One night the phone rang during dinner. Ed answered it. "For you," he said. "A man."

She knew who it was. She wanted to talk to him and she didn't. Ed watched her.

"It's been a long time," Richard said.

"Yes, it has," she answered.

Richard's voice was quiet. "I heard you were living with someone so I didn't call. I didn't think I should."

"Yes," she said.

"Are you all right? I just called to see if you're all right."

She heard music and laughter in the background.

"I'm all right," she told him.

"I miss you," he said.

"My mother has come to live with us."

"You sound funny. Can't you talk?" he asked.

"I'm okay," she answered. "I just don't have much to say."

They said enough more words to get them to goodbye, and then she hung up the phone.

"It was Richard Larson," she told Ed's raised eyebrows. She bent her head and began eating whatever was on her plate.

In March her mother broke her hip. When she came home from the hospital, she was someone else. She no longer slept at night. Instead she called Del's name, and when Del woke from heavy sleep to go down to change her, to bring her a drink, her mother said, "I hate you."

April finally came. She sat in the tub. Alone. It was good to be alone. She lay back and looked at her body drifting just below the water. She was drifting too. She didn't love this man. She felt no desire, no desire for anything. There was a kind of freedom in this. Only every now and then did he invade, ask something she didn't want to give. She had wadded the red underwear in the back of the drawer after that one night, and he never mentioned them again. But sometimes he yelled at her, Del, that's not how you feel. You say fine, all right, yes, but that's not true. What could she say? I'm tired. I don't feel anything. Leave me alone. Instead she went along with him— when he was strange, when he was angry, she was careful, careful like a cat.

One day he said, "You need a break. Get Mrs. Morgan to stay with your mother and we'll go to Tanglewood for the weekend. We'll lie on the grass, drink wine and listen to Brahms."

So she got Mrs. Morgan. She kissed her mother goodbye. "Please help with your grandmother," she said to Mark and Aaron.

They drove off. Then they got lost somewhere down around Hudson and ended up stoned at a drive-in movie watching *Road Warrior*. Later they went to a motel. Ed turned on the radio and stretched out on the bed. She decided to go in to take a shower. He looked at her funny.

"Dance," he said. "Take your clothes off slowly and dance."

She laughed, figured he was kidding and started into the bathroom.

His face darkened. "I want you to dance for me."

She believed if she didn't do what he asked, he would act crazy, jump from the bed and come up close to her. He would yell. She was afraid. She knew she should get it straight once and for all, but she didn't. She danced. She slowly took off her clothes and danced. He watched her from the bed. She looked at him with loathing. Then they were two strangers fucking in an empty motel room.

The next morning her body felt so heavy, it was hard to stand.

On the drive home Ed Dugan sang and banged his hand against the steering wheel just off the beat of the loud radio. She sat by the window and thought about how she got herself into this and how to get herself out.

Ed pulled into a mall and opened his door. He looked back at her to follow.

Just a little longer, she thought.

They went into Jamesway. He headed for the hardware section and picked out a glue gun. On the way to the cash register they passed through lingerie. He slowed. She felt sick. He began to push the hangers aside, to lift out things and put them back. She walked on a little, showing him she was ready to leave. Finally he pulled out a red nylon, one-piece thing with ribbons and net and lace, and a diamond shaped hole at the center.

"Get this," he said, walking toward her, the red slipping through his fingers.

She backed away.

"Get this for me," he said.

"It's too small," she said. Jesus.

He said, "Try it on."

Hating herself, she walked to the fitting rooms. A young girl opened one of the doors with a key hanging from a string around her neck. "How many?" she said.

Del didn't want the girl to see the thing she was trying on, the thing with *Teddy* stitched on the red label. The girl looked at her suspiciously and handed her a yellow plastic card with a big *1* on each side.

She hung the red thing on a hook and started to take off her clothes. Everything was so heavy. Then she sat down on the little seat and watched herself slowly rebutton her sweater.

"No," she said.

She stood up and lifted the underwear from the hook.

"Teddy. No."

When she came out of the little closet, Ed was waiting by the bin of sale bras.

"This isn't right for me," she said and pushed the red underwear into the rack. She made herself meet his eye, and then she walked toward the checkout aisles.

Ed said nothing. He drove. She looked out and breathed. She glanced at the speedometer. 60. It was a narrow, sometimes winding road. She forced herself to keep her hands loose in her lap and concentrated on the black metal handle of the glove compartment. She prayed. For miles they drove like that. On the turns she braced her feet to keep from sliding across the seat. She tried to decide which was more dangerous—to say something or to keep quiet.

When they were almost to Marwick, she said, "I'm sorry."

Ed slammed on the brakes and twisted toward her. The van skidded across the highway, turned in the other direction and banged along the guard rail. They stopped. They sat for a minute, silent. Ed got out. He looked at the tire on her side. He slid the door open and found a jack. She got out. The tire was flat.

"Can I do anything?" she asked.

And then it happened.

He raised the jack handle above his head. "You lying cunt," he screamed.

She turned and ran, past the van, down the road a few hundred feet to where there was a turn to Marwick. He was still screaming in a high-pitched nasal voice. A car went by. When she moved onto the side road, when the trees blocked the view to the van, she kicked off her sandals ahead of her and scooped them up. She could not feel him behind her, but she did not look back. She thought she could hear his voice. She heard her breath, the slap of her feet on the blacktop.

The edge-of-city business, a Gulf station, Burger King, Midas Muffler were in sight ahead, a red brick Dairy Cooperative building beside her. She looked back. She didn't see him. She ran down the driveway, through the shrubs to the rear. She hid in a doorway, shaking. It started to rain. Soft spring rain. She sat down on the concrete step. She thought she could hear yelling. She waited. Then it was quiet except for the sounds of traffic. After a while she felt safe. She looked at her watch. It was 7:00. She would stay one more hour, then she would walk to the gas station to use the phone. By then she'd figure out how to get home.

"He was here," Mark said when she called. "Came in frantic, looking for you, wanted to know if you called."

"So where is he now?" she asked.

"He said he was going back to find you, to tell you he's sorry if you called. Are you okay?"

She told him she was not okay, not hurt, but angry with Ed, that she'd be home soon. She spoke to Mrs. Morgan for a minute. Her mother was fine. The kids had been helpful.

Next she called her friend Sally. Sally said she could pick her up in half an hour.

The gas station was closing. She had no money. She was cold and wet from the rain. She crossed the street to watch for Sally's car inside the entrance to the Burger King. Just as she went to step off the curb, Ed's van pulled up. He leaned across and rolled down the window.

"I frightened you," he said.

She looked at him and said nothing.

"Please get in. Let me take you home."

She told him Sally was coming to get her, but she wanted to talk to him so why didn't he park and meet her inside.

She sat at a table, felt the warm air blow from the vent. Ed brought coffee. For a minute she wrapped her hands around the cup.

Finally she said, "I'm angry about the red underwear, about the dancing."

He looked tired. "I wanted you to stop being ashamed of your body, to not say what you don't feel."

She thought about that, and then she said, "When you first came, it was going to be a visit. A day or two. I had no plan to live with you, with anyone."

"We get along," he said.

"No," she told him. "I'm afraid of you."

He said, "Del," but she stopped him.

"Please stay somewhere else tonight, come and get your things tomorrow when I'm at school."

He stared at her and was silent. She looked at him.

Sally's car pulled into the gas station.

"She's here," she said and started to rise. "I'm sorry."

He took her wrist and leaned across the table.

"That's not what you're feeling right now," he said and let go.

She hurried out. When she passed the window, a man she'd never seen before sat staring at two empty cups.

She would have liked for that to be the end, but it wasn't.

When she got home from school, all his things were gone. His tools, the copy of *Ulysses* from the bedside table. She lifted her eyes to the hills, the just-budding maples, the chickadee on the branch just above the picnic table. "Thank you," she said.

"Yeah," Aaron and Mark said.

Mrs. Morgan said, "Such a nice man. So friendly. So kind to your mother."

Thank you, thank you, thank you, she said for days. That and May I never do that again.

Monday after school she stopped at JAKE's to get milk. She was standing at the counter, waiting to pay. She felt someone too close behind her. "Del," the voice of Ed Dugan said in her ear. A wave of nausea.

She moved a little down the counter so that when she turned she'd have some space. "Ed," she said.

"I got an apartment in town, up above the hardware. Come on over and I'll make us some coffee."

Us? She was glad she was in the store, glad that Lois was listening, that Lil was behind her putting cans on the shelf. Witnesses.

"No. I want to make this a clean break," she said. "That's the best way. Please understand."

She turned her back on him. She paid for the milk and picked up the bag. She looked at him and said goodbye. He didn't speak. His jaw locked, his lips tight, his eyes flat. She opened the screen, went out to her car and drove home. Crazy. Crazy.

When she walked in the door, Mrs. Morgan was chatting on the phone, "Oh, here she is right now … Yes, nice to talk to you too." Mrs. Morgan moved the receiver toward her.

"It's Ed," Mrs. Morgan said.

Which was better? To talk to him or not? Safer to talk. She filled herself with air and took the receiver.

He told her surely they could be friends could get together for dinner occasionally she was being silly it would be better for her spirit he was going to be around town he certainly wasn't going to suddenly stop existing she was being irrational did she think for one minute she could end it all as easily as that?

She said, "Please Ed, don't call me again. I don't want to see you or talk to you." And she hung up.

Don't call, she kept saying. He sent her letters. One said, I've booked us two flights to Mexico City when school gets out. I know we will have a wonderful time. She didn't answer the letters. He came to the house and she said, Please do not come here. When he wouldn't leave, she opened the door and went up to her room and sat trembling on the side of the bed, ready to call someone for help until she heard the door click. Sometimes he sat in his car out in front of the house. She was frightened. She thought about contacting the police. For the first time she understood about having a gun, how someone could say, Get off my property or I'm going to shoot.

One day she saw an *Apartment For Rent* sign in the hardware window.

"Is it the apartment upstairs that's for rent?" she said to Bud Baker, as he weighed her up a pound of nails.

"Guy moved out this morning. Said he was going to Ithaca."

16
Circling – 1984

Oᴛʜᴇʀ ᴛʜɪɴɢs are on my mind when the Tupperware lady says, "First, let's move your couch over by the door and the table here."

Before her words reach my brain, she's got one end of that maroon monster, a cast-off from Steve's mother, waist-high and swinging away from the wall. I register the crap underneath: a package of Zig-Zags, a pizza crust, a dried puddle of something.

"Get under it good," she directs.

And just like that, I've got the other end up. I believe in those mothers who lift cars to free trapped children.

"You know," she says, as she backs me toward the corner, "a successful Tupperware party doesn't just happen; it has to be orchestrated."

This is what they all keep telling me: all those teachers all those years, the judge, last week. Like it can all be organized into an outline:

    I. Get Straight
     A. Your Drawers
     B. Your Life

"Okay," the Tupperware lady says, "put it down right there."

As I'm trying to remember what comes next *1.* or *a.,* she says, "While you get the vacuum, I'll start clearing the records off the table. They'll be here in an hour."

     a. Radically change
     1. Do what other mothers do

It's this kind of outline thinking that got me into having a Tupperware party in the first place. Me, Carla Morletti, once a distinguished member of the Pagans Motorcycle Club Women's Auxiliary, taking directions from this middle-class matron in a flowered shirtwaist in my own living room.

From the closet where I'm searching for the end piece of the vacuum and sorting through the events that brought me to this moment, Madeline, that's the Tupperware lady's name, calls through the distance, "Mrs. Morletti, I'll bet you went to Woodstock."

Imagine the numbers needed to go back that far. *XXX* No. Surely the recent past is enough to explain why I'm in this closet and the Tupperware lady is in my life:

> ~~*I. Get Straight*~~
> *I . Recent Events Leading to T. P.*
> *A. Plumbing*
> *B. The Other Woman*
> *C. The Gun*
> *D. PINS Hearing*

Again the distant voice, "Mrs. Morletti, where are you?"

I resist yelling, I don't know. The silhouette of Madeline's life flashes before me—a neat staircase of Roman numerals.

But for me it always happened all at once, fast. Plumbing. A few weeks ago I was on my back underneath the sink, trying to get into the trap, when it came to me: Another Woman. The reason for Steve's distance. My leavemealone leavemealone of the last few months about to pay off in big-time pain. I was just getting my breath after that bulletin when the front door started banging. A stranger. Only strangers go to that door.

I yelled to my daughter, "Tess, see who's out front." She made no response, as usual, so I struggled from under the sink. Out the front window I saw a state trooper car; out the back I saw Tess headed into the woods. Bang. Bang. What now?

The trooper eyed the wrench in my hand like it was loaded. "Mrs. Morletti?" he said.

I thought of Steve's marijuana plants blinking neon, a tropical bright yellow-green, on the window seat.

"Is your daughter Teresa here?" the trooper asked.

Madeline reaches around from behind me and retrieves the vacuum brush from under a boot. "Here it is," she says, handing me the hose while she juggles the canister. "As soon as we get the Tupperware out of the car and displayed, we have to set up the games." She gives me a you-can-do-it smile and heads back to the living room, me attached to her by the cord. Should I tell her she has lipstick on her tooth?

I fill in Madeline's life: tie-backs, dresser scarves, a Betty Crocker kitchen and a polyester husband. No policemen at her door. The trooper at mine told me that someone saw Tess leaving Dutton's trailer a few hours earlier. Dutton reported a pistol missing from a bedroom drawer.

We found the pistol in the weeds not far from where we found Tess, her body curled into Steve's leather jacket, my bread knife tied to her waist. "Why? Why would you do such a thing?" I asked, trying to pry her arms away from her face.

She tightened, became even smaller. Then it came to me. "Rambo. Are you Rambo?" I said.

I picked her up, her tensed body weighted down with Steve's jacket. The trooper helped me rise and steady. "It's going to be all right," I whispered into the darkness where she hid.

She uncurled against me, her wiry head emerged from the jacket. "I didn't mean to be bad," she cried.

"We need more chairs," Madeline says, starting for the kitchen. "How many definites are coming? You know, day parties are not recommended."

I've thought of all that. My neighbors do the night shift so they don't have to pay a sitter or they're on unemployment or they've never worked. I count: Mrs. Dutton, Mrs. Johnson, Mrs. Washburn and her three daughters. Not the woman who lives in the cabin. But down on the next road, every single woman. A few of my friends. You're kidding, they said. A what kind of party? Please come, I told them. And act normal. I'm reorganizing and I want the firemen's auxiliary and the Presbyterian church to know it.

"Twelve. Twelve definites."

"Oh, that's a nice number," she says.

The judge said, Mrs. Morletti, unless Teresa's behavior improves significantly, it may be necessary to place her in foster care. But of course I knew he meant Steve and me, unless our behavior improved significantly; I knew PINS really meant Parents in Need of Supervision.

The interior of Madeline's station wagon is not quite what I expected, doesn't quite fit my outline for her. I'm expecting immaculate, and what we've got is marginal, heading toward the edge. A bag of returnables, something yellow staining the back seat, and a pile of *Good Housekeeping* magazines. On the bumper there's a ripped sticker; only half of its message remaining: *ife?* I can no longer guess what it said. Still her car's a couple circles above the Maverick, but coming soon to one of those decisive forks in the road.

The Maverick. It's so often in our yard with the hood up that even though I cajoled Steve into pushing it into the barn in preparation for this party, I still see it like a missing puzzle piece in front of the grandfather maple. Loss. Like when someone goes and isn't in the places where they used to be.

Madeline puts out her arms. Her fingernails are bitten, red, chewed down as far as you can go. If this keeps up, I'm going to have to revise my idea of Madeline.

"Just stack the boxes on top," she says. "Tupperware is light. But very durable. Keep piling them up. Between the two of us we can make it in one trip."

And what a long strange trip it's been to me following Madeline's straight back down this path. But it isn't a straight path. I don't outline; I spiral. Circling, circling. A Slinky. Being pulled, finally lifting into another place when the weight becomes great enough.

Steve should see me now, a bag of Tupperware party favors in either hand.

He said, There is no other woman. What would I want with another woman? My life's complicated enough already. But I don't believe him. Whenever I look in his eyes for truth, I see myself, falling through dark space, groping for a ripcord that isn't there.

Madeline starts unpacking the Tupperware onto the table. Green, pink, blue. Big, small, tall, thin.

"What's this weird one here for?" I say.

"That's for pretzels."

"And this?"

"A patty shaper."

I point to a thick green one.

"To grate and store."

I am glad I decided to do this party straight; otherwise I'd think I was hallucinating.

Behind the display, Madeline looks across the living room as though speaking to an audience. "No matter what you want to save and keep fresh, there's an appropriate piece of Tupperware," she says.

For a second the stack of pastel vessels glows, caught in a passing ray of September sun.

"Ahhh, I see," I whisper.

Madeline takes a crumpled yellow sheet from her pocket and spreads it out flat on top of the Tupperware pyramid. She looks at her watch and takes in a big gulp of air. "My notes," she says. "Forty minutes and we'll be putting this show on the road."

"Right," I say. I can see she wants more, but I don't know what to give her. I notice the paper is trembling.

Madeline looks me full in the eye. "I've got a confession to make," she says, and she draws herself up. "This is my first Tupperware demonstration." Then she looks down at the floor.

If she wasn't behind that mound of containers, I know I could give her a pat or something, but from where I am, I can't quite reach her. I hear a distant rumble. It grows louder and sputters to silence just outside where Madeline and I are standing. Madeline moves closer.

"What's that?" she says.

"My husband," I tell her. "And he's parking his Harley in the front yard."

We square our shoulders. "Things don't always go as planned," she says.

The back door bangs open and an angry voice fills the house and starts toward us. "That cocksucker. He's lucky I didn't take him by the throat. Carla," he bellows.

He has had a fight with his boss. Enter Steve. I see him through

Madeline's eyes. Dark. Hairy. Tattooed.

For a moment she's a small creature, caught; then a look of calm determination takes over her face. Like an underwater swimmer, she pushes through the space between them. The Tupperware Party will go on as arranged. "Mr. Morletti, I'm Madeline Lowry, the Tupperware Demonstrator. Your wife and I are just setting up for the party. Perhaps you'd like to join the preparations. The ladies will be here soon."

Somehow she has gotten hold of Steve's hand and is shaking it up and down. His body softens, his eyes laugh. "Pleased to meet you," he says.

Madeline lets go of his hand and gestures toward the window. "Mr. Morletti," she falters.

"Steve," he says. He takes off his cap and gives his ponytail a tug. "My bike," he says. "You'd like me to move my bike." And he's out the front door.

II. Eighteen years of marriage

A. Surprises

"What a nice man," Madeline says. She beckons me toward the kitchen. I follow.

Steve's a painter. Houses, bridges, church ceilings. He can climb to the top of anything and go out on the ledge. He can look down. Even when he calls the foreman names and walks off the job, they always take him back because he will go where no one else will. But he doesn't talk and he doesn't listen.

Madeline surveys what I've set out for the fancy dessert part of the party. Cherries Jubilee. "Good, you got diet soda and Sweet and Low. That's important."

"I followed the list of suggestions to the letter," I say.

"That is the least risky approach."

Approach. I feel I've been circling for hours, years, and have just gotten the message to make an instrument landing.

The judge said, Teresa is to behave on the school bus. She is to use no profane language. She is to enter the building by 8:30. She is not to

leave school. She is to do what she is told to do when she is told to do
it. Do you understand? Yes, we said.

I start a pot of coffee. Madeline begins to lay out the favors on a tray.
"Let's go through the order of things. First, after everyone arrives and
gets seated, we'll play the name game."

"The name game?"

Steve's bike roars by on its way to the barn.

"I've never ridden on a motorcycle before," Madeline says.

"He'd probably be pleased to take you for a spin."

Madeline giggles. She refocuses. She turns the favors, twenty pastel plastic bottle stoppers, all in the same direction. "The name game
is an icebreaker. We go around the room and each person picks an
adjective, a word to describe themselves that begins with the same
letter as their name. Like Sincere Sara or Nice Nora. Ms are hard. I
always have trouble with a good M-word that feels like me.

Captivating Carla. Cagey Carla. Careless. Contrite.

Steve comes in the back with a case of Budweiser. "How about a
beer? Loosen you up for the party."

"No, thank you," Madeline says.

"Give everybody a couple at the beginning; you'd sell a lot more."

"Steve," I say. Seductive. Self-centered. Secretive.

"Only kidding." Again he takes off his cap. He bows slightly. "Really," he says, "do you need any help?"

Madeline is gone; she would eat out of his hand. Isn't there anyone
normal left? Where am I to find a role model for the new me?

"You could put all the items in that bag out on the other tray."

Steve lifts the bag and dumps the contents into a mound.

"Now spread them out."

Steve looks puzzled.

"It's another icebreaker game. Everyone gets to look at the tray for
ten seconds. Then you cover it back up and the person who remembers the most gets a Tippy cup."

"A what?" I ask.

Steve has put both hands over the mounds. Steve has good hands,
pliant, the fingers long and sure. "A stopper. A green plastic stirrer. A
what's-it with a little purple strap, a ..."

"Steve."

I hear the front door creak and soft footsteps sneaking up the stairs. I know it is Tess. She has left school two hours early. She has not done what she was told to do when she was told to do it. "No, no, no," I shriek to the ceiling.

Madeline looks alarmed.

"My daughter has run away from school. The school will be calling any minute to inform me that she has been suspended for leaving without permission and that she cannot return until I go in with her for a conference where I must promise, in no uncertain terms, that Tess will never misbehave again."

Madeline touches my arm. "I have children," she says. "How old is Tess?"

"Ten," Steve says. "She's only ten."

"I just can't deal with it right now," I tell them.

Madeline looks at Steve. He finishes spreading the favors. Then he leaves. I hear his tired tread on the stairs.

We carry in the trays, the cups, the glasses, the spoons, the forks, the plates, everything that can, should, be in the living room for the Beginning. I hear the murmur of child and man above.

Madeline glances at her watch. "Ten minutes," she says. She looks pale.

"I guess we're ready," I say.

Steve and Tess come down. They are both quiet.

"Tess, this is Madeline," Steve says, "the woman who's helping Mamo."

"Tess," she says. She raises her hand. To touch her cheek. To smooth her hair. Her hand hovers, makes a nervous blessing, then retreats.

Tess looks tired. Dusty, with a clean spot around each eye. Probably she has run all the way up Fyler Hill.

"There is one thing you could do for me," Madeline says.

I imagine her blue flowered shirtwaist blowing behind her as she disappears down the road on the back of Steve's bike, me in the doorway as the first ladies arrive, the telephone ringing in the background.

III. Desertion

Madeline reaches into her pocket and takes out her notes and once again sets them on the stack of containers.

"If the three of you could sit on the couch over there and pretend you're the audience and I could just go through the first few minutes of my demonstration, I think I could stop shaking before they get here."

Steve moves across the living room and sits down. He motions Tess to sit beside him. I sit next to Tess. Madeline clears her throat and pulls down on her dress.

"Just one small thing before you start," Steve says.

What now?

"You got a smudge of lipstick on your tooth."

"Oh no," Madeline says, scrubbing her finger back and forth. She shows us her teeth.

"It's gone," Steve says. "Now we're all ready." The three of us settle into the soft maroon cushions. Land. For this moment, come to rest.

Madeline begins. "First, before I demonstrate for you what a fine product Tupperware is, I want you to know how much I appreciate being able to get together with all of you today."

Steve takes one of Tess's hands and I take the other. We smile at Madeline and she smiles back.

17
Water – 1984

DEL WATCHES THE WOODS. So far, from the outhouse, she's seen a red fox, a great horned owl, and what she swears had to be a coyote. Another one of the things she loves about being here at the cabin, being the only person who lives on this dirt road, is that Sally's outhouse doesn't need a door. Every trip to the john is really a chance to commune with nature. Del's original idea, when she first rented the cabin from Sally in June, was to draw the changing woods when she went to pee. Take her pad and pencil, sit long enough to do a quick study—eventually do a series: *The World from the Outhouse*. But now what she likes to do is just sit and watch the woods. Drawing is too distracting. Like right this minute—not a foot from toilet-seat level—a dime-sized black spider, with a yellow zipper down her back, is building her web between two stalks of goldenrod. She's attached the guide wires and now she's spinning out perfectly spaced cross-webbing. So that's how they do it.

And it isn't just watching the woods, the privy itself is a thing of beauty—a turned-on-end cigar box structure of weathered clapboards with a tarpaper roof. Fastened to the side is one of Sally's beaded rope hangings, bleached the same gray as the planks. When it's time to dig a new hole, the whole thing's light enough for two people to drag it to another spot. She's done a pad of drawings of the outhouse as well.

When people wrinkle their noses at the thought of no indoor plumbing, she tells them, I love the outhouse. Richard says, Maybe you won't feel that way come winter.

Richard. Richard, your *maybe*s are the one thing throwing me off. Aaron's okay, boarding with Lee's cousin's family, doing his senior year at Lawrence High in Massachusetts. Even though Antioch didn't work out, Mark's now got a job in Brooklyn delivering cars. So Richard, it's just you—this never really knowing one way or the other. When you get home from the city tonight, maybe you'll stop by. Maybe you won't. Don't say it would be easier if I had a phone. I am not ready for a phone, those middle-of-the-night calls. Besides, it was still *maybe* when I did have a phone.

In the distance there's the whine of a chainsaw, then the sudden staccato of a woodpecker. Sam barks. He's had enough of being gated on the porch, but if he comes to the outhouse with her, he ruins her chances of seeing any animals.

Del puts a new roll of toilet paper in the holder, another example of Sally's ingenuity. To keep the squirrels from getting at it, the toilet paper is housed in a peanut butter bucket with a slit cut in the side to pull the sheets through. The interior décor of the outhouse is a trip as well—Sally's trip. Every inch of the walls is decoupaged with quotes, many of them from *The Teachings of Don Juan*. All summer, each time Del sits here, she works her way a little further around. She's finished reading everything on the left and is now starting on the other side:

> *You think and talk too much. You must stop talking to yourself. What do you mean? Think about it. Whenever you are alone, what do you do?*

Del laughs and reads the last part out loud, "I talk to myself." More like, I talk to Richard.

Though Sally now has a baby and has moved to her husband's where they have electricity and running water, she'd spent years improving this place. In her tiny garden, in with the corn, Sally grew her own pot and stoned in the evenings, she played. This outhouse only one of her many projects.

Del watches pale leaves let go to drift to the floor of the woods. Goldenrod and lavender asters bloom by the edges. Only a few more weeks until school starts again—lesson plans, papers. The world as seen from the blackboard. On the way back to the cabin she eats a few berries. When the thorny canes grab her, she manages to pull free. She stops to once again take the cabin in: how it squats a little crooked on its foundation stumps, its leaning cobblestone chimney, its small porch with the sprung rocker where she eats her breakfast.

Sam's big paws drape over the railing, his white flag of a tail beats the boards. "Well, if you didn't rush at the blue jays this wouldn't be necessary." She turns him loose.

Dinner. If Richard comes it won't be before seven. Traffic out of the City is so heavy on Fridays. If he doesn't turn up, well, she'll draw. Or write him a poison-pen poem. She reaches into the cooler that stands in the darkest corner of the little hall between the porch and the main room. The frozen jugs of water are half-thawed. Have to exchange them with the ones she has in Sally's freezer tomorrow. By touch she locates a bag of vegetables, a bottle of apple juice. The celery feels soft, the leaves wilted. It makes a good thermometer. She leans the stalks up against one of the jugs.

She dusts the mouse droppings from the counter and makes herself a lettuce and a first-from-the-garden tomato sandwich. Sun's down behind the trees, but still plenty of light to read outside. She straddles the hammock. With a glass in one hand, the sandwich in the other, and a book under her arm—the book Richard brought her two weeks ago, pulling it from his jacket pocket just before he left. I'm surprised you've never read it, he said, grinning, when he handed it to her. She eases down, feeling for balance before she settles her full weight and swings her legs up. "Don't upset me, Sam," she says as he noses the sandwich now resting on her belly. Once again she opens the book to the title page:

Lady Chatterley's Lover
The Complete and Unexpurgated 1928 Orioll Edition

All week she's been book-marking passages she'd like to read to Richard. What might Richard's response be to Connie Chatterley thinking that sex trespassed on her privacy and inner freedom. Del chews on the tomato—and what a sweet tomato it is. Had she ever felt that way? Of course she knows what Lawrence is up to. Will Richard? This is Connie Chatterley pre-orgasm talking. Connie, before her passion with Mellors. Then BANG one does one crazy thing after another. Who cares if one's a love-slave? She marks that page with a blade of grass. Trouble is Richard comes and goes so quickly.

Each time Del pulls down, the braid on the pump handle dances, the two small bells ring. The water pump is her favorite of all the cabin wonders. Sally has painted the handle scarlet and attached to it a rawhide braid, woven with beads and bells and feathers. The water splashes over the sides of the bucket and sprays her bare ankles as it hits the large stone under the pail. The grass along the edge grows thick and green from chance watering.

Del carries the bucket to dump into the big reserve ten-gallon can that sits at the end of the gas stove. Three more buckets will fill the canners on the back burners for a bath later. Once she counted—forty-two pumps to bring up enough water for a bath.

Back outside the sun's behind the beeches now. The leaves starting to glow. If Richard doesn't come soon, well, then he probably isn't coming. Del contemplates the mound of wood ready for stacking. Most of this load is black walnut and the smell of wintergreen is thick as she leans toward it. The last time Richard was here, he had praised her stacking. With this last load, she has at least twenty face cords. Richard said fifteen would do it, but she wants to be absolutely sure there's enough to get her through to next June. She'll sleep in the big room near the stove and close the bedroom off once it turns cold.

Way after seven. The birds are starting to flit and disappear. A bat circles. She sinks onto the porch steps to watch the sun go down, rests her back against the logs. Her muscles let go. Not a single car has passed by all day. Her closest neighbors live over on the next road—a motorcycle couple who streak by now and then, wave. What is it Sally said when she rented her the cabin a few months ago? May be more reclusion than you're ready for. After these last few years—Mark's trouble, her mother's illness, Ed Dugan—she is oh-so-ready. Forty-five, but this is the first time she's ever lived by herself.

Sam stands with his head on her knees. She scratches his ears absently. When she stops, he presses his cold nose against her hand. It reminds her of how she and her mother used to tickle each other's feet. They would stretch out on the long green couch on rainy Saturdays, each at opposite ends, each off in a book. If either one of them forgot, the other pushed with her toes as a reminder. When her mother died—that terrible chasm. The one who had always been there no matter what—gone. For a long while she sits, listening to the faraway chug of an engine.

She lights the kerosene lamps and sets two of them on her drawing table. Evening at the cabin is her favorite part of the day. Maybe Richard will still come, but if he doesn't, well, she'll have a good time anyway.

How long have she and Richard been in this *maybe* world? Off and on for three years with Ed Dugan mixed in, and the relationship hadn't changed much. His divorce hasn't made a big difference. He appears, they talk and laugh, sleep together. The morning comes quickly. Richard—always his touches when she passes; pours him juice, lifts his plate. He kisses her and leaves. Too bad people aren't as easy as water and wood.

The hall has gotten so dark she needs a flashlight to put things away in the cooler. When she shines the light down, there's her toad. That is how she's come to feel about him. He has taken up residence in the hallway and most nights when she flashes, he's there—fat, warted, and big-eyed. He never moves, just stares back at her when she squats to talk with him.

Does she want to draw or write? When Richard began working in the City, she began to write poems to him, the first real writing she's ever done. The poems: what she wishes she'd said. Poems she carries to the mailbox on the main road, proclaims by hoisting up the little red flag. Poems she sometimes later retrieves before the mailman comes.

She gets out her notebook and sits down at the table. She looks over the poem she's been working on, a poem that started one day right after Richard's truck disappeared from view. She was setting a bag of trash into the burn barrel, full of the joy of Richard and the morning. Then that immediate flash of just how vulnerable this makes her:

Could I cache your kisses? Run them stuff-jawed
to some dark stash. Braid blisses of these cornucopian

dawns to hang vaulted in golden hoards. Vacuum pack
certain smiles. Line them for winter on warehouse walls.

Secure from February snow, I could be a prodigal spender;
what would I care about income, outgo? Risk extravagance,
tipsy dance till frogs, spring dervish. Then peep out like
crocus, a winter stowaway impervious.

No, she's not in the mood to work on a love poem to Richard. He's there; she's here. She closes the heavy split-log door and builds a fire. The kindling roars up, the bark on the bigger logs crackles. All the corners disappear. She turns the back burners until the flames lick blue around the big speckled canners. Brewing the bath. Then she lifts her bag of marijuana and papers from the hiding place in the secret compartment of her pencil box. Richard's not coming. She flattens the paper and sifts a mound down the center, the perfect amount not to be too stoned. Richard doesn't smoke. Too freaky, he says, having once gotten paranoid from grass that must have been soaked in LSD or something. If by chance Richard comes knocking on that door, she doesn't want to be so high she ends up floating, with Richard planted solidly, rationally, below. She twists the ends and lights up, takes the smoke down and holds it. She smokes and rocks, the heat from the stove, warm on her legs.

She sets Sally's battery record player on the counter, with her three records: Bob Dylan, David Bromberg, and Buffy St. Marie. She puts on the Dylan. *It Ain't Me, Babe* plays and she dances while the water gets hot, dances with her eyes closed and the windows black, around and around the islands of light. Her shadow sways and slides along the walls. Sam sleeps by the fire. When the steam rises, she takes the tin tub off the nail behind the stove and places it inches from the heat. She pours in the hot and then some cold. Balancing on one foot, she tests it with her toe until it's right. She sheds her clothes and steps in, then squats on her haunches and sinks. Knees splayed, she sits. For a long time she thinks of nothing beyond the heat of the water, its soft wash against her chest when she breathes.

Sam raises his head and thumps his tail. There's a light tapping on the door. Startled, she reaches for a towel and rises. Her heart banging. "Who is it?"

"Me."

Richard. Wrapping the towel around herself, she tracks across the room and lifts the latch. Not his usual smile. She sees only his face, his silent face, suspended in the dark hall. Richard, a warrior, his green eyes black in this light. She moves aside and he steps in. "Is something wrong?"

"No," he says. "Go on with your bath if you want to." He pulls over a chair and stretches out long, his shoulders low. He props his boots on the kindling box. "It complicates things, you not having a phone."

She turns, her body still jumpy. "I'm not ready for a phone," she says. Not ready to open a funnel so the world out there can pour through. Mark in crisis.

Richard sniffs. He thinks it odd that she gets high alone. It's not like drinking, she's told him. "I was thinking about you earlier," she says, swaying back and forth by the warm stove, her voice sounding calm. "You seem sad."

"I was thinking about you too. That's why I'm here."

Again she sways before the stove, her arms across her toweled chest. Sam's breathing, the only sound. Richard pushes up in the chair, leans over and opens the door to the stove. "So what's new?"

What's new? This is the first time Richard has ever used this kind of conversation starter—not even when they first met and needed such conversational bridges. Maybe if she gets some clothes on, it'll all feel less awkward, less *who is this intruder in the night?* "I'm on my second reading of Lady Chatterley," her voice rises as she moves into the bedroom. "Such a wonderful gift, Richard." In the darkness she takes her nightgown from beneath her pillow and pulls it over her head, then goes back in the big room. "I've marked some places I want to read to you."

She sits in the rocker and opens the book to the part she finds astounding—that Lawrence can so fully know how a woman feels. More fully than she knew herself until she read the words. But just as she tilts the page to the light, Richard reaches over and closes the book. He gets up and stands behind her chair, puts the book back on the table. He rests his fingers on her shoulders. She breathes. She sits with her hands open, tries to let go of feeling that what she wants has been snatched away.

Richard leads her toward the bedroom. She follows, her hand still in his. He sits down with her on the side of the bed. Neither of them says anything. He pushes her back. He takes off his boots and stretches out beside her. The quilt feels damp. He strokes her hair. She wants to open like a flower, turned toward the sun, but she doesn't and she's not going to pretend.

He sighs. He sits up and slowly pulls off his shirt, his socks, his jeans, his underwear. He stands and rolls back the covers. "Get under," he whispers. "It's cold."

She does. All the while breathing, keeping her body loose. When she first dances with someone she doesn't know, this is how she follows—lets her body become liquid and then she goes where he goes. He holds her. She puts her arms around him too. He touches her breast, the inside of her thigh. He kisses her neck. She stays turned toward him, her eyes closed, her body still, her breath even and slow.

"What?" he finally says.

"Nothing," she answers.

He rolls away a little. For a long time they're still. At last he sits on the side of the bed. He reaches for his clothes and slowly begins to pull them on. She listens to each of the sounds: the zipper, the leather belt against the buckle, the laces knotting. He turns and touches her face. "I'm going," he says, his voice tired.

She feels his weight lift from the mattress. "Richard ..."

He stands at the foot of the bed. "I'm working on it," he says.

She hears the heavy door open and close. The latch drop into place. The car start and back out.

Part II
Castanets
1985-1986

3

Scenario:

They meet on the midway.
His arms leave her breathless.
He hits the ball to the top,
rings the bell,
and gives her the Kewpie doll.

She's got nice tits
which she gives to him
along with "the best years of her life."

They marry:

After a brief honeymoon, they move to the edge.
While she stands washing diapers and thinks, Is this it?,
he works at a job he does not like and fears he's missed
the last train to the Elysian Fields, but maybe not if he
hurries. Then he won't be able to get the car started
and it'll ALL be her fault.

To be continued …

18
Trouble – 1985

D<small>EL PULLED UP TO</small> JAKE's, put the car in Park, and turned the key. Milk and butter were on her mind, but when she stepped out, a surge of current hit her … WHoooost. It almost pulled her across the street. Her eyes met the eyes of a man. She lowered her head and hurried to the safety of the store. Once inside she leaned against the screen door: What was that?

At the cash register while Lois tallied up her groceries, Del said, "What's going on at the Inn?" As president of the Inn Restoration Foundation, Lois would know.

"Some men from Camp Parmela are painting the trim for free?"

"Camp Parmela … the prison?"

"Yes," Lois said. "Want these in a bag?"

Outside again, Del did not look toward the Inn.

A few hours later Carla pulled up to JAKE's. She left the engine running—"damned car." Coffee and cigarettes were what she needed. As she stepped out, a bolt of energy zinged her … ZZiihhhst. Her eyes met the eyes of a man. A man with wonderful shoulders and arms. She raised her hand in greeting and went into the store. Who was that?

On the way to the cash register, Carla looked at herself in the darkened glass of the soda cooler. She smiled her Beautiful Smile and waved; her reflection waved back approvingly. While she waited for Dot Frazer to unload a full cart, Carla leaned against the counter. She ran her fingers along the edge, thinking of his ribs.

"How you doing, Carla?" Lois said, not breaking her rhythm as she punched the price of Dot's order on the cash register with her right hand, and with the left, pushed aside another counted juice can.

Just my luck, thought Carla, surveying Dot's still half-full cart. "Had to leave the engine going. Trouble with the starter." Carla smiled toward Dot who took the hint and emptied the basket faster.

Puffing from bending her round body over the cart, Dot said, "Catering a big wedding at the Inn tomorrow. Hoop Dawes's oldest daughter." She directed this at Carla who had flipped open the *Sun* to check her horoscope. Then Dot turned to Lois and whispered, "You're sure it'll be okay to go over to the kitchen while *those* men are there?"

Carla stopped reading, but kept her eyes on the paper.

Lois gave the ceiling a give-me-strength look and began loading the bags. Everyone knew that for the last twenty years Lois had almost single-handedly kept the Inn from falling down by writing grants, running raffles, and renting the place out for weddings.

"Know you only have eleven Hawaiian Punch? Twenty percent off 'cause it's an Inn function. This go on your bill?"

Over the clank of the cans, Dot said, "Ten men and only one guard."

Lois stopped, put her hands on her ample hips. "Dot, you're on the Inn Restoration Committee. Free labor. All we have to do is furnish the paint. The men from Camp Parmela do the rest."

Carla's eyes riveted to *CANCER*.

"What kind of crimes are they in for?" Dot said confidentially.

"Third time DWIs, Failure to Keep Right? I didn't do a background check when they arrived this morning." Lois raked her fingers through what looked like a new perm and began putting the cans into bags again. "Got somebody to help you with these?"

"My husband will get them later."

Carla helped Dot carry the bags to a shelf by the door. The rough idle of her car had upped a notch.

"Why thank you, Carla." Dot huffed her way back to Lois. "'Course it doesn't bother me, but you know some people in town aren't going to like all those black ..."

"Really?" Lois said. Then she stabbed Dot's total onto her bill and shoved it across the counter for an initial. "Dot, I spent a couple of hours over there earlier, talking about what they need to do first, where they have to caulk. Camp Parmela even supplies the ladders."

Carla wanted to say, What about the gorgeous conquistador with the heavy black beard?

Lois turned and opened a cigar box on the shelf behind her for the keys to the Inn kitchen. Dot tucked them in her apron pocket and hoisted one of the smaller bags. She pushed the screen with her buttocks. "Well, if you're sure ... " she mumbled as the door slapped shut.

"I should have told her Rape and Riot," Lois said.

"A pack of Marlboro Lights. A large Tylenol."

"Extra Strength? On your bill?"

Carla didn't even want to think about that bill. End of the month for sure. "The paper too." She had to finish her horoscope. "How long will it take to paint that much trim?"

"Three or four weeks."

Three or four weeks. That sounded like an interesting amount of time. The man was gone. She slid into the car. The needle was just above E. Maybe there was enough mower gas to get back down tomorrow. Maybe Steve would get the child support money to her today. She wasn't going to worry about that now. Carla put the paper on the dash to read as she drove.

She turned the corner by the Inn. There they sat. Waiting warriors beside a Tudor manor. One, like some Zulu Chief, rode a concrete lion that guarded the entrance. She didn't see the ... electric man. The rest lounged on the porch steps, railings, benches. Lunch. Without seeming to look, she took in as much as she could: the guard—paunchy, white, a revolver; most of them black—striped muscle shirts, bandannas around a few heads, late twenties, thirties. No one smiled or waved, but they were watching.

She made a right up Fyler Hill. The Maverick hesitated. "Come on, Bessie." She shifted into Low; it gained strength, struggled on, made it. Carla glanced at her horoscope with one eye:

CANCER

Today is your day for adventure.

"All right!"

You will have an opportunity to meet someone unusual.

Who said there wasn't something to this stuff?

Don't be overly concerned with the advice of friends.

"Okay."

Employ good money sense today.

Wonder what his sign is? Maybe a Scorpio? So intense. April had been a downer. An empty, yes, an empty, celibate spring. But May was looking better. "You're insane," she told the eyes in the mirror. Carla lit up a Marlboro, chuckled, and began to make a plan.

"You're joking." Del laughed. "You're kidding, right?" She looked intently at Carla. "You're *not* kidding."

"Cross my heart. I'm going down tomorrow, same time, and I'll look at him, and he'll look at me. That's Phase I. Plus, I'm 'employing good money sense' by using the refund I got in the mail today—talk about an omen—to pay my grocery bill and get my car fixed. Since JAKE's will be the center of my operations, I want to be on the good side of Lois."

The two women faced each other across Carla's big kitchen table, a place they sat at often. Before, During, and After. Already they had laughed long about their different responses to the swarthy, muscled man with the mad eyes. "Chicken," Carla said. "Nuts," Del replied.

"I know what your horoscope said about advi ..."

"I'm not listening."

Rudy came in the kitchen. "You ought to listen to someone rational," he said, gently punching his mother's shoulder as he passed through to the back deck, a rickety floor on feeble supports, all that was left of a former back room.

"Would you like to hear," Carla called after him, "something rational about your and that cradle robber's," the screen door clicked shut, "relationship?" She turned to Del. "He's eighteen years old, sleeping with someone thirty who's got two kids, and he wants to talk about rational?"

Del decided not to push Carla too far today. "Okay. Phase I: Staring. Then what?"

"We can see how we feel about what we see. Then Phase II. Contact."

"Contact? You, the guard, and ... at least find out his name. We can't keep calling him 'electric man.' Carla, what do you think he might be in jail for?"

"Jeez, Del, you sound like Dot Frazer."

"Don't you need to know that? Before you start messing with this guy?"

"Uhmmm," Carla murmured, absently doodling a string of connected hearts on the back of her refund envelope.

Del leaned toward Carla, spoke a little louder, "Carla, this man is not in prison for too many traffic tickets. I'd guess he's in his thirties. Think of it."

"Yes."

"He hasn't seen, been with a woman in a long time."

"How do you know that?" Carla said, finally looking up.

"The same way you know it."

"More coffee?" Carla said, but she made no move to get up and instead began writing the letters *E.M.* in each heart.

"Don't you want to consider the scenario?"

Carla put down the pencil and looked at Del. "No," she said. "He's very attractive. He's lonely. I'll get to know him a little. I'll find out what he did. It can't be anything real heavy or he wouldn't be on a work crew. If he's too crazy, I'll back off."

Tess clomped through as Rambo: fatigues, a hunting knife tied to her waist, Steve's old motorcycle boots. She leaned on the back of her mother's chair and rested her chin on her head.

"Yes, Teresa, what can I do for you?"

"Food."

Carla kissed her cheek. "How about some chips? They're behind the noodles." Tess got them out and came back to lean again. "Tess, I'm trying to talk to Del. How about going outside for a while? Go bug Rudy." Tess didn't move, appeared to be looking at the funnies over her mother's shoulder. "Come on, Tess. Go find Nool. Get him to play cards, go to the pond with you." Carla almost always had other people living there—cousins, sad-story people. Del's son, Aaron, even hinted about returning to finish high school in Danford, bunking in with Rudy until college. Tess shuffled out, the knife drawn. "Thank you. Be careful with that."

"I've got to go," Del said. "Maybe Richard will come by this weekend." She rose and poured the cold coffee down the drain, ran water to rinse it out. As Del started out the door, she turned for one last word, "Like they say ... "

"Yeees?"

"When you play with electricity, you may get ... "

"Laid."

Del shook her head, "I'm going to tell you, I told you so." She started down the walk, but then she turned and went back. Carla, still on the porch, wearing the look that said further advice was not welcome, a look that always made Del retreat, a look Aaron had been giving her since he was little.

"What?" Carla said, the joke gone out of her.

"It's about Aaron. Nothing I say is getting through. If he calls Rudy to work on some songs, maybe you can get a word in. Since he's started practically living here whenever he's on break, maybe you can encourage him to stick it out in Lawrence High school. Seems crazy to come back here to school when he's only got seven weeks until graduation."

"Infidelity," said Carla. "His first love. Never quite get over that one. As you well know."

Lee.

Looking GOOD, every morning at ten o'clock, Carla drove down to JAKE's. Even that second day the man knew and managed to be working on the side of the Inn that faced Fyler Hill. He signaled *okay* if the guard wasn't around. On those days she sat in the car at the foot of the hill and they stared at each other across the road as long as they dared or until someone pulled up behind her. When he looked at her and then quickly away, she knew the guard was watching. Then she didn't wait. He certainly was one beautiful man, narrow-hipped and long-thighed with the shoulders and arms of a weight lifter. But mostly it was his eyes: merry one minute, with a dark flash the next. She wondered about his mouth beneath the beard.

Some days he managed to be on the other side when she came out of the store. Like that first day, she felt his energy the minute she pushed open the screen. If no one was around, they stared again. On nice mornings Carla began the ritual of sitting out on the bench in front of JAKE's to read the paper, have a cup of coffee, smoke a cigarette. Sometimes there were kids and dogs and bikes. Sometimes, if things were slow, Lois joined her to chat about the weather, the polo crowd, and even occasionally, "the men from Parmela." The trick was to try to bring the conversation around to the electric man without being obvious. If he'd popped into view across the street, Carla might have been able to zoom right in with a direct comment like, 'That guy up on the ladder seems to be a good worker,' but the man was never around when Lois took a break on the bench.

For Carla these mornings spent in front of JAKE's were a kind of delicious foreplay, a dance she did for him. When she moved to the trash barrel, talked and gestured with her hands, bent to set the groceries in the trunk of the car, always she felt him watching. The best was when he worked on the side that faced the store. Carla pretended to read the paper while she watched him climb the ladder, hand over hand, his calves flexed, his bare back swimming; watched him hammer the window frames, his arm rhythmically raising and lowering when he pounded in a nail. Above the paper she followed the flow of his long body stooping and straightening as he brushed brown paint on all that Tudor trim. Secretly her eyes tracked him and imagined.

After about a week of what Del called the "starings," Carla finally got lucky. Lois brought her out a warm cinnamon bun and elevated her legs on the bench. "Varicose veins," Lois said.

Carla gave her own legs a worried survey. But after all, like Del, Lois was at least ten years older, pushing fifty.

While she worked through the top layer of icing, Carla decided to pump Lois from a different angle: "I don't know how you do it, Lois. Run the store all week now that your husband's not well enough to do much and still get over to the Inn every morning to make coffee for the Camp Parmela crew."

"Poor Jake," Lois said. "Even before the diabetes started taking such a heavy toll, dealing with the customers was never his thing. People like Dot and the rest of the snoopers making comments about the Parmela guys would have sent his blood pressure to stroke level."

Carla saw that this last approach was not getting her any closer to her major objective: the man's name and bio, but before she could fire off a better shot, Lois put her feet flat on the sidewalk and balled both hands into fists.

"You know what I told them at the last Grange meeting, some of those grand citizens who worry every time a stranger shows up in town? I said, The men from Parmela have strict orders to have nothing to do with the local inhabitants. If there's even the slightest bit of a problem, Parmela is going to pack up their ladders and return to camp. End of project. And if this town, with its narrow-mindedness, its snide remarks, is the cause of the trouble, I'm going to resign as president of the Restoration Committee and you can see how you feel about watching the Inn fall, piece by piece, before your very eyes."

Seeing that Lois was on Code Red Alert, Carla figured she best be cool, but then Lois sank back again and said, "Besides I've come to really like most of the crew. You know what they call me? Boss lady. Jackson—he's kind of the leader—he says I'm one tough cookie."

And there it was—the opening she'd been waiting for all week: "Isn't it too bad that people you say are so hard-working and nice have gotten themselves into trouble? It's got to be a terrible thing to be in jail."

With this, Lois told *All*. Which, though it wasn't a lot, was sure more than Carla knew. She was careful to hide how she was hanging on Lois's every word. "Artie, the tallest black man— the one who wears a jean vest—I guess he's my favorite. He always asks how my mother's doing since she broke her hip." Lois leaned toward Carla and lowered her voice, "Funny, but I feel kind of like a mother to some of them. Especially Bill. He's the youngest, the only other white man besides Raoul. Raoul, the one with the black beard. Raoul Santano. He's very quiet." Lois touched Carla's arm. "Maybe too quiet. His parents are Spanish. They live in the Bronx." Lois went on about the others with Carla seeming to be listening, nodding her head. But really she was thinking—Raoul Santano. Yes.

May 21st. Contact. Monday morning of the third week Carla made her daily trip to JAKE's. Time was running out. On Friday Lois had said they were going to finish the painting on Monday or Tuesday. Carla decided somehow, some way she was going to speak to, going to touch Raoul. As she started down Fyler Hill, she began to search for his distantly familiar body. It had become a kind of game. How far up the hill could she be before they saw each other? Then she looked deep into his eyes and barely watched the road the rest of her slow descent. But today he was not there. Anxious, disappointed, she made the turn. He stepped out from behind the van and moved in front of her car with his hand up to stop. She did. Her heart pounded.

"Don't be frightened," he said. Reaching in the window, he touched her shoulder and looked into her face. With the other hand he gave her a note. Their fingers met. "Go," he said and disappeared behind the van.

Carla didn't remember parking the car or going into JAKE's to get the paper, the coffee. She sat on the bench, the headlines a blur. She felt the corners of the note poking her hip through her shorts pocket. Her shoulder and fingers tingled. Indeed he was an electric man. She was surprised by his face, even frightened. A craggy face. For the first time she seriously wondered what he had done. Carla glanced up and down the street, across to the Inn. She looked at the print shop, the antique store, the post office. There was no one in sight. She sat and slowly breathed. Then she reached into her pocket and drew out the note. She opened it carefully, smiling at the tight precision of the folds. Her hands shook.

May 21, 1985

Dear Woman with the beautiful smile

This is how I think of you. Tomorrow I am going to give you this letter. See you up close. We have it worked out. Please do not feel I am being to forword. I want so much to get to know you better. I hope you will write to me. That you will tell me your name and your address. I am hoping that after you get to know me better in letters you will come to visit me some Sunday. We could have a picnic. There are tables and trees and the last of the spring flowers. When you read this we will be packing up. Tomorrow is our last day. I will miss seeing you every day.
Please write. Ask me anything you like.

Always
Raoul

Raoul Santano
Box 343 Camp Parmela
Marwick, NY 13445

She read it over and over. The woman with the beautiful smile. Today their last day. Already she saw two of the men, Artie and Bill, loading the ladders on a truck. She did not see Raoul. She ran her fingers over the square, exact letters and began to think of her answer.

May 21, 1985

> ~~*Dear Electric Man*~~ *Dear Raoul*
> *I am very glad that we final...*

"Del, two ls or one in the word *finally*?"

"Two." Del resisted her teacher impulse to say, just write, worry about the spelling later.

Carla sat high atop her big double bed, chewing on the end of a pencil, discarded beginnings around her. Right after Steve left, Carla moved up to this room. I'm starting over, she said. This is *my* room now. Entrance by invitation only. She painted the scarred iron bed lavender, piled on another mattress and topped it off with ruffles. The end result was a combination love nest – mother's council chamber. A pink shaded lamp cast a rosy glow over the décor and the gallery of family pictures: her mother, smiling as she cut into a huge cake; her brothers, Bobbie and T.J., sitting on the hood of an old Pontiac; a younger Tess, holding their pet raccoon, Harry; Rudy, all in black. There were no pictures of her father, no pictures of Steve.

"Damn. It is so much easier to say it. I can't make it come out right on paper, can't get the smile in the words."

When Del stopped by to talk, Carla had rushed downstairs with Raoul's note and pleas for advice on her reply. She charmed Rudy and Nooley into taking Tess with them so that now Del and Carla were sequestered in Carla's boudoir while Carla wrestled with the muse.

Del pulled the rocker to the window to look out across the valley. The lushness of summer coming on. Carla resumed her struggle, her head bent as she wrote. It was strange to see Carla at a loss for words, Carla who was always ready with a remark, Carla who always had a story. Funny, Del thought, for her it was just the opposite: so much easier to write than say. Or better still, draw what she didn't even know she felt.

Once again Del reread Raoul's note. It still surprised her. She had assumed that this man was a crazy. But there was a gentleness in what he said, what he didn't say. *Ask me anything you like.* Surely he meant, Ask me why I'm in prison. I understand that you will want to know.

Del still felt the urge to try to persuade Carla not to become involved, but now it was more complicated.

"Here's what I have so far," Carla said. She crossed out as she went along:

"Dear Raoul, I am ~~very~~ glad we finally met. I am sorry that today was your last day at the Inn. I will miss seeing you too. I ~~sure~~ am glad you found a way to get your note to me. If you hadn't, I'd made up my mind I was going to talk to you some way." Carla paused to add something. She continued. "I am finding it hard to write this. In fact I have started several times. I'm a better talker. I have enjoyed staring at you the last few weeks. It's funny, but I feel like I know a lot about you just from that. Just as you probably know a lot about me. I think it would be best if I told you a little about my present life. I have recently separated from my husband. (Feb.) After being married for 18 years. I have two children. Rudy who is 18 and Tess who is 11. I am 35 years old. This last year has been a crazy one for me. I still am mixed up. I tell you this because I want things to be honest between us. Right now I am not involved with anyone. You have probably already figured this out from the vibrations I've been sending you. I would like to have you write to me and tell me more about yourself. Yes, we could get to know each other better in letters. I am curious to know what sign you were born under. When is your birthday?" Again Carla paused to make a change. ~~I hope to hear from you soon.~~ ~~Love Always~~ Take care. Carla

"Well? What do you think? I didn't mention going to visit. You know, in some ways I've liked the distance, the slow motion—kind of a dream. I've had a dose of reality. Steve and That Woman, frozen pipes and bad cars. Know what I mean?"

"Yes."

"I didn't want to ask about Camp Parmela. I'm offering friendship here. Nothing heavy-duty. Think that's clear?" Carla searched around trying to locate her cigarettes beneath the papers.

"You might make the friendship part more ... definite. But I don't think it's going to matter much how you try to make it ... less intense."

"What do you mean?"

"The idea of you is probably the center of this man's life. You're what he thinks about."

"I suppose."

"I wonder when he's going to get out?"

"Lois said people don't go to Parmela until the last couple of years of their sentence. I figure he had to be there for a while with good behavior to get put on a work crew."

"What do you think Lois meant when she told you Raoul was 'too quiet'?"

"Who knows? It doesn't feel right to ask him why he's in jail in a letter. How about this?" Carla crossed out a section and wrote again. "Instead of saying the part about not being involved, I'm going to say, 'I think it would be good to have your friendship.' I cut out the vibrations stuff too."

Del sat staring out the window. Carla sighed. She knew Del was ... what was it she called it? Taking a look at the scenarios. She was big on options. Del, Del, thought Carla, shaking her head. She found a fresh sheet of paper and carefully copied the letter over. She folded the letter and pushed it in an envelope. It wouldn't fit so she bent it in half and stuck it in again. She licked the edge and pressed the flap tight. Across the front she neatly printed Raoul's name and address. Then she leaned it against a picture of her and Vicky, from back when she was sixteen and working at that go-go sleaze-joint in Monterey—the beginning of her long career of depressing jobs, including her current stint bartending. She turned on a tape and with the other hand gathered up the wads of paper and dumped them in the trash. She smoothed the bedspread, plumped the throw pillows, and then turned to rummage around in an old wardrobe that stood in the corner.

When Del looked over her shoulder, all she could see were Carla's bare feet below the wardrobe door and clothes being tossed to the bed. All the while Carla singing along with the Dead: *"When the shadows fall it'll do you fine. When the cold winds blow, it'll ease your mind."*

"Carla, what are you doing?"

"Thinking," she said from beneath a flowered sundress which she pulled on and adjusted so there was a hint of cleavage. She stepped before the long smoky mirror of her old-fashioned dressing table and raised the thin skirt to curtsy position.

"What are you thinking about?" Del said.

"Oh ... what are you looking at out that window?"

"TROUBLE."

"I figured. You know, Del, the trouble with you, the trouble with you is ... you're a Virgo. I'm thinking," said Carla, "I'm thinking is this summer dress right for a May picnic?"

All the while she was wrapping the fried chicken in foil, fitting the brownies into baggies, she felt a fat toad of doubt squatting in her gut.

"What you doing, Mamo? Where are you going?" Tess said, leaning over the picnic basket, fingering the little packages.

"Oh, just going to visit a friend, a friend who's lonely." She didn't say a lonely man who has made me the center of his life.

"Maybe he's a killer. Maybe he'll try to hurt you." Tess searched her face.

And Rudy said, "Don't take any knives or dope the brownies. Guards and dogs are going to check you out."

"Stop it. Both of you."

CAMP PARMELA
New York State Correctional Facility

The minute Carla saw the sign, she knew it was the wrong dress. It was more than friendly. It didn't say "Take care" it said "Take Me." Now as she made the turn into Camp Parmela, she wasn't sure about anything. She pulled up the front of the sundress, wished she'd worn a bra.

The entry road was long, lined by tall pines. It looked more like a drive into an estate. Carla didn't know what to expect. She had visited Steve in jail once. The time he got picked up for having an unlicensed weapon. That had been the real thing. Glass between them with chicken wire pressed inside. She tilted the rearview down a little. Why? she said to her eyes. Why do I seek to fill my bed with desperadoes? It's not like they're great lovers. Why not a nice insurance agent? But Del said three-piece-men could be crazy too. Maybe all men are mad. The eyes in the mirror said, *And you are the soul of sanity, right?* But it wasn't Raoul's possible madness that worried her; it was his love.

Camp Parmela stretched out before her. It looked more like an army base than a prison. No fences. No bars. Rows and rows of barracks painted brown with several two-story brick buildings on either side of the drive. Carla pulled into the parking lot marked *Visitors*. She was glad she had Del's car, better than pulling in with the Maverick, the muffler teasing the blacktop.

She wondered if she should take in the basket. Perhaps it was true; they might want to look inside. She lifted it out. She knew Raoul was expecting her, had signed her up on the visitors' list one week in advance. She had received a letter from him every day since the work crew left Danford two weeks ago. Sometimes they were cards; sometimes they were detailed accounts of his routine at the camp: his work in the greenhouse, his weight-lifting, the TV shows he watched, what they ate. He told her he was a Scorpio, that he was thirty-three years old, and that he'd been in jail for seven years. He still didn't say why he was in jail and she didn't ask. The letters were affectionate, never sexual or mushy, and usually signed Thinking of you—Always, Raoul. Pressed between the pages, the purple petals of some sweet-smelling flower and pulsing between every line, the beat of "us." She wrote back several times, but she found it hard to think of new things to say and JAKE's had the sappiest collection of cards she'd ever seen. Plus she had just done eighteen years of *us*.

A sign on the door of the brick building on the right said *Visitor Registration*. Carla adjusted her straps and started up the steps. She opened the screen door. The room was full of people sitting on benches lining the walls. Even some children. It was quiet, only the whir of a big fan and a soft blur of music from one of the offices down the hall. The looks of quick pleasure from the men confirmed her doubts about the yellow dress. She moved to the long counter where a man in a khaki uniform, with a gun bulging on his side, leaned reading a paper. He looked up. "I'm here to visit someone," Carla said. A baby cried behind her.

"Have you ever visited before?"

"No."

"Name?"

"Carla Morletti." She felt like the counter was a platter for serving up her boobs.

The man checked the list on the clipboard. "You here to see Raoul Santano?"

"Yes." She felt the room come alive behind her. Like it was frozen when she came in, but now it flowed: chairs moved, people coughed, a child whined for candy.

"First, I need to see photo ID."

She gave that to him.

"Okay, now fill this out," he said and handed her a form and a ball point. "You'll need to bear down hard to make three copies."

Jeez. They sure wanted enough information. Date and place of birth, U.S. citizen, social security number, place of employment, marital status. Were you ever arrested? She filled it out and handed it back to Sgt. Burke, as it said on the name tag below his badge. He looked it over and went to the phone in one of the little offices behind the counter. She couldn't hear what he said.

He returned in a minute. "I need to check your purse and basket." He looked down into the interior of each and then handed them back to her. "Just wait here until they bring the men to the picnic grounds at two."

The clock on the wall said 1:50. Carla took a seat by a woman with a stroller wedged between her generous thighs. She could talk to the baby because the rest of them didn't seem too cheerful. They looked like people who'd walked the long road to the jail and their shoulders said it was not a good trip. No three-piecers in this crew. Mostly Jamesway-Laundromat. She smiled at the kid and the kid blessed her with a burst of joy.

Raoul Santano. Did his parents visit him from the Bronx? It was true she was coming to see a lonely friend. For even if there were no bars, how would it feel not to be able to leave when you wanted to? But the trouble for her was that coming here was a little like going to the grocery store hungry. She hadn't slept with anyone for months. God knows how long it had been for Raoul. Only their longing would be a lot riskier than a cart full of junk food. Plus she knew she was going to drive out of these gates at six hungrier than ever. It did not form the basis for a rational relationship.

The guard stepped around the counter. "All right, folks. I'll walk you over to the picnic area—though many of you know the way. Just a reminder: no drugs or alcohol."

And no getting laid.

When they got to the road, everyone fell into a ragged line behind the guard as he walked beyond the brick buildings, past the ends of the barracks where men watched from open windows, then into the large park. Raoul was right: there were trees and flowers that Carla had never even seen.

He was sitting at a faraway table. His heavy black beard and curly head. For a moment it was as if she was in the Maverick coming down Fyler Hill and he was on the roof of the Inn. They stared at each other. It was a distance they knew. He rose and moved toward her. She remembered his shoulders and arms, the muscles of his thighs. She was surprised he wore a khaki uniform and saw the other waiting men did too. She smiled and he laughed. And then he was only a few feet away. She put the basket on the grass. He took both her hands and held them up. He stepped back to look at her again. Then he bowed a little. "Ahh," he said and looked into her face, "such a pretty dress, the woman with the beautiful smile." Never had anyone seemed so happy to see her. He took the basket and holding her hand led her to the farthest table. She could hardly breathe.

"Sit down," he said and gestured toward the bench. And then he moved to the other side and slowly sat. Again he took her hand. "I must sit here for now. This is difficult for me. It has been so long since I have been with a woman. So long since I have been with a woman like you. Well, what I am saying is, we must take our time on this wonderful day. What are you thinking?"

"Yes," she said.

"Ahh, you are feeling it too. Very strange. How about a tour of my summer beauties? Let me show you. For I have helped grow most of them from seed and transplanted them to these beds."

And that was what they did. Walking softly beside her, a few fingers guiding her under an elbow, he led her around the grounds. "Copper Iris, Iridaceae ... Early Saxafrage, Saxifraga Virginiensis ... This one you must water daily; this one, weed carefully around its fragile roots ... Each time you visit, you will see the miracles of change."

Soon she found she was no longer listening to the words; she heard only the rhythms, the rise and fall of his voice. She smiled and nodded and said "lovely" but all the while she watched his fingers gently lifting the drooping head of an orchid-like flower to reveal the delicate carving of gold inside, his hands pushing down the soil as he talked. She thought of those fingers on her body. And it was true there was something desperate in his face, eyes light and then dark, like the moving of sun and shadow through the leaves above them.

And then he stooped before a bed of purple blossoms. With his back to her he said, "I must tell you." He turned and curved her fingers around the stem of one of the flowers, the petals just beginning to furl back from the bud. He looked at her with sad eyes. She was afraid. "Seven years ago I killed a man." He stepped away. "He was my friend. I found him with the woman I loved."

He turned and walked slowly toward the trees along the edges. She went and walked beside him. She touched his arm. They moved along the borders of the woods. She listened to his breathing. Heavy and uneven. He was a man who knew without words. She had not given him the quick look, the touch of reassurance in those moments of telling that would make it all right. The doubt she'd felt for days found its way to her head. Somewhere in the reading of his daily letters, like Del, she'd seen the scenario: She would feel closed in by his love, put on edge by the touching at the Sunday picnics, would find reasons not to go. She would sleep with someone she met at the bar one Saturday night. She would write a final letter filled with honest lies about why it must be this way, and then cross her fingers that when he got out he would not come to get even. And oh, the trouble.

They circled the grounds many times. His breathing was more

peaceful. He took her hand and brought the tips of her fingers to his lips. Then he put his hands on her bare shoulders. He was trembling. He stared at her with his black eyes and said, "Now you know what kind of man I am. Could you accept that much love?"

She felt his fingers tighten. She returned his look and shook her head. She saw him flinch, saw his tears, felt her own. He let go of her shoulders and for what felt like a long time, they stood without moving. Then he turned and walked across the field. She watched his fingers open and close, saw him put his hands in his pockets. She watched his body as she had secretly tracked him on ladders most of May. He never looked back.

Carla stood there for a while, the purple flower in her hands. Then she walked to the picnic table and lifted the basket with all the little unwrapped packages. She walked to the car and set the basket on the seat beside her. She drove back to the main road.

Well, she was leaving before she wanted to, but she was leaving.

19
Sunshine – 1985

"HERE SHE COMES."

"Who?"

"My mother." Aaron reaches up and pulls Rudy's curtain closed. Her car, her flashing signal, vanish.

Rudy laughs. He peeks out. "Hey, it's not like we're up here shooting smack. No, we're doing our homework. Good boys."

Aaron opens his notebook, lingers on the last lines of the song he's working on:

Take my words home to your point of view
and see them change.

This is what he should be writing, not some lame Health report. He flutters through the pages until he comes to where he and Rudy left off:

Lysergic Acid Diethylamide
Rudy Morletti and Aaron Merrick
Health Report   *June 9, 1985*

His mother's voice drifts up from the porch. Carla's cigarette cough. He skims the first section. "All right, let's finish this sucker."

"So was your mom pissed when you told her you were moving in with us?"

"My mom doesn't get pissed; she gets disappointed."

"Disappointed?"

"After my fateful return from Lawrence to live with her in that shithole cabin, when she found out I was only going to school a couple of days a week."

"I wish my mom got disappointed. You ever see Mamo pissed?

Busts a gasket. What'd your mom say?"

"That I had to go to school on a regular basis or move out."

"She knew you could bunk here. You only got another few weeks before graduation anyways."

Aaron tips his chair against the wall. His mother and Carla still buzz, buzz, buzzing below.

Rudy gives him a probing look. "Does she know what happened about your girlfriend?"

Aaron kamikazes his pen down, ready to write. "Like I said, Rudy, let's bring this baby home. Soon Health, all this crap will be behind us."

"For you maybe. One more year before I'm out if I'm lucky. Besides you still got college."

"Music school. And surely they are not going to spend a week doing fucking gerunds."

"Gerunds?"

"Believe me, you don't want to junk your remaining brain cells with such."

Rudy plays the opening cords of "Born to be Wild," then he flops back on his bed. "Hit me," he says.

"Here's where we left off: 'When LSD was first discovered, some researchers thought it might be an extremely useful tool in the investigation of psychosis and mental illness.' Okay now what we're going to do is set this next part up as interviews. I'm going to ask you a bunch of questions. Then I'll do one on myself. Teacher will be thrilled by our resourcefulness."

"Resourcefulness, shit. She reads the stuff we say, she'll send out the narc squad to bust us."

"Rudio, it's going to be anonymous. Live research we've gathered from the streets."

"The streets my ass."

Aaron skips a line and prints the next heading neatly across the page. "Got to do this carefully so we don't have to copy this mother over. One draft is all I'm up for." He reads the title: "Personal Interview with LSD User: (confidential)"

Rudy hangs upside down from his bed.

"Quit fucking around. We've got to knock this off before class tomorrow. Ready." He writes the letter Q. in the margin and then prints out his first question. "What's the most LSD you've ever done and what kind?"

"You're serious? You want me to honestly answer these questions?"

"Go," Aaron says and places an A. on the next line.

Rudy straightens up, plants both feet on the floor, his guitar across his knees. "Let me think. Three and half hits. Two orange sunshine, rest black."

"I'm going to put it down like notes. Real authentic." Slowly Aaron asks and Rudy answers, strumming on the guitar each time Aaron stops to write.

"Okay, now I'll quick interview myself." Carefully he enters a new set of questions, prints his responses, all the while humming along with the wash of words floating up from the porch.

Q: *How many times have you done acid?*

A: *Couple hundred*

Q: *How many bad trips?*

A: *Plenty*

A big laugh from below. His mother. A fireworks laugh, bursts of silver—pow, pow, pow. Not a sound he's ever heard her make. He leans toward its shimmer.

Then her voice, dead serious, nightdaynightday, "When Aaron was little he always ..."

He reaches over and pulls the window down.

Aaron steps out on the porch. The boards warm his bare feet. An end of June morning, his first Monday out of school. On the rail he balances a glass of milk with two pieces of toast on top. Strawberry jam drips onto the peeling paint. He stretches out in the old rocker and raises his feet to rest on the edge of the railing. The sun splashes hot across his winter-white chest. He eats and rocks and thinks of nothing.

He goes back inside. The house is quiet. Rudy and Nooley and Tess are still sleeping. Stuck to the fridge, there's a note from Carla: *Store / Peggy's / Happy Vacation, Mamo XXX*. Retrieving a rubber band from the floor, he twists it around his tangle of hair to keep it off his face and flips the oven dial to 300. He pushes open the screen to the back deck. Cold. Not enough meat on his long bony body to insulate him. The morning sun hadn't gotten to this side yet. Fog still hangs in the valley. Down on his knees he reaches under the greenhouse tent he and Rudy made from two old windows. Just room enough to protect six healthy marijuana plants, each a foot and a half tall in their compound buckets. Six beauties grown from excellent seeds. Probably transplant them this weekend, little danger of frost now. Carefully he prunes away two of the smaller lower leaves. Got to stop robbing them though, or they'll be naked by harvest time.

Back inside he places the two leaves on a cookie sheet and slides it in the oven. Papers? He rummages through a can of miscellaneous junk on the counter. Nothing. He checks the leaves, already beginning to wither and curl. He ambles into the living room and pokes through the stuff neatly arranged on the coffee table. Finally he finds a crumpled E Z Wider marking Carla's place in her book. *Lady Chatterley's Lover*. A loan from his mother, no doubt. This friendship between his careful mother and Carla, their bonding during the changing of a flat tire—still trying to fully grok that. He turns down the corner of the page, smoothes out the cigarette paper.

He checks the oven. Smells good. The leaves are brittle. He takes a clean bowl from the drainer and carefully crumbles each of the crisp leaves into a mossy mound. Exactly enough for a generous joint. Next he sticks his notebook under his arm, lifts his guitar out of the case, and with the bowl and cigarette paper in his other hand, maneuvers the door open to step out onto the front porch. Lola, the Morletti's aging beagle, follows. He pulls the rocker over to sit full in the sun. He eats, then creases the paper, drops pinches of flakes up and down the little trench, rolls it tight. Perfect. From his jeans he pulls out a book of matches. *Earn $1000 a month from your home*, it says. He sprawls out. With his bare feet on the rail, he lights up and sucks in. What does he want to do when he grows up? THIS. He rocks and smokes and watches the sun dapple his pale belly. He opens his notebook and reads what he's got so far:

Take my words home
to your point of view
and see them change.
Is your sky close and comforting
or deep and empty?
Is it time to go
or are you stuck?
Do these words seem numb:
a junkie doctor
or a train that never moves?
Mind-surfing ...

His mother's car pulls in. She retrieves a big paper bag from the back seat and starts up the walk toward him. He holds the burning inch-long joint between his thumb and finger, rests his wrist on the seat of the rocker. She doesn't look at his hand. She would never get stoned at 9:30 in the morning.

She rests the bag on the porch steps. "How are you?" she says.

"Fine."

She only wants to know what's *fine*. The few times he remembers starting to tell her anything real, she got that anxious look he hates, the one she always had when his father was silent, when Mark was in trouble. The look that said, Not you too?

"You're up early," she says.

"Yep."

The smell of the burning pot fills the space between them.

"Is Carla around?"

"No, she went to the store."

"I brought over some lasagna. Lots of hot sausage. I thought I'd come by and have dinner with all of you tonight. Only a few more weeks and you're going to be gone."

Months, a few more months.

She lifts the bag and starts for the door. Then she turns back toward him and sets the bag by his chair. "Better still. Could you put it in the fridge after it cools down? Tell Carla I'll come by about six." Halfway to the car, she stops. He knows exactly what she's going to say. "Aaron, did you mail your financial aid application to

Bramley yet?"

"Not yet."

"Aaron ..."

"I'll put it in the mail tomorrow."

"Aaron, if that application..."

"I said," his voice is hard, "I will."

She flinches, then turns and heads down the walk. He doesn't look her way again. He concentrates on his notebook, waits till he no longer hears the car.

Mind-surfing:

The next line slides from his pen:

> *When it gets too rough*
> *lower the sails.*

He draws on what's left of the joint.

July: his Survivor's Benefits run out. He's eighteen and finished with high school, so the government says, That's it. Well, it was sure nice while it lasted. He calls his mother from JAKE's Grocery. Can't sponge off the Morlettis the rest of the summer. "Okay if I stay at the cabin until college starts?"

"If you get a job," she says.

He walks the one mile with his guitar and backpack and crashes in the little side bedroom. He tacks sheets of brown paper to the walls, scrawls stuff he likes:

> *Krsna is the lover of Radna. He displays many amorous*
> *pastimes in the groves of Vrdavana. He is the lover of*
> *of the cowherd maidens, the holder of the great hill*
> *Govardhana, the beloved son of mother Yasoda, the*
> *delighter of the inhabitants of Vraja, and He wanders*
> *the forest along the banks of the river Yamuna.*

Dirty glasses, his Chinese checkerboard with cigarette butts to the rim, wads of discarded works-in-progress, all the clothes he owns, form a moat around his bed.

"As long as I don't see it," his mother says.

"A little disorder's good, frees your compulsions."

"What about the job?" she says.

He hitches to Marwick and fills out applications: bagging groceries at P&C, part-time janitor at a Unitarian Church, ticket taker at the Northside Cinema. Now that she finally has a phone, he lists the number. We'll call if we need you, they say. But they don't. He hangs out the month of July. "I applied a lot of places. I'm waiting for a call."

"The Moores need someone to paint the trim on their house," she says.

So he paints the month of August and he and Rudy play music and tend their crop, smoking it along the way. The night before he leaves for Bramley, she picks him up at Morletti's after he says his final goodbyes.

"Where's your trumpet?" she says.

"Sold it."

Of course she knows he smoked it up. But what can she say, given her own predilections? Instead she gives him anxious advisories about getting to bed early enough so he doesn't miss his morning classes, about having something better for breakfast than M&Ms and Mountain Dew. Her words fill a cartoon bubble floating from her mouth, but he hears only a soft swish of sound lapping against his warm darkness. Tucked in the big pockets of his army jacket, he feels the lovely weight of at least two ounces of very fine homegrown.

20
Holes – 1985

THE MINUTE STEVE PULLED INTO THE YARD, Carla taped the hot-pink flyer to the front of the refrigerator:

Biker Benefit For Muscular Dystrophy
Spinners September 10

Hot enough to screech Steve to a halt on his way to hand her the support money. He stabbed the flyer with his finger and said, "What are you crazy? I better not see your face there."

Then he slammed out. Intent on roaring away on his Harley. Intent on becoming a speck disappearing down that dusty road. He pulled on his gloves and swung onto 1000 lbs. of might. He raised his tight, square body and came down hard with his right foot on the starter. Klisssh. Nothing. He jumped up higher and came down full force again. The engine kicked in, sputtered, quit.

Carla watched from the doorway, smiling.

"Revenge," she said later to Del over coffee. "What's that they say about revenge?"

"It tastes like dirt?"

"No, about it being sweet. Well, when Steve said that to me, you know what I was thinking?"

"Whether you should wear the white top with the fringe or your black undershirt."

"Nothing, I mean nothing's going to keep me away. Imagine. He walks out of here nine months ago. February and half a cord of wood on the porch. After eighteen years, he's feeling encumbered. Only comes to see Rudy and Tess when it suits him. And he still thinks he can roar in here, park his motorcycle in my yard, and tell me what to do?"

"You know what I'm going to say."

"Yes." Carla squeezed her eyes shut, then popped them wide. "You're going to say, 'Do you think going to Spinners is wise?'"

"Well, do you?"

"I can't wait to see his face when he shows up with That Woman. I'm trying to decide how I want to do the scene:

> "Why, Steve, what a surprise, and this must be
> Marion. Then I extend my hand graciously.
>
>   or
>
> I call drunkenly across the bar, 'Well, well, get a
> load of what my old man just dragged in.'"

"Really, Carla, are you going to go?"

"Yes. Want to come?"

"Are you kidding? Just the thought of three hundred bikers and you and Steve and Marion is enough for me. You can tell me the whole juicy story Monday or I'll read about it in the papers. Besides, Richard and I are going to the Fire Department Clam Bake tomorrow."

"Speaking of trips. And you know what else, Del? I'm thinking seriously about getting blasted and entering the wet T-shirt contest."

Saturday Carla got her neighbor to jump-start the Maverick and drove off, grinning. When she pulled up to Spinner's at 3:00, the benefit was already big with hope. She heard the band playing a block away. An Indian summer afternoon with the sun turned on full. The big blacktop parking lot was crowded with bikes and torpedoes. She didn't see Steve or his motorcycle. Bikers and biker women were everywhere—biceps and hair and navels. Well, it ain't the firemen's clam bake.

She pulled into a *NO PARKING* zone and let the car die. Then she tilted the rearview to check herself by sections: black mind-of-its-own hair, dark eyes and pink cheeks, a beautiful smile and nice throat. The white fringed shirt was the right choice, more subtle. She threw the car keys under the seat, folded her T-shirt into her bag, and took a deep breath. Here I come.

On the way from the parking lot to the bar, Carla waved to some people she knew: Jewel, in a long flowered skirt talking to some desperado; Tillie Kuhn, dancing barefoot in the street, and others she'd seen around at the one Harley Rendezvous she'd been permitted to go to with Steve. Steve. But she wasn't ready for chitchat yet.

The band must be on break. Through the open door she heard the whoopees of the crowd above the juke box. As she entered the cool darkness of the bar, she almost bumped into the chest of a man with a tattoo on his weight-lifter arm that said *NAM*. A man with flowing gray hair and interested eyes. He turned aside and with a broad flourish, bid her enter. "Well, well, well," he said, looking at her with approval. She flashed him her smile and swept on to the bar. She wasn't ready for that either, but later, definitely later. The bar was three deep and already the floor was splashed with beer from the two kegs pumping to a steady lineup. She went to the end where she knew she could catch the bartender's notice.

"Carla. How you doing?"

"Good, Charlie, real good. I'd like a shot of tequila."

Charlie turned, and without looking, lifted the bottle from the pyramid backed by big smoky mirrors. Biker bars—you could count on the jar of sausage, on the sign that said, *You don't have to go home, but you can't stay here.* Charlie upended a shot glass in front of Carla and poured to the rim. "On the house, one bartender to another," he said.

"Much obliged." She downed half the shot. A warm rush of heat hit her belly. "Whooee. Fire."

"You still working at the Edgewater?"

"Two nights a week. I close Fridays. Ugh."

"Know what you mean. Catch you later."

Carla shut her eyes and swallowed the rest. A muffled blast exploded under her ribs, bliinnnged to her groin, her breasts, the tips of her ears. Okay. Ready. She floated out. People everywhere. Standing around their iron horses, their hogs: Sportsters, Panheads, Triumphs. A 1940s Indian. Standing around sucking up the sun and bullshitting. Bullshitting full dress vs. stripped, Gull wings vs. V 65s.

Bullshitting drugs and speed and sex. Carla wandered around in a happy haze. Sometimes as she passed a group, someone offered her a joint, "Toke?" No sign of Steve. She was glad and not glad. The sun was so big and hot, didn't seem right to waste it on revenge. Now and then she felt NAM in the distance, felt him watching.

By 9:00, from a mixture of tequila, dope, and friendly nips out of tendered flasks, she was on the edge of drunk. On the brink of shit-faced. Drum roll. Time for the WET T-SHIRT CONTEST. Line up to get splashed. Why not? With much concentration Carla managed to get into the ladies room, to get her blouse unbuttoned, to get her bra off, to get the sleeveless white T-shirt over her head, her arms in the right holes.

Back in the bar she saw Jewel in the line. Jewel looked blurred. Carla found her way to the end. Through the haze, she tried to decipher the scene: a roped off ring, crowds around the edges, drum rolls, a tall blonde in a transparent T-shirt steps into a spotlighted circle, she turns, stretches out her long white arms, shimmies, hoots and hollers, she disappears. Another woman and another. Strange. Next. Carla's turn. She gave her name and they pinned a 6 on her back. She didn't feel so good. "Lift your hair," said the girl as she began to squirt water at her. My god, it was cold. To make the nipples stand out. Could she back down now?

Then she saw Steve. There was no one with him. She took in air. Drum rolls. She walked out into the spotlight and turned to the background beat of *Ripple*. She looked at Steve and laughed. He smiled. The man with the interested eyes was right behind him. Carla raised her arms and clapped them above her head, then walked off to cheers. It was all pretty unfocused.

She couldn't find her clothes or bag in the Ladies Room. Forget it. Drink anymore and you'll puke. She glanced at herself in the mirror. Not subtle. She pulled the moist T-shirt away from her skin, pushed at her hair, and went out. They were just announcing the winners. Coffee. That's what she wanted—coffee. She heard her number. "Number six. Please come forward." She was no longer in the mood for this. Thick. Numb.

Just then someone touched her lightly on the arm. "Aren't you going to collect your prize?" It was the man with the NAM tattoo, covered now by a dark blue shirt. "You won second place." Carla leaned against the end of the bar, tried to work her way up through the heaviness.

"Are you all right?"

"Hey, where's the pretty lady who won second place? Number six?" a voice on the speaker called.

"Here, let me help you. Then some air. My name's Murphy." He put his hand under her elbow, led her to the spotlight. She took the prizes—a small bottle and a shiny box.

"Congratulations."

Carla faked a smile. Murphy moved her toward the door and got his jacket. She saw Steve's face signaling some message she couldn't decode. She followed Murphy outside. A light mist of rain, but the air felt good.

"Put this on," he said. She did. He pushed her prizes down into the pockets and zipped her up. Then he lit a cigarette and handed it to her.

Just what she needed. "You'd make somebody a good father," Carla said.

Murphy laughed a laugh that filled the street. "First time anybody ever told me that. Looks like you're feeling better. Want to take a little sober-up walk around the block?"

Carla reached out to shake his hand. "Murphy, I'm Carla. Carla Morletti."

Murphy backed away a little, gave her a close look. "Any relation to Steve?" he motioned toward Spinners. "Steve Morletti? Not his wife, I hope."

"Separated," she said. "Do you know Marion?"

Just then the door to Spinners opened. Steve. This time she recognized the look—worry. Well, well. He motioned to Murphy. "I'd like to have a few words with my wife."

Murphy leaned toward her, became larger.

Carla moved between them. "It's okay," she said. She stepped off the curb and leaned against one of the cars, the jacket pulled down over her rear. Things were still a bit wobbly, but a lot less blurred.

"I'll be right by the door," Murphy said and disappeared inside.

Steve lit a cigarette and gave her one of his shrugs, the one that always made her want to hit him. Gave her his *How can you be so dumb?* twist of the mouth.

"Where's your little friend, Steve?"

He flinched. "Carla, do you know who you're with? He's ... he's ... a very unstable person."

Carla pulled the prize bottle out: tequila. She unscrewed the cap, took a hefty drink and stifled a cough. She extended the bottle toward Steve. "Let's drink to your sudden and deep concern for my welfare."

"Don't be a bitch," Steve said. "Looks to me like you've already had more than enough."

"Really?"

"Carla, this is serious. This person is unpredictable. Vietnam did something heavy-duty to his head."

Rain now. Hard rain. Carla moved past Steve and pulled the door to Spinners open. "I hope you're going to get it together to come see Tess and Rudy Sunday. Breaks their hearts when you don't show up."

Murphy was right where he said he'd be. She handed him the bottle. "Revenge," she said, "you know what they say about revenge."

He took a long swallow, emptied the bottle. "'Nothing which we don't invite,'" he said and together they moved toward the bar.

"And, oh, Del, if only I had left right after I'd landed that parting punch at Steve. Gone to my car, slept it off in the back seat ... But ... "

"I feel a little queasy already," Del said. "I can't imagine what you felt like Sunday morning."

"Don't," Carla said, pressing her hands to her temples. "Anyway things are going along good. Murphy being charming, lighting my cigarettes, laughing at my wit, etcetera. Steve has disappeared himself after telling me how dangerous Murphy is ..."

Del stopped laughing. "Carla, who is this Murphy?"

"Of course, he's got a few loose wires. What else are you going to meet at a biker bar? If I wanted respectability, I'd have gone to the clam bake."

"Carla?"

"He's a forty-five-year-old Vietnam vet on full disability who's on a double dose of lithium to keep his head together."

Del set her cup down carefully. "Why get involved with someone like that?"

Carla watched Del closely. "Why did you get involved with Lee?"

Del searched the top of the table. Then she said, "I was seventeen."

"How about Dugan?" Del didn't answer. "Same old story, Del. Like that book you gave me. Like Lady Chatterley. Remember when she's looking in the mirror at her body, after she hasn't slept with anybody for a long time. Remember how dried up she feels. So I meet Murphy."

"Okay, I know the story."

"The guy who wrote that book understood. Anyway, I haven't *seen* Murphy crazy. You never believe it until it happens."

"Till he takes you by the throat."

"Del, remember I told you how my father treated my mother, how he controlled her. I watched that. There was always a kind of terrible sameness about it: his mean voice, her tears, his big hands grabbing her. Her whimper. I hated him and I hated her for not fighting back."

Carla rose. She stretched her hand up and gave the carved bird hanging from the ceiling a little push. It glided back and forth and then began to spin. She dumped the coffee dregs in the garbage, then lifted the burner grates from the top of the stove and threw them in the dishwater. She began to scrub each one. "No one's *ever* going to do that to me."

"How do you know?"

"Because I'm not afraid. Because when they look at me crazy, I look crazy right back. I see my father in their eyes and I've still got a dose of venom saved up. I'm ready."

"So then what happened?"

"Next thing I know I'm in the car, kind of draped over the steering wheel and Murphy is banging on the windshield, but in a friendly manner, though very drunk. And he's saying, 'Carla, unlock the car.' Now this is very strange because I don't remember locking the doors. It's something I never do. But there I am on the inside so unless some fairy godmother sees me drunk and stashes me for protection until I come to my senses, I must've done it. I think some animal instinct made me lock up before I passed out, probably all those stories about biker gang bangs."

"Weren't you frightened?"

"No. So I open the door. We talk about going to Nick's for breakfast. This is fantasy. It's pouring rain. There is no way my car will start without a jump. I don't feel good. Somehow we get the lunatic idea that we'll go on Murphy's Harley. We find it. Even this is almost beyond us. The bike starts—which is truly amazing. I hop on the back and away we go. At least it has stopped raining and Murphy goes slow."

"Carla, you are making this up."

"I wish. Not too far down the road I know that I'm going to be sick. Somehow I convince Murphy to pull over. Imagine puking into the wind. We're on the edge of the woods. I get Murphy's jacket off and to him before I start to throw up. I'm good and sick and he's nice enough to keep his distance, saying, 'I'm right here if you need anything.' Eventually I feel better, but not much. I am cold and reeking. 'How about a hot shower and a warm bed?' Murphy says. Never has anything sounded so good. And we tool right over to The Holiday Inn."

Del placed her hands over her ears.

"It is now maybe 3 a.m. We go in. Only the night clerk is there. Thank god. Think what we looked like, Del. He doesn't bat an eye. Treats us like we're normal. A shower. Sheets. Comfort. We both pass out. That's the story."

"So what was the other prize?"

Carla lifted a box from the top of the refrigerator. She took off the lid and held the contents before Del's eyes: a pair of black silk bikini underwear—stitched on the crotch, Harley wings; embroidered in scarlet, *You've had the best.* "So tell me, how was the firemen's clam bake?"

All that fall every week or two Murphy drove his Harley up over Bear Spring mountain to stay at Carla's. He'd pull in unannounced with a case of Genesee and a bag of groceries on the back. More often than not Carla was happy for the company and the food because times were hard. At 110,000, the Maverick served what might be its final notice. And one day when it was full to the brim with every heavy dark thing in the house, the washing machine stopped spinning. For days anyone who wanted jeans, a sweat shirt, or a pair of socks had to reach down into the icy waters to search. "It's every man for himself," Carla said.

Getting to the Edgewater Tuesdays and Fridays and getting home again sometimes took most of the morning to arrange. "It's a test," Carla said, "but at least the kids are in school." Rudy in his senior year, Tess in sixth. Then, that very day, the bus dropped them off early.

"Cooties," Tess said.

"What are you talking about?"

"Not us," said Rudy, "but a lot of kids. They're closing down till Monday."

"What next?" Carla said heavenward.

On days like this, the roar of Murphy's bike was welcome. But Rudy and Tess were wary. Murphy was sometimes jumpy and silent. When Carla said, Bring in wood and they didn't, Murphy spoke, Didn't you hear your mother? Murphy was the first man Carla ever brought home. Their shoulders and elbows said, We don't like him much. Carla's chin said, Tough.

When Murphy came, sometimes they went for walks in the woods and he pointed out buck rubs and explained to her the glacial contours of the valley. But more often he sat around and drank beer and he and Carla played gin into the night. Murphy's medication put him on a strange edge and a funny schedule. He couldn't sleep and when he did, he had horrible jungle dreams. Sometimes Carla woke in the darkness to see him shaking in the rocker beside the bed, his body wet with sweat. "Murphy, are you all right?"

"Go back to sleep," he said from some distant swamp. Then he slept most of the day.

Carla was always an early riser, had prided herself on getting up in the dark to make eggs for Steve all those years. Murphy's schedule went against her grain. On those mornings when he slept heavily in the bed upstairs and after Rudy and Tess went off to school, Carla brought a quilt down. With this wrapped around her on the couch and a cup of tea on the table, she read, really read for the first time since she ran away with Vicky when she was fifteen. Now on those cold fall mornings while Murphy slept, Carla went through the stack of books piled by the couch. "Give me some more stuff by men who get it," she said to Del. So she read *Madame Bovary.* "How about some stories by women?" Carla said. And she read Grace Paley.

Sometimes she copied down words she liked: *miasmic, voracious, skew.* "How do you say this word, Del?" and she'd point to the list taped to her door. She started writing about what she was thinking and she hid the notebook under a board in the upstairs hall. Some days she said, "Is this it?"

Early one morning while Murphy slept, she took her coffee out to the back deck. The rickety floor was cold under her slippers. Air blew her thin gown around her ankles. A white frost covered the grass that sloped below the porch and rolled down the valley below. She pulled her robe close, cupped her hands around the hot mug. The steam warmed her face. A few rays of cold sun cut through the trees on the hill across the way, sparkled on the frost.

How long had she lived here? Ever since Tess was two. Nine years since they left California to make a new life in the country. She and Steve never really changed things, but they'd started over a lot. She looked at the doghouse where Tess wrote the words L OL A above the door. At their old gingerbread farmhouse that Steve painted halfway up but never finished when he got to the scalloped clapboards. Steve.

Then she heard them. If there had been any doubt the verdict was now final: WINTER.

She looked up. Flying almost directly above her head and low. She saw the movement of their wings, their long necks stretched in flight. Maybe two hundred in a long dark V, with another line of fifty or more beating to catch up. A few stragglers. She set her cup on the window sill and spread her arms out above her head. Her robe and gown blew softly back. She fluttered her fingers and danced across the floor almost to the edge. "Take me with you," she called. Then she dropped her arms and watched them disappear.

Murphy got up earlier than usual and in foul humor, but she didn't pay him much mind. She stood at the sink and washed the dishes and thought about Emma Bovary.

"I'm heading home," he said. "My disability check comes tomorrow. And I go to Long Island to the V.A. for my yearly evaluation next week."

"Bye," Carla said. "Drive carefully."

Once Carla asked, "Want to meet Murphy?"

Del declined. She passed by Carla's every day on her way home from school. If Murphy's bike was parked in the yard, she didn't stop.

Right from the beginning Carla said, "It's not a heavy-duty sexual thing. He's company." Oh ... and, of course, it pissed Steve off.

Then one Saturday Del got a call. "Del, we're supposed to be at Reese's wedding at two."

Del's clock said 2:15. "You're not going to make it."

"Murphy can't get his Harley going. Rudy and Tess are already over there with Steve. Could you give us a ride?"

When Del pulled up to Carla's, Murphy was kicking his motor-cycle. A muscled man in a pure white sleeveless undershirt and pol-ished black boots. Carla was swinging in an old tire caught by a thick rope that hung from a limb far up in the old maple. Her flowered skirt sailed behind her. In the background the bondoed body of the long-faithful Maverick. It reminded Del of a Salem ad. Sort of.

Carla waved and dropped her cigarette in the dirt. Murphy stopped kicking the bike. He got in the front seat. Carla in back. "Murphy, I want you to meet my friend, Del. She's the one who's writing that poem about women and men I read you."

Murphy nodded.

"How they don't even speak the same language." Carla squeezed Del's shoulder. "My sentiments exactly. Better take the back way."

Murphy brushed the dust from his jeans.

Del started the car and put her left blinker on even though no-body was coming. Richard thought this was funny, to signal when there were no cars.

Carla leaned over the seat to check the clock. "By the time we get there the wedding will be over. They'll be drinking and the band will be playing. Good timing, eh? At least Marion's not going to be there; Steve's got some sense of decency."

"Hmmm," Del said as she turned onto Cobb's Road. Amazing the power of this man's silence, and talky-talky Carla must be registering this as well.

She tried to get something on the radio, but ever since she made the last payment, she had to either play it at full volume or listen to static. Richard said it was a contact problem. She switched it off. "It's probably fastest to go up Ostawa," Del said and shifted the car into 2. She finally had the rhythm of this engine.

"So you write poems," Murphy said.

He speaks. She had expected his voice to be lower. "Well, mostly I draw, but lately I've been doing some … writing."

"Do you like men?"

She laughed and shifted back to D as they crested the hill. "Do you want a yes or no answer?" No reply. She glanced at his silent profile. "I thought I gave women and men about equal time."

"Ball busting," he said, still looking straight ahead.

Del tried the radio again, but when she turned the select dial, it crackled.

Carla broke in. "Say the one you said for me the other day, Del— the one about being crazy. Not anything anybody would figure coming from respectable Ms. Merrick. Say it 'cause I got a surprise for you."

Del slowed for the curve.

"Yeah," Murphy said, "do me something. Do me something." He did a drum roll on the dashboard.

Del jumped. He had nice hands.

"Come on, Del, say that one."

"Carla … it's pretty … provocative."

Murphy turned, leaned toward her. "Provocate me," he said.

Del swallowed. Here she was speeding down the Ostawa being asked to recite an angry poem to Carla's latest angry boyfriend. What the hell. "The name of this poem is *You Are*." Her voice reminded her of the time she did *My Old Dog Tray* back in fourth grade.

"Some, the morning after, join the army or the Jehovah Witnesses.

'Let somebody else deal with for a while, man, I'm tired.'

'Think I'll hole up till the millennium. It's Dangerous out there.'

Amen!

Some rave: Big fists banging on the Big door 'Hey, who the hell's in charge. I'm pissed.'

And if one of *them* says, '*You* are,' you can always freak which'll getcha 14 days off and make it clear you aren't putting up with any of this Personal Responsibility bullshit …"

Del hesitated, best to end there. God knows where this was going. But Carla poked her in the shoulder. "Go on, go on, you're getting to the best part."

"Yeah," Murphy said.

Del shifted back into overdrive at the bottom of the hill. Another block and she could eject these two and return to her own well-ordered universe. She took a breath, and forged on:

"No doubt you're saying, 'Whew, this certainly isn't me.'

Okay, so you and Sid Vicious don't trick or treat in the same space. And you don't make your exit on a Harley, wearing leather emblazoned UpYoursQuietlyDesperateAtLeast I'veGotBalls."

Del paused again.

"Come on, you didn't get to the shopping cart yet," Carla said, urging her on as though if she goes a few more feet, she'll score.

She pulled into the parking lot of the Carriage House. A blue and white striped tent full of people sat under the trees. The music played.

"That's enough of that," Murphy said and stepped onto the blacktop.

Silence.

Murphy hesitated; then he leaned into the car and gave Del a long look. He closed the door and walked away. They watched Murphy—his white shirt, his boots shining—as he moved toward the tent.

"Carla, what were you thinking asking me to say that poem?"

"Oh, him. I was going to surprise you by joining in on the last part.

Why that poem, that poem is something I can dance to. Ready?"
With that Carla began:

> "But don'tcha wanna come clean? Declare the mind-mines
> you're patrolling, the bombers you've got on alert, how often
> you take your cart to the Mall of Life and fill it up with nothing."

Carla motioned Del to join her for the finale:

> "Who's the drummer in your Looney Tune Band?"

"You are," they said.

"Gin. Read 'em and weep," Carla said as she fanned out her cards
on the kitchen table. "Royal flush besides." She wrote down her
points. "That's the game even without your hand. Let me see your
money." She made the gimme sign beneath Murphy's nose. Murphy's
only response was to withdraw slightly as he continued to rest his
head heavily on his fists amid a dozen crushed Genesee cans. Carla
checked the clock. 2 a.m. Surely he would sleep now. She wanted to
get up early. Since Murphy got back from the V.A. evaluation, he
wavered between morose and nasty. Quite a while ago she had second thoughts and mixed feelings when she heard the Harley roar in
uninvited. There's more to life than Gin and Genesee.

"Cheer up, Murphy. You remind me of that shirt of Rudy's: 'Life
sucks and then you die'." Sometimes Murphy's silence got to her,
urged her against her better judgment to prod him.

"Murphy, you know what I think?"

Murphy looked up. "What do you think, Carla?"

She felt the jolt. Watch your mouth, my dear. Not now. Not now.
Carla carefully gathered up all the cards, shuffled them, placed them
in the box.

"What do you think, Carla?"

"I think you drink too much. I think whatever they've got you on
now is messing up your mind."

Murphy lowered his arms. He grew larger. The muscles of his face
hardened. She knew now he would stand up. Murphy lifted his body

and pushed the stool back with his legs. It scraped against the floor. Carla stayed in her chair. He placed his hands flat on the table and leaned toward her. His eyes were two dark holes.

My father. The eyes her mother pleaded to. Her body tightened. She returned his stare, unblinking and neutral.

Neither of them moved.

She saw his body give.

She reached forward and touched his hand. "I'm going to bed," she said. "There are blankets on the couch."

Slowly she went upstairs. She stopped in the hall to listen to the breathing of her son and daughter. In the morning there will be a way to end things with Murphy. She closed her door and slid the bolt hard into its socket. Leaning back against the frame, she spoke to the darkness that would soon be morning, "I am not her. Remember that."

21
Castanets – 1985

AT 1 A.M. Route 205 is empty. Del drives. Carla sits in the darkness with the directions to the Nassau County Jail on her lap, ready to switch on the light to tell what bridge, what exit, what lane.

Carla's voice startles the silence. "Just as he goes out the door I remind him, 'Rudy, be smart. No trouble. Think.'" She begins to poke around in her purse. She searches her pockets. She starts to grope under the seat.

"What?" Del says.

"Matches."

Del pushes in the lighter.

"Busted," Carla says, the cigarette between her lips, ready. "Nineteen, and he gets busted at a Dead concert." For a second both women are caught in the glow from the lighter's fiery tip. "Del, what if I couldn't have borrowed the money from you to make bail? What if you hadn't been able to drive me? I know this much: His father's coming up with the money for the lawyer."

"Carla, Rudy said they're treating him okay."

"It might be better if they knocked a little sense into him."

Wells Bridge, Franklin, Walton. Everyone is sleeping. They do not see a single car. Carla smokes. Del watches for deer. She knows they come from the side, from nowhere. Both feel the strangeness of being the only ones out in the world. They do not talk. Just the back and forth, back and forth of the windshield wipers. Each worries her own private pain, like a hole in a tooth, touching it again and again, wondering at its size. Roscoe. East. New York—117 miles. They make the turn onto 17. Still no traffic. Del spreads out a little, pushes back in the seat, flexes her fingers on the wheel. She can be on cruise for a few hours. They float through the night. Every now and then a big truck passes, pulls them as it rumbles by.

From the stillness, Carla speaks, "I figured it out. When God told Eve she's going to be punished by having pain when she brings forth children, I thought that just meant birth. No, Baby. It means this." She spreads her arms to gather all of the distance, everything from her bed a few hours ago in Danford to the Nassau County Jail. And everything before and beyond that.

"Del, if you had known that screwing in the backseat of a Pontiac when you were fourteen …"

"I was not screwing anywhere when I was fourteen. Ronnie Legler was dry humping me in the dark on our living room couch. A Catholic boy who sweated a lot while he was involved in an almost mortal sin. And I was filled with guilt about messing up a beautiful experience and fear that he wouldn't respect me."

"Fucked up," Carla says.

"I kept my clothes on until I was twenty-one. Finally they came off because I was too exhausted to hold on to them any longer."

Carla rolls this around in her brain. Her clothes have been off since eighth grade. Not to say it went well. Mostly she knew crazy people not too far along in the art of living. "Okay. Del, if you had known that getting laid at twenty-one would lead to this," again she gathers the space in her fingers, "would it have made any difference?"

"No," Del says and turns on the radio.

But Carla knows Del's cool no to her question is just Del running away to some other room in her mind. Mothers. Motherhood. How? Not like her mother. Carla guesses she loved her mother back then, but it's been hard to forgive her for not protecting her and her brothers. But where did she go wrong with Rudy? Hasn't she tried to keep him safe from the world? Right from the start; back when she was seventeen and she and Steve were living crazy, doing anything that turned up. Staying with a for-sure-insane artist and sleeping in his closet. She remembered when she got her first contraction. She was standing in that six-by-six room, painting a window on the wall, with Steve asleep almost under her feet.

She nudged him with a toe. "Time my pains," she said.

Steve jumped up like he'd been shot, almost knocked over the blue paint for the sky.

"I haven't got a watch," he said.

"Well, then count because I'm not going to the hospital until I get in a yellow sun and some tree branches and you put up these curtains."

When she got the next contraction, she only had the leaves to do. Steve stood behind her counting and rubbing her back and begging her to go to the emergency room.

"Go call the taxi," she said. "By the time it gets here, I'll be done."

The day she brought Rudy home, the closet looked like a little nursery—peach walls with a big window and curtains covered with fuzzy ducks. He was a beautiful baby, with lots of dark hair and big black eyes. "I'm going to take good care of you," she told him. And she did. Except for that one terrible winter in Oregon. She'd kept him safe. They'd grown up together, and if anyone messed with him, school or street, she had straightened them out. She was not like her mother. But now Steve's living in Utica with someone else and her first born is in jail. What had all her fierce protection come to?

And Del knows her quick no to Carla's "would it have made any difference?" is not the way it is. Knows her instant negative is a way to close the lid. She's already crammed all that stuff in a box labeled *Mother-Love No Matter What.* Anyway we can't do things differently. No point looking back.

But lately, at forty-five, she almost wonders. Driving to school last June, end of the year, 1. 2. 3. on her mind, up ahead two robins standing in the road. She knew the birds would fly up and away when the car got a little closer. The car came up on them; she started to brake when she saw a small foot raised in the air to take the next step. Babies, dumb baby robins, with half-ready breast feathers, walking across the road. They flew up just as the car reached them. She heard the soft thud of their bodies. In the rearview mirror—two small heaps on the black road. She thought of the thousands of up and down trips the mother robin made. Tears. By the time she drove up the hill to school, *15 mph Children Crossing*, she was sobbing. She sat in the parking lot, her arms folded across the wheel, her forehead resting on the backs of her hands, and cried like she had not cried for years. Cried for her children. For herself. The inexorable guilt.

But mostly for Mark. When he was little, his sharp shoulders, his raised pointed chin, always sticking out just enough to register his complaint. Mark, refusing to go mum on the periphery of his father's silence. Once Lee snatched him by the arm, lifted him from his seat to dangle above the refused scrambled eggs while she stood paralyzed and mute, while his brother stared into his plate. The rest of the silent breakfast Mark ate the cold eggs with his left hand, his thin white arm, as though disconnected from his body, motionless on the blue plastic cloth, the five red marks turned toward them. He kept making them see: This is happening; this is happening. She repaid him with anger.

That winter when Mark was five, they had moved to the tiny apartment in Marwick after she had gathered enough energy to leave Lee the first time. Gathered, from the despair of two or three binges running into each other as regularly as Friday night paychecks, enough … enough *flight* … to pack up what she and Aaron and Mark needed. To carry the boxes up the stairs, trip after trip, to unload in the dark furnished rooms. Mark's cries woke her every night. Exhausted from hard days at school and late nights of marking papers, she groped her way to his room. She would not turn on the light.

He would be sitting in his wet bed. His pajamas, his sheets, often even the blankets soaked. She would not speak. She would lift the child from the bed and stand him on the linoleum. In the dark she would yank off the clammy bedding, wipe the rubber cover, put on dry sheets. Finally she would pull off his wet clothes and maneuver him into another pair of pajamas. She would place him back in the bed and leave the room. Often in a few hours Mark's crying would wake her again. Again she would stumble to the little dark bedroom. The child, the bed, wet once more. She never yelled at him, but each snap of his pajamas was an accusation.

Now Mark calls collect from a pay phone. He has lots of credit: his father's suicide, the way his own mother lifted him from the bed.

I've just been mugged.

I'm in Port Authority and I have no place to sleep.

I don't want to be anywhere anymore.

He means, You are responsible for me.

Some days she can answer, I'm sorry. Other days she unplugs the phone.

Carla and Del going down Route 17 in the middle of a rainy November night, trying to find their way. Del drives and Carla peers through the darkness. Out the black window, Carla sees colonies of weathered bungalows closed for the winter. The sign says *Liberty Next Exit*. The radio plays a soft fuzz in the night. She turns to Del, senses she's crying. Carla leans toward her. "Are you all right? You sure you don't want me to try to drive?"

Del sniffles, laughs. "No, scared as I am, it's better I do it. Have you got a tissue?"

Carla searches, pulls out some Kleenex. "Do you want to tell me?"

"Oh … just thinking," she blows her nose, "how it's so not like I thought it would be—all of us decorating the tree on Christmas Eve, singing carols and joking around while we string popcorn."

"So you don't want to talk about it?"

"I feel okay now. What I want is a cup of coffee. Where are we? What time is it?" She hands Carla her watch, realizes she's been on automatic for a while. She rolls her shoulders, stretches her legs.

Carla switches on the light. "2:30." She pours Del coffee from the thermos between them. "The last sign said Liberty. I'm almost out of cigarettes."

"There's a diner just beyond Middletown, not too far. We can stop there." Del notices it isn't raining, turns off the wipers.

"I was thinking about mothers," says Carla. "Bringing up kids."

Del turns from the wheel slightly, catches Carla's eyes, laughs again. "Jeez, Carla. Maybe it'd be more comforting to sink into a father-topic: inflation or the hostages, how much gas mileage I get with my car."

"Yeah, right. Really, I was thinking about my mother." Del turns off the radio. "About how pissed I am. I wish one of those times when my father came at her, she'd had a gun ready and as she'd backed out the door with us right behind her, she'd said, No more, you bastard, no more. And that we'd gotten in the car and driven away forever. But since he died … I don't know. Maybe it doesn't matter as much. It's not like I've forgotten, but well … what a couple of sad cases, my parents." Carla reaches over and turns the radio back on, tunes in a station.

"Rock 107 where the music is right all night. How are you doing out there, you strange people?"

"Great," Carla says to the radio. "Jim Dandy." She flicks on the light for a minute, glances down at herself, over at Del and puts them back into darkness. She reaches in her bag and pulls out a brush. "We look pretty bummed. Living proof of parental neglect." She attacks her hair, wild black curls that refuse authority. She tucks in her shirt. "What's that you're wearing?"

Del has on a long underwear top that she sleeps in and jeans. The back of the cabin is cold and damp in November. The wood stove doesn't do much in the bedroom. Over that she has on one of Richard's wool shirts. It was there on the hook by the door when she rushed out at twelve. Rushed out to get Rudy's message to Carla: Rudy's being held at the Nassau jail; he tried to call, but the phone company said your phone was disconnected. Please come and bring at least five hundred for a bail bondsman. Del checks her clothes. "Don't worry I've got something else for when we see the police."

"So if it's 2:30 now, what time you think we'll get to Mineola?"

Del figures with her fingers on the wheel: 12:30 to 1:30 … "Probably get there around 5:30 or 6." She pushes the car to 65 just thinking about what the Cross Bronx will be like at 6:30. She's never done that kind of driving. She's only been a passenger in rush hour and the only way she's dealt with even being in a car that was doing 60, five feet behind another car, in the middle of four solid lanes, with suicidal maniacs weaving in and out, plus horns and occasional obscenities, was to close her eyes, fold her hands in her lap, and center on breathing.

She's felt mostly okay until now. Since Roscoe, the only evidence of another world beyond this highway is an occasional glimpse of a little side road snaking its way through a break in the scrubby oaks. Otherwise it has been just Carla, Del, and the truckers, and many of them are asleep in their semis, lined up in the rest stops, their engines running, the cabs outlined by lights.

Now suddenly they hit signs of civilization: Arthur Glick Truck Sales, Monticello Racetrack with a moving neon sign—a sulky driver whips the horse on and on and on. Carla lights up her last cigarette, wads the package and throws it into her purse, "I'm ready to get out, walk around for a minute, pee."

"It's coming right up, but we can only stay a few minutes. We have to get to the Cross Bronx before it starts pounding."

Just beyond Middletown, The Quick Way Diner appears. Del pulls in front of the seen-better-days Quonset and they fold out. Like leaving a dark movie, nothing is real. They go in. It is exactly as they knew it would be—the chrome, the Formica, the fluorescent lights. Behind the counter, leaning against the cooler, the plump old-gal waitress who does understand. The tired truckers, drinking it black out of heavy cups banded with blue. Even the one lone piece of lemon pie under a scratched plastic cover—the meringue shrinking from crayon-yellow cream, beads of egg white sweat on its stiff tan swirls.

The only thing out of place is a young girl who sits at the far end of the counter. Carla and Del both register her: maybe sixteen, punk, a disheveled Mohican growing out maroon, black everything—leather, boots, pants, eyeliner—except for a white satin scarf that wraps round her neck and furls down her back. Carla and Del go into the bathroom. When they come out, the girl is gone. They are relieved. Carla gets cigarettes and a can of Coke; Del, milk. Five minutes and they are back in the car.

"Do you have the directions?" Del asks.

Carla lifts them from the dashboard and places them back in her lap. "Yep."

"Well, start getting ready to navigate. It's going to be tricky real soon." Del pulls onto 17. Neither of them mentions the girl in the diner. It's busier now.

NEW YORK THRUWAY – Toll Booths 1 mile.

Just the sign is enough to trigger a reaction in Del's body: sweat on her palms, pulsing on either side of her throat, saliva gone, a rock wedged under her ribs. She sits up straight and turns off the radio. It's a switch from one place to another.

"What's up?" Carla says, leaning forward.

"Nothing. I see a Thruway sign and my brain broadcasts emergency to my entire body." Del takes slow, regular breaths.

"Do you want me to try and drive?"

"No, it's better I do it."

And then off to the right, standing with her thumb out, the girl from the diner. Carla looks at Del, her eyes straight ahead, hands at 10 and 2 on the wheel. Though Carla already knows, she says to Del, "What do you think?"

"I think I am close enough to freaking as is." Del slows. They pass the girl.

"Karma," Carla says.

"Yeah, but what kind?" She thinks of Mark and pulls over. They see the girl running for the car. "Tell her I'm going to get in that middle lane and stay there. I can't let her out except where I feel comfortable stopping."

Carla rolls down the window as the girl comes even with the car. "Where you headed?" Carla hollers above the sound of a passing truck.

"Anywhere," the girl answers.

"We're going to Mineola. We can't let you out except when there isn't much traffic and it's easy to get off."

The girl opens the back door and gets in. Carla moves around in the seat so she can really see this kid. "You understand that?" she says.

"Yeah."

Del moves back onto the highway. "Give me some change. I don't think it's a ticket."

Carla hands her some quarters. She has a fistful ready. They pull into a booth and Del drops 75 cents in the basket. The green light goes on.

NEW YORK - 40 miles

This is it. The traffic is different. Steady. Lots of out-of-state cars. New cars. Food trucks and milk tanks going to feed the city. Del feels the pressure to get up to 60, to stay there. Otherwise she becomes an island in the moving river. When she feels she can do two things at once, drive and speak, with her eyes still riveted to road she says, "What time is it?"

"4:15. How are you doing?"

"Okay. Now turn on the light for a minute and just give me a quick rundown of the directions."

Lights. Carla smiles at the girl, but gets no response. Then she studies the paper for a minute. "Okay, we're going to go across the Tappan Zee Bridge; that will take us to Yonkers where the Thruway turns into the Major Deegan. Then we take the Cross Bronx Expressway ..."

Del interrupts, "Bad idea. You can turn off the lights. I know the Tappan Zee's next. After we cross there, just tell me the one that comes after that."

From the darkness a voice speaks, "I know the way to Mineola. I can tell you ahead of time when we're coming to those points, tell you what lanes, and when you have to get over."

"No shit," Carla says, laughing.

"No shit," the girl responds.

Del's body gives a little.

"What's your name?" says Carla.

"Janice."

"Are you in some kind of trouble?"

"Nothing like that," she says and looks out the window.

Carla sees this, but she holds the connection a little longer. "We're on our way to the Nassau County Jail. My son just got busted at a Dead concert."

Janice still looks out the window. "I know the way. I'll tell you in plenty of time," is all she says.

And that's the way it is. They cross the Tappan Zee where the road dips them down low into a cement trough, with Yonkers rising above them. Still in this trough, they hit the Cross Bronx. The traffic is pounding now with the concrete wall one foot from her fender. Del grips the wheel and keeps the car at the same speed as everybody else, saying over and over in her head, godhelpme godhelpme. They streak by miles and miles of trash: fast food cups boxes bags sodden newspapers an old athletic sweater a black lace slip. Janice does what she says; she knows it cold. Finally, at the Throgs Neck, they break free, rise up from below, see the lights of the city. The traffic thins and Del breathes. Then east on the L.I.E.

"This'll be good," Janice says. "I'll get off anywhere along here that you can pull over."

Carla and Del look out to the "anywhere along here." There is nothing but dark and highway and sleeping houses across a gully.

"You just stay in this lane. Mineola's the next right."

"You need money?" Carla says.

"No."

Del sees a pull-in, checks the rear, and swings over. There's a flash of satin, the jingle of jewelry. As Janice opens the door, Del reaches to touch her sleeve, but doesn't. "Thank you, Janice," she says.

The girl steps out and then leans back in a little. To Carla she says, "Your son'll be okay. It's a big bust. Probably a Nassau narc in tie-dye says, 'Got a hit.' A setup, makes a lot of money for the county. He'll get a fine, but that's all that's going down." To Del she says, "Be easy," and smiles. She closes the door.

They watch her jump the guard rail, watch the white scarf disappear down the slope. They sit for a moment, let go. Del moves the car back onto the road.

"Well, she sure knows the way to Mineola," says Del.

"She knows a lot, but she doesn't know the way," Carla's hands gather the spaces again, "she doesn't know the way from Mineola to where we are."

And they can't tell her.

"Okay. Are you ready for this one?" Carla says.

Del giggles. "I'm ready."

"Could you be sixteen again?"

"Well. At last. Finally you give me one I can do." Definitive and eloquent. Just tell sixteen to sashay her sweet can in here so I can look her in her pale blues. Say to her what I say to you. Could I, would I, be sixteen again? And Del looks at Carla. "No, Baby. No."

Carla whoops and bounces in her seat. She lifts her arms above her head and makes castanets of her fingers. "No, Baby, no. No, Baby, no," she sings.

22
Rope & Bone – 1986

His shirts he hangs on the back of the chair, one on top the other so they won't wrinkle. On the end of the kitchen table he begins to fold the rest of his clothes, piling them up by kind: underwear, jeans, bandannas. Like the women in the laundromat do. As the stacks spread, Carla's friend, Del, moves her papers over to make room. While he folds, he listens to his daughter's laughter above the TV. For a moment he feels like he lives here again. All the dents and cracks are familiar. The half-stripped table he started last winter waits. While he stands in this kitchen, sorting socks and rolling them into lumpy wads, he watches Carla. He watches Del.

"You do good work," Carla says. "Did Marion teach you that? You never did laundry when you were with me."

He looks up at her to see if she's being nasty, but she just smiles and goes on rinsing the glasses.

He watches Del cross off and write, chew on her pencil, and write some more. She says she's fixing a poem. Fixing a leaky hose, fixing the toilet. Fixing a poem? She shifts in her seat, pulls on her hair, says, "Carla, see if this makes sense so far."

He puts the sock down, inches toward the words, words strung out down the page.

> "*They marry:*
> *Rope and Bone.*
> *Sunday and Saturday.*
> *That and this.*
>
> *He said, 'It was our finest hour.'*
> *She wept.*"

Carla butts in, "The 'She wept'... sounds like Jesus." Then Del X's out a line and looks at the ceiling like she's waiting for words to drop from above.

He tosses the last ball of socks on the pile. His shirts need buttons. Carla used to do them. Marion doesn't. "You got any thread," he says. Carla turns and drops her jaw. He ignores this. "I need white thread and a needle."

She goes up to her room to find them. He follows her as far as the foot of the stairs and calls, "And dark thread. Dark blue thread." He pulls Tess's hair lightly as he passes her chair.

"What you doing, Papo?" Tess says, not looking away from the screen.

"Sewing buttons."

"Well, when this is over, I'll help."

"All right."

Carla returns with the whole sewing box and a crack about how she's fresh out of thimbles. He ignores her again. He checks each of his shirts, sets aside the ones missing buttons. Several have rips in the elbows, torn pockets. Maybe next week. He smiles at the picture of himself—Steve Morletti, Pagan Biker, busy with his mending. He settles himself into a chair and pushes aside all the piles, careful not to disturb Del's papers. When she looks up, he motions her to go on. Everything's under control.

No buttons. He searches through the box. None. He does not want to get into this business with Carla again. He explores the box, layer by layer, once more. Not one button. Besides they have to be small and like the rest. He sits and stares at the shirts spread before him.

Then he laughs and looks down his front. He counts the buttons from his neck to his waist and the empty spaces on the shirts before him. With a tiny pair of scissors, he snips off the buttons he needs from the parts he tucks in his pants. He lines them up in a row, ready.

He looks over at Carla. She sits by the window, smoking a cigarette, staring out at the blue sky. The sun touches her white blouse, her black hair. He'd forgotten her hair—hair that always gets away from clips and scarves.

In the little pincushion he finds a bunch of needles. He chooses one with a small golden eye and lifts it to the light. He pushes his cap back and, squinting, pokes the white thread through the tiny hole the first try. He pulls the thread down to make it double and ties the ends together in a knot at the bottom.

Putting on a button shouldn't be too hard. He straightens the shirt in front of him, lines the little white plastic circle up across from the button hole, then slips the needle under, lightly holding the tiny rim with the nail of his forefinger. In jabbing for the opening, the button shifts a little. Once it's fastened down, it'll be easier. As he recalculates the exact spot, he notices there are three tiny punctures. Tracks left by the missing button. This changes things.

He lifts the shirt onto his legs and pushes back from the table. From underneath he pokes the needle through one of the little dark holes and slips the button over the point. Carefully, so as not to tangle the long thread, he pulls it all the way out. He puts the needle in another hole of the button, finds the second dark speck with the point, pushes it part way in, and from below draws the thread down with one final tightening tug. The button is trapped.

Then he notices Carla looking at him. He keeps sewing, keeps his brow wrinkled. The kitchen is quiet. TV voices murmur in the distance. He sees Carla turn back to the blue sky, the kind of blue that only comes in February.

February. One year ago this month he ran out of this kitchen, on Carla's voice, on Carla standing with a maybe loaded gun screaming, You ever touch me again and I'll kill you. Left Rudy and Tess, on the dark stairs, listening. Slammed the door so hard, the old window cracked. A late icy February night. No bright blue sky, no pretty Carla then. Somehow he got to Marion's. The drive from Danford to Utica is still a blank in his mind, but the next morning there he was passed out on the front seat in the alley behind Marion's apartment.

The thing with Carla was that every new fight, she brought it all up again. Sometimes before he even got in the door, she screamed, You son of a bitch. Then she always got to how many years they'd been married. She'd look up like she was talking to God and say, Five years. Ten years. Eighteen years—real disgusted. But the night she got out the gun, she didn't bother reminding him of the years. Somehow she'd found out about Marion. When he came home late, she was waiting on the stairs. She jumped on him and started clawing him in the face like a crazy person. He ended up slapping her. She went nuts, started biting and throwing stuff. All the while yelling, I'm not like my mother. I don't have to put up with your shit. Then it seemed like out of nowhere she had his gun, aiming it right at him. That was when he got the hell out.

After a few days at Marion's, he went home. Piled on the porch, all his stuff: boxes and bags, all his pictures. Everything. And a note. Something about how she was done with living with someone who couldn't hear, how there was a person inside her body. A note that said if he tried to get in, she'd call the cops. That the next time he heard from her, it'd be through her lawyer. That this time she meant it. When he started banging on the door, he saw her go to the phone. He left. Let her cool off, start to miss him. Three days later, painting up on a scaffold, he got a registered letter from some woman lawyer in Marwick. Lot of big words he never did read. Boiled down to a legal separation, a visit with the kids Sundays, and fifty a week.

But that was a year ago. Most of the war's over. Today he feels good. Home for his Sunday visit. He's given her the promised fifty, plus fifty from before. He's painting full time, even though it's winter.

He watches Carla. She lights another cigarette. She looks at him and smiles. He goes on sewing. The second button's easier. Yes, today Carla's being friendly. She may change any minute, but today she's got the white flag up. She crosses the kitchen, reads over Del's shoulder.

"I'm almost ready," Del says. "Then I'll read it to you, see if it's clear."

Carla starts pulling stuff out for dinner. "Well, I like the last part, 'mutually generous.'" She raises her arms and laughs.

He's always liked Carla's laugh, every part of her moves. He remembers the good times when she laughs. He watches the rise of her breasts, the curve of her belly. Out of the corner of his eye follows her ass as she bends to get potatoes out of the bin. Yes, today he feels fine.

"When you finish that, I got some socks you can darn," Carla says.

"Okay," he answers, biting the thread, "but I have a price."

"You're right about that. Morning, noon, and night. I'm aware of your rates."

He looks in her dark eyes, wants her to remember some of those times. "How about getting me a beer?" he says.

"Get it yourself. And don't start drinking so early. Next you'll be getting loud and obnoxious. Start telling me what to do," Carla says this while she's reaching in the refrigerator, opening him a beer.

He sits and drinks and sews. Only three more buttons to do. Carla peels potatoes at the sink. Del sits across from him, her small hands at rest on the table now. She reads softly to herself, her lips moving, her head bouncing a little. Then she begins to copy it all over, her tongue reaching out to lick her upper lip every few lines.

Del, now here's a woman hard to figure. Different. Her slanted eyes and bony cheeks. Del, always a little distant. Maybe a couple years older than him. Forty-five, forty-six. Stayed in that cabin all alone. Her man only there some weekends. He never had any teachers like her. He talked to her husband right before it happened. Him walking along the road. The eyes of a man not right in his head. Burning up. Always with his kids, seemed to love those kids. Shot himself. Should've stopped by his place and smoked some good weed with him, told him ... yeah, life's a bitch, but it can be fine. Once he asked Del, How come a lovely lady like you isn't married? I didn't like being married, she said.

"Ready," Del says. She clears her throat, raises the new paper from the table. Carla stops cooking. He puts down the shirt and leans forward. Del's eyes touch his and blink, like she only just realized he's there. She smiles and starts to read.

He likes the sound of it. They marry ... rope and bone ... speaking in tongues untranslatable. Del reads on. It seems like Del's as pissed with the woman as she is with the man.

Del stops. Right away Carla starts with the questions.

He leans his chair back and, balancing against the shelves, pulls another beer from the fridge. He tosses the cap into the basket by the sink and drinks. He sews and listens to the women, but they don't tell what he wants to know: Who's the rope? Who's the bone?

He watches Del. What would Del be like in bed, her cat-stretching body, her teardrop tits, rising and falling? But she never sends him any signals. A flick of her shoulders says, *I don't do one-night-stands.* Hey, he's serious, too, but, well, another kind of serious.

Still pushing the needle back and forth through the little holes of the button, he asks, "Is that how women feel? That they're so different from men?" He sees Carla's surprise, the jerk of her head, the widening of her eyes. She stares at him.

"I don't know about women," Del answers, "but I've felt all those things."

"Amen," says Carla, and turns back to the frying chicken.

"Well, I don't know, darlin's. I don't know about us being so different. Look at it out there—the sun shining, that bright blue sky. Why I could just take the two of you into that big old bed. We could have a fine afternoon."

Del laughs.

Carla laughs too. "You must be smokin' some good stuff, Baby. Dream on," she says.

Steve hangs another finished shirt on the back of the chair. "I'd like a copy of that poem," he says. Del hesitates, looks over her first sheet, then with a smile, pushes the new copy across the table to him. "Thanks," he says and folds it into many squares to tuck in his wallet.

"He wants it for That Woman," Carla says, banging the lid down on the potatoes. "As if she could relate to 'standing at the sink washing diapers.' She doesn't know anything about that—having kids *or* having no money." She jerks open the refrigerator door and pulls out the milk.

"Carla, don't start," he says and caresses her bottom, feels her familiar warmth in his palm. She moves away. Leaves his hand in mid-air. She gives him no chance to fan any fires. That night with the gun, it was like Carla went around a corner and she never came back. She must have told him she meant it a dozen times through the years. This time she did.

He tries to push a dark thread through the eye. His aim is careful, but each time only part of the thread enters the hole. He wets the end to a point in his mouth like his mother used to do. He is surprised by this memory. He sees her sitting in an old rocker sewing. Curving over her shoulder is a tall brass lamp with gold fringe hanging from a big white shade.

"You know what I just thought of Carla? Back when I was maybe seven or eight, living on Ramsey Street, and every night after dinner my mother sat down under an old brass lamp and mended our clothes." He shuts his eyes. "I see all the rooms. Up in the attic where me and Jimmy slept. In the mornings I listened to the pigeons."

"Oh," Del whispers, and her hands move in the air, "that's one of the things I remember most. The pigeons up under my grandmother's eaves, right outside my bedroom window. Did you ever try to make that sound? I used to listen and listen and try."

He tilts his head and leans forward like he hears something, something off in the distance. He smiles. Then slowly he draws his head down into his shoulders. His chest swells. He begins to wobble his neck and out of his throat there comes a gargled coo.

Del laughs, "That's it." She tries, fails totally, tries again.

Carla comes to the edge of the table. She bends toward him over the piles of clothes and really looks at him. "Steve?" she says. Then she sits down in the chair beside him. She begins to pull her neck into her shoulders.

Tess appears, wearing her father's black leather jacket. "What's that funny sound?"

"What's it sound like?" Steve says.

"Sounds like a pigeon."

"Well, that's what it is. A pigeon."

"A pigeon here in the kitchen?" Tess says and begins to search.

When Tess turns away, Steve coos again. Carla and Del laugh.

"What's so funny?" Tess says.

"It's your dad, Tess. Show her, Steve," Carla urges, wrapping her arm around the child's waist. Again he lowers his head, swells, waggles his neck, and coos.

Tess snaps her fingers. "Cool, show me how."

"Show us all," says Del.

Tess sits down on her father's lap. Tess has Carla's beautiful face—the same big, soft mouth and dark eyes. But her movements are all Steve. Ready and quick. Steve moans. "You sure are getting big."

Tess grins. "Do the pigeon."

Steve sets aside the shirt. "First of all, you don't just *do* it. To start you have to, you have to become a pigeon."

Carla's eyes widen again. They are all watching. The phone rings. The pigeon disappears.

"Answer it, Tess," Carla says. Tess doesn't move. It rings again.

"Tess," she repeats, her voice rising.

Steve pushes her lightly from his lap and Tess creeps to the hall.

Carla yells, "One of these days, Tess, one of these days." Almost to herself she says, "They're threatening to turn off the phone. They'd be doing me a favor."

Tess calls from the hall, "Mamo, it's Rudy. He wants a ride from town. He's at his girlfriend's."

"Cradle-robber," Carla yells in the direction of the hall. Then her look is all charm. "Steve, the Maverick isn't running. Could you?" She gives him her Beautiful Smile.

"Tell him I'll come get him if my car starts," Steve hollers to Tess.

Carla leans toward him. "You having trouble with your car?" She shakes her finger. "I told you not to buy that car. I mean it already had 130,000 on it. It was a torpedo when you got it."

How quickly she turns. He shrugs. He is not, goddammit, he is not going to get into it with her today. He wishes he had a dollar for every fight they've had over old cars.

"I can go if you have any trouble," says Del.

"I think it'll run. Come on, Ramboette," Steve says to Tess. "Let's go get your brother." He takes the last beer from the refrigerator and eyes the bottle on top. He'd like a shot for the cold, but Carla stares at him hard. Instead he takes his jacket off Tess as Tess starts for the hall. "Get your own coat," he says to the whines of protest. He sets the beer on the edge of the cabinet and begins to rummage through a drawer.

"What are you doing?" Carla says.

He lets her wait. "Where's a screwdriver? What'd you do—rearrange the whole house?" He means to keep it light, but just the thought of the carburetor puts him on edge.

And, of course, Carla doesn't let it go by. She never does. "You got a problem with me rearranging the whole house?" she says, her hands go to her hips, her chin angles toward him. He knows her fingers will curl into fists. They do.

"A screwdriver, Carla, all I want is a screwdriver."

"In the hall closet," she says, her back to him now, her hands stirring something on the stove. "Steve," he can hear she's sorry, "talk to Rudy about the woman. No good's going to come of a nineteen-year-old messing with someone who's thirty and got two kids." She faces him again.

"Carla, you know he won't hear it."

"Talk to him anyway. Please."

He nods puts the beer can in his pocket. He moves into the hall, passes his and Carla's old room, empty now, closed up for the winter. The closet surprises him: an old saw, a hammer, a screwdriver, a rusty pair of scissors hang on the wall. Beneath, Carla has nailed a sign, *Return Or Else*. Here's another Carla he didn't know. He sticks the screwdriver in his pocket and squats to help Tess pull her boots over thick socks. His throat tightens where Tess's small wiry head rests beneath his chin. He looks for gloves, doesn't find any.

They go out the front. Carla has fastened a long strip of duct tape across the cracked glass. Maybe he'll fix it one day. It's probably been Exhibit A for her story about how he slammed out one February night, leaving her with half a cord of wood on the porch. He's heard it himself four or five times.

"Shut the door," he reminds Tess who leaves it wide. "And Tess, do what your mother says. When she asks you to get the phone, do it right then." Tess doesn't respond. "Tess, do you hear me?"

"Yes," she says, cocking one shoulder just like he does.

The daylight is gone, taken over so quickly by February darkness. It's a lot colder out. They get in the front seat. He opens the beer, drinks, places the can between his legs. Again wishes he had a couple shots to dissolve the knot in his throat, something to lift the heaviness he now feels.

He pushes down on the pedal, turns the key. It starts up and immediately dies. He bangs the dash lightly with his fist. A rebuilt carburetor costs $150. He doesn't have that kind of money this week. He's not going to ask Marion. He finishes the beer, his fingers numbed by the freezing metal. Tess drums softly on her knees, hums.

"All right when I holler, I want you to turn the key like this." He mimes the motion. "Then right away push down on the gas like this … When it starts, kind of flutter it like this … Listen and I'll tell you when to start and when to stop. We've got to do it just right." On Tess's face is a look of complete concentration. "You have mittens in your pocket?"

Tess shakes her head no.

He pulls the seat forward and gets out. Tess slides over, the top of her head barely visible above the wheel. He rolls down the window a few inches so the kid can hear him and closes the door. He zips his jacket as far up as it goes and moves to the front of the battered Chevy.

Through the kitchen window, he watches Carla and Del moving around the table, putting on cups and plates, the knives on one side, the forks on the other. He watches the flow of their arms, the swing of their hips.

Their lips move. He leans toward them.

23
Edgewater – 1986

DEL CRUISED BY THE CARS lining both sides of the street in front of the Edgewater Bar & Grill. Carla's recently resurrected Maverick wasn't among them and it wasn't in the lot behind the bank either. Del toured the block again. Friday night. Richard not home from the City. She wanted the solace of human companionship. Still no Maverick or any other cars she knew.

Maybe Carla had finally given up her part-time bartending job. She often said, Serving shots and soothing drunks is not my idea of the good life. After which Del always intoned a line on the value of work: some variation linking freedom and responsibility, independence and employment, morals and getting up early. I've heard this before, Carla said. Or maybe the Maverick was ailing and Carla had hitched a ride. Del pulled in by the fire house and parked.

The Edgewater resides in a small one story frame house. On the front porch there's a swing and a blinking *Coors* sign. On the left the bar's jammed up against Main Street's row of businesses: Mang Insurance, Valley Video, The Stanton Luncheonette. On the right the bar teeters toward Onango Creek. A couple years ago, a drunk fell in and drowned.

Del opened her door to sounds of a juke box whining a did-me-wrong song and wails of whoee. A short man and a tall woman bandied threats on the steps. Del tried to pass around them, but they motioned her to go between. She offered them a conciliatory smile which they refused. There were some young guys shooting pool in the little front room. Del threaded through, greeting a few she'd watched go from round and ruddy on skate boards to lean and dark, with sinewed arms aiming cues sticks, cigarettes hanging from their lips.

She slipped through the double door into the dim back room. Carla wasn't behind the bar; instead a large man in a black cowboy hat was busy filling pitchers. Del squinted through the dark toward the kitchen, but Carla was nowhere in sight. She'd have one drink, see if Carla was around, and leave if no interesting talk turned up. She slid onto the last stool. As she pulled out of her coat, she saw her reflection, more and more the image of her mother: good cheekbones, but also the same short chin. Bold eyes caught her startled ones in the glass—a white-faced woman staring at her in the smoky mirror. "Mirror, mirror on the wall," the woman said to Del's reflection.

Just then the bartender's large presence broke the spell. "What'll it be?" he said.

"Bring me another Manhattan, and this lady whatever she's drinking," the voice beside Del said.

Del turned and looked directly at the woman on the next stool: shockingly short dark red hair framed a marble face and blue eyes, a chin and brow arched for combat, all haloed by a plastic stained glass lamp dangling above her head. The woman laughed and Del, instead of objecting as she'd planned, said, "An Amaretto on the rocks."

The bartender swiveled and moved away before Del could ask about Carla.

The woman leaned a little toward her. "I know your story," she said. Del started to speak. The woman raised a silencing finger.

Del resisted drawing back. Instead she smiled and nodded. The woman stared at her, reading her face as though it were a palm. Del willed herself to stay easy and made some observations of her own: the woman's black leotard, the dark printed skirt, the perfect teeth, the manicured nails the same color as her hair, the sapphire ring the same color as the eyes—eyes with a few lines webbing from their corners. The woman reminded her of someone. Pale, pale Moira Shearer running down the stairs to throw herself from the balcony beneath the speeding train, tears flowing onto her porcelain face, her red shoes still dancing.

The bartender set the drinks in front of them, and the woman tapped the stack of bills spread carelessly beside her glass. Del waited while the woman lit a long brown cigarillo and sipped her Manhattan, delicately retrieving the cherry with her sharp nails.

Then she smiled at Del's smoky image, a smile that curved her lips, but changed nothing in her cool blue eyes. "Here's what I see: You took the Whole Earth microbus. You bought an Ashley stove and sent away for pamphlets on homeschooling, home burial, and homegrown." She raised her glass to Del's surprised mirror eyes. "But," she continued, "being stoned by kerosene gave you no special dispensation from the void." She turned away from the mirror and looked at Del up close again. "You've got what I call the Funny-Lucky-Look: Funny you didn't know this before, but lucky at least you know it now."

At this, both of them leaned back and laughed. "Now," said the red-headed woman as she slid from her stool and drained the last of her drink, "when I get back, you can tell my fortune." Then she moved gracefully through the Friday night congregation toward the back to the rhythm of Willie Nelson's *Crazy*.

Who was this woman? Again Del looked at herself in the mirror. Her white thermal underwear top with the pink rosebuds, her long brown hair pulled back with a barrette, no makeup. She did look pretty back-to-the-land. Still. Del raised a twenty and motioned to the man tending bar. "Could you get me another Amaretto and a Manhattan? Isn't Carla working tonight?"

He glanced at the clock. "She was supposed to be back by now," he said. "Everybody's looking for her including your friend there." He pointed to the empty stool beside Del. "Carla's ex has been calling every five minutes. Very intense."

Then Del knew who the woman was. She looked back through the crowd toward the bathrooms. Tell her fortune indeed. Marion. That Woman. But she was not at all what Del had expected. Wouldn't Carla be surprised. What would Carla do?

Del had never been able to put Marion all together from the pieces that erupted out of Carla's volcanic tirades. Marion: forty-two, no children, married to a hippie minister named Nathan, a man she hadn't slept with for seven years, who was diplomatic when Carla once called him on the phone to say, Do you know your wife is fucking my husband? Marion: a big honors graduate from Cornell, a computer analyst, who now managed a business office in Utica, who met Steve at a Harley Rendezvous. A woman Del had heard Carla scream at, Don't you ever call here again, after she wrestled the receiver from Steve, and then a few weeks later down this same wire, instructed Marion, Steve, and Nathan how to can their tomatoes while the three of them stood together in that Utica kitchen waiting for the water to roll in the big porcelain hot bath.

Del had expected a dark Cleopatra with a snake around her neck, not Moira Shearer. She felt an arm go lightly around her shoulders.

"Del, darlin'," Steve said in her ear and kissed her on the cheek.

She drew back a little, just enough. "Steve, I haven't seen you for a while."

"Where's your old man?" Steve eyed the cigarillos, the Manhattan, and sat down on the stool. Marion's stool. He called down to the man tending bar. "No word from Carla yet, Randy?" The man shook his head. "So Del, do you know who you were sitting by? The redheaded lady with the blue-blue eyes?"

"Yes, I do."

"Well, I'm glad you're here. Talk some sense into Carla if she shows. I got nowhere with Marion. She just rears up a few hours ago, says, 'I'm going to have a little friendly get-together with your estranged wife.' Before I can get my pants on, she's in the car and gone."

"Where is Marion now?"

"I sort of kidnapped her out the back. Left her at Nina's waiting for a pizza. She'll be waltzing in here soon."

"Where's Carla now?"

"Do I know? But when she does show …" Steve looked up. "Speaking of the devil."

There was Carla, at the end of the bar, loading beer in the cooler. The man in the black cowboy hat was gone. Carla, in a long red sweater and black jeans, had already taken control of the bar, bantering with the row of men, while she pushed in the bottles.

Steve got down off the stool as he folded Marion's money and cigarillos into his pocket. He squeezed Del's arm. "I'm counting on you to prepare the way. No doubt we'll be back."

"But …" she said. Del watched Steve's graying ponytail, topped always by the soft leather cap, weave out through the double door.

Carla saw Del and waved. She closed the cooler and moved down the bar. "Del, I didn't know you were coming over." From behind her, she lifted a bottle of Amaretto and topped off Del's half-full glass. "What are you up to?"

"Carla."

"What's wrong?"

"Carla, how would you feel if right this minute Marion walked into the Edgewater Bar & Grill?"

Carla's hand flattened on her heart as she looked toward the door.

"Hey, Carla, how about a beer?" hollered a red-nosed man a few stools down.

Carla gave the man her charming smile and reached for his outstretched glass. "I'm getting ready," she said to Del and went to serve the waiting men.

Del watched Carla working the bar like there wasn't another thing on her mind.

There had been a time when Carla made it clear to Steve, to Del, to the world in general: If I ever get my hands on That Woman. But lately her talk had been more benign. Once she told Del, I got to be Who I Am dancing with him for eighteen years; she's welcome to the next go-round. One time she said, Isn't it strange how a city-lady is so caught up on a dude like Steve? When Del reminded her she'd been pretty caught up on him herself since she was sixteen, Carla said, Well, you know without the rosy glasses. What I mean is when I stopped sleeping with him, I noticed this and that and the other.

At the far end of the bar, Carla came to a full stop. Del turned. Marion, and behind her, Steve, shielded by a large box of pizza. They all looked at Carla. It was her movie. Her head was back and laughing. She did not look their way.

Steve lifted the box over Del's head and cleared a space to settle it on the bar. He ripped open the cover to expose a large pie, covered with mushrooms and peppers and anchovies. Marion slid onto the stool and raised her Manhattan.

"Well," Steve said to Del. "Which way is she going to blow?"

Del flattened her hand on her heart.

"I'm willing to give her the scene," said Marion. Marion extended her hand to Del. "Del Merrick, I'm Marion Greenberg. I liked the poem you gave Steve. I thought it was fine." She pulled a cigarette from Steve's pocket.

Carla moved down the bar and stood opposite Marion, both her arms on the counter. Her chin, angling their way. Then she pulled back a little and her eyes filled with tears.

The two women looked at each other. No one moved.

"It isn't like I thought it would be," Carla said. She turned and took a bottle of tequila from the shelf. She filled two shot glasses and extended one toward Steve. She raised her drink to them. Marion and Steve and Del followed. The four glasses touched.

"To love," Carla said.

24
Graduation – 1986

"WHAT DO YOU MEAN you 'invited everybody'?"

"Guess," Carla said, her eyes big. "Del, you'll never guess." With that she climbed up on the old spool table and began to circle it, beating out Saints with her bare feet while she blew through her lips on an imaginary trombone, "Pu Pu Pu Pu ... Pu Pu Pu Pu ..."

The old deck trembled and Del raised herself on an elbow where she had just sprawled in the sun. "You better quit bouncing around up there or this whole porch is going to collapse."

Carla slipped down off the table and stretched out on her stomach. "Ah, summer. At last."

Del waited. She gave Carla a long look, but Carla was silent, her eyes closed. Del reached over and slapped the board beside her ear. "Okay, you got me. *Who* did you invite?"

Carla sat up and slowly lit a cigarette. Then she leaned back against the clapboards.

"Carla!"

"Well, here's the way we did it. Rudy sent graduation announcements to everybody he wanted to come, you, Aaron and Mark included, and I sent birthday invitations to a special group. I think it's some kind of sign that Rudy is graduating from high school on my 36th birthday. I feel like I'm kind of graduating too."

"And who did you invite?"

"Oh, just every person," Carla hesitated long enough for Del to lean forward expectantly, "I was ever in love with."

Del jerked up. Carla laughed. "*All* the people you were ever in love with?"

"Yep, I made a list. I started with Babylove Stewart back in eighth grade. The first boy I slept with, and kept on going for twenty-two years right down to the present." The "present" was someone she would not name. 'Too soon to tell' was all she would say. "Of course," Carla continued, "there was a big gap in there for the eighteen years I was married to Steve, and Rudy already invited him. Just imagine if everybody came. Almost all the players in the whole drama here at once. Sweet Jesus."

"Do you really mean 'everybody'? Even people you don't like?"

"Everybody. If they made my heart go beat-a-beat-beat once, I invited them. Think of it, Del. Think. Who would you invite?"

Del was silent. She looked out across the valley to the hills of green trees, all the gray skeletons gone. "I'm not sure I even want to think about it. How did you know where some of these people are? Like what's his name ... the boy you loved in eighth grade?"

"Babylove ... Billy Stewart's I sent to where his parents lived. I woke up yesterday. It was raining. The idea came to me. I went down to JAKE's and bought a package of twenty little invitations ...'I'm going to have a party. I hope that you will come. We'll laugh and jump and play some games and have a lot of fun.'"

Del winced.

"I know. Knock-out awful? I spent the whole damn day going through old letters and Christmas cards, racking my brain to come up with streets. Some I sent to bars. Told them all to R.S.V.P."

"Carla, what if they actually come?"

Carla looked heavenward. "Hummm. But it sure will be fun waiting for the mail every day. Maybe I could make a speech, a speech of appreciation. Not really appreciation, more ... Del, what's the word for, 'I've done what I've done ... and now it's done'?"

Del thought. "Affirmation."

"Affirmation. Yes, that's it—A Speech of Affirmation." Carla rose, stood behind the spool table, calmed the bursts of black hair, and adjusted her shorts. Then she cleared her throat as she banged a spoon against a coffee cup. Her face was beatific. She fixed her gaze beyond Del to make eye contact with all those long-ago and many recent lovers. "I've asked you all here today to express my thanks, my heartfelt appreciation for your help in becoming what I am."

"Which is?"

"Wiser than I was." Carla walked to the edge of the porch and began to reel in the laundry.

"You sent one to Raoul in jail? And Murphy and …"

"Everybody. It took me over an hour at the post office just finding all the zip codes. But I came up with something for every single one."

"How many?"

"I had just enough cards. Another sign."

"Twenty?"

"Wait till you make your list. You'll be surprised how many."

"Who says I'm going to make a list?"

"Come on, Del. You will, you will, I know you will."

Driving home from Carla's, Del thought about the new yellow-green of the leaves, her lesson plans for tomorrow, Richard's arms. She sang *Lullaby of Birdland* in French, but just as she made the turn around Grat's Bend, she began to make her list. Well, not Jack Griffith, the boy with no front tooth she sat next to at the Rialto every Saturday in seventh grade. Visvaldis Puzulas, the boy whose parents escaped from behind the Iron Curtain. She used to watch his arms in a short sleeve khaki shirt, an army shirt, used to imagine tracing the back of his neck, downed with light hair, the pink ridges of his ears, from where she sat behind him in Miss Durlong's algebra class. And once she and her best friend Marcia walked him home. That's 1.

Carla wrote out the numbers 1 through 20. Then she added a 21. She was going to try finding her old friend Vicky one more time. Why she'd give anything to know that Vicky O'Mara landed safely somewhere. Beside each number, in a neat column, she listed the initials and added the heading *M. I. L.* She tacked it to the back of her bedroom door.

The first card came from Blacky Baker, a Pagan biker who helped her out when everything with Moss fell through. The card said in big jagged letters, *Baby, I'll be there. Bringing a couple of friends. Black.* Carla put a check by 6. B.B., and for the first time began to imagine these men, some still seen in boys' bodies, standing in her kitchen, leaning up against bikes out front, talking to Tess, to Rudy, to her. She had a moment of doubt, but swept it aside as she spring-cleaned the living room.

Eight invitations came back stamped *Address Unknown* and the invitation to Moss folded inside a note from Dave Beale, the bartender at the bar in Monterey where she go-go danced for a while. Said he hadn't seen Moss in at least ten years, heard he was dead. So far she had drawn a line through ten initials and put checks by four: *19. B.M., 15. S.S., 13. J.R., 6. B.B.*

The party was still two weeks away. Carla began to think about food. To the list on the back of the door she added: *Things to Do* and *Things to Buy.* Under this she wrote: *clams shrimp potato salad.* Under *Do*, she printed *$ Steve.* She would get him to kick in extra with the support payments. He was painting steady now that it was good weather again. After all Rudy was his son too. Maybe Gary would let her tend bar three days a week instead of two this summer.

When Steve heard about Carla's idea, he roared in on his motorcycle and said, "What kind of fucking mother are you anyway?"

"That's a fairly accurate description," Carla said, dumping the boiling spaghetti into a colander delicately balanced on the rims of the sink and the dishpan. "And one capable of," Carla ran water over the noodles, "taking care of these children since you walked out of here in pursuit of same two years ago February, leaving half a cord of wood on the porch. Are you staying for dinner?"

"Will the story of that wood ever end?"

"Never."

"What are you having?" Steve said, removing his leather jacket. He leaned up against Carla while he diverted the stream of water onto his hands. She moved away as she lifted the colander to rest it back in the pot on the stove.

"Still, Carla, where did you get such an idea?"

"Just a rainy day whim. An impulse. Why do you care really?" Carla handed Steve an onion and rummaged around the drawer for a knife, many of which she noted Tess had taken for god-knows-what new adventure. From the refrigerator she brought out tomatoes and some wilted lettuce. "I guess that's all there is," she said and Steve began to chop. "Is it that you're jealous?" Carla said.

"I guess."

"Dinner," Carla hollered out the kitchen door across the road to where Tess was stretched on her stomach, listening to the activity in a huge ant hill. She swore she could hear them singing. "Bring me my knives and get your brother. He's up on the hill."

She turned back to the kitchen and caught Steve in her dark, laughing eyes. "Who, Steve? Think. Who would you invite?"

After days of putting on and taking off, of *but I didn't really love hims*, Del's list was done, and it hung in the back of her brain. She planned to watch from a distance. Then she zoomed in close on twelve of them sitting around Carla's big kitchen table. Twelve of them and one empty chair. She thought of Lee, of his death. She was surprised by her anger. The power this man, who killed himself almost ten years ago, still had in her life, in the lives of their children. She had bad dreams filled with images she'd cut long ago. "I'm not enjoying this," she said to Carla.

"Ahh, Del. Boo and hiss. Or get up and leave. You keep forgetting it's your movie."

Del was pensive, unconvinced.

Carla lifted a bottle from the top of her refrigerator. "Have a shot of tequila. A jolt of affirmation."

Del shook her head and Carla replaced the bottle with a sigh.

"Well, let me read you my quote for the week." Carla was always placing wise sayings on her refrigerator. "Ready? Here's what it says, 'For we all share the same human condition: we are born, we suffer, we die.' Now, if that isn't cause for one hell of a big party, everybody invited, I don't know what is."

June 24, 1986: Rudy's graduation. Carla's 36th birthday. And it was going to be beautiful. When Carla woke up, the fog had already rolled away, the sun was in the room, a thrush piped in the woods. Graduation at one o'clock, the party right after.

Everything was ready. Huge bowls of potato salad and two triple-decker cakes made. She and Rudy and Tess spent all evening the night before baking and decorating. Rudy, usually Mister-too-cool-to-care, had razor-bladed his portrait from the *Morning Sun* page that printed pictures of all the graduates in the county. He'd then pasted his head onto a muscular cardboard body wearing a sign that said *I'm outta here*. It had taken Rudy an extra year to get there because of the problems with reading, but with his usual hustle he'd pulled it off.

Steve and Rudy set up the big rented red and white tent in the side yard. They figured where they'd put the beer—one keg by the tent, one in the field in front, and one by the clams. Nooley came with his truck and they winched the Maverick out to tuck it away behind the old barn. From time to time they drifted through the kitchen to lick the spoons, to run their fingers round the sides of the stacks of pans. The house smelled of chocolate and lemon wax, the outside of wild roses.

"Now if we, and our distinguished guests, just don't get too shit-faced to appreciate—to affirm—this work we've wrought," Carla said.

Del dreamed of a snake, a dark snake thick as her arm, long as her body. A black snake with a pale green belly, the same snake she saw when she was eleven. Their counselor, the girl with tiny golden freckles all over her face, said it was a King snake, a good snake. They had squatted on the edge of the woods and watched it for a long time until suddenly it was gone.

"But I'm forty-eight. Why did I dream about that snake now?"

"I don't dream," Richard said, his back to her, his voice muffled by the pillow.

"Everybody dreams," she said and curled into his body.

He brought his hand back and rested it on her hip, his fingers drew on her thigh.

"Don't go to the party if you don't want to," he said.

"It was a beautiful snake, a good snake."

He turned toward her, and with a flicking tongue, licked her nose.

By the time Del got to Carla's, cars, trucks and motorcycles lined both sides of the dirt road. She had to park far away, but even at that distance, she heard the twang of Bob Dylan telling her to trust yourself, you're on your own, you always were.

Here and there people sat and leaned on hoods and tailgates, laughing, drinking beer, sharing a joint. The air was rich with dust and dope and heat. In the big treeless field across from Morlettis', a softball game was in progress with bare-chested, barefooted men looking for the ball in tall summer grass. Rudy was catching. He had let his Mohegan grow in. At nineteen he'd turned into a younger version of Steve, his body compact and ready. So different from Aaron and Mark ... Lee ... lean, loping, glancing off to the side. Just ahead another circle stood in the middle of the dirt road playing hacky sack; the soft little bag a blur in the air, lobbed from a knee to a foot to a chest. No hands allowed.

If it feels crazy, I'll be home early, she said to Richard as she walked out the door. I'll be here, he said, his green eyes mocking her fear.

Yes, the party felt friendly. Del took a few deep breaths, tried to loosen the coil around her gut. Were any of these the men Carla loved? Three were coming from before Carla married Steve and maybe none from "after." Carla's secret amour, a man she was still silent about, would not attend and there was no word from Raoul or Murphy.

A man was curled up on the hood of Nooley's truck, his head resting on his hands, mouth open. Michelangelo's David with a full head of yellow ringlets and finely sculpted features. Del would like to have drawn those delicate nostrils, his pale paper lids. He opened his eyes. The irises were so light he seemed sightless. "Buzzed," he said, and closed them again.

Over by the big washtub of clams stood four people. People who didn't fit. They stood talking to several Hell's Angel types with a couple of women in leather. The man was short and balding, with seersucker Bermudas and pale legs spindling down into black silk socks and very white sneakers. Around his neck, hanging from a Hawaiian lei, a ukulele. The woman was round and pink and fluffy and held an accordion. With them were two pastel children, a boy about fourteen and a girl about ten.

A motorcycle roared in the distance. Del turned and saw the dust swirl. The hacky sack players moved to the side. Del stepped behind the truck. A big Harley flew by, but did not stop. Del recognized Murphy's flowing gray mane and on the back, hugging his leathered torso, a girl, with blond hair flying. Del stepped out to look after them. The girl was not wearing any clothes. Del hadn't seen Murphy since she gave him and Carla a ride to the wedding reception. Provocate me. She did not want to see him now, hoped he would keep on going.

Just then Steve appeared from the bushes, Marion right behind him. Del started to call hello, but then she saw Steve's face and stopped. They crossed the road, got in Marion's car, slammed the doors. Steve squealed out, Marion's profile dead ahead and unsmiling. Del hadn't seen them lately either. They were living together was about all she knew. That, and what she saw now.

Del was making her way over the final rise when she heard an engine. Again she moved over close to the parked cars to make room. A green van went by. A familiar green van. Just as Del was about to place it, she saw the small discreet sign on the back. *Camp Parmela.* Raoul.

Del hurried. The van signaled and double parked in front of the house. A beefy man in a khaki uniform with a revolver on his hip got out—the guard who supervised the work crew last year. He vanished and appeared again on the other side. He opened the door. Del caught her breath to see Raoul descend. She tried to locate Carla, but could not see her. Raoul did not appear. Instead the guard leaned in and drew out an odd shaped package, wrapped in bright green tissue. Flowers.

Del came up on the Morlettis' aging gingerbread farmhouse just as the guard handed the package to Carla. He said a few words that Del couldn't hear, bowed slightly, walked quickly back to the van and pulled away. Carla did not see Del and Del made no sign. She stood still in the road watching. She saw Carla glance at a note, saw her slowly push herself back and forth on the tire swing, her toes trailing in the dust, the roses cradled in one arm. Yes, she did look lovely in a white peasant blouse and long skirt trimmed with lace.

Then she saw Del. "Aren't they beautiful?" and she held the roses up. "Guess?" she said.

"I know. I saw the van go by."

Carla handed her the card to read:

> *Your beautiful smile sometimes comes to me. I'm going home soon. I wish happiness for you.*
>
> *Goodbye Raoul*

"Carla," Del said, holding the card to her cheek.

"I know. Probably the only poet to pass my way." Then she bent her face to the roses and took a deep breath. "Del, I'm so glad you came. I was wondering where you were. See, everybody's happy. All your worrying for nothing."

Del did not mention Steve and Marion. Murphy. "What about the ... people you invited? How's that feeling?"

"Complete anticlimax. Not even a vague flash for any of them. A complete *How could I ever?* Which is just fine with me. All except Babylove. He came with his wife and kids this morning. You will freak when you meet him."

"Babylove?"

"Billy. The backseat of my father's Pontiac when I was fourteen. Babylove Stewart."

She led Del to the corner of the house and pointed to the pastel group. Of course the family that didn't fit. "Billy Stewart, his wife Fan, and their two kids. What do you think?" Carla said in Del's ear. "Me and Babylove Stewart?"

Del laughed. She looked at the little pink balls that peeked out of the backs of Fan's baby blue Keds, then she looked at Carla's bare feet. "I don't think so," said Del. "I just don't think you could."

"But don't they look good? Happy?" Carla said and sighed. "Del, before everybody gets totally wasted, we better do the cake and presents." Carla handed the roses to Del. "Would you put these in water and could you get Rudy's present out of the trunk in my room? There was no way to disguise a guitar case, but I wrapped it anyway. I'm going to find Rudy. What a shame Aaron and Mark couldn't come. Rudy's disappointed."

Del had tried to reach them both: Mark in New York. Aaron in Boston. Left messages on machines. No response. Another thing she wasn't thinking about.

Carla turned toward the road. There was the roar of a motorcycle again. Carla laughed. "Probably Murphy. Did you see him go by with Godiva?"

Murphy came tearing into the yard and cut the engine. No girl and no helmet. It was clear he was messed up. He stared at Carla and then at Del and he didn't seem pleased with what he saw.

Del started up the front steps. Carla shrugged, "Welcome to the party," she said. Murphy's bloodshot eyes followed Del to the door. Carla waited a minute for him to react, but he just sat on his bike, his boots planted to balance the weight. "See you. I sure can pick 'em," she said and headed toward the field.

Del found a big jar in the kitchen and set the roses out on the deck. She was glad to be in the house away from Murphy. He was the kind of thing she meant when she told Richard she might be home early. Jerry Garcia was singing. She went upstairs to Carla's room. Carla was a re-arranger. A way to work out of a blue day was to push the dresser from by the window to where the bed was. A visitor could mark Carla's depressions by the number of different places the couch had been that year. And since it was a big old house, when she ran out of walls or when it was a black month, a grim season, she just changed rooms altogether, which is how she came to this place at the top of the stairs. When, two Februarys ago, Steve moved out, she moved up. Del laughed to see the reversible sign that hung from a nail on her door. Today *Yes* was turned out. Del flipped the sign over to the big *NO* in black magic marker. And printed in the corner, *Tess I mean it!* She envied Carla's absolutist approach to order.

Del stuck the card from Raoul in the edge of the mirror along with snapshots of kids and dogs and kittens. She looked at herself in the long glass. She reached up under her skirt and pulled down on her blouse, then leaned forward and inspected her face. She used to hate it when people said, My, you look just like your mother, but those last few years when she visited her mother in the nursing home and everybody said it, she didn't mind anymore. She liked her face.

There was a soft click behind her. Del turned. Murphy. His back to the closed door. He stared at her and then lifted a chair to place it in front of the door. He sat down, tilted the chair against the frame, and swung his feet up on the trunk at the foot of Carla's bed. His lips and jaw, even the pouches beneath his eyes, drooped. "Well, well, the poet."

Del thought he probably saw her heart jumping in her throat. Her first impulse was to scream out the window, but even that was on the other side of the bed and Murphy's legs. Besides, who would hear her above the Dead? She just stood there and breathed. Rudy's guitar was in the trunk beneath Murphy's boots. She wanted to get that and get out. She sat down at the dresser and opened the side drawer as though she must find something. A needle, a gun. A cover for her shaking hands.

"How about a poem? Yeah, do me a real poem. Maybe a love poem. Not some fucking thing about getting thrown in the looney bin." Murphy pulled up on his shirt, scratched his hairy stomach. All the while his eyes traveled her body. "Yeah, do me a love poem."

And now his hands drummed on his thighs as they had that day going to the wedding when on Carla's request she had recited a poem she just wrote. She knew by the way he looked at her as he left the car, that she had pissed him off. Murphy reminded her of the coldness that could flash up in Lee, the rages of Dugan, their taking control, and she hated how she turned into a creature that crept along the wall pretending to be invisible. She knew the fright in her eyes seemed to set them off more. She had never been beaten, only grabbed a few times, slapped on the head once, but she had looked into the eyes of insanity enough to know that she would do anything if only, if only, they wouldn't hit her. She lifted out a pair of scissors, closed the drawer with a bang. She rose. "Murphy, I have to open that trunk to get the guitar Carla bought Rudy for a graduation present."

Murphy lowered the chair to the floor as she approached.

She slipped the scissors in her pocket and lifted his feet from the trunk to set them to the floor. "Here, hold this for a minute," and she handed him the afghan folded on the top. She undid the two heavy latches and pulled up on the lid. It would not give. She smelled Murphy's body behind her, heard his breathing. She banged her hand under each latch and tried again. Murphy got up and moved to her side. He gave her the blanket and reached down to lift hard on the lid which gave a little. He grunted and gripped the sides of the top, the veins in his arms stood out as he bounced the whole trunk one hard knock on the floor. Then he pulled up again. The trunk opened with a scrape. Wedged in diagonally was a huge package wrapped in smiling Santa Christmas paper. Murphy lifted the package out. Del closed the trunk and spread the blanket back. She moved the chair away from the door and took the wrapped guitar case from Murphy's hands. "Thank you." She looked at him. "I couldn't have gotten it open without your help." She turned and went downstairs with the Dead singing:

> "Sometimes the lights shining on me
> Other times I can barely see
> Lately it occurs to me
> what a long, strange trip it's been."

Her hands were sweating; it was hard to breathe. Her car seemed far away down the road. She felt for her keys. She could hand Rudy's gift to Carla and plead illness. Then the woman in the blue Keds smiled at her and motioned for her to join them. Del turned and walked straight for that group. She set Rudy's gift beneath the first table. The man acknowledged Del's approach, reached out for her hand and drew her forward. "I'm Bill Stewart and you're Del. I knew that when I saw you moseying up the road. Carla told us you were coming. This is my wife, Fanny. And Grif, our son. Our daughter, Lou."

Everybody grinned. They watched Carla cross the road.

Bill motioned to Carla to hurry along. "We were just about to get the party singing. Pass 'em out, Grif. What do you think, Black?" Bill said, giving the biker's generous stomach an affectionate pat.

"I'm with you, man. Let it roll," Black bellowed, raising his beer in a toast.

"Give everybody one," Fan said and she began to squeeze out some notes on her accordion.

Everybody clapped. Del too. Yeah, Whoeee.

The boy handed Carla and Del, everyone else in the group, a kazoo.

"Oh, I always wanted to play one of these," Del said.

"Well, what'll it be?" called Babylove Stewart.

And Del began to blow out Saints as she headed for the deck.

"All right," Carla yelled and took hold of Del's waist. Rudy and Tess slid in behind her.

They formed a line, snaking their way to the back of the house: Black and his friends singing, Babylove strumming, Fan squeezing, everyone kazooing.

Del left her sandals in the grass and moved up those fragile stairs, the worn boards hot beneath her toes.

"Do you think it'll hold us all?" hollered Carla.

"Who knows?" said Del.

Grateful Dead played at full volume and they all danced.

From the upstairs window, Murphy looked on.

Part III
Shelter
1987-1993

4

Alternate endings:

She smokes, becomes thin, and drinks from a bitter cup,
pouring the dregs out day after day to someone similar.

He drinks and takes his comforts where he can.

Or/And:

She gathers the children together
(whom the sins of both shall be visited upon later),
throws the stained mattress up over the old Pontiac,
and heads out for godknowswhere.

To be continued …

25

Hitch – 1987

Comparative Music 200   *Aaron Merrick*
January 9, 1987

Several types of rhythmic Ostinato span 6 centuries The term isorhythm was originally applied to certain 14th C motets???????!!!!!!!!!!!!*&·*%$*#

Joe Doe
He ain't no friend of mine.
He doesn't laugh at my jokes
and he doesn't get high.
When I'm out on the road,
he passes me by.

B<small>RAMLEY WAS NO DIFFERENT.</small> Aaron hocked his guitar and hitched home. A guy named Goose picked him up in his '70 Van, with a full set of Pearls and two big speakers in back. When they got to the house, his mother was at school. They set up in the loft. He reassembled his old electric guitar. They were jamming when she walked in the door. He saw her face and decided to explain the situation before they played anymore. "Mom, this is Goose."

Goose rose from his drums, made a polite bow.

"Aaron, what are you doing home? What about school?"

"The teachers are on strike. We haven't had any classes in two weeks. And I don't think I'm going back even if they do settle."

She sat down.

"I'm interested in playing, not the fifty fine points of each note."

"What are you going to do?"

"We wondered if we could stay here for a few days until we figure things."

She took a breath, let out the air. "A few days, but no longer than that unless you get jobs. Take care of the wood while you're here," she said.

No jobs. They wheel-barrowed the wood in, stacked it in perfect rows by the stove.

Winter.

In April Goose went home to New Hampshire.

"Aaron, you can't stay any longer," his mother said.

"I thought maybe I could camp out. Go back and forth to Boston every couple of weeks, play drums in Harvard Square. Make enough money to get by."

"No," she said. "Go out and get a real job. I'm not going to support any part of a plan I don't believe in."

"Can I camp out on our land even if I don't come up to the house?"

"No."

"What are you going to do? Call the police?"

"Would you camp on the land when it isn't okay with me?"

With a wooden tongue drum under his arm and a backpack, he headed out to hitch to Boston. Figured he could play in Harvard Square, on the subway. Set down the striped engineer's cap he now wore on his long tangled hair and pick up twenty-five to fifty a day. At least in good weather. He'd figure winter later. He got as far as the turn to 88 when a state trooper cruised by and pulled over.

Two troopers slid from the opened doors and walked toward him. "Put your stuff down and raise your arms," the younger one said.

"You got a search warrant?" he said, not moving.

"Listen kid, there's a law against hitching; plus I saw you give me the finger. You want me to tell the judge you resisted arrest as well?"

"I didn't give you the finger. I'm not stupid," he said, looking the trooper in the eye. "I resent you hassling me when you should be out after criminals." But he did what they said. When he was five, a police car forced his father to pull over. He was drunk, speeding, weaving on and off the road. His father resisted. It took four policemen to get him in handcuffs. While they struggled with his father, he and Mark hugged each other on the floor of the car. If he let himself, he could still hear his father's screams.

They put his father in the state hospital at Marwick for observation. His mother took them to visit. His father looked normal, not like the other people who shuffled and kept glancing around. When his father came to live with them again, at night from his bed he heard him tell his mother stories about the people on the ward. Then his parents laughed. They were happy for a while.

So Aaron didn't resist. The troopers went through his pockets, looked in his boots, made him set out his stuff along the edge of the highway: copies of the *Bhagavad-Gita* and the *Bible*—which they fingered suspiciously. They paged through his notebook of lyrics. "A poet, what we got here is a fucking poet." Then they unrolled his jeans, his winter coat, his sleeping bag. No dope, no toothbrush, and no underwear. They got back in their squad car and drove off.

He walked to the next 88 entry road and stuck out his thumb. His first ride was with a trucker who had spent four years in Nam. "Yeah, I did any drug I could get hold of: heroin, cocaine, grass, of course. How I got through the pacification of the villages. Consider yourself lucky, kid—Don't ever go to a war."

"I wasn't planning on it," he said.

The second ride was with a gay guy who lived on Beacon Hill. "You want to stay at my place?"

"No thanks," he said.

When he got to Boston, he slept in the park the first couple of nights. Then he met a girl at the Hare Krishna eatery. He was sitting there getting the indoctrination that came with the free food when an aristocratic girl pulled up a chair next to him and put down her bowl so close her hand was almost touching his. "I'm Chase Manley," she said. "I heard you playing your drum by the Commons exit."

They talked. He thought about telling her how after his father died, he started to have stomachaches. His mother took him to a pediatrician. As he was being poked with the stethoscope, the doctor said in a way he might have asked about the weather, How did your father do it? Chase lived with some people in Cambridge. She said he could crash there for a while.

Where could I get one of those drums? the people said after they stopped to listen to him play for a while, after they dropped some change in his cap. I always wanted to play an instrument, they said. He wrote down their names, made some vague plans of how maybe he could call the drum man in Marwick to see if he wanted to venture into a small business. Mostly though the names, scribbled on scraps and backs of matchbooks, tangled with the stuff in his pockets and slowly transitioned to trash.

The drum was a thing of beauty, an oblong box of cherry wood, fastened with pegs. Each slit sanded to perfect roundness and played with two superball sticks or the fingers. The sound was unusual, a muted xylophone echoed through the moan of a dove.

The best times, the most money to be made on Saturday evenings in Harvard Square—people out to walk the summer night. During the week he went to the Trenton subway exit just as people were getting out of work. He got a little following, blue-eyed Aaron with the beautiful wooden drum. Regulars who smiled, stayed for a song or two, dropped some loose change, sometimes a single, in his hat. On a good day he made thirty to forty dollars. True, there were a lot of days when he didn't play. When it rained or when he had enough ahead for a pack of Camels, he worked on songs—he didn't feel any great urge to amass money. He got high, did a lot of pizza, and didn't get overly excited about personal hygiene. He got by with a corner of an apartment to sleep in right around the block from the square. Chase Manley and some other people were having a rent war with their landlord so for now they were living free.

Still—the leaves were all down. November took its usual grim view of the future. Business in Harvard Square dropped off. He was thinking about thinking about winter soon.

Then they lost the war. The landlord said they better be out by morning or they could answer to the police. He took his drum and left.

A few hours after he crushed his last empty pack of cigarettes, he met Syl Bead. Syl had a car and a carmine Mohican. She was back from a year hanging out in Amsterdam and she'd worked in a greenhouse long enough to buy a rusted-out Subaru that housed her clothes; her laboratory rat, Precious Thang, who nested in and chewed on the wires up behind the dashboard; and several works-in-progress sculptures. There was enough room for his pack and drum in the back. And they figured they had just enough gas to get to Danford. It was only six hours if they took the Mass Pike. "Shouldn't we call ahead and let your mother know?" Syl said.

"Nope. Better to just go. Probably be able to stay there for a while."

"Cool."

"'Course, we'll have to get jobs," he said.

"Definitely. And we can set Precious Thang free in a healthy environment."

They got jobs delivering *Pennysavers* two days a week. It was sort of working—just enough to keep his mother from getting enough anxiety gathered to ask them to leave. Anyway his mother liked Syl. Syl raked leaves unasked, made a fancy coffee cake out of cherries and Bisquick, and sat and talked. He figured in one week, Syl talked more with his mother than he had in his whole life. He wandered in and out of the words. He never really listened to what they said, but their murmur splashed like the waves on the beach where he and his dad camped one soft summer night.

Winter was coming on. But Precious Thang would not leave the inner workings of the Subaru. She had already done some pretty extensive damage to the electrical system. Aaron had black taped a lot of it, sometimes with bizarre results. You had to signal when you wanted to turn on the wipers, and vice versa. And the interior lights no longer came on when you opened the door, but then it no longer screamed to put your seat belts on either so they figured it was a fair trade.

Every day they left the door ajar with the broken end of a canoe paddle as a little ramp leading from the car to the November grass. At the foot, they placed a bowl of various delicacies: dry dog food, bread—soft and toasted, milk and egg mixed. But no meat. Thang was vegetarian. None of it ever looked touched. And still she refused to come out. Once when Syl grabbed at her as she disappeared up behind the glove compartment, she was left with the end of Thang's little white tail. Syl cried. "This is not working out," she said and blew her nose. "I begin to doubt the wisdom of taking her out of the shelter."

One afternoon when they got up, they found the Marwick *Sun* opened to the employment section, with magic marker circles: *Waitress Wanted; Man to assist in Home; Car Wash attendant.* They knew his mother had gathered the necessary energy. Syl did three loads of laundry. He vacuumed the loft, dumped the Chinese checker ashtray, put the milk glasses to soak. They loaded the car, made the decision to leave the sculptures up on the rafters of the barn. As they were putting the last load in the trunk, his mother's car came up the road.

"What's up?" she said.

"Time to head out," he told her.

Syl said, "We thought we might go to Jersey, maybe visit my father. I might be able to get a job helping this guy I know do stained glass," and while she talked, she poked behind the dashboard with a maple branch. "This is it, Precious Thang. Your last chance at clean living for a while," she called upside down, the branch rasping back and forth around the hanging wires.

"Or maybe we'll go to Florida," he said, banging the trunk closed on the overflowing bags and boxes. "Syl's mother lives in Tampa. I can probably get work painting. Well, we better get going," and he slipped into the driver's side, rolled down his window.

Syl gave his mother a hug. "Thanks for everything," she said and got in too.

"So where are you going?" his mother said, bending down to the window.

"We'll decide when we get to Marwick."

Syl leaned across the seat. "Oh, I forgot. I've got a favor to ask."

"Yes?"

"I'm hoping you can take care of my spider plant. I left it by the sink. It's just too unstable for all this travel."

His mother laughed. "I can handle that." And she touched his arm, then stood back. "Take care," she called as he began to back down the drive.

"So long," he said. When he made the turn-around at the barn, he saw her still waving, still standing by the edge of the road.

Shit. He tried to pull the door of the telephone booth closed, but it kept hitting the corner of his drum. The man at the ticket window watched him, his face set on *blank*. Screw it. Have to call her. There was no other way. He pushed the drum away with his foot and pulled the door tight. He counted out his money. $4.28. Nothing to do but make it collect. He placed the call, told the operator to let it ring and ring. He was just about to give up when he heard her voice from what sounded like a long distance. Yes, she'd accept.

"Hi, it's me."

"Where are you?" she said.

"I'm in Tilson, Missouri."

"You're where?"

"I'm stuck in Missouri."

"What are you doing in Missouri?"

"I'm hitching to Oregon to a Dead concert, but I'm having trouble getting out of Missouri. Red Neck country."

"Are you okay?"

"Yes. But I was wondering. I can't get Syl. I keep calling her at her father's. No one home. I hate to ask," he hesitated and then started again. "Do you think you could arrange for a ticket from Tilson to Denver?"

"Denver?"

"I figure I can hitch from there. If you pay in Marwick, Greyhound puts it through to Tilson on the computer. Ninety-four dollars. I'm in the Greyhound station now, been here all night."

There was a long silence. "Okay." Then another long pause. Then her voice so low he could barely hear it, "I can leave in a few minutes."

"I've got a job lined up calling people on the phone when I get back to Boston. I'll pay you back."

"I hope you will."

"I will."

"Five, ten dollars a week would be fine."

"Really, I'll send it all first pay day," he said.

And that was about it. He didn't know what else to say. He said goodbye and hung up the phone. He just stood with his hand hanging onto the receiver. Probably she was thinking he'd never send the money. He knew she'd go right out to the car, drive straight to the bus station, both small hands tight on the wheel, sitting a little forward, like she couldn't quite see, like some animal might jump out any minute. He knew all the while she'd be thinking. What would she be thinking?

He didn't know.

26
Potato – 1989

Del felt Richard sitting on the side of the bed, his flesh warming her thigh. "I was dreaming about a potato," she said.

He didn't say anything.

"I dreamed I *was* a potato."

"Oh," he said. Not Oh, tell me about it, but Oh, I'm not listening.

Usually Sunday nights when she felt him get up, she slid over into his warmth and smell to sleep again, the shower turning to rain in her dreams. When he returned to the edge of the bed to put on his socks, she curled around him, nestled him in the curve of her belly and legs, her breast pressed against his hard thigh. Sometimes in half-sleep she licked the ridges of his bony knee or traced the hollow of his hip with the tips of her fingers. Sometimes he ran his hand down the long distance of her ribs or softly tongued her ear, his breath blowing the hair on her neck. Then he finished dressing in minutes, the quiet tread on the stairs, the click of the door. Gone until his Friday return.

But this night was different. His silence egged her on. "A potato, with a withered paunch and little dark eyes sunk in wrinkled skin." A potato that looked a lot like her mother. Her mouth shriveled and pinched, just before she died in the nursing home. She pushed her thigh against him, wanting him to turn, to show he heard her. Instead he reached for a can of talcum. The bed vibrated as he shook the powder first on one foot and then on the other. "Are you listening?"

He set the can back on the table, the metal bottom scraping on the wood, the only sound in the darkness. "Yes," he said.

She felt his weight lift a little to open the dresser drawer, to pull his socks and underwear from where she always put them, always ready when he needed them, folded neatly in the front. He settled back against her again, but said nothing more. She moved her leg slightly, no longer touching his body. Let him sit there, doggedly going on with his usual routine. He pulled on a sock. White cotton socks he always put on before anything else, even before his underwear. Did first what she did last. Then he bent to tug on the other sock. She rolled over to her side of the bed. He lifted his arms to drop his T-shirt over his head. Then he stood to put on his underwear, his pants. The hangers jangled when he took his shirt out of the closet. She pushed the pillow up against her ears with her fists.

Once a few years ago she sat right up in bed and said to him, Richard, why don't you turn on the light? He hadn't answered her until the next Friday when he returned. He said, like there'd been no week in between, Driving through the night I breathe in the quiet. By the George Washington Bridge, I'm ready. I have just enough to last me for the week. So far.

She heard him zip his pants, begin to brush the change for tolls off the dresser into his palm. Heard the clink of his keys, his gropings for his wallet. The thump of each boot as he set them on the floor. He sat on the bed, lacing. If she didn't make some move now, he'd go down those stairs. In a minute she'd hear the click of the latch, the headlights would flash on the ceiling and flee. He'd be gone a whole week and she would not have touched his face or smelled his hair or felt his mouth on her skin.

She was just turning onto her side to move toward him, when his hand came down on her hip. "Gather ye rosebuds," he said.

"That's not it."

"I like potatoes."

"That might be part of it."

Then down the stairs. The door closed. Gone. She moved over onto his side, burrowed into the hollow left by his body. She nuzzled his faintly damp pillow, breathed in the smell of him. Richard, even his sweat smelled clean.

Usually in August, just before school, she had anxiety dreams. She saw herself talking in front of a large class of noisy students not listening to anything she said. Sometimes without any clothes on.

When she went in, organized her room, made a few plans, the dreams stopped. But getting older wasn't quite the same. House cleaning and making a few lists were not going to do it. She squinted at the distant orange face of the clock. 3:00. At least tomorrow was a holiday.

She turned over onto her back and stretched her toes for some new place in the bed. A cold spot. She threw off the sheet. A while ago she'd glanced through an article on sunbathing. In a colored box, set off from the rest, it had listed *Don'ts* to prevent wrinkling: *Don't sleep on your side. Don't rest your face in your hands when you talk on the phone,* and the funniest: *Don't frown.* It's a wonder it didn't say, *Don't laugh.* On her side was when she noticed it the most. She brought her hand up and touched her breast, her stomach. The soft sag, the loose folds. It didn't show much when she was upright, but when she bent over, when a bunch of skin got together ...

Fifty in September. Fine. But what would it be like to walk around in an old body? Richard's stomach was flat, his skin tight. At least his hair was thinning. Women: babies and breasts. Potatoes withering, full of eyes sending out shoots searching for light. Life. Mark already twenty-four, starting to get a little gray early like Lee did. Aaron twenty-two. And both of them, both of them still so shaky.

She turned on the lamp, swung her legs over the side of the bed and looked down at her body. She stood up, sucked in her stomach, and laughed. She rolled the window out. A May-luscious night. Mud. Peepers. An ooze orgy. The moon full and bright. A few drifting clouds. She pulled on her jeans, a heavy sweatshirt, her boots. Her body felt loose and alive inside clothes without underwear or socks. Maybe it was the faint smell of decay, swimming up through her unconscious, that spawned the dream. Maybe she should clean out her cupboards. Do a big throw-away. As good as a tummy tuck. Certainly less futile.

She went downstairs. Sam raised his head and stared at her. She opened the cupboard and the vegetable bin under the sink. Something rotten for sure, but not too messy. She lined up the garbage bag boxes, combined two bottles of Windex. The onions looked fine. No question it was the potatoes. She lifted the heavy sack onto the counter, careful not to break off the shoots that crawled from the opening. Almost a full ten pounds; they were old when she bought them. She wrinkled her nose. A wet spot in the corner. She imagined the withered brown contents mixed with mush. Might be best just to dump them straight into the compost.

She hesitated, then reached into the bag, working her hand down the cold waxy shoots to find the potato that fed this strange growth. She shivered when her fingers made contact. How like human skin. Rough. A heel. An elbow. And cold. She lifted the potato to the light. Looked closely for the first time. Four downy lavender fingers, paling to translucent tips with tiny black claws, twisted from the now shriveled potato, its russet skin filigreed like the faces of the very old. She set the potato on the table, let the shoots trail over the edge. Her fingers itched to draw it. On butcher paper, much larger than life, all browns, hatchings of yellow and purple. She lifted all the shoots so they rested on the table. Then slowly she tipped the bag to empty it onto the big bread board, Lee's writing "table." The potatoes rolled out. Near the bottom of the bag she located the rotten one and dumped it in the garbage.

She opened the door and stepped out. Warm. The air sweet with lilacs and approaching rain. The brook was loud, rushing. Dangerous even. Aaron and Mark, so vulnerable. And not one goddamned thing she could go back and undo. She moved through the shadows of the big maple and out across the yard knowing there was nothing menacing in the pitchy blackness of the woods beyond. She stepped to the edge of the garden: last year's tomato vines, sodden heaps of hay mulch, a few drooping sunflower stalks rose up. The garden.

Back inside, rotating both hands, she spread the potatoes over the top of the board. With a large knife, she cut the first one. Again she was surprised. Soft white flesh opened to the light as the blade split the brown skin. Sam rose and stretched, his nose sniffing. Then he came to sit beside her, his plumy tail beating on the rug.

She worked her way down the counter, cutting each potato into three sections, trying for an eye for each part. So they could find their way up through the dark? She considered again the potato with the searching fingers, but did not cut it. With her arm she gathered the pieces into piles and swept them into the big basket she held below the edge of the counter.

She reached down two kerosene lamps from the shelf beside the sink where they'd sat since her move from the cabin. She lifted one of the chimneys, raised the wick a little and lit it. The wick caught with a sputter, releasing a curl of carbon. When it burned evenly, she put back the fragile glass and lowered the wick. Then she lit the other lamp with just as good luck.

She made several trips back and forth from the house to the back yard.

"Watch your tail," she whispered to Sam as she placed the lanterns on the ground, then took the rake and pick from the shed. The light from the lamps cast sharp shadows on the garden. Aaron and Mark. Mark and Aaron. Sure, she would give anything … if. The brook rushing now, but by the end of June it would be dry.

The moon disappeared behind a cloud. She let the rake drop so suddenly Sam rose up with a start, followed her so closely she almost tripped on the stairs to her room. Lying on her side, she slid her arm under her dresser until her fingers touched cold metal. With an effort she worked the box forward enough to finally cup her hand around one corner. Sam stood above her, his head tipped to one side. "Goddamned right, it's ridiculous," she said. With a grunt, she rose, gripping the box. She pried the lid up and breathed in. Marijuana. Such a lovely smell. She smiled—remembrance of things past indeed. Too bad Richard didn't smoke, didn't like the feel of it. Still what a pleasure it had been to get high and play alone. She put the bag in her sweatshirt pocket along with the papers and a pack of matches.

Outside again, Sam still right on her heels, she lifted a lamp up and made her way, one step at a time, down to the brook, more of a river now from the rains. Sam sniffed the water, but knew enough not to go any closer. She side-stepped the tangles of brush and set the lamp on a stump, then moved right to the edge. She fanned out the pack of papers and set them on a rock, then held the match until they flamed up all along the edge. She watched them burn till only ashes remained. Then she opened the plastic bag and, one pinch at a time, sifted the contents, all the flakes, all the twigs, all the flower heads, onto the dark water. The plastic bag fluttered up and disappeared. "Goodbye," she said.

Back by the edge of the garden, she set the lantern down again. Sam sank to the ground and rested his nose on his paws. With the hoe she raked away the ruins of last year, pulling the piles to the sides to cart away in the sun. Of course it would have made more sense to wait for Richard to rototill. She cleared enough space for about five rows, set two feet apart. Plenty of room to hill up the soil as they grew. Half the garden for potatoes? The brook said, Why not? She stacked stones on one side to mark the first row, and then, from the other side, eyed a straight line and piled another. Five trenches. Hours of digging. You have the rest of the night, the morning, the afternoon, next week, the May night assured her. True. Look, Richard, she'd say when he returned on Friday. She brought the pick down into the winter-softened earth.

27
Soup – 1989

DEL FLICKED A SMALL RED BUG off one of the potato leaves, but she didn't see any signs of damage. Then she walked the rows. Of course she wouldn't know the true measure of all her labor until she went underground. One year she'd made the mistake of taking the easy way—covering the potatoes with straw in order to avoid hilling, but when she went to harvest them, almost every potato had been bitten into. Moles. Well, soon enough, she'd know how they'd all done. In two days on her fiftieth birthday, she was going to break ground, dig the first ones up and make a big pot of potato soup—lots of butter and cream and onions just like she grew up on. Sit out under the maple in the calm of living alone and celebrate: Here's to coming through.

Potato soup—not something Richard would eat on the weekends. Bad for your cholesterol.

Del leaned the hoe by the door and removed her shoes before stepping into the house. The damp smell of carpet shampoo mixed with Lemon Pledge. The house cleaned top to bottom. Too bad her birthday was also the first day of school, but somehow the harvest of the potatoes had to be when she actually turned fifty. What was it Marion once said? Funny-lucky. Fifty, the funny-lucky turn. Funny, you didn't know sooner, but lucky you do now. Once again she checked her school bag: her new grade book, her lesson plans, her box of sharpened # 2 pencils. Everything was right where it was supposed to be. She was all set.

The phone rang. Only a mild upping of her heartbeat.

"Hi, it's me."

"Aaron? Where are you?"

"I'm at Carla's."

"You're at Carla's? I thought you were in Boston doing marketing calls for Sprint."

"Rudy and I have gotten jobs at a sawmill. We start tomorrow." Ominous pause. "I was wondering if I could live at the house for a while. Just till I get a little money together."

One swallow of hesitation. "All right."

"And could you stop for Rudy mornings, drop us at the Quickway in Stanton on your way to school? Guy's going to pick us up there. We'll chip in for gas."

"Yes. Yes, I can. But Aaron …"

"Temporary, transitional," he said. "Got time to pick me up now?"

She backed slowly down the drive, on her periphery caught the green swell of potato leaves when she made the turn at the barn.

Del hadn't seen Carla, hadn't talked to her for weeks. The few times she'd passed by Morlettis' there was a big red truck in the yard, signs of yet another love interest, and well, she didn't have the energy. One bad guy after another just wasn't as fascinating as it once was. When she made the turn onto Chicken Farm Road, she realized she was hoping she didn't have to meet up with any of that crew, that she was sorry Aaron and Rudy would even be working together. Too late to be the kind of parent who was a den mother, who took the kids to church on Sundays—Aaron was twenty-two, Mark twenty-four— yes, it was a little too late now.

Aaron was waiting on the Morlettis' steps with his guitar case and a beat-up backpack. Pretty much *it* for his worldly goods. He looked terrible. Thin and unwashed. Raggedy cutoffs and tangled hair. She rolled down the window and waved. Do not cry and do not go on and on about how awful he looks.

While he got settled in the loft, she put on water for spaghetti, cut up tomatoes for a salad. Too late for *Jesus Loves Me*, but at least he could eat, wash his clothes. Have the comfort of some order. It was too quiet up there. She listened at the foot of the ladder, heard only his breathing. A clean place to sleep.

Food, a shower, a nice flannel shirt she'd tucked away to give him for Christmas. He didn't seem quite so destitute. He needed to go to the dentist. She had dreams about his teeth. She listened to him playing his guitar while she got ready for bed. She and Aaron and Richard on the weekends. And sometimes Richard's kids, but just for day visits. Well, that should work out okay.

She called to him from the hall, the whole house dark. "You might as well take my car in the morning since I don't have to start work until Wednesday. My last day to sleep in. You've still got your license?"

"Still got my license."

"Well, good night then."

"Good night."

"Aaron."

"Yes." His voice wary.

"I'm glad you're home for a while. Glad you're safe."

She woke to the screaming of the phone. The sound of heavy footsteps. For a minute she thought someone must have broken in. Then she heard Aaron's voice. She switched on the light. 12:00. It felt much later. She listened for the tones. But she couldn't catch any words. Then she heard Aaron come into the hall. She got out of bed and went to the top of her stairs.

"It's Mark. He says I need to come and get him. It's an emergency. He needs to come home for a while. Says to tell you he'll find some work."

"He wants you to drive to New York tonight and pick him up?"

"Yes."

"He can't take a bus in the morning?"

"No."

"And you're willing to do that?"

"Yes."

"What about your first day at the sawmill?"

"I'll take care of it."

She handed him the keys, money for gas. In a few minutes, she heard the car door slam, the sound of gravel, saw the headlights turn away at the barn.

A red truck came tearing up the driveway. She was about to jump for cover when it skidded to a shrieking stop, one tire flattening a big bag of potting soil. Then she recognized the driver and resumed hoeing. Just Carla Morletti on another rampage. Really she wasn't in the mood for a *he said this, then I said that* tirade, didn't really want her potatoes subjected to all that turbulence, but … Mark was still sleeping and Aaron had gone to the sawmill as soon as they arrived so there was no one but her to listen, deflect the volleys.

The truck door slammed and Carla came charging right through the onions. "For two cents I'd join a nunnery."

She considered saying she'd be glad to fund the conversion. Carla plopped down at the picnic table and began digging through her purse.

"Marriage to Jesus, who's there in spirit only … for less than two cents."

It was just like they were continuing a conversation from that morning rather than weeks since they'd talked. Del tidied up a hill in the last row. Going to take a final picture of the potato plants before the big harvest tomorrow. "Think of it, Carla, every single potato I planted made it to the light."

"He says I can't use the truck to get to work this week like he promised because his wife needs the car and blah, blah, blah."

She could say, His wife, he's got a wife? but she does not want to add any fuel to the furor. "Tomorrow I'm going to dig right down into this soil and find potatoes." She does not mention that it's her birthday. With the arrival of Mark and Aaron the solitary soup beneath the maple scene has dimmed, but she does not want to add the Morlettis to the mix.

"I got to drop the truck over there before they get back. Provide my own ride home. Be discreet. That's what he says to me, 'Be discreet, Carla.' Discretion the last thing on his mind when he comes wheeling into my yard middle of the night anytime he feels like it."

Del put down the hoe and wiped her sweating face with the tail of her blouse. "I actually dreamed I *was* a potato." She stretched her back and then began to weed the last corner. "You know I wouldn't be surprised if I ended up with a couple bushels."

"I was hoping maybe you or Aaron or Mark could follow me over to Wynn's, give me a lift back. When Aaron gets here with your car. Where's Mark? Rudy said Mark's going to be around for a while. Wynn might be able to use him to help clean up his sculpture barn. He's got a big commission."

She did not want to get anywhere near this Wynn situation, have Aaron or Mark anywhere near it either. Wynn. Even the sparest of clues indicated stability was not his strong suit.

Carla practically had her head down in her bag now. "What time is it? What time you expect Aaron back?"

"I don't know." This was true for the time. She'd stopped wearing her watch for the summer. But she did know when Aaron was getting home—around five which the sun said was soon.

By now Carla was systematically unpacking her big pocketbook. "Oh, here it is. Before I have a heart attack thinking I left it at the Quickway. That's all I need. Get arrested on top of everything else." She set a plastic baggie and a pack of rolling papers on the table and began reloading her purse. "Robbed this from Rudy's plants this morning, dried them in my new toaster oven—a gift from Wynn. We might as well relax while we wait for Aaron. Can't be long now."

"No thanks," Del said, "I've …" She tosses the weeds onto the pile. "Given it up for the duration."

Clearly Carla didn't register this, just went on expertly sprinkling flakes into the crease she'd made in the EZ Wider. Then she made a deft roll, licked the edge to seal it, gave a twist to each end. "Ehh," she said, holding it up to the sunlight. Her entry in the joint rolling contest. And then Carla began rooting around in her purse again.

Del glanced down the road.

"Got any matches?" Carla said.

"No." Further she did not want Aaron to arrive to the smell of pot. Or to have it go wafting in to Mark either. Not when she planned to make it very clear that if they wanted to live there for a while, as long as they were both working, there was to be no drug activity. She knew what they'd say, You call smoking a little grass "drug activity." Yes, I do, she'd reply. Tomorrow evening after the potato harvest the three of them could sit down and clear the air.

"Want some onions?" she said, stepping carefully over the potato rows.

"Now how am I going to manage to get to the Edgewater tomorrow? Wednesday's one of the busiest nights. Volunteer Firemen. Best tips for the week. No matches anywhere?"

Del pulled up three good-sized onions and peeled back the first papery skin, pinched off the tiny roots to drop back into the garden as she moved down the row. Then she bent to harvest a small bunch of garlic. Something moved. A praying mantis's large eyes stared at her from a grassy reed the same color as its body. "Oh look, Carla." Del set the garlic and onions on the grass then slowly reached her forefinger down and slid it between the mantis and the reed. The mantis's four back legs secured to her finger. She extended the mantis for Carla to inspect. For a second Carla hesitated and then rested the joint on the table and held out her hand. Del pushed the insect onto Carla's palm.

The mantis caught hold of the soft flesh of her cupped hand. Carla started. "What a grip." Then she scraped the creature onto the table.

Del straddled the bench across from Carla and lifted the mantis again. The insect, almost as long as her finger, reared up and wiggled its two short front arms together.

"Praying," Carla said.

"Pregnant," Del said, turning her finger to look at the bulging pouch, beating beneath the mantis's jade wings. "I remember when my belly was like that." Her empty hand outlined a huge arc in the air. "So big with Aaron that when I put the seat back far enough to fit behind the wheel, I couldn't reach the pedals." She bent and lay her hand onto the grass. The mantis hopped and disappeared in the green.

Just then her car appeared. Carla tucked the joint in her pocket, slung her bag over her shoulder, and started down the drive. "See if he's willing to follow me over to Wynn's, give me a lift back to my house. Shouldn't be more than an hour or so."

Del set her book bag on the seat and gave one last look toward her classroom on the second floor as though her mind could scoot around checking: Had she forgotten anything she needed to get ready for the real first day tomorrow? Today only pretend. Just twenty-minute sessions for each class, half a day to get oriented. Everybody still on their best behavior. Four sections of high school art, two sections of remedial English. 6B the only group likely to make her neck ache. There were still lots of teachers' cars in the parking lot. She was determined not to fall into her old ways of being the last one to leave, staying late day after day preparing, preparing in order to try to keep one step ahead of kids like Stan Morgan or Neil Hayes. As though yet another seating chart was going to do it.

She made the turn onto Main Street. The school loomed up on the hill, its terraced lawn sweeping her way. Its WPA architecture speaking for all that was traditional and upright. The sixties never even happened here. Of course in a few days she'd whip up some energy, some excitement for the new classes. She always did. But right now her potato plants beckoned. She'd have to pick Aaron and Rudy up at the Quickway at five. That gave her all afternoon to dig potatoes, spread them out to dry. Maybe even get things started on the soup. She'd left Mark looking at yesterday's want ads, but leaning toward Wynn's offer of a month or two of doing clean-up work for him. She'd wanted to caution against that, but this evening, laying out what she expected in terms of them living at home was as much as she could do.

When she passed JAKE's Grocery, she hesitated for a second, but no, she was sure she had everything she needed: the butter, the cream and milk, lovely bunches of parsley blooming in her window ... She turned into the gravel bank and headed for the rise of her road at the back. Unless you knew it was there, you'd never guess that tucked in along the brook, there was a stone house. Her stone house. Get the newspaper and mail on her way out later. She steered to the right of a couple of big pot holes. Get Aaron or Mark to fill those in with gravel before they got any worse. Fix some garlic bread and salad. No birthday cake needed. Then her stomach lurched—parked in front of the house, the red truck. And she knew, as you come to know these things, that this was not going to make her happy.

Del put the car in the barn and began the walk to the house. Oh well. Oh well. She opened the door. Carla looked up startled. The man who must be Wynn looked at her with cool eyes. Mark's back was to her.

Carla stood, her hands flashed up, two flushed birds, "Del, I thought you were at school ..."

On the table the mirror she used to check for creosote in the chimney, on top of that a line of white powder. The man made no move at all. Mark did not turn.

"Jesus, Carla," was all she said. Then she closed the door.

Del lifted the fork and hoe from the bucket and walked around the house to the garden. Her school pants, her school shoes. Fine. Her foot settled solidly on the fork; she pushed it deep into the soil far enough away from the first plant not to do any damage. She heard the truck start up and back down the drive. Important to fork in around the whole thing before she lifted it out. On the final plunge, she levered the plant up. Potatoes, lovely brown-skinned potatoes, dangled from the roots. Some of the dark soil dropped away when she gave the plant a shake. She reached in and pulled a beauty out. Rubbed it back and forth in the grass until its smooth skin gleamed. Then, she took a bite.

28
Dogs – 1989

Christ, what had Tess done now? Carla took a breath, then made the turn into the door marked *Office*. How she hated this place, the heavy chairs lined up for the truant. She looked toward the two secretaries who sat talking across their desks. They didn't appear to notice her standing at the counter. The barrier. The principal's door was closed. The new principal. Maybe Tess was in there.

Out the large window, beyond the two women's heads, the playground. Carla watched a little girl's legs pump fiercely until her sneakers reached the highest possible spot, then she dropped her head all the way back to catch the world upside down. Tess used to do that. Before the time-out corners, the pencil-stabbing, the fat guidance folder. Before the principal's weekly warnings of more and more dire consequences. Well, it was a new principal, a new year. Maybe she and Mr. Vincent could come up with a new plan. For a moment Carla leaned in, felt the tired ache in the small of her back. Enough of this bullshit. "Excuse me," she said, as she rounded the end of the counter like she might barge on by.

Both women turned, gave little jerks of their heads.

"I'm Carla Morletti, Tess's mother. Someone left a message where I work that Mr. Vincent wanted to see me."

"Yes, of course. Mrs. Morletti," the older woman said, rising and smoothing out her pantsuit. Carla glanced down at her own clothes, her bartending garb—black jeans and a scarlet sweater. Tip clothes. She gave the secretary her *let's get on with it* smile.

The woman looked over her glasses and bent the corners of her mouth up. Then she pulled a card out of a file box marked *9th Grade* and set it down between them, pointing to the telephone number.

"We tried to get you at home," she lowered her voice, "but a recording said it was no longer …"

"What's the problem?" Carla said.

The secretary glanced at the principal's closed door. "Mr. Vincent is busy, but if you'll take a seat over there, he'll see you just as soon as he's free."

Carla looked at the clock. 1:30. "Someone's covering for me at work. Is it something I can call him about?" Plus Wynn's goddamned dogs—she had to feed them on her way back.

The two secretaries looked at each other, frowned, made little no head shakes. Clearly they'd already reached a verdict on Tess's latest offense. "I don't think it will be too long," the other secretary said.

Carla sat down. She'd like to duck out to the parking lot for a cigarette, but instead she began to thumb through a copy of the school newsletter, a thing she usually put directly in the trash when it arrived in the mail. Ever since she saw she wasn't going to get through to them about Tess, she took all their blah-blah words and dumped them right in the burn barrel. If she let even the first paragraph of the Superintendent's Greeting into her brain, she'd be pissed off all morning.

Attention Deficit Hyperactive Disorder, they kept saying. ADHD. How they seemed to love that neat little diagnosis. Tess only in third grade when they started wadding it all together, tossing ADHD at her every time she went in for a parent conference. I don't think so, she told them. When Tess was little, didn't she make Carla read *Charlotte's Web* to her over and over until all the pages fell out? Those baby spiders ballooned from that barn hundreds of times. Teresa can't focus, the psychologist said. Focus? Couldn't she take long stories in and give them back almost word for word? She wasn't like Rudy or her father who turned all their *d*s into *p*s, couldn't read the signs on the Thruway. No, Tess could read your socks off. Okay, so she had to wander around the room while she did it. Let her. The point was when they weren't boring her, droning on and on about the rainfall in the Amazon, Tess could pay attention big time. As long as you didn't try to make her. Trying to make Tess do something was like trying to get out of a muddy ditch, the more you accelerated, the further down you went. Her report cards called her *difficult, dis-*

ruptive, distracting; the teachers' anger etched on the yellow cards in the slashing of *T*s, the stabbing of *I*s. Didn't she, Tess's mother, understand this anger? Didn't she sometimes want to take hold of Tess when she flipped into make-me mode and shake her, but whatever was going on with Tess, it sure as hell did not all fit into four letters of the alphabet. Jesus. Carla honed in on the *Monthly Menu*. All that fruit cup and tuna delight calmed her down.

At two o'clock, just when she was ready to light up, leave, press for some action, she was ushered into Mr. Vincent's office. He was not what she expected. Not like the last principal, a pale little man with a small rounded belly protruding just below his belt. No, Mr. Vincent was a different specimen altogether—trim and tan with perfect hair. He reminded her of the teachers in Wynn's prep school pictures. Sociopaths, everyone of them, Wynn said.

"Mrs. Morletti." Mr. Vincent moved smoothly from behind his large desk and extended his hand.

She hesitated, then managed to reach out to be caught in his firm grip. First principal who'd ever done that. Yes, maybe they were going to get somewhere.

"Please have a seat," he said. "Theresa will be right down."

"What happened?"

Mr. Vincent took the top off his pen, made a notation on his yellow pad. "I'd like Theresa to be here before we begin."

He looked different, but she had this down-dropping feeling he was the same.

Mr. Vincent leaned back his chair, but he didn't quite look at her. Like someone behind her had just raised a hand. "Mr. Ross is bringing her to the office," he said slowly, deliberately like there was plenty of time to get to the bottom of this.

But there wasn't plenty of time. She needed to get going. Dirk would be pacing the bar.

Mr. Vincent opened a thick folder and began to glance through it as though she wasn't there. Carla felt a burn moving up her neck. She leaned forward and folded her arms to rest on the edge of this man's cool desk.

He looked up. That flicker of surprise. Then the squint of authority.

"Is that Tess's folder?

Mr. Vincent hesitated, closed the file. "Why yes, yes it is."

"Mr. Vincent, how well do you know Tess?" Another flicker. "My guess is, it will go better if you fill me in a little. Tess can be difficult. No one knows that better than me, but ..."

Mr. Vincent put down his pen. "Theresa is on in-school suspension right now. She had an altercation with one of her teachers."

She wanted to bend across the desk and bite his aristocratic nose. She willed her voice to remain calm. "Perhaps you could be a little more specific."

Just then a large man appeared at the door with Tess. Tess, with her spiky haircut, black, black, everything black. Tess didn't look at her. The man nodded to Mr. Vincent and left.

"Have a seat, Theresa," Mr. Vincent said. He rose and closed the door.

Tess stood motionless, then she moved slowly to the chair beside Carla, slid down, her shoulders low, her legs sprawled out. Both of her sneakers untied. Tess's upside-down version of sitting up like a lady. She wanted to reach over and squeeze her knee, to say, Tess, enough; I am so tired.

"Theresa." Mr. Vincent's voice was deep and full of patience. "What happened in English class this morning?"

Tess did not speak.

She said, "Tess."

Tess turned toward the window. The playground was deserted now; all the swings empty.

Mr. Vincent read from a yellow sheet. "Mrs. Crowley said she asked you to copy a sentence from your book on the board and underline the nouns, that everyone in the class was taking a turn. Then what happened?"

Tess sat up a little in her chair and shrugged her shoulders, her Igiveashit shrug, the one that always made Carla want to reach out and smack her.

Mr. Vincent put down the paper. He looked at Carla for the first time since Tess's arrival. He gave his own little shrug and began to drum his fingers on the arms of his leather chair. Carla read his mind: Here they were lined up before him, mother and daughter.

Two truants. And what was he to do with them? He shook his head.

Carla knew she should say, Mr. Vincent, I'd like to speak to my daughter alone. Then she should try to get Tess to tell her side of the story. Then she should try to negotiate some end that would simmer things down. But just the thought of trying to put that all together made her teeth itch. And, dear god, she was tired of it all, so instead she leaned toward her daughter and said, "Tess, I need to get back to work so I don't lose my job. And I have to stop and feed the dogs on the way."

Tess stiffened. Why had she said exactly what was bound to make it all worse? Time, work, the dogs? Why did she keep turning her weariness, her frustration on Tess?

Mr. Vincent picked up the paper again.

Tess stuck her fists under her thighs and began to jiggle her legs. "Do what you're going to do," she said.

Mr. Vincent sighed, returned to the yellow paper. "You refused to do the task. You ended up swearing, calling Mrs. Crowley a name. And you left class without permission."

Tess stared at Mr. Vincent. "My mother has to go feed Wynn's dogs," she said.

"Theresa, unless you apologize to Mrs. Crowley, you …"

Tess stood up in a flash of black. At the door, she turned and looked at Carla. Fury. Then she was gone.

Mr. Vincent placed the cap back on his pen. "Mrs. Morletti," he said.

Carla pointed out the window. Beyond the swings, loping toward the parking lot, Tess, all darkness against the Indian summer sunlight.

"Out of school suspension until she comes in and apologizes to Mrs. Crowley. Theresa can't have it all her way, Mrs. Morletti. She has to learn."

Carla rose. She too turned at the door. "Mr. Vincent, for this," she spread her hands to take it all in, "what sort of grade do you think you and I deserve?"

The buzzer to change classes blared in Carla's ear, then muffled as the heavy side door shut behind her. Tess was nowhere in sight. Across the crowded parking lot, Wynn's truck flamed red in the October sun. At least she had the truck. A good trade off for feeding three crazed Dobermans until Wynn got out of jail. A registered, inspected, insured vehicle with good tires. She wished she had a dollar for every crisis that included a car that wouldn't start.

She slid onto the hot seat, looked back at the school, its red brick exterior squatting smugly on its knoll, its shiny windows decorated with cutouts of colored leaves. I hate cutting along all those blue lines, Tess used to tell her. Carla backed, looking carefully both ways.

Once when Tess was ten, and the then-principal called to say Tess dumped the trash can on top of her teacher's desk when everyone else was out for recess, she went in and asked to read Tess's file—today even thicker sitting on Mr. Vincent's desk. The guidance counselor didn't want her to see it. She insisted. They brought out a folder, full of scores and teacher comments and psychological reports. After only a few pages, she couldn't see the print anymore. Fastened to every new year's awful words were Tess's class pictures: her dark eyes and big mouth, Steve's jaw, a dear little child face smiling at her. The same face she still saw when Tess was sleeping.

Traveling slow, she checked the side streets. Then up ahead she saw her, her black Jimmy Hendrix T-shirt rounding the corner by the post office. Carla lit her next to last cigarette and pulled up. Tess didn't stop, didn't look her way. Creeping along beside her, Carla stretched across the seat and cranked down the window. "Let me give you a ride up the hill home."

"Go feed your lunatic boyfriend's dogs," Tess said. She crossed in front of the truck.

"Tess," she called, "I'm sorry." But Tess did not turn. She did not let her explain. She just kept moving away from her until she disappeared behind the Inn.

The post office clock said 2:40. Dirk would be hopping. The beasts would have to wait. They wouldn't starve overnight. Cerb's eye infection could go one more day. As she made the turn toward Stanton, she glanced up Fyler Hill, but there was no sign of her daughter. All along 51 she watched the black and white cows crowding together under the trees. Sometimes they turned to look as she went by, their huge bags swaying as they moved, their barrel sides hanging from jutting hip bones. They were mothers, but what did they know of any of this? No principal lined them up to say, Shame on you.

In one of her last attempts to get through to Tess's teachers, she took Tess's cardboard box kingdom to school to show them. See how the doors and windows to the castle open, how the drawbridge lifts up, she said. See the unicorns hiding in the forest mountains. Tess works on these for hours, she told them when they said Tess wasn't interested in anything, that she couldn't be still for five minutes. She did not tell them how Tess slept with the kingdom by her bed, her little knights facing the dark. Four hand-carved knights found in a box, marked *Rudy and Tess*, long after Carla's father died.

And when Tess's own father, when Steve left, when Tess was in fifth grade, it all got worse. Tess. She was out of hand. Mr. Vincent made it clear she must make peace with the English teacher. She must apologize. How to manage that? Tess's father. An hour away living with his girlfriend. Maybe Tess should be with Steve. A daughter and her father. Tess with Marion? Tess full time, instead of every now and then for a weekend, a movie at the mall.

She made the final turn to Stanton and lit her last cigarette, crushing the pack into a tiny ball. A ball that blurred in her fist. She stuck the cigarette in the corner of her mouth. Tomorrow she'd say, Tess, you have to go in and work it out with Mrs. Crowley. You have to do what I say or … Or what? Up ahead in the window of the Edgewater Bar and Grill, the neon Coors sign blinked.

The next morning when she went through the kitchen, Tess was hunched over a bowl of Fruit Loops. Carla hadn't talked to her since she disappeared behind the Inn yesterday. Had only seen her face, half under the covers, one clenched hand almost touching her kingdom when she peeked through the darkness last night.

Carla swung the big bag of Kibble 'n Bits onto her hip and opened the door. No point getting into the conditions of her suspension now. "I'm glad you got home all right," she said.

Tess didn't say anything, just shrugged and turned the milk carton around to look at the pictures of missing children on the back. She would not hit her. For the last three years every time Tess gave her that shrug, she put her hands in her pockets and took a walk. "I'll be back by noon, so don't go ramming around on your bike because when I get back, I want to talk to you."

"Talk to me about what?" Tess said, filling up her bowl so full that the pastel loops cascaded over the sides.

She could've said, Talk to you about how tired I am of dealing with you. Talk to you about how I'm thinking of sending you to your father's. But she just shifted the heavy bag. "Noon. If the monsters don't eat me up."

"So why don't you put them in a kennel?"

"I told Wynn I'd take care of them. I promised." Plus of course she had the use of his truck. Anyway didn't Wynn say his lawyer was going to get him out any day, how no way can they prove he filed a bunch of phony tax forms. White collar crime. Steve would have a few things to say about that.

Holding the sack tight, Carla stepped out onto the porch and slammed the door hard in reply. She hoisted the bag onto the truck seat and pulled herself up. She studied the house: the weathered clapboards, the drainpipe broken off and leaning against the side. The front door glass taped where it cracked when Steve slammed out the night he left. Three years ago.

The house fit Tess's folder. Disordered. Disadvantaged. Dysfunctional. Hey, she knew all the big words. She wasn't dumb, just dis … located. But there wasn't any junk in the yard and she wasn't on food stamps. She had to do that once, but she hated the faces behind that counter too much to ever do it again.

She shoved the big bag over and started to back out. Cerb's eye drops. She turned the truck off. Tess was gone. The bowl of soggy Fruit Loops surrounded by the piles of unfolded clothes, her black pants bunched on the drain. She set the empty milk carton on top the overflowing wastebasket. What a mess. What a life.

She rummaged through the piles again. No drops. The G.D. things cost fourteen dollars of the fifty Wynn sent her. She was not buying any more. Let Cerb go blind. Anyway how the hell was she ever going to get him to let her put them in his eyes? Tess was right. Why was she taking care of those friggin' dogs? She went upstairs. Bits of mud and curls of dust littered every step.

The eye drops were right on the top of her dresser beside her last year's birthday gift from Tess. As she lifted the box, she knocked off one of the cymbals. Carefully she balanced the little disk back on its stand. She stopped, studied again Tess's gift: a miniature full set of drums with a tiny rock drummer, delicate hands holding tiny sticks, all at perfect proportion and tilt, made of cardboard and lids and spools and screws and disks and foil, all fastened to a shiny black platform. She remembered again Tess's head bent over the kitchen table, her lips tight in concentration as she glued and cut and painted. Mrs. Crowley should see this. She picked the board up, carried it over to a far window, and set it down gently on top of an old trunk. Out of sight. She jammed the drops in her pocket.

Downstairs she pulled the back door to. Enough. Enough. Why shouldn't Steve deal with it all for a while? She jumped into the truck, ground the gears, and screeched onto the road.

Look out, you beasts, I'm in no mood for trouble.

Wynn's was the only place on the dead end. She pulled into the driveway beside his house, a tall gaunt Victorian job with a backyard full of dismantled cars—all neatly stacked for future sculptures: piles of headlight eyes, stacks of fender-hips, rows of door-handle-mouths. Is this what you think of women? she said when she saw his first sculpture. What the 21st Century thinks of everything, he answered.

Her lunatic boyfriend. But that first night last year when Wynn sat at the end of the bar and drew her eyes was the best she'd felt in a long time. I'll help you close, he'd said. All the while they put up the chairs and stood together to wash the glasses, she had talked, and he had listened, his head leaning to one side, his eyes watching her. She had talked about anything that came into her mind.

Would we really want to know where it's going? Del tried to clue her in: Think it over, Carla—another trip through the Horror House of Love? The more she saw of Wynn, the less she heard from Del. At first she chalked it up to Del going straight, putting her life in alphabetical order, living with Richard Larson. Ms. Recovery. An Alanon groupie. But was she on the money about Wynn? Yeah.

She surveyed the house again and sighed. The dogs. She took a deep breath. Last week, the first time she'd fed them, she'd smoked a joint before she went in, thought that might make the whole thing more fun. Instead she'd been paralyzed with fear as the dogs lunged, afraid they were going to tear her to pieces. Especially Cerb. There was something not right with that dog even before the infected eye. She hadn't fed them stoned again.

Today the minute she opened the truck door, she heard their maniacal howls. Bub, Lucy, Cerb. God, how she hated those dogs. While the dogs leapt and smashed against the front door, she sprinted around behind the house, let herself in the back room and tested the kitchen door to make sure it was tight. She dug around with the bowls in the bottom of the wooden bin. Next she opened three cans of Alpo and spooned that on top the mounds of dry stuff that looked like those mixes in the baskets on the bars of nice little restaurants. Finally she poured water down over the whole mess and pushed a cod-liver oil pill into each gooey center. Wynn's formula.

Instinctively, she braced herself. Sure enough, at that moment Cerb's large body hit the kitchen door, glass rattling, with Bub and Lucy right behind. The floor vibrated. She turned and gave them her most sincere smile. "Simmer down, Boys. It's just about ready." Cerb's eye looked terrible—swollen, blood red, and even from here she saw there was stuff caked all around it. What she needed was a muzzle. Crooning nonsense and smiling again at the dogs, she slowly opened the door, pushing her weight against the impact of their banging bodies. She got it wide enough for Bub to squeeze through. She knew Cerb and Lucy would follow; she didn't wait. She ran out the back door around to the front. Watching where she stepped, she went quickly through the house to close the kitchen door and pen the dogs. Then she collapsed into a chair.

Jesus. But she didn't sit long. The stench. She rose and moved into phase two of the operation. Cleanup. From the front porch she brought stacks of *New York Times*, still being delivered daily, a Christmas gift from Wynn's Westchester mother. Evidently she knew nothing of his present confinement, and clearly he didn't want her to know. No contact from the estranged wife either. Don't answer the phone, he said in his letters.

She raised the windows in the kitchen and pushed open the swinging door to the pantry. Close putrid air filled her nostrils. The windowless pantry smelled like something had died in there. Maybe a poisoned rat decomposing in one of the cupboards. She flicked a switch, but no light came on. Maybe Con Ed had turned off Wynn's electric. She wouldn't want to be the meter man.

Braving the smell and still holding the pantry door open a crack with her toe, she stretched and groped around in the darkness of the nearest cupboard for the leaf bags, ready to recoil if she touched something furry. Her fingers settled on a box, next to it the paper towels and the can of Lysol spray. Back in the dim light of the kitchen, she let the pantry door slap shut against her rear. How'm I doing? she said to the ceiling. Whatever was stinking up the pantry, it could rot until Wynn returned. The promise had not included the disposal of dead rodents. On her hands and knees she began to roll all the dirty and ripped newspapers as tight as she could. With the towels she picked up the piles that had missed the paper. She sprayed liberally and breathed through her mouth. Actually the dogs had done better the last few cleanups.

Systematically she worked her way through the house, rolling the paper, packing it down into the plastic bags, and opening windows as she went from room to room. It wasn't long before whining and scratching came from the back, but they seemed much less desperate. As she cleaned up and spread fresh paper, she made up her mind. She was going to find a kennel for these dogs. Send the bill to Wynn. Well, at least she'd look into it. She finished spreading paper in the hall. Done. She checked her clothes and shoes for dog doo. Now just Cerb's eyes. Wynn had told her, You must be in command at all times. Should have dumped some dope in his food—like brownies.

The dogs scratched and whimpered. She went upstairs to Wynn's room to call Steve. Let the dogs jump to get in. Wear Cerb out. She opened Wynn's door. His room still fascinated her. After the weird sculptures in his studio: bright blue praying mantis females clutching beetle babies to their headlight breasts, she'd expected a dark bedroom, soft and thick, maybe blacks and reds, with furry insect patterns crawling on the walls. That's what she was ready for when he said come on in that first time. Then he led her in to white walls, straight back chairs, a pewter pitcher. Pale rugs on polished wide board floors. Every surface bare and clean.

Then surprise again. Look up, stretched out on the pure white bed—you looking at you, a huge mirror mounted in a curly golden frame. More what I expected, she said, smiling at a self she'd never seen.

That was last year. Things change.

The dogs scratched downstairs. If she took them to a kennel, a great weight would lift. She climbed onto the white white bed and stretched out. She looked up at her body, lying open and inviting. She smiled seductively. She didn't really want Wynn to get out of jail. He was too volatile. She reached over, lifted the phone, set it on her stomach. Too bad she couldn't just call him up and get it over with. Please give me Wynndel Barringer, the Third out of cell block 9. Well, maybe you could just give him a message: Tell him Carla called, that I took the dogs to a reputable kennel because … Because I just couldn't manage it anymore.

She dialed Steve's number. Marion answered. "Hello. Hello." Carla imagined Marion's mouth making fishlike Os against the receiver. She just didn't have the strength to speak to Marion. She put the phone down. How good it would feel to be able to talk to Del, to be able to pour it all out to somebody. So dumb, dumb, dumb again.

Downstairs when the dogs saw Carla through the glass, they all three raised up and barked. She took their big kitchen bowls and filled them from the other sack of food in the pantry. Still the rotting smell. She took the box from her pocket and removed the bottle. She filled the tiny dropper. One perfect drop formed and plopped onto the tip of her trembling finger. She filled the dropper again and laid it on the table next to a chunk of bloody hamburger. Ready.

It was harder to control the door from this side. Usually she just flung it wide and let them rush in. Now she opened it a crack, calling sweetly, "First you, Cerb." But instead Bub got through and immediately went over and started nosing around. She got the door shut. Cerb's red eye glared at her. "All right now, Cerb." But this time when she opened the door a bit, both dogs leapt at once and it smashed back against her. All three dogs began to race through the house barking. She took a deep breath and called in her most Wynn-like voice, "Cerb." He came to the door and stood looking at her, his red eye glowing. She held the meat toward him. His nose raised and quivered with interest.

"Come here, Cerb," she said, feeling more confident.

He turned his head to look around.

"Cerb. Come," she repeated. She waved the bloody chunk slowly back and forth, hypnosis, the dropper trembled in her other hand.

Once again he looked around and then started slowly toward her, his ears raised, his tail still. His thin, powerful body on neutral. In command at all times. When he got to within a foot of her, she said, "Sit."

He didn't sit, but he stood still, looking up at her. She tried to hold him with her stare. She could hear Bub and Lucy bounding around upstairs. She'd forgotten to close the hall door.

She set the meat on the edge of the table. The dog turned his head to look at it. She extended the dropper toward the red eye. Slowly, slowly. He grabbed her hand.

"Drop it," she screamed. He growled, but let go. He took the meat. She stepped back. Cerb crouched. He continued to snarl, his teeth huge and white. Her hand ached, but she did not look at it, did not take her eyes off of him. "Stay," she commanded in a voice surprisingly steady. Her body shaking.

"Stay," she said again and began to slowly back away. Cerb crouched lower, his teeth bared, but he did not move forward. Carefully she reached her bitten hand back behind her, hoping to guide herself to the outside door. All the while she tried to fix the dog with her eyes. Her fingers touched wood. She leaned back a little. Then the door moved. The pantry.

Cerb started to slink forward.

"Stay," she said softly. She felt the swinging door's slight give against her. Then she saw Cerb shift his weight. He vaulted, and as his body rose in the air, hers instinctively jumped back and through the dark opening. Now in the pantry, both palms flat against the door, she braced her legs, ready to lock against the force she knew was coming. As Cerb hit, she held the weight of him, his snarling and gnashing vibrating up her arms.

For the next few minutes the door balanced uneasily between them, leaning open a few inches against Carla's straining body, and then pushing back against the Doberman's raised strength. Just when she felt her tensed legs could bear no more, the dog's weight gave way.

He sniffed around the door, and then she heard his toenails click on the linoleum and the lapping of water. She listened to Cerb's nails as he moved back toward her and braced for another lunge, but the dog merely snuffled nosily at the crack and then slumped down, his body wedged against the door, his panting breath inches from her tired legs. Overhead Bub and Lucy ran from room to room.

It was hard to feel how much time had passed, entombed in this darkness. She felt cold. She rubbed her hands up and down her arms, hoping to stir some warmth. She rolled her aching neck. Cerb sniffed. How much longer might she be trapped in this foul airless room? She placed her nose to the sliver of light and breathed in. Only Tess knew where she was. It must be heading toward 2:00.

The phone above in Wynn's room rang. It rang and rang and rang, and though each ring jangled her nerves and set the dogs upstairs to barking, she recognized in it some hope. Maybe Tess had told someone she was here. Cerb's weight shifted, the wood pressed against her a little more, but he did not rise. The phone stopped. She didn't know how long she waited, ready to lean against the door, every few minutes sucking quietly at the small space around the wood. But she was afraid to move much, afraid to drag the large bag of dried food over to reinforce her position.

The phone rang again. This time Cerb scrambled up as if suddenly about to dash to get it. As before, it rang many times, each one an accusation: I know you're there; I know you're there. Yes, yes, I am. Come and get me. Her throat tightened, restrained sobs for this ridiculous situation, for her problems with Tess, for her life lately, and done with an awareness that she must weep in a way that used up the least amount of air. Cerb whined in unison, on the other side of the door. Then all was quiet. She waited.

Waited. Then she was startled by loud banging. Cerb leapt away and began barking and jumping. Glass rattled. "I'm here; I'm here," she screamed. "That crazy dog has me trapped."

"Mamo, where are you?"

Tess, in the back room, the voice loud and clear, the other side of the pantry wall. By now Bub and Lucy had raced down the stairs and the den of howling and crashing dogs made it impossible to hear anything beyond that. Still Carla beat on the wall and continued to scream, "Go get someone to help." She felt the vibrations of Tess's return pounding, a heart beating between them, but could not make out what she was saying. Then the pounding stopped. She sensed Tess was gone. Surely gone to get help. The dogs barked on. They seemed to be everywhere. Sniffing through the crack, leaping against the glass of the back room door, racing back and forth. Never did she feel she could count on Cerb to be gone.

Time passed. She continued to yell now and then through the racket. Surely Tess would realize the best thing was to ride her bike the half-hour to town to get help, but the dogs' nonstop barking made her think Tess was still there. Then she heard the kitchen door open and bang against the wall, the dogs somehow out in the back room. Next she heard the slam of metal. And the dogs' voices diminished as though closed up in a box. She pushed the swinging door open. Tess stood there in the kitchen. The dogs were gone.

All the way into town, with Cerb, Bub, and Lucy held captive in the back of the truck, she pressed Tess to recount her every step: how she knew something was wrong, how she called from JAKE's, her bike ride over, how she saw she could lure the dogs into the truck by pouring out the entire bag of Kibbles and across that scattering a dozen mushy steaks. "I figured the meat was going to be frozen. Instead they were all yucky and running blood. Perfect." The freezer must have been off for days. All the while she told of her adventure, Tess turned toward Carla, her eyes large, thrilled.

"But how did you know how to put the truck into gear and back it to the door?"

Tess gave her a secret smile.

"I see," Carla said, "But how did you get the cap door open and those fiends in the truck without Cerb attacking you?"

"That's the best part." With the trap all set, Tess had opened the kitchen door a crack and wedged in a piece of cardboard that kept the latch from catching. Cerb's red eye staring at her all the while. Then she slid a board across the rafters and climbed the shelves until she could hoist herself up. Holding tight, she rammed the door full force with the board. It popped open and the dogs rushed out. Just like she planned, they went right up into the bed of the truck to sniff around the food. She dropped down and slammed the tail and the cap window shut. "Nothing to it," she said, punching Carla lightly in the arm.

Carla made the turn at the corner and came to a stop in front of JAKE's Grocery. The dogs rose. She reached across the seat, and pulling Tess to her, held her for a minute, feeling that wondrous ache that the child she once carried in her body, rocked, maneuvered into snowsuits, had grown so large. Then she let go.

The dogs began to bark.

"So what shall we do with these beasts?"

"We'll take them to a kennel," Tess said.

"And what shall we do with you?" Carla asked, touching Tess's cheek.

Tess looked away.

"You know what you have to do."

"You mean about school, about apologizing."

"Yes, about that."

Tess sat and said nothing for a few minutes. The dogs calmed. "I don't know," she said.

"Yes, you do."

As Carla turned to back out, she saw the dogs reclining around the pile of Kibbles, their noses resting on what was left of the meat.

"Look," she said.

Tess laughed. "I guess I can do it," she said.

Carla drove around to the front of the school. The buses were starting to load on the blacktop in back.

"You know, Tess, it's not so much to apologize. It's to face her, to tell her what made you so mad."

"I can't do that," she said. "You tell her. Explain about the itching to go, the trembles. Nasty nouns, vomiting verbs. I can't. I won't."

She slumped against the seat.

"Tess."

She sat up and looked back at the dogs again. "And after we do this, we'll take them to a kennel?"

"Yes."

Tess opened her side and climbed down. She started slowly toward the main entrance, waiting for Carla to catch up. Then Tess turned, her shoulders raised, her palms open in front of her. Pleading.

Carla rolled down her window, her view of Tess's face blurred. She shook her head.

Tess looked at her for a long moment; then she swiveled and walked up the steps. Carla watched Tess see herself in the big glass doors. She bent and tied her shoes, and then, she disappeared inside.

Carla got out of the truck and stretched her tired legs. Across the field on the empty playground, one swing moved slowly back and forth, stirred by some hidden current. Carla moved through the tall grass. She shed her shoes. Her fingers curved around the chains, she pushed off.

Under and up, under and up.

29
Rain Songs – 1989

Del knows something's going to give, but she doesn't know in which direction. She keeps seeing herself and Richard and Aaron and Mark as dominoes standing in a row. Or maybe cards balanced one on top the other to make a little house. Whichever cliché it is, if any one of them breathes normally: Fwam.

She watches Richard's taillights until they disappear down her dark road—probably he'll make the George Washington before rush hour. She takes in a chestful of October air and steps back into the reek of cigarettes. At the same time she got Mark and Aaron to agree to no drugs on the premises, she should have told them no smoking in the house either. Above her in the loft—Mark's adenoidal breathing. From Aaron's room—the low fuzz of the radio. One thing at least, with them here, she knows they're safe, no emergency phone calls in the night.

No question it's easier when it's just the three of them. The addition of Richard on the weekend and occasionally his children—Candid Camera. Or like one of those recovery writers says: He may mention the hippopotamus in the living room. Still it's not like they have to hold their breath too much longer. Mark says he's going back to the City as soon as he puts together a little money—hard to do only working a few days a week at the sawmill. He doesn't say that's because Wynn's in jail, but she knows that's true. Aaron's looking for a place in town or he says maybe he'll build a little shack up on the hill. Is he serious? Maybe she should get herself a one-bedroom apartment in Marwick, rent the house to reliable tenants. Room for Richard on weekends, the day visits from his son and daughter, but too small for it to be an option for Mark and Aaron. She opens her bedroom window and slides back into bed. 3:30. School tomorrow. Mondays always the scariest. English 6B. Stan Morgan—probably going to have to kick him out permanently. Maybe she'll get lucky and he'll be absent.

Five minutes before they have to leave. She hears Aaron go into the bathroom. His bedroom door is open. She'd like not to look, but she can't help herself—the disorder both appalls and fascinates her. It's the way Aaron has always kept his room, the floor by his bed changing only in particulars: hunks of play dough becoming balsa model plane pieces becoming wads of song lyrics becoming crushed Camel packs amid glasses of milk in various fungal stages and lumps of gray-white tube socks, no two having the same color bands. An upside down Chinese checkerboard overflows with butts. Aaron spends two minutes in the bathroom, pulls a baseball cap over his tangled hair, swings on his jacket and is in the car by the time she gets there.

"Hey," he says and turns on the radio. The radio hadn't worked for a couple of years, emitted a staticky buzz whenever she turned it on, but the first morning Aaron rode with her to get to his sawmill job, he folded an empty matchbook strategically up under the ON dial. All it needed, he said. By the time they make the turn at the barn, they're listening to Hot Pajama Party, WOUR Utica, Jethro Tull's "Bungle in the Jungle." The twenty-things-to-do when she gets to school list fades. Bob Marley's stirring it up by the time they take a right onto Chicken Farm Road.

Rudy's waiting on the Morletti's steps when they get there. She pulls up beyond the big hemlock so the house is partly blocked from view. She doesn't want Carla blipping up on her periphery. "What's up?" Rudy says when he climbs in the back seat. A big paper sack lunch his girlfriend just packed settles in his lap. A lunch he often inventories for them: PB and marshmallow fluff on a hamburger bun—his favorite, diet Pepsi, Fig Newtons, and a note which this morning he doesn't read to them.

Del glances back at Rudy when she makes the turn onto Route 8; his ponytail, the red bandana he's wrapped around his forehead make a bright spot that bobs up and down while he sings along with the radio. Today he makes up his own little song: Just back from selling T-shirts on the Dead tour, going to work for a tree-cutting man, in twenty-six more weeks he'll have enough time in to collect unemployment.

The tempo picks up. Laughter. She laughs too. "Sure is grand to be up at the crack of dawn, going to work," Aaron says. He surveys the gray sky. "Maybe it'll rain."

"Yeah," Rudy says, "Get there, work a couple of hours, eat lunch, smoke a joint, go home."

"Can't beat that."

Rudy chants and drums his fingers on the back of the seat. "My praying-for-rain song," he says.

Aaron and Rudy confer. Del eavesdrops. Rudy's girlfriend may be pregnant. She and Carla are talking into the night. He's leaving it up to them; it's their decision. They come to the Quickway in Stanton. It's a frosty morning and she's early so they sit in the car with the heater running to wait for their sawmill boss.

"Want anything?" Aaron says on his way into the store. He returns with breakfast: a large Mountain Dew, a bag of peanut M&M's, and a pack of Camels. His boss arrives in a shiny new pickup. He's a warm, teddy bear-looking guy in his early thirties.

"Nice truck," she says.

"Credit cards," Aaron tells her.

"Credit cards?"

"Money from one makes the payments on another makes the payments on another."

Del turns on the lights in the high school art room and pulls out a white sheet of paper. Her first period art class will arrive soon, only sophomores, but all of them wide-eyed and willing. Polar opposites of 6B, her Language Skills group. How she wishes she only had the art students, but in a small school, several of the special subjects teachers had to fill up their schedules with a remedial class or two.

She places the objects she wants to use for a contour drawing on another white sheet—a pair of her favorite sandals, the leather worn in wonderful ways. She lets the sandals flop down the way they might have fallen if she had kicked them off as she stepped into bed. Beside the sandals, she places a pair of men's heavy workboots. These she lines up side by side, two stolid soldiers in formation as though they've been nailed in place. Lee's boots that she's kept all these years knowing that one day, when she's ready, she going to do a drawing of these two pairs of shoes: hers and his, touching.

She wants to be drawing when the kids start to drift in. The paper is cool and smooth on the heel of her hand. Now she looks at the bottom ridge, how its dark edge lifts off the white. Slowly she moves the pencil as though it is tracing along that first bump, that bit of rough. She'd like to rush ahead to where the back begins, but no, she must stay with this knot on the curve.

Students start to arrive. She ducks her head slightly in greeting, but she continues the slow blind inching of her fingers across the page. Just as they've been doing for several weeks, they start getting out the pieces they're using as models for their contour drawings: the engine parts, bicycle brakes, egg beaters, pine cones, hunks of barnacles. She feels them start to draw, feels the stillness of imagined pencil points slowly tracing the outer edges. Yes, yes, she can do this.

All morning she gathers her energy for English 6B. At the beginning of the year, seeing how much 6B hated reading and writing, for a few days she tried drawing with them. Their language skills so off the track, each taking his or her own strange detour, she'd thought maybe contour drawing might be soothing. Fun. Contour drawing of their hands—the wrinkles of the thumb, the rounding of a nail. Like going back to crawling before they got to words. Hadn't drawing negative space led her to writing love poems to Richard? But right from the beginning 6B had been furious, had refused to turn their hands as models, refused to pick up their pencils. What did this have to do with English? Fuck that. The whole class close to mutiny. She had to go back to fill-in-the-blank ditto sheets to calm them down.

6B starts to seep in. First, Kathy and Calvin. Calvin orders his papers and folds his hands on the desk, ready. A few more wander in: Cindy, Stan, Neal. Neal sits down on Del's stool at the podium and pretends to be studying the Daily Attendance list, the one that every day says at the top *Learning to Care; Caring to Learn*. She starts to move toward him. Just before she penetrates his space, he slides into his seat and slouches down, his shaved head sunk on his chest. He and Stan start to laugh. Joe jives in. The last thing Joe wants is to be sitting in a desk for the next 42 minutes.

Everything the class will need is already on their desks. She stands at the door as-if-ing ease. She welcomes Patty, who's been out for four days. Patty whose black nails will flutter up all period like pirate flags of warning. As usual Vic and Jerry hang outside in the hall until just after the last possible second. As she's about to close the door, they push themselves in.

"What's this?" Jerry says.

Del sees she's accidentally put the wrong book on his desk, a copy of *Where the Red Fern Grows.* "That's Joan's. Please put it on the table."

Just then Joan comes in. Jerry sweeps the book onto the floor and holds his nose, "I'm not touching her book."

"Fuck you," Joan tells him.

Del retrieves the book and hands it to Joan. "That's enough, Jerry," she says.

Joan sits down and the room gets mostly quiet. Del breathes and takes in the back rows, the October orange of the hills across the valley. "All right, let's get started," she tells them.

Only Vance and Lori are absent. She introduces the new composition unit: Process Writing. On each desk, there's already a packet of five pieces of composition paper with a bright yellow sheet stapled on top stating the objectives. Yellow like the suns they drew in kindergarten, back when maybe they believed. "You know," she says, "things like How to Drive a Tractor, How to Make a Cake."

"How to ..." Neal moves his fist rapidly up and down under his desk. Jerry and Rich laugh.

"I'm sick of writing," someone says.

Vance comes in. He's wearing his coat. He's always wearing his coat, his navy jacket, zipped to the neck. He hasn't been in class for a couple of weeks. She fishes his folder out of the box and hands it to him. "All right, I want everyone to list five things you know how to do."

"I can't think of anything," Patty says. Her nails flash up.

"Things you know how to do." She reads them five of hers that she's already written on the board: build a fire, make bread ... She tells them not all topics have to be dead serious. "You could do something like How to ..."

"Skip school," Vance says.

"All right," Del says, "whatever, but make some of them be things that have a real process. The idea is to try to explain each step clearly to someone who's never done it. Like you're writing a manual."

"A sex manual," Neal says.

Her neck aches. "All right, now I want to go around the room and have everyone tell one thing they know how to do. I'll write them on the board. If you see any you can use, write them on your list. You start, Calvin."

"Mow the lawn."

Meanwhile Joe has turned around so he's sitting backwards at his desk. He's trying to engage Vic in arm wrestling.

"Are you going or staying?" she asks him.

"Let me think about it," he says.

She continues around the room, writing down one for each of the students: track deer, clean a gun, change the oil in the car, do the laundry. She notices only Calvin and Kathy are copying any.

"Change a baby," Joan says. Joan has a one-year-old daughter. Joan is fifteen.

"Now I want to have us do one together on the board that you can copy as we go."

"That's dumb," someone says.

"That way you'll understand how to write your own instructions. Let's do How To Change a Tire." A sudden sadness swells her throat—she and Carla changing her tire on Chicken Farm Road. She swallows. "How many of you know how to change a tire?" Not one of them raises a hand. She writes the heading on the board and the words *How To Change a Tire* and under that *Steps*: She advises them to copy this on the first sheet of composition paper. Mike, Rich, and Vic make no move to write. She taps Mike's desk, catches Vic's eye, whispers, "Get going" to Rich.

"I haven't got a pencil," Mike tells her.

Del hands him one from the bunch she has ready. In this class an idle hand is indeed a devil's workshop. "You'll be the experts because this is something I've only done once with someone else's help."

Cindy moves closer to the board.

"Okay. what do we do first?"

"Loosen the lugs," Cindy says.

"No," Jerry says, "first you better tell them to get out the jack and lug wrench."

"Good." She sees that every single kid in the class is engaged, even Vic, from an ironic distance. "Let's take Jerry's first and Cindy's as the second step. Now copy this exactly. Full sentences. Skip lines so we have room to fix it." She starts writing on the board. *1. Remove* then she crosses that out and writes *Get ...*

"Make up your mind."

"That's the way it is," she tells them. "When you write, you have to keep changing things." She continues printing: *Get the jack and lug wrench ...* "What's a lug wrench?"

"What you use to remove the lugs," Vic says.

"Every idiot knows what a lug wrench is," Jerry says.

"Maybe I didn't," she tells them.

They all laugh. Slowly they proceed. Vic, Cindy, Rich, and Jerry really know. Their bodies are on Alert. They are discussing it between themselves. Everyone else is listening and diligently copying. She is the secretary. She writes and crosses out as they negotiate the language. Sometimes she asks questions. "Yeah, but what happens when you can't get the lug nuts off? That happened to me once. When I couldn't get them off, after struggling for an hour, screaming and near tears, I walked a few miles in the freezing cold to a friend's house. She came and helped me and you know what she did?"

"She jumped on the wrench," Cindy says.

"That's right." She goes back and writes, *(If the lug nuts won't turn, you can try jumping ...*

"If you keep adding stuff, we're never going to finish," Mike says. She glances at his paper. He is only a few numbers behind the rest of the class. This is perhaps the longest he's stayed with any writing task so far. She looks at the rest of them. They've been at this for twenty totally focused minutes. She sees by a few bodies, time is about to run out. She cheers them on with, "Hang on. We're almost done. Okay, we've got the spare on and the car back down on the ground. Now what do we do?" She writes *10.*

"Tighten the nuts hard," Vic says.

"Not too tight, you'll strip them," Jerry interrupts. "Just get them snug."

She writes the instructions. Then she goes back and adds 'ly' to snug. "Snugly."

"That sounds stupid," Jerry says.

"Yeah, it does," she agrees. Tighten snug. Tighten snugly. She's trying to decide which way to go with it. She erases the 'ly'; then adds it back on. "I can't decide which way is best," she tells them.

"You don't know? You're the teacher and you don't know?" several say with indignation.

Finally the tire is on; the car is down.

"Maybe you better tell them to put the stuff back in the trunk," Joan says.

"No," Kathy tells her, "that's just common sense."

"Maybe you should remind them to get their tire fixed so they'll have a spare," Patty says.

"No, no more, enough," they call out. The room starts to wiggle.

"All right, pass in your sheets. You did really well with that. Now tomorrow you'll pick your own topic and do the same thing." Most of them are not listening. The lunch bell is in one minute. Rich and Mike try to go up to put their folders away early. She pushes them back with her eyes, her hands extended in a Stop Right There signal.

Most of them lean out of their seats like runners crouched for the gun. The bell rings and they are gone.

At the end of the day she's one of the first teachers out of the parking lot. She's making progress on her new school year's resolution to not be such a drudge. She takes the back way up through the hills to be right in with the trees, all that shimmer. Maybe something's going to give, but it doesn't feel like it's going to be this afternoon. She parks the car in the barn. Sam comes bounding down the drive, his white flag tail waving. That's the thing about dogs, about Sam especially—no ambivalence.

"Hello," she calls when she opens the door. She can hear the washing machine agitating. Overloaded. She goes back through the hall. Mark is standing knee-deep in piles of dirty clothes. He's wearing a black ski cap. She steels herself. Something's up. "You cut your hair." No way his long hair could be up under that.

"Yep."

She backs out of the laundry room. She doesn't want to crowd him. Whatever's coming, she wants it to move toward her in slow motion. Mark's done the morning dishes. She can't stop scouting along the trail for what's ahead. He passes through, goes up the ladder to the loft. "Thanks for cleaning up," she says. She hears him dragging things around up there and begins to open the cupboards, the refrigerator, the bin—something to do to calm *her* down. She bends over and takes a good whiff of the potatoes, pushes her hand down through them. They feel cool and dry. Have to be on guard against one going rotten way under. She pulls out a few and begins to peel them.

Mark comes down with several large garbage bags, full to bulging, and sets them outside the door to take to the barn. "I'm going back to the City tonight."

"Tonight?" The knife cuts the potato into quarters, four perfect white sections. Maybe the house isn't going to come down around her after all.

"Well, middle of the night, got a ride with Nooley. One of the guys in the band called this morning. He's got a place where I can stay."

She looks at Mark head-on, risks the news that may bring. Thin, the black ski hat makes his cheeks look even more hollow, but no other evidence of decline. "They've lined up studio time. Good possibility we're going to make a record. On an independent label."

She goes back to peeling. "That sounds good. Especially about the record." She doesn't say, What about a job to support yourself? The last time Mark called from the City for emergency money, she said No. He hasn't asked for money since.

"Cold," he says. "Let's have a fire."

Her hands have steadied, her breathing calmed. Relief, now only the tightness in her neck, 6B fatigue. "Aaron should be home soon. I'll make a big dinner. Chicken and mashed potatoes."

"And gravy," Mark says. He uses the small ax to split a few pieces of kindling and sticks in a few logs.

She checks the sky, clear, almost no wind, the sun getting low on the hills. It'll be easier with just Aaron, one less potential complication on the weekends. She dips three chicken breasts in crumbs. She hears the fire roar up. Mark closes the vent partway and goes down the hall. He comes back with a bunch of clothes which he begins to stuff in Lee's big army duffle.

She'd like to suggest that he fold them, offer to do it for him, but she knows from other times what his answer will be: What's the difference? Lee's duffle—somehow with all the hitching and relocations, it's one of the few things Mark hasn't ended up leaving behind. She quarters more of the potatoes and puts the water on to boil.

Mark stretches out on the couch, presses his sock feet close to the stove. "I'm thinking of getting a track bike, of getting another job as a messenger."

"Oh," she says. He has tried this several times before, has had several bad accidents: flown over driver doors that have opened right in his path, been thrown onto the hood of a jeep that cut him off rounding a corner. Stitches. A concussion. Bikes stolen. Somehow it always ends in disaster. "No work that's a little less dangerous?"

"Not that I can do," he says.

She thinks of 6B. How she can't do that; how every day she does it.

Mark used to tell her tales of his track bike: how it had no brakes, how by turning the front wheel, he could balance without moving. How sometimes he held onto buses and got pulled along. He rode stoned and listened to music through his headphones. All she could do was ask him worried questions—How can you hear what's behind you? She shakes the chicken to coat it in bread crumbs.

"Sprinkle on some of that Lawry's," he says.

She sets the oven at 350. For once let them have a normal family dinner. No trying to wedge in advice between the lines. She pulls on the toes of Mark's socks as she goes by, a small tug, to give you wiggle room she used to tell them when they were little. Mark smiles. "What kind of record are you going to make?" she says.

He sits up, lights a cigarette. "You know what Velvet Underground is?" She shakes her head no. "I don't think you'd like it," he says.

She gets out the plates and silverware. The red placemats that Lee's mother made for her. "Don't you have tapes of some of the songs you're going to do for the record?"

He goes up the ladder, brings down his old messenger bag. He pulls out a tape and sticks it in the deck. She sets the pan of chicken in the oven and lowers the heat under the boiling water, then pulls the rocker up close to the stove.

Mark reaches up and skims off his hat. Thinner, but with his hair buzzed short, he looks so much like Lee, it's always a jolt. "Ready?" he says. "Not your kind of music, but ..." He pushes the button, turns the speakers. "I'm not going to play it as loud as it would be in a club."

The music—everything all at once, no spaces anywhere. It is strange and dark, with a haunting dissonance pulling at its edges. No maple trees, no blue October sky in this song. She hears the drums in the background. "That's you," she says. "I can feel the City, the grit, the concrete rising up."

They listen until it comes to the end. "I hear the subways roaring through black tunnels."

"Want to hear the other side?"

"Yes," she says.

She checks the chicken, slides the potatoes into the water. The City fills the room, the great bridges swing across the river.

Mark arranges the three placemats around the table. "Maybe we'll go on tour. There won't be any real money in it, but there'll be the experience of the road."

She sees him try to decide about the placement of the knives, the forks, the spoons.

"What we're hoping is that the record will get picked up by a European label. If it does, we'll go all over to help promote it."

The main thing is just to listen. Listen.

He takes three glasses from the shelf. "I get along with the guys in the band. Now I have some friends in the City I can rely on."

Because no matter how she steels herself, what's going to come, will.

He looks it all over and moves the salt and pepper to the middle. "This time they'll probably only cut six thousand, more records than cassettes and disks." He pulls three paper towels from the roll. "Next month we're supposed to play at the Paradise Club."

He sits down in his place by the stove. She sits across from him, tucks her hands into her sweater sleeves, to keep from reaching over, to still their warning urge.

"You'll see," he says, folding each of the towels into a perfect square napkin the way she does. Then he anchors one under the pile of silver by each plate.

"Yeah, you'll see. You'll see: We're all going to be okay."

30
Shelter – 1990

Richard pulled into the driveway right behind Ellen's car, but even if he nosed her back bumper, his truck still blocked half the sidewalk. Every other weekend, Saturday morning, 10 a.m. is always his pick-up time for Lisa and Andrew. Could she have accommodated him by parking in another five feet? He resisted reciprocating with a blast of the horn.

Andrew signaled from the door "two minutes" and Richard knew one way or the other, even if it meant Andrew dragging Lisa out, they would not keep him waiting. Early on there had been a few scenes with Ellen when he had to go up to the house to get them. Since then, Andrew made sure they were always close to ready.

He opened the *Sun*. If there were any movies that the three of them would like—maybe even Del—then he'd keep them until after the early show. *Batman. Driving Miss Daisy, The Little Mermaid*—not looking too promising.

Lisa appeared first, Andrew right behind, carrying her jacket and both their backpacks. Lisa, twelve, going on twenty, designer everything, the dark curls of Ellen's family. Going to be pretty. Andrew, Larson genes, the awkward of fourteen, and pale from sitting in his room most of the time, with headphones in his ears listening to blow-up-the-world music. At least today he'd get them both outside. Go canoeing after lunch.

Richard reached over and rolled down the window. "Want to go see a movie tonight if we can agree on something?" Both faces remained open to further negotiation. "Lisa, run in and tell your mother you'll call later about what time you'll be back." She opened her mouth to make a *why me?* protest. "Lisa," he said.

She turned and went back up the steps. Slowly. He resisted suggesting that she put her brand new ten-speed up on the porch. Andrew got in front. No arguments there since Andrew tended to motion sickness. He flipped Lisa's pack and jacket over his shoulder onto the back seat.

"How's it going?" Richard said.

Andrew shrugged.

"School's starting in a few weeks. How are you feeling about that?"

Maybe a shrug.

9th grade. Richard remembered his general science classes. Brutal. He had to lock up everything in the lab that could be used as a lethal weapon. One of the main reasons he got out of teaching. He tried to catch Andrew's eye, but Andrew looked straight ahead. "Did you get to hear the Cubs' game last night?"

"Yeah, there's a good chance they're going to take the National League. The Cardinals suck."

Finally a connection.

Lisa got in the back and slammed the truck door. "Mom said to tell you the dentist thinks I may need braces and you have to pay for them if I do."

Richard backed out and switched on the radio to WQXR, maybe catch the weather report for tomorrow. The announcer said, "There is increasing concern over Iraqi buildup of troops along the Kuwait border." He switched the radio off. Concerns that are going to ramp up to stealth bombers soon. He turned onto 23 rather than taking I 88. No hurry. Straight ahead one of the maples had already started to turn orange. For a while they drove in silence.

In some ways the visitations wouldn't feel so artificial if he had his own place, rather than bringing the kids to Del's, but with him working in the City all week, owning a co-op in Brooklyn, it seemed crazy to run a house upstate as well. One good thing: The weekends are easier now that Del's sons were off on their own again.

Right after they made the turn toward Danford, Lisa leaned over the seat and waved a plastic case back and forth. "Dad, you want to hear my new CD? It's awesome."

Andrew made a thumbs down motion which Lisa missed.

"Is it country and western? My favorite, George Jones?"

"Ick. Country and western. That's disgusting. You're just saying that, Dad."

"Well, what is it?"

"New Kids on the Block. Come on, Dad, please."

"No CD player, but maybe you could sing me one of the songs. Andrew and I can do backup."

Andrew laughing now. First laughter he'd heard in a long time.

"Okay," Lisa said. "First, I'll teach you the chorus. The words are easy. Not like rap. Ready?"

Richard took Back River Road. "I'm ready," he said.

Lisa leaned up to his ear and began to sing,"'Oh, oh, oh, oh, oh.' Okay, now you do that part."

Richard angled the rearview so he could watch her reaction. Her mouth was open, smiling, coaxing him on. He sang out with gusto, carefully repeating the five ohs in Lisa's rhythm. He poked Andrew to join in. Andrew shook his head and covered his ears.

Lisa went on, swinging one finger as though she was conducting, "'Hangin' tough, hangin' tough. Are you tough enough?'"

Richard joined in.

"Okay, good," Lisa said, "Now, the next part. 'Oh, oh, oh … Listen up everybody if you wanna take a chance, just get on the floor and do the new kids' dance.'"

By the time he pulled up to Del's, the two of them had it down. "'Hanging tough, hanging tough.' Take this on the road," he said. "You can be our roadie," he told Andrew, reaching over to squeeze Andrew's shoulder.

"Oh, Dad," Lisa said, then jumped out and ran toward the house; no doubt to see if she could listen to the CD on Del's player.

Andrew opened his door, but instead of getting out, he said, "Mom's up to something. All kinds of long distance calls. Going into the other room to talk. But don't tell her I told you."

Richard opened his door too. "I won't," he said. He watched as Andrew headed toward the woods.

October and a heavy frost on the last of the chard. The big maple had finally shed most of its leaves. Since it wasn't Richard's weekend with the kids and he planned to do wood all day, Del was going to make herself clean the gutters. She felt around behind the tool box for her gutter gloves to lift the handfuls of gunk that had settled in the bottom of the trough. And there the gloves were right where she so smartly left them last fall.

The phone rang. No surge of adrenaline. Mark and Aaron registering low on her Richter.

"I want to speak to Richard." Ellen, Richard's ex-wife. Her once good friend.

"He's down at the barn splitting wood. Could he call you?"

"I want to get this over with," she said.

Del hurried to the barn. "Ellen's on the phone," she shouted over the roar of the splitter. Richard continued forcing the log against the blade. It cracked, broke into two sections, and dropped heavily to the ground. She turned and started for the house.

Del was not in the kitchen when he opened the back door. He knew she had fled upstairs. He took a long breath and picked up the receiver. Here it comes. "Ellen."

"I got a job in North Carolina. We're moving next week."

"What about Andrew and Lisa? They've already started school."

"You can come to Raleigh."

"It's a fourteen-hour drive."

"The agreement says I can relocate for employment reasons. They can come visit you vacations."

"Ellen, don't do this."

She hung up the phone. He dialed her number. The line was busy. Finally he put the receiver down. He went to the foot of the stairs. "Andrew and Lisa are moving to North Carolina next week."

"Richard," Del said. She came to the railing. She started down toward him. She was wearing her white underwear shirt, the one with the pink roses. Her breasts were soft, the nipples faintly outlined beneath the flowers.

"I'm going to finish this load before dark," he said.

She watched him walk down the drive. He put on his gloves and flicked the switch with the toe of his boot. The splitter started up. He lifted a big log and placed it on the belt. He pulled down on the handle, slowly driving the wood into the wedge.

She leaned her head against the cold glass. "I'm so sorry," she said.

***

He arrived home early from the City. Catch the kids before they left for North Carolina. Del wasn't around. The phone rang. He hesitated for a minute and then he picked up the receiver.

"It's me," Andrew said. "We're going."

"I'll come over."

"We're leaving right now."

"Andrew ..."

"Lisa says goodbye too."

Richard drove by the empty house. He parked in front. Lisa and Andrew did not come out. He drove back to Del's. She met him down by the barn and put her arm around his waist. They heard the first geese. They watched their V turn over the stand of pines on the hill.

"I've decided to build a house up on my land," he told her.

"What?" she said. She'd decided she'd start putting the plastic on her windows and some weather stripping around the front door.

"I'll get Harvey to help me lay the block. Get Pearson to do the excavating, spread a few loads of gravel so we can get in there with the truck."

"Are you hoping that Ellen might let them come to live with you, Richard?" When he didn't answer, she said, "When are you going to build a house?"

"Now."

"In October you're going to start building a house? When you only have Saturdays and Sundays to work on it."

"You could meet me there weekends when it's done," he said. "You could live there all the time if you wanted to."

"But it works fine you staying here. Especially now with Mark and Aaron off on their own."

"It's not that," he told her. Then he kissed her neck and got into his truck. She curled her fingers over the edges of his open window and looked into his green eyes. "I'll be back," he said.

She watched him go down her road, watched for the moving dot of blue to appear on the distant hill across the creek, watched him disappear into the dark spot of hemlocks that fronted his land. She watched with her head tilted to one side, moved by sporadic little shakes, like she had water in her ear or like she was trying to jiggle something back into place that had rattled loose.

Richard called Raleigh.
    "How's it going?" he asked Lisa.
    "I made cheerleading," she said.
    "What do you think?" he asked Andrew.
    "I don't know," Andrew said.

Pearson bulldozed a flat grade the next weekend and Richard and Harvey put in the footers. By the end of October they'd laid up a thousand blocks for the basement and poured the ten yards of concrete to do the floor. From his sister's house, snaking up through brush and trees, he stretched two hundred yards of heavy electric cord to bring power for lights and tools. Richard podged the basement walls, watching the last maple leaves float down while he smeared on the thin layer of mortar to smooth the blocks for the tar. Black and gray, the structure made a strange arena, his boots on the concrete echoing to the empty woods.
    "While you backfill the north side, I'm going to frame up the big windows in this back wall," he told Pearson.
    As he hammered, he looked over the edge where the land dropped away into the deep gorge full of water rushing to the valley. Lots of light for a family room later, plenty of space for all of Andrew's books.
    The next weekend Richard capped the void with a deck of plywood, insulating between the joists under that. He set the windows in place and put in a temporary back door. He borrowed a chunk stove and rigged up a pipe. Weekend fires would help to keep the basement dry. He unloaded twin beds he'd stored in Del's pole barn and set them up in one corner, careful to keep them pulled out from the cinder blocks. He stood in the doorway and surveyed the space. Shelter. A hole-up for a hermit.

Richard called the guidance counselor every few days.
    "I'm concerned about my son."
    "Could you keep an eye on him?"
    "Maybe get him to join the band, play some sports."
    "I'd appreciate knowing from time to time how he's doing."

"It's hard to get through to him."

The first flurries blew out of the gray November sky. Del covered her carrots with a foot of straw and contemplated the wood swelling her shed; she noted the cracks in the ends, lifting the well-seasoned logs at random to feel their lightness. She checked the fire extinguisher and poured antifreeze into her radiator for the twenty below nights ahead. She sent off a winter box to Mark in New York, to Aaron in Boston: heavy sweaters and plaid shirts from the Salvation Army, woolen mittens and thermal socks from the racks near the checkout counter at the Big M.

Richard passed through on his way back from Raleigh to check on his house, to sleep a little.

"How are they doing?" Del asked.

"Andrew's missing a lot of school. He stays in his room."

That night Richard told Del, "I'm going to put on the roof."

She unwound a towel from around her wet hair.

"The roof? You didn't build the house part yet."

"I'm going to build the roof on top of the basement. I want to protect it from the weather. I don't want to put tarpaper on the sub-floor and have that collect snow and leak all winter. I'm going to put on the roof and jack it up to frame the house under it next spring."

"Couldn't you just spread a big tarp?"

Richard didn't answer.

"I don't get it," Del said. "Richard, are you thinking Ellen might let Andrew come to live with you?" Or just hoping if you fill every waking moment, you won't feel anything?"

Richard added another log to the fire. If he needed to he could make the place livable in a hurry.

Del stopped brushing her hair. "Is it possible to lift up something so big and heavy?"

"Archimedean," he said.

"Is it?"

"It's possible."

"And are you going to be in under that heavy thing when you're jacking it up?"

Her hair fell over her shoulder down onto the lace of her slip.
"I'm going to be careful," he said.
"Can I do anything?"
She fastened it away from her face. She smelled clean.
"No."

Bingham's Lumber delivered twenty-three trusses, forty sheets of plywood and enough bundles of shingles to do thirteen squares. He picked up a fifty-pound box of tenpenny nails. He nailed down a rat sill all around and on top of that he built courses four boards thick; these forming a giant twenty-four by forty-four foot frame, not nailed to the sill. *Andrew had been such a good-natured baby. Willing to go to anyone.* The weight of the roof would keep the frame in place until he was ready to lift it. The trusses, awkward, but just manageable alone, he set onto the frame every twenty-four inches, slapping in braces to keep them straight until the plywood could be nailed on top to make the structure rigid. *He used to sit up on his bed in those sleepers with the feet, his toes kicking back and forth into the light from the hall. I'm thinking, he'd say.* When the shingles arrived, he helped unload them from the truck.

Del got out her long underwear and her flannel sheets.
    Richard got the last shingles on just before hard winter hit.
    Ellen called to say Andrew smashed the bathroom mirror with his hand.
    Richard asked why.
    She said she told him he had to go to school.
    Richard asked was he all right.
    Ellen said yes.
    Richard drove to Raleigh.

Pussy willows, April's first soft signal, appeared along Richard's road. Del's crocuses pushed through the layers of sodden leaves. Shad blossomed. Hoop Dawes drove his manure spreader by Richard's squat little structure and tried to fathom what on earth he could mean by putting up such a building. The people in town said Richard Larson was planning on raising the roof up to build the house underneath.

Hoop told them, "Hogwash, only a fool would do such a thing." Anyway it couldn't be done. No way to lift such a weight and hold it steady,

Richard spent a week in North Carolina.

The next weekend he told Del, "I won't be back till dark."

"What's happening with Andrew?" she said.

"We're going to try a different school."

He picked up his two hydraulic jacks from down in Del's barn and took the back way to his land. He figured he needed twelve concrete blocks for each column, six columns for each side—*He learned to walk before he was a year old. He pulled himself up and took books from the shelf to look at the pictures.* Seventy-two and seventy-two. One hundred and forty-four blocks. Plenty of scrap boards to start the temporary piers. *He moved around from room to room holding on to the furniture and the walls.*

It'd take three or four days to raise it and one to get the corners framed to make it stable. Get it up halfway this first weekend. Safe to leave at four feet. He'd take the next Monday off for when he'd reached the critical stage. *Andrew had no friends.*

She pulled the rotted black plastic off last year's garden and watched the green spot of hemlocks on the hill beyond the creek. He would be under thousands of pounds of moving weight.

The space between the roof and deck was dark and cramped, dank and airless, with only a little light coming up through the stairwell cavity. For a moment Richard hesitated at the top of the ladder; then crawled onto the deck. *Andrew had always been afraid of the dark.* Hunched. Careful not to get caught on the hundreds of roofing nails which pierced the plywood, he worked his way up and down through the trusses, setting the two heavy jacks and several piles of scrap lumber over each hurdle first. He pulled off his tan coveralls. To lighten, to better feel the rhythm of the roof. On his stomach he released the valve on the lift and placed the first jack two feet down from the inside corner on the long side. Slipping the lever under the end of the first truss, with a whine of wood on wood, he slowly pumped the handle to lift the frame one and a half inches above the sill. A crack of light lit the space.

He placed the second jack under the frame two feet further down the long wall and raised that section one and a half inches. Then he moved carefully back through the truss to place one of the scrap lengths of wood in the space between the sill and the roof frame made by the two jacks. He hopscotched the first jack down to two feet below the second lift. Slowly, weaving between the trusses, he worked himself down the forty-four foot length until there was an inch and a half space of lovely light glowing along the whole side, interrupted only by the six blocks of wood. Methodically he repeated the process down the other long side, his body and mind finding the rhythm. By the end of two hours the entire roof was raised the thickness of one best-selling supermarket novel. He breathed deeply, leaned against the truss, and smiled. The smell of mud. The time that he always went hunting for mushrooms with Lisa and Andrew. They could all do that again. Del, too.

He heard a tractor laboring up the road, the clank of metal. Hoop Dawes going to spread manure on his upper forty. Spring.

Beginning in the place where he'd just ended, he started to work the jacks back down the side. *The winter he was four, some nights Andrew curled up in his closet, with Baa, his stuffed lamb.* At seven and a half inches, he replaced each pier of two-by-sixes with the flat side of a cinder block. It all felt steady.

By twilight, the roof sat solidly on twelve columns, each two cinder blocks high, fifteen inches above the basement level. Exhausted, he stretched his cramped body out full on the deck. He looked up at the trusses. Just under the outer lip of the roof, he saw Venus blinking above the trees.

Del watched the lights of Richard's truck come up her road, watched his dark shape unfold and move up the stone walk.

She opened the door.

"Well?" she said.

"Maybe," he said, dropping his weary body into a chair.

"Maybe?"

He lifted one of her fisted hands from the table. He uncurled her fingers and nuzzled her palm. "By tomorrow night the roof should be up four feet. Halfway there."

At 3 a.m. Monday, just as Richard was getting into his car to start his middle-of-the-night journey to New York, he looked back to see Del's white nightgown flying through the darkness toward him. He rolled down his window.

"But what if there's a big wind?" she said.

"It's six thousand pounds, still sitting low and stable. Go back to bed."

The guidance counselor at the new school said he'd keep his eye on Andrew. The school had an excellent jazz band.

By first light Saturday Del watched Richard's back receding as he moved toward the barn. She did not open the door, did not call after him, Be careful. Did not shout, Do you want some help? Still in her nightgown and one of Richard's old shirts, she took a compost bucket back to the garden and began picking up the largest rocks winter frost and Richard's rototiller had heaved to the top. When Richard's truck made the turn at the barn, she waved, but he didn't see her. Maybe it would be good to live where there were people. All those years growing up, her mother had listened. Now she and Carla had turned their separate ways. Even Sam was gone. Hit by a car. Maybe she could get another big old dog.

The roof sat just as he left it. Dwarfed by the tall maples, their tips lit with spring's first red glow. Richard lifted the jacks from the bed of his truck and moved down the slope to the back door. Inside, the basement was cold and dank. Balancing one rung at a time, he went up the ladder far enough to set the heavy jacks onto the deck, giving each one a push to roll it away from the edge. *Maybe Andrew would make friends with some of the kids in the band.* It was so much easier to move about under the roof now; for though he must hunch and bob his head beneath each truss, he could stand much of the time. He hummed, a kind of raising a roof tune, a pumping song. Up-downupdown. *Maybe Lisa's room would go in this corner, with big windows for lots of light, and Andrew's across the hall. Del would like to watch the woods change. Soon they would be green with new leaves.*

Richard moved to the eastern end of the house, looked down and out onto the drive; then he crossed to the south and studied the ground as it dropped away into the ravine. From each section, he decided where he would jump should he feel the roof start to move, to shift its massive weight on its lengthening fat legs. He targeted places to leap. If it happened, he figured it would be slow, figured he would have time to escape over the edge.

He pushed the first jack to the corner. He was ready. He turned the valve, raised the handle, fastened on the extension, placed the lever two feet from the corner and began to pump. Gently, evenly, he continued to raise and lower the handle. The roof lifted, with a complaining creak of old bones as the whole structure flexed.

Over the chugging of an engine Richard heard a man's voice yell down from the road. For a moment he looked up from his crouched position over the jack.

"How's it going?" Hoop Dawes hollered.

"Fine," Richard called. "Just fine. I figure I'll have it up with the corners framed out in another couple of days."

Hoop shook his head and yelled back over the rumble of his tractor, "I'll include you in my prayers."

Jack. Rise. Place the piece of wood. Lower the jack. Fall. Rise. Fall. Begin again. Soon his body learned the dance. He raised the entire roof another one and half inches in just under an hour. Outside, the morning sun jeweled the dew-beaded webs woven on the grasses that were already creeping back to reclaim the scraped land.

Now in overalls and work gloves to keep the weight of the bucket from scraping her calf, from blistering her fingers, Del hauled another load of rocks over to the edge of the woods and dumped them in the hollow she and Richard had been filling as they had cleared her land the last few springs. Is there no end to the rocks the earth keeps spewing up? As she carried the bucket back to fill again, she searched the dark trees across the hill. She listened hard, wondering if the fall of such a weight would sound like thunder. She bent and began to pick up piles of the smaller stones. If she lived in a neighborhood, she could listen to children playing, people mowing their lawns. Maybe even get a little dog.

By 12 o'clock Richard had completed five cycles of the dance, had raised the roof another seven and a half inches and added one more block to each of the twelve columns, with each column now seven blocks high. And still the roof felt very bounded by gravity, each column fixed. At the rate of one cinder block every five hours, he should be able to have the next set of blocks in by five and the last for today in by ten. Only three more blocks in each column needed tomorrow to reach eight feet. He breathed deep, did a little shake-shake jump, loosening for the long day ahead. Hunger. He would make a quick food run at five if he had time after he got the next block in. He pushed the jack into place and began to pump.

She was already in bed when he came in. She heard him in the kitchen, the clink of glass, the water running. He came slowly upstairs and sat down on the side of the bed. "Well?" she whispered, reaching her hand under his shirt to touch his warm back.

"Six feet," he said. He pulled off his boots, his clothes. Within minutes he was asleep.

His body beside hers, from time to time the muscles of his legs, his arms jerking, he slept. She curled against him. She touched the flesh of his hip, his thigh, careful not to wake him. Each time the wind rose up outside, she started from the dream that was just beginning.

She heard him in the darkness pulling on his pants. "So early. You have to start so early?" she said, heaving her body up to sit on the side of the bed. "It's raining."

"I have to get the rest of the way up today and brace the ends," his voice said.

She stood. "I'll fix some breakfast, make some lunch for you to take. What about the wind?"

"No time," he said. "I'll grab something."

She watched the lights of his truck move across the wall and disappear. She could sit talking with new friends at outdoor cafés.

* * *

Just as he levered to place the eleventh block in the north corner, he heard a low moan, felt a tremor along the frame. He stopped pumping and froze.

Del swung her mother's picnic basket onto the seat and reached into the pockets of her yellow slicker for her keys. Her lighted kitchen, a lantern in the night, moved away as she backed down her road. At the edge of vision, bright green numbers flashed time's disappearance: *11:56. 11:57*. Without leaves it was hard to judge the wind. The rain seemed to be falling straight. Her headlights caught the swollen creek, Hoop Dawes's lower forty under muddy water. The road up was slippery, clay-red streams deepening all of winter's cracks. Through the dark trees, now and then, a glint of light. Richard.

She made the turn. Her car nosed down into Richard's drive, settled into mushy ruts. And there he was, moving back and forth beneath the roof, her view of him broken by giant wooden Xs that braced the end. Bright lights dropped from orange cords on either side. She saw him see her, but without the loss of a single beat, he continued his steady rhythm.

She swtiched off the engine, the lights, put up her hood and breathed. Her boots, sinking in mud, carried her to the other side of the car. She lifted the basket and made her way down the hill to the back. She pushed open the basement door and stepped in. Above, she heard rhythmic pumping. She started up the ladder and swung the basket onto the floor above her head.

"You can't be here," his voice said. "You can't be under here. Go back to the car."

She remained on the ladder. She could not see him. The pumping stopped. "I couldn't stand it any longer. Not doing anything. I was lonely. I brought some food."

His steps came across the floor. He pushed the basket aside, crouched down, and touched her hair, her fingers wrapped around the rung.

"One and a half more inches. One hour. And I wouldn't put money on it either way."

"There's chicken soup and coffee."

"Good," he said.

"I'll wait in the car," she backed down the ladder.

"Del."

She looked back up at him.

He laughed. His heavy boots, his tired face rose above her.

"Don't slam the door."

31
ROADWORK – 1992

THIS IS HOW SHE DOES IT: Forward ....Reverse .... Forward .... Reverse ....

This, on a section about as big as her kitchen. She goes over the same area on an average of eight times. Compacting, compacting, compacting. It's got to meet specification. A little college girl, paid by the state, runs around checking. She's affirmative action just like Carla. Carla's the night crew percentage for women on heavy equipment. The roller she runs is the easiest, most expendable, big machine. All she does is roll fill. There are a few women on the daytime blacktop rollers, but she says she could never do that—we're talking real skill. Those women come to work in make-up, looking pretty, and run that blacktop roller back and forth like they're crocheting. What would be best for the company is if Carla was black: kill two birds with one stone. This is hard to come by upstate. The big boss takes the quotas seriously. If you don't have the right percentages working, you can get shut down. They can't afford that. If they don't meet their contract date, they lose the money they put up when they made the bid. This is a private contract, not like civil service where people take a week to fill up five potholes. The company's already got crews going twenty-two hours a day. Everybody's pushing like a maniac, especially if the thaw came late. You know what you're supposed to do and you do it. Even if you don't.

Running the roller is a lot better than doing flag or picking rock eight hours a day. Flag is dangerous. Carla almost got run over by a guy on a motorcycle who blew by the flag person at the other end. And it's unbelievably hot; you're standing all day in the sun with a half-hour lunch and a couple of fifteen minute breaks. It's not cool to say you've got to sit down 'cause you feel a little faint. Picking rock, well, picking rock, you can imagine.

Her first night on the big roller, Red, the foreman, gives her ten minutes of instruction: do this and then this and then this and she was on her own. No kidding. No safety course. No hitching along for a day, looking over some guy's shoulder to see how it's done. Red switches this on, he pulls this to the left, he pushes this down. "Like that," he says, and he climbs off and never looks back. No good luck and no goodbye.

At first when the big roller goes up on a rock the size of her head, she's sure she's going to tip over. Her first few nights she thinks she may have to stuff her shirt in her mouth to stifle her scream. Though actually it's usually so noisy no one would hear you if you screamed bloody murder. DO NOT CHANGE GEARS WHILE TRANSMISSION IS ENGAGED is about all you have to remember and that's written in inch-high letters right under your nose. There are just two gears: slow and fast. She only found out there was more than one after she'd been on the job a month when Red peered up at her through the 4 a.m. glow, after she'd brought the roller to its final stop for the night and said, Carla, tomorrow give fast a look over. Hearing Red's voice coming up out of the dark was a shock—most communication is by sign language. Plus most of the time you're wearing ear plugs.

Doing roller you have two completely different work situations. One is when you're part of the beehive. The trucks go in and dump the gravel, followed by the bulldozer that distributes those piles, followed by Carla on the roller. Not too far ahead are the earthmovers—machines as big as her house—totally changing the geography, pushing the hill that was here into the chasm that was there. Unbelievable. And the noise—the ground shakes like some polka hall for giants.

Or you can be all alone. Because the big roller is the last thing to shut down, you can be the only one, except the foreman, still on the site at four in the morning. Whatever's been leveled has got to be rolled because it might rain. Then the site is quiet except for the back and forth clank of her own machine. Forward.....Reverse.....Forward......Reverse..... This is when you can fall asleep. Every now and then you kind of jerk and you realize you've been out and already you've had these little bits of dreams, usually dreams that have some sort of clanking at their center.

It gives you a lot of time to think.

What Carla thinks about is this: She wishes she hadn't started right off yelling. She wishes she'd gone into the kitchen, sat calmly down across the table, taken a couple of breaths, and said, Eighty-five dollars is missing from my room, and then just waited. Or even if she started out all wrong, when Tess said, What? You think I'd lie to you? she wishes she hadn't backed away from that, that she'd been able to say Yes. This isn't the first time. It's happened three or four times before. At least. But this is the biggest amount. The first few times she just kept dumping everything out of her purse and carefully sorting, piece by piece, through every section of her wallet, even the hidden compartment which she absolutely never uses. In between the pictures in the photo fold-out. Down in the bottom of her reading glasses case. Ridiculous. And already that heavy stone dropping like what she's got is a deep well from just below her throat to somewhere just above her pubic bone. Tess. Then hiding her money under the cushions in her room and finding it gone. She's pretty sure she knows what Tess is doing with the money. That's the main thing. It's not just the money—that she's stealing from her—the even bigger thing is what she's pretty sure she's doing with it. She can't keep backing away from that. Eighteen and heading for adult-time trouble. No more juvenile offender. Name in the paper, on your record, everything. Tess, I want to talk to you … Tess, I want you to know … Tess, I'm concerned about … If her brother still lived home, she could lean on him, but he's off on his own; there's no more counting on Rudy. Sending Tess to paint with Steve in Utica didn't last three weeks. Well, sure, Steve says, why should she work when she can sponge off you? Father love. And she knows Steve's right, but she's afraid of what will happen to Tess if she kicks her out. She's been reading a book one of the sad-story people left behind. It's by this Zen monk with a name full of letters in weird places she wouldn't even pretend to pronounce. Little bitty readings for each day, and some of it makes sense—the part about leaving no shadows. That's what she wishes she could do when she talks to Tess: Leave no shadows. The way she does it, she casts dark blotches every which direction and Tess ducks in behind one of those, and she follows her and they never end up where it was she thought they needed to go in the first place. In fact, after the fight often she can't even remember where that was.

How she got working on the road crew, the last thing she would ever have imagined herself doing, well, maybe one notch above driving tractor-trailer, was that her neighbor's husband says to her one day, after he's heard her bitch for years about what a drag it is never having a car that starts, Why don't you apply for the roadwork out off Route12? What? she says. You could be the flag lady ... ha, ha, ha and collect unemployment all winter. The ha, ha, ha revved her up; she knows about how they have to hire a certain number of women and working with a bunch of road guys checking you out surely can't be all that different from tending bar. Easier, in fact, since they won't be loosened up with booze. Part-time at the Edgewater Bar & Grill isn't enough to keep things running and the thought of unemployment, of not having to lug her battery in on dark February nights to bed it down by the wood stove so her car will start the next morning, is her idea of going to heaven.

So one day on her way into the Edgewater, she swings over to Route 12 and pulls in by the trailer at the Four Corners which she thinks is maybe the on-site headquarters. She's expecting whoever's in charge to kind of give her the look down his nose or at best, the once-over to size up her biceps, but no, right away after she rap-raps on the door, this man—turns out he's actually part-owner of the company and probably worth a million dollars—greets her in a courteous, business-like manner, and when she states her name and that she wonders if they have any openings, shakes her hand, gives her an application and moves some stuff off the table so she's got room to write. She's floored. The last time she applied for a real job at Marwick-Eaton Pharmaceutical, there was a glass window between you and some receptionist and you were lucky if you could catch her eye and get her to make direct human contact. The roadwork application is straight-forward, no none-of-your-business questions. They do not ask you *What is the highest grade completed?* which actually she minds a lot less now that she's got her GED than when she should've said 8th. They do not ask *What is your marital status?*, always an eeny-meeny-miny-moe question for her since they don't have *estranged* or *occasional*. They do not ask if you've ever committed a felony. Here she can give a straight No, but it always gives her a long pause, wondering who in their right mind would say Yes? There's no place for references; no place for who they should call in an emergency. On the *Previous Employment* lines, she lists the *Edgewater Bar & Grill* in *Stanton,* the *Macumber Box Factory* in Marwick and a go-go bar in Monterey. The application doesn't include a *doing what* slot, but she wouldn't have put down go-go dancer even if it had. She finishes the application, Bill DeStefanoto takes it, tells her they've got nothing right then, but she should keep checking back because something might open up. She stops by every three or four days, and lo and behold a few weeks later she's doing flag: fourteen dollars an hour, time and half if it's over eight, bringing home five hundred a week and likely to get back anything she pays in taxes. With unemployment compensation not so far down the winter road that she can't spot it on the horizon whenever her wrists, her muscles, are aching so bad she's not sure she can drag herself out of the bed.

Way past eight and the sun's going down. It gets a lot harder to judge the distances at dusk. Up ahead she sees that one of the earthmovers is waiting for the electric company to finish rerouting a line, so the whole beehive has come to a halt. Red is giving her the open hand back and forth under his chin which means *turn off* your machine. She does. The two dump trucks and the bulldozers do the same. The site becomes almost quiet. Now you might think that given this unexpected lull, there'd be a bit of conversation, a few jokes hollered across the way, maybe an update on Ralph's new baby, how Clem's wife's coming along after her operation, what happened at Berton's son's hearing. No. There is no talking while you're working. Usually it's too noisy, but even when it isn't, these men don't seem to feel the need to reach out with words. At first she tried to stir up a little chit-chat during the waiting-around times, thought maybe all their voices needed were little jump-starts of interested questions. How many kids do you have? Been working on the roads long? You from around here originally? And though they were polite and gave her brief responses, the conversation sputtered to a stall right away because they never returned with anything near a What about you? Okay, she got the message. You know the word *taciturn?* Yep. They do talk during the midnight break, but it's pretty much always the same conversations: past years' hunting stories told again and again with amplifications and what's the present game situation—bucks sighted, where the turkeys are feeding. At least three times she's heard Clem's story about the most beautiful ten-pointer ever that he had dead in his sights up on state land, how he didn't move and watched the buck coming on, a perfect shot, and then saw a flash of red just beyond—his brother-in-law making the drive from the other side. He had to lower the gun and let that buck go. The men all shake their heads, yeah, they know the feeling, his loss is their loss, and she's getting so she feels it too. Or they talk about vehicles: current problems with and advice on, hot items called about in the automotive section of the *Pennysaver* that are already gone, fond memories of faithful trucks or tractors or cars that just wouldn't quit.

Except for Scott, right from the go, they've all been polite to her, treated her like a daughter or a sister. Moved over to make room on a tailgate. Cut way down on the swearing and been apologetic when they forgot. She's had to watch her language lest they be disillusioned. Occasionally when some personal topic forced its way to the surface—Clem's wife's cancer, Berton's son's DWI—the sympathy was there in the slow nodding of heads, the pained looking away. She's said a little about Tess, her concern. How tough it's been for Tess not to have a father living home. Kids, Red said, shifting his position, like he was grounding himself for a blow. There seems to be a general consensus—the less said the better. Words make it worse.

The electric company's still jockeying with the line. Red signals. It'll be about ten more minutes. She shifts around a little to see if her bladder could use a quick trip to the woods and when she feels it doesn't, she stretches her legs and does some neck rolls. She lights up. They're allowed to smoke during temporary shut-down times. She sees Clem and Berton are doing the same. Red's chomping on some vegetable; what he chews on since he quit smoking in June. His doctor said if he wanted his heart to take him through a few more years, he better quit smoking, quit drinking, quit running after fast women. He gives a big laugh at that one since everybody knows he's been married for forty-five years, and he'd get the frying pan right on his head if he ever, if he even, well, it just wouldn't have been worth the trouble he'd have stirred up at home. He says he's starting to get orange from all the carrots. Red—what a nice man. He's more talkative when he runs her back to her car in his truck at the end of the shift. Usually they're the last ones to go.

She sees that the men ahead of her have gotten down off their machines, out of the trucks, checking their tires. Scott is looking off toward the hills. Just above the stand of pines, that kind of—red, so flat, such a perfect circle stuck in the sky—it doesn't seem real. Like that picture on Del's calendar. That fiery spot up there might be the just-before moment of Del's picture, with its blue-black sky and its pasted on moon, and under this sun, the gypsy would still be playing his lute. The lion watching, the lion exactly the same. That lion and Scott. Yeah.

Men. All of the years she's been studying men as a daughter, lover, wife, mother, and even lately as friend, she still feels like she arrived in the middle of the movie, that she must have missed some important scene or clue that propels the action forward, that convinces you, in due time, it's all going to come together. What they're doing and why they're doing it is going to, within the larger story, make sense. Be Logical. Be Rational. Isn't that how they've billed themselves? No. That's *it*. This is her latest theory: There are no threads, no dropped hints that when looked back on from the final shot will lead her to exclaim, Oh, gosh, now I get it. Nope. Men are moved by random impulses just like the rest of us, but they square the goopy consequences off every day so they fit into two or three different compartments they've smacked together for storage in order to leave a little space for future maneuvers. And there you have it—the male mind. To her it looks sort of like a combination garage/local post office. At least with women, you know you're in a giant junk shop right from the go, no deceptive advertising, and the most you can hope for is to keep a running inventory, an inventory that never promises to really list everything in stock all at once.

Men. Of course there are many good ones like Red and Clem. But here's the thing: How come with a nice guy, she never feels any electrical activity whatsoever? Besides the book by the monk, somebody left this article around about women who always go for rotten guys. Not rotten exactly, maybe more like *No Vacancy* whenever you're needing a room.

It's that time of evening when all the trees have started to glow, a kind of light, a spell, a shimmer it's hard to describe—pink-gold, lavender-lemon, a time when the gods or ghosts may speak. The trunks and branches stand out black against the mowed fields. She likes the way the farmers roll their hay and leave it hunched along the ridges. July is the time of Queen Anne's lace. Hundreds of pale, luminous disks feather up on the banks. And when you look at them close, each one is made of ring upon ring of tiny flowers and at the very center there's a purple blossom, one drop of blood. She never saw that dark center before doing roadwork until one evening when she was squatting off in a private sea of lace, some distance from the crew.

Red motions her to turn the roller back on, a fisted knock on his chin with his right hand and every one climbs back in and fires up. It reminds her of those TV concerts where the conductor waves his stick to the side and all the violins begin. She rolls forward in slow, positioning herself so she can watch Scott's profile as he works the dozer. She knows he will not signal when he's done; she'll have to pick it up from the way he turns his head, by his now familiar final checking each side before he swings out of the line. He does not like her, and she doesn't know why, but from the beginning he made it clear she can expect nothing special just because she's a woman. He doesn't do anything active; more it's like he looks right past her. A real son of a bitch, she once told somebody, and then for the first time realized what that meant and ever since she's rephrased her description—a real son of a gun, Scott can be a real son of a gun.

Scott swivels to check each side and turns the bulldozer in the direction of Clem's truck. Of course he leaves barely enough room for her to squeeze by. Screw you, Scott. She doesn't grant him the satisfaction of a glower. She'd like to give his arrogant profile the finger, but instead she smiles and raises her hand in a cheery *hey, no problem* wave which he pretends not to see. She moves up onto the piles of gravel and, without any wasted maneuvers, begins her steady roll.

Del Merrick should see her now—working, really working. Maybe she should give Del a call.

The first couple of passes over the area, she'll keep it in slow, but after that she can speed up. No question that after three months of this, she getting more expert. At forty-two she's holding her own, her body's still generating interest, but by Friday the muscles of her wrists, her neck and lower back get so tight, she has to keep up a diet of ibuprofen which she can sometimes feel having its way with her stomach. Running the roller on average of fifty hours a week means that pretty much all she does is work and sleep. Even so, there's the constant fatigue; good sleep is hard to come by in the daytime. Just as well she isn't in love at the moment; she's too knocked out for sex. And it's hot even with the fan. Impossible to get it dark enough to fool her sleep system. If you want air, you've got to have a little light too. Usually she's so wound when she first gets home around five, she can't settle. She does a couple of loads of laundry, defrosts the fridge. She doesn't vacuum since Tess is still sleeping. Later when she finally drops down into that exhausted heaviness where she dreams she's being run over by something with enormous tread, the noise of Tess racketing around on the stairs pulls at her. She wants to yell out her great need to be allowed to stay under, and maybe she actually does, but usually it feels like her mouth cannot pull itself open, that her arms are encased in an oily black ooze.

She overlaps a foot or so the roller mark of her last pass and creeps steadily forward. Around the smell of dust and exhaust, there's the smell of rain. Something's moving in that the sky doesn't know about yet. The lights come on; the big generator hums beneath the clank of her machine, the swash of gravel, the roar of the earthmovers, followed by the scraper's raking screech. Roadwork is noisy business even through her plugs. The roller lifts as it climbs over several rocks as big as basketballs. There are those tense seconds of imbalance and then the machine settles again. Ahead of her stretch three sections, each the size of her living room. Compacting, compacting until an early break at eleven and then only an hour or so after that on her own—word's come down they're knocking off early with full pay. A reward from the company—they're ahead of schedule and tomorrow's the Fourth of July. Until then all she has to do is roll.

The monk says it's good to follow your breathing. Breathing in, I am going forward. Follow your breathing and just let your thoughts float up. Like a guard at the palace gates, you know what is coming in; what is going out. In the distance, backing the flanks of the biggest machine, the final red glow of the sun. Carla rolls forward and breathes......one......two.......three...... It's hard to hear who's coming in and who's going out in all that roar.

Yesterday she found the back of the old dryer dented, the top beaten, the control dial smashed. On the opposite side of the barn, a rocker she'd hoped to fix up, broken to pieces, as though it had been hurled against the wall and then stamped into bits. Lying in the middle of the floor, Steve's wrecking bar. She knows what has happened—this is the scene of one of Tess's rages. So far she's never witnessed her furious smashing, has only come upon the broken results. Her first feeling is always relief. It's been things and not people she's hurled. So far. She knows, has known for a long time, Tess is not okay. There's a misfire someplace. And what Tess is doing is making it worse. Less spaces between. A constant jitter. Steve thinks she's making a mountain out of what's just being eighteen. He can't see it, was out of the house before it started: the going off over nothing, the angry eruption of dislocated words, the spooky silence after. Now the stealing, the coming home after she's gone to bed and still sleeping when she leaves. Of course Tess is hiding, avoiding interrogation. But this weekend, enough hours off in a row to gather her strength, she'll get Steve to come, Steve without Marion. She'll present him with the evidence—the morning-after fury in the barn. She'll tell Steve the part about no shadows. Maybe, calmly together, her mother and her father, they can find a way in.

Red's making the rounds, signaling time to shut down. That means everybody but the roller. He motions her that he has info. Up ahead Scott's leveling the last sections she'll do. There's the final mutter of dying machines. She turns hers off too and comes to rest in the quiet, scans her body, the shooting pains in her wrists. Clem and Berton flash her a wave and head out for home. Red cuts the lights along the line, all but the sections she'll roll. She slides down. After her butt and her legs have been vibrating, bumping along for hours, the return to earth surprises her feet. There are a few weightless moments, a shifting of gravity, time to convince her limbs they're of equal length.

In this semi-dark state of imbalance, Red's voice makes her jump. "Carla, I figure you've got about an hour to go. Take whatever break you need and then get that final section good." He sniffs the air, raises his hand like he's checking the breeze. "Feels like rain and we won't be back till Monday."

She nods and sways from side to side, stamping her feet to bring the blood down.

"Scott'll be done by the time you finish your break and then he's going to hang out and close down for me here after you've rolled. He'll give you a ride back to your car."

"Is that all settled?" she hears her voice say. It's been hours since she's spoken. And what she wishes that voice said is, Red, don't leave me.

"Yep, everything's set." He looks over his shoulder, leans his head to one side and closes his eyes, like he's going through an is-there-anything-I-forgot routine. Then he gives her a smile and moves off in the dark. "Have a good long weekend," he calls. "Get yourself out on a picnic. See the fireworks. You deserve it."

"You too," she answers. Then she hears the slam of a door, watches his taillights recede. The scraping of the bulldozer pushing gravel stops. Just her and Scott, alone on the road. She breathes. Her guard at the gates is making the moves to calm down.

Scott backs the bulldozer in beside the two trucks. He gets off and starts toward the roller. He's a tall man, maybe fifty. One of those men who hasn't started to age. Lean. A man who never sits down. No, he isn't what you'd call good-looking, but he's got that, whatever it is, you know he's there without even turning around. The only man on the job who gives her that jolt. Just like the magazine said. She knows he's married, but he's got the eye, that flicker of current; he's still testing the air.

When he's within range, she calls to him, friendly, no edges, she hopes, "Going to duck into the woods for a minute, and then get rolling. Get us out of here as fast as I can."

"Okay by me," he says. His face is in shadow, his back to the light. In the three months she's been on the crew, this is their first trade of words.

She leaves him leaning against the machine and with her flashlight locates her path, jumps the ditch and heads for the turf she's marked as her own. There's the smell of wet grass and manure from the cow yard just down the way. She hears an occasional sighing moo, the thud of heifers bumping the fence. The thicket of pines is her perfect close spot. Portable toilets back by the trailer are too far to do her much good. When she first started working, she'd expected joking asides on her returns from the trees, but instead there's been that same respectful distance, a shy looking away. No question, the bathroom breaks are easier for guys, but with practice she's got it down to an elegant bit. The monk says, whatever you're doing, be doing it. Breathing in, I'm unzipping my pants. He's big on the present, says that's all there is. Sounds simple, but no, it's hard to stay *here*. From where she squats in the dark, she sees the fiery glow of what must be Scott's cigarette. Crickets, frogs, some rhythmic chub-chub no one can name, the love songs of night once the roadwork shuts down.

She scrambles up the bank and heads for her roller's familiar dark hulk. No irregular lumps, no signs of Scott. One cigarette and then hit it and then the drive home—to sleep in the cool dark of night, the pleasure of that. And no electrical detours. Remember, she's fasting: No More Men. For a while. She pockets her flashlight and reaches up for a match. It's then that she knows he's somewhere there in the dark.

"Scott?" she moves away from the roller, back into glow of the lights down the line.

His flashlight goes on. "I'm here by the generator. Just making sure I'm going to know how to shut it all down."

She puts her light back on, too, even though she doesn't really need it here. Is she imagining it or was he spooking around? "Got a match? One quick cigarette and then I'll get going." Just the patter of words stills the bump of her heart. By now he's moved out of the dark. He strikes a match for her and takes out a cigarette for himself.

"Got any big plans for the Fourth?" she says.

"Not really."

She is going to have a conversation with this man. Words, any words, will do. Drain the current out of this situation, her attraction. "Me either. I'm just looking forward to being off that roller for a while."

He steps back a few paces and haunches down, braces himself against the bumper of the dump truck, but he doesn't offer any response.

Okay, forget the chit-chat; she'll try something real, "Well, actually I'm getting my strength up to deal with my eighteen-year-old daughter. She's heading into some serious trouble and I'm hoping I can get her father to come down, that between the two of us, we can help her make some kind of turn."

"What kind of trouble?"

Carla, don't blow this. "Well, for one thing, drugs. But, not just that, she goes into these out-of-control rages." She's telling this man stuff she has trouble telling herself.

"And you can't get her to see anybody?"

"Just the mention of it sets her off. She says nobody's going inside her head."

Scott settles full on the bumper and bends forward a little, shakes his head like he's in there thinking. She scoots onto the step-up to the dozer cab.

He turns a little more in her direction, "My brother's son had a lot of problems. Billy, my nephew. Looked like he was just a screwed-up kid at first. Problems in school. Drugs, stealing, you name it."

Up out of nowhere, tears. And they just keep coming. She wipes her eyes and nose with her sleeve.

"You okay?"

She nods, gets out another cigarette. He hands her the pack of matches. No, she isn't okay. Tess's been pretty much morning, noon, and nighting through her brain for weeks. Oh, longer than that. How many years? And how many years more?

Bugs sputter around the big light poles over by her last place to roll. They sit and smoke. Feels like there's no hurry; the night has slowed down.

"My brother and his wife have actually had to call the police a couple of times to get Billy to a crisis center."

"My god, I don't know if I could do that. Tess'd never forgive me." But that's not quite it.

"That's what my brother said, but he was afraid Billy was going to do himself or somebody else real harm. Well, he just went to the phone and did what he had to do. He knew there was no way of getting him in the car. But here's the thing: Billy's doing better now. No miracles; it took a long time. He goes to this clinic in Marwick."

She knows Tess'd never go to any clinic.

Like he's read her silence, he says, "Yeah, my brother and his wife figured Billy wouldn't ever get help, but after a couple of late night trips to the hospital, he started taking some medication. One of the crisis people got something going with Billy. This young counselor."

Maybe if she'd been there when Tess smashed the rocker, her fear for her, for it all, would have got her to the phone.

"The clinic and the crisis center are listed under Onango County. My sister-in-law said she started sleeping better just having the numbers handy."

"I am so tired of it," she hears herself say.

Scott shifts away a little. "We don't have any kids. So I can't ever really know what any of that feels like. Having to pick up that phone. The rest of it." He rises and looks toward the last section.

"I'm going to start making the final rounds, but I'll be within earshot if you need anything."

He's already passed back into darkness before she jars loose. She steps up onto the roller and shifts into low. The lever is cold in her hand. The roller begins its steady roll. There's always more give until it packs down.

Tess. Something has lifted.

It isn't until she shifts into reverse that Scott's words actually enter her mind. *And all the rest of it.* The longing. And she didn't even respond. No children. She can't begin to wrap herself around that. She creeps the roller forward again, squinting to see, with her back to the light. There's an orange glow from an upstairs room of the farm house down below. This new road, running so close, must be a sad sight for them.

One of those funny moons is just coming up over the barn. It's then that she sees the white spots moving, bobbing about two or three feet from the ground. And hears mournful groans. It's then she realizes what those flashes of white are. She turns the roller off.

"Scott," she calls, trying to throw a calm voice back into the dark. "Look toward the barn." The monk wouldn't have missed this one for anything.

Up on back legs, a white-spotted cow. Mooing. Moaning. Crying and dancing under a lopsided moon.

32
Message – 1993

Mark shifted his messenger bag and veered the bike to the right—catch the fast lane down the center. The bus on his left pressed him. Squeezed him. He banged hard on the door. Fucker moves over another foot, bike's going to be on the hood of the taxi. He banged again, "Check your mirror, you mother." He dropped in behind the limousine and glanced at his manifest: *5565 Madison Ave. Suite 816. Rush.* He needed a signature. That'd slow him down. He ran the light.

No batteries for the walkman, a drum payment due on the 15th, whenever that was. Down to rolling his own. Lyrics for a song: *Messenger Blues*. Plus the major motif—*And my girlfriend's pregnant.* Only four thousand songs exploring similar heartaches. Everybody rolling their own.

Kid about to step off the curb. He swerved to the left. "Look out, Buddy." 4556, 4560. Next block. Traffic lighter now. He made a U-turn—honking of horns—gave the driver a smile and a wave, flipped his toe clips, and eased the bike to a stop by a good pole. No need to remove the front tire in this neighborhood. Doorman across the way had the eagle eye. He wrapped the chain twice around the forks and pushed hard on the U-lock until he heard the click, then glanced back at the bike while he slid the bag to his chest to keep it from catching in the revolving door. Even though he'd sprayed the bike black to cover the brand name, to tone down its resale value, a good thief could tell what a beauty of a track bike it was just by its silhouette.

He pressed 8 and stepped to the back of the elevator. The thing was he and Marlene should not have a child. Level of chaos so extreme it'd already zoomed off the chart. Have to X every *No* on the

Ready to be a Good Parent test.

"Excuse me," he said to the coats and ties and stepped out. His own fashion statement—padded bike shorts over his best navy long johns. His sneakers squeaked on the marble floor. People beavering away beyond the opaque glass. Gnaw ... gnaw. Floating it all over to the big lodge. 812, 814, 816. *Berlinger, Smythe, and Co.* He unzipped his bag, thumbed through to the right envelope and turned the shiny brass knob. No one at the reception desk. Rush, rush, here I am. All the doors closed. He checked his sheet. Next delivery only a few blocks away. Still having to prove himself to his new employers: Meteor Messenger Service. Needed wings on his Converse All Stars. Especially since he had no money to get high, his preferred means of travel. He drummed out a catchy little number on the desk. No response from the doors. No perky *May I help you.* Give it a couple of minutes before he upped the volume. He set his bag on the floor and settled into the padded chair.

No ifs, no buts, they had to get the money for the clinic together immediately. No time to wait around for the whole welfare trip. The longer they put it off, the sadder, the worse it got. Him, forced into the *Let's Be Rational* part of the duo. Him? More proof of how truly off the charts the situation was. Marlene? Marlene kept her toe shoes in the oven for gods sake. Not that there were any less roaches in there. Maybe because the neighborhood junkies might not consider it. Whenever she wasn't practicing or headed to dance class, into the oven they went. She wouldn't say why. But for him, it was just one more piece in the pile of evidence that they could not have this baby. Got to call the clinic, see how much it costs, and come up with the money somehow. Aaron? Address unknown. No hope there. And he absolutely was not going to ask his mother. No windfalls headed Marlene's way either. Tell my father I'm pregnant, ask him for money? Marlene's frequent refrain when she'd been talking enough to do any refraining. Hadn't even let her dad know when she was in the psych ward. One thing in their favor: It wasn't February.

West 28th quiet. Flower shops all closed, but still the smell of roses. Roses and rain coming. And of course the smell of gutter garbage, always the gutter garbage and exhaust. Overall not a bad beginning at Meteor. Impressed them with his speed. Rough no pay coming for the first two weeks, but clear no amount of could-you-possiblies was going to change that and he could hardly lay the abortion thing on them. No gig money in sight either. The group just trying to find the time to put together some new stuff, put together a new demo. He hoisted his bike up onto the stoop and checked the windows on the fourth floor. Open. Marlene was back from the diner early. No dinner tips, but maybe she'd gone to a payphone, made the call. If she wasn't too low, got to put together a plan. That evening. Not tomorrow. Now.

The last flight was always a killer. Finding this dog-sit in a loft with them only having to kick in three hundred a month, a place where he could play his drums, room for Marlene to work out, a streak of unusual good fortune—a vast improvement on squat-living where they'd had to go in through the steel doors in the sidewalk. But with each flight of stairs, his bike always gained another fifty pounds. No sympathy forthcoming from Marlene if he came in huffing—smoke, smoke, smoke them cigarettes all she'd say when she was still saying much of anything. Twenty-seven and already his lungs black, his hair going gray. Just like his father's. Just like you, Dad, in I don't want to count the ways.

As soon as he put the key in the lock, Lovely began to bark, the thud of her Great Dane bounce against the other side sending a tremor through the frame. "Hello, Lovely, it's me." He turned the key and when the door didn't open, he unlocked the flange-lock too. Quadruple the barricade, but if they wanted to steal his drums, all they had to do was blow-torch the center panel of the door out like they did the sculptor's on the first floor. And he could not bear to spray-paint his new Pearls to cut down on their resale value. He kept them under a ratty old comforter, but that was even more lame than the oven.

Lovely embraced him, her paws planted on his shoulders, her wet tongue covering him with kisses. Marlene's leg stretched along the barre, her chest to her knee. Her pale, perfect arm extended. She did not turn her head. "Hey," he said. "You got off early. That's good."

Her only response a sigh of breathing correctly. Almost three months along, but her body in denial too. He lifted Lovely's paws and once all of her was down, gave her a good scratch under her chin. Then he wheeled the bike over by his drums. He pulled off the comforter—just looking at them helped. He surveyed the rest of the room—place needed some attention. Trash can spilling over. Sink full of dishes. Mattress, stacked with a mix of dirty clothes and wadded covers. Been a while since either of them had been up for playing house. Have to do a thorough before Gregory returned from his parents' in Oregon. At least Gregory's space on the balcony, still tidy. Nice guy, Gregory. Going to give his mom and dad the ultimate bad news—HIV positive. Gregory willing to let them continue the share if the three of them could keep it together. Along the *Let's Be Rational* lines, this seemed like a stretch.

Marlene shifted to the other leg.

"Had an okay day on the bike. No fuck ups. Made good time. Told me to come in tomorrow."

Marlene looked past him—sad—but said nothing. Marlene. Marlene. Low, but not so low she couldn't make herself do her work-out. A good sign. But too late to call the clinic today.

"Going to take Lovely for a w-a-l-k." Lovely began to leap. "You want us to wait for you?"

Maybe a twist of the knot on the back of her head, her black hair pulled so tight it slanted her eyes.

Lovely's leash was not on the hook by the door. Not on the sink. The refrigerator. "Lovely, be lovely and stop jumping. Please." He lifted random piles of stuff. What he wouldn't give for a pack of Camels. Flip the box open, pull out a firm smoke, flick his lighter, suck in, ahhh. "Any idea where the leash is?"

Maybe another shake of her head. Marlene was balanced on one leg, her other leg raised behind her. Swan. She could do this forever.

Either of them remembering to put the leash on the hook was another matter. Mark took a piece of clothesline from the drawer and fastened that to Lovely's collar. "Be good if we could talk when I get back," he said. "You don't have to bother with the flange." But before they got to the first landing, he heard the bar drop into place.

Marlene was a lump under the piles on the mattress when they returned. Lovely joined her. The message was clear: I don't want to think about it. She'd been like that for weeks. He opened the Bugler

can—getting low—dumped a bunch of tobacco on a sheet of paper
and began to roll the cigarettes he was going to need for tomorrow.
Progress for sure. He'd even scrounged a couple of Camel boxes from
the trash to carry them in. "Marlene, it'd be good if you came up out
of there. I think you know what we have to do."

She didn't answer. Only Lovely's tail beat up and down whenever
he spoke.

He clipped off the ragged shreds on the ends of the first cigarette,
lit up, and then started to roll another. He'd like to beat out some
of this on the drums, but that was not the best strategy for getting
Marlene to surface. One foot in front of the other—forward was the
direction he needed to focus on. He sat and rolled, phrases of a song
bleeping up, then flattening with each drag, his heart beat, beat, beating in the quiet.

He carefully placed the cigarettes in the boxes. Then he bagged
up the trash and set it by the door. The dog rose. "Not yet Lovely."
He turned on the light in the bathroom and turned it off again—the
condition of the tub and toilet beyond his current level of pretend.
Instead he began on the dishes. First he emptied the sink quietly so
as not to jangle Marlene, Marlene who was only a few months back
from Bellevue—delusions extraordinaire. Her name was Mary and
somebody kept fucking up the message the angel Gabriel left on her
machine. Made the approach to ending this pregnancy tricky indeed.

Once all the dirty dishes were up on the drain, he needed to scoop
out the glop that had slid to the bottom: strings of spaghetti, bits
of Chinese Take-out, Cheerios, and hunks of Lovely's Kibbles had
all glommed together. He held his nose with one hand and used a
spatula to shovel out with the other.

Once the dishes were done, all but the soakers, he began to sort
through the piles to figure out what was dirty, what was clean. He
gave Marlene's tights, his black pants the smell test and stuffed them
both into a raunchy pillow case. He put together three loads. When
he began to count out five dollars in quarters from Marlene's tip
money, there were signs of life beneath the blankets. Another good
indicator. "I'm taking five dollars for the laundromat," he said. No
response. If he'd said for cigarettes, maybe she would've popped out
to protest.

He folded everything else and sorted it into neat stacks: mine, hers, towels, other. Then he swept, wetting the edge of a newspaper to create a dust pan to push the mouse turds and tobacco, the dead water bugs, the city grit onto. Little trick learned from you, Dad. Though something more substantive might have been in order, eh?

He sat down at his drums, made a few adjustments of the cymbals—his top of the line Zildjian—and mimed a roll. Place was looking better. A little breeze lifted the sheet they'd tacked across the window. Still the smell of roses four flights up. Maybe when he coaxed Marlene out into all this order, her mind would clear long enough to hear what any benign angel was bound to say: Call the clinic.

The sound of a car alarm woke him. Lovely went to the window and looked out. Marlene was curled up so tight he had trouble lifting her arm, turning her wrist to see the time. 8:30. Shit. He had to be at Meteor by eleven. Marlene was probably supposed to work lunch. She'd been basically comatose since he got home yesterday, so she might not even go to work. Not much time to pull the whole thing together. "Marlene?" Her back to him, her back always to him these days. He jiggled her shoulder. She remained limp. "Marlene, how about if we go down to the corner and at least call, see how much it costs, tell them you're almost three months along?" He felt her body tighten. She was in there. "Find out, if you decide to do it, about how long you'd have to wait?" Her body still rigid, but no words forthcoming.

He got up and pulled on his bike shorts, his shoes. "I could call, but they're not going to let me make any arrangements. They're going to want to talk to you. You're the one who has to say, This is what I have to do."

He tied the clothesline around the meter and gave Lovely a sorry pat when she tried to press into the phone booth behind him. He checked his list of questions. He didn't want to forget something and have to get up for this again. Already having to quell the rising urge to walk over to West Side Highway and stick his thumb out, the urge to turn his back on this situation until it disappeared. He dialed the number.

Four hundred dollars. Since she was heading into the second trimester, since the situation sounded difficult, they could probably see her for counseling in the next few days and go from there. Yes, of course, she had to be the one to make the final arrangements. He pressed his forehead against the cold metal: get the money, zap Marlene out of the zombie-state, arrange the time off from work. He pushed the phone booth door open slowly so as not to catch the dog's nose. "I don't know, Lovely, but somehow, we've got to bring this off."

Black strands of hair over the pillow, the only proof that Marlene was still part of the heap. He reached in and found her arm: 9:15. He had to be headed uptown by 10:30 to get to Meteor by 11. Marlene needed to do lunch if there was any hope of putting together the rent on time. "Marlene, I just called the clinic. They seemed to fully understand our situation. I've figured out a way to get the money. If you call this morning, chances are good they can talk to you, help us this week." He slowly lifted off the first layer of blankets. She didn't move. He folded back the sheet.

She opened her eyes, the first time she'd really looked at him in days. Tears. "If your father had made your mother do this, you wouldn't even be here."

He didn't say that at this moment, such a release didn't strike him as such a bad option.

"Marlene, what about your dream to be a dancer? We're struggling just to take care of ourselves. Look around you: Is what we've got going here a world you want to bring a baby into?"

She sat up. He took hold of her and set her on her feet. He led her into the bathroom. "See if you can get yourself together enough to make the call. Just make an appointment to talk to the counselor, then see what you feel up to from there." He pulled the door closed, heard the water running. He counted out the money for the calls, then gave the snare a pat, threw the comforter over the set, and tucked it under the edge of the bass.

The quarters, the dial tone, the number, the extension. He kept his eye on Marlene, so she wouldn't fade away. "Could I speak to Katherine Barker?" He put his hand on Marlene's shoulder while he waited.

"This is Mark Merrick. I spoke to you about half an hour ago ...Yes, my girlfriend Marlene Dashel is right here." He handed the phone to Marlene.

Marlene listened for what felt like forever. Then she said, "Nine o'clock tomorrow." She left the receiver dangling and started back toward the loft.

He bent and gave Lovely a reassuring scratch. Then he dropped in the last quarters. A sleepy voice answered. "It's Mark. Yeah, you know the Pearls, are you still interested? ... Got two more fifty dollar payments ... I'll know definitely by tomorrow ... I could let you have them for six hundred. Have to get the money to me in the next day or two."

The drums or the bike—without the drums, he can't make music; without the bike, he can't work. He untied the leash from the meter. "Just a few more days of faking our way through, right Lovely?"

See why you weren't quite up to it, Dad—this going on, one foot in front of the other, a real heavy-duty effort.

A few hours for the whole thing is what they said. Then a few days of rest. Been three hours already. The woman working at the desk, answering the phone, older, no-nonsense face. At least that was heartening.

Place full of waiting women. Women went in, women came out. Young and not young, all colors. None of them smiling. Him, the only male. Every half-hour or so, he went down to the street to smoke. Woman at the desk always saw him go, always saw him come back. Main thing when Marlene came out, he should be there.

"Well?" he said as soon as he got off the elevator.

"Go on down and flag a taxi," the woman said. "By the time you get back up here, she'll be ready to go home."

He stepped out into the street, raised his hand. Home? Home? Marlene might be about to walk out that door, but going home wasn't what they were about here.

"Clean sheets," was all she said. Then she curled on her side and within minutes little puffs of breath the only signs of life. He watched her face, her lashes black against the faint blue skin below her eyes, the rest of her white, see-through pale. She hadn't burrowed in. Maybe in a few days she'd come through this, be steady enough to be on her own.

Because, Dad, one lesson you taught me for sure: not much further along this road, it's all going to bust up and go down.

33
Vessels – 1993

Carla drops a dozen packs of Juicy Fruit and a large bag of Gummy Bears by the cash register. Chewing—how she plans to get through this hospital thing. The counter at JAKE's is so loaded with Christmas lights and holly, it's hard to find a place to lean. She resists the urge to give the plastic Santa a smack. Instead she checks her horoscope in the *Sun* while Lois rings her up.

> *CANCER (June 22-July 22) You will be able*
> *to right a wrong today if you are mindful.*
> *Remember first things first and that for the*
> *moon, there is the cloud, so don't try to do*
> *everything all at once.*

Whatever happened to 'You're about to meet someone exciting: Go for it?' What's this horoscope person on? 12 Step or Zen? She can't decide.

"That it?" Lois says.

"Better give me a carton of Marlboros too. I was going quit while I was in the hospital, but according to my horoscope …" She stops before she gets to 'everything all at once' because Lois will nose right in on that.

Lois eyes the brace on Carla's wrist. "My cousin had it—this carpal tunnel surgery—and they didn't even keep her overnight. Gave her a local and shoved her out the door. You got to be dying before they'll give you a bed."

Carla roots around in her purse not really listening. She doesn't listen as well to people now that she doesn't owe them money—one good thing about her roadwork job. But if she can't get herself on disability when her unemployment runs out, probably have to start tuning back in. She fishes out her last fifty. Feels a twinge in her arm, a tingling in her thumb. About time for a little something to ease her. Important not to arrive at the hospital in a lather.

Lois checks her own wrists. "How'd you get that carpal thing anyway?"

Another pain right up to her elbow. "Running the roller." Just the thought of Forward .... Reverse .... Forward .... Reverse ups the throbbing. "Plus it being congenital," she adds. Lois'll love that.

"Only a few days till Christmas; no time to be in the hospital. Big storm on the way besides. They going to let you out this afternoon?"

"Well ... probably not. My condition's a little more ... complicated." She is certainly not going to get into complicated by what. Lois would have that on the wires from Danford to Stanton before closing.

Lois pushes the bag toward her. "I hear Del Merrick has cancer."

Carla hears that. A pang of guilt hits her. She hasn't heard anything about Del since Del rented out the stone house again and got herself another apartment in Marwick.

"I heard she's at Memorial. Isn't that where you're going?"

Carla looks at her, even though she doesn't want to know any more.

"That's all I heard," Lois says, "but you know how cancer usually goes."

Carla turns and starts for the door.

"Hey, don't you want your groceries?"

She takes what Lois hands her.

"Why don't you call Richard Larson; he'll be able to tell you. Those kids of hers, lord only knows where they are."

"Right," Carla says. At least she knows where Tess and Rudy are, sort of, but right now given this whole detox thing, just as well they aren't around.

"Merry Christmas," Lois calls.

Carla pulls the door closed on the jingle, jingle of the goddamn bells. She slides the bag onto the seat and takes out her keys, but instead of putting them in the ignition, she sits looking at the Budweiser sign. Breast cancer. Ovarian cancer. Colon cancer. She feels random pulses of malignancy secretly at work in her body. She rips open the carton and gets out a cigarette. Definitely not the time to quit smoking. Zen or whatever—Carpal tunnel and this little over-doing of the Vicodin for pain, well it's a lot better than having cancer. But, hey, Del Merrick's twelve years older than she is.

Carla starts up her new, well new to her, car—a 1985 Dodge Dart. Only 90,000 miles. Four tires with tread. Even a little Saint Christopher medal dangling from the mirror. Not having cancer and a car that runs—Count your blessings would have been more like it. No matter what Rudy says about vintage, finally she's going to send the Maverick to the crusher.

What was it her horoscope said? 'Right a wrong.' Right a wrong? Didn't she already apologize big time about bringing Wynn over to Del's? Like she had any real say in the matter. Wynn and Mark were going to do what they were going to do. It's not like she was snorting that stuff.

Maybe she could go back and get one of those sappy get well cards. Del might think that was funny. She still owes Del the five hundred from when Rudy got busted at the Dead concert. Hell, maybe she can even go visit Del right in her hospital room once the tunnel surgery's over, before they really get her going on the other thing. Go in there and give Del a twenty-five-dollar installment.

The sky's heavy and gray—big snow coming for sure. She can smell it even through the smoke. Carla checks her rearview, gets a hot flash of Raoul painting the Inn. Raoul, his muscles rippling as he climbs the ladder. Raoul, about a hundred years ago. Well, at least she'd been smart enough not to go for that. She starts to back out. Her wrist shooting pain now. She puts the car in Park again and pulls out the vial she has taped under her seat. It's a little too soon, but she's starting to sweat. She dumps six pills into her shaking palm. That baby doll doctor better not start poking around again about where she's been getting this stuff. Certainly he hadn't believed it was just something her mother left in her medicine cabinet. A year's supply of a controlled substance? Somehow, Mrs. Morletti, that doesn't quite compute. Real bedside manner this guy has—doesn't quite compute.

She makes a left at the Inn. Might as well take I 88. Get there a little early, find out what room Del's in. Scope the situation out. Maybe she's imagining it, but her wrist feels better already.

Tess jiggles the knob and pushes hard. Locked. The kitchen and back locked too. No smoke coming from the chimney. No car in the driveway. Only the long-dead Maverick in the barn with the hood up. Maybe her mother doesn't even have a car now that she's been laid off for the winter. Tess bangs on the door. No sounds of movement. She raps on the glass again, then stoops to peer under the duct tape. Something's up. Her mother never locks the house unless she's going to be gone for a long time. Someone wants to come in and steal my K-mart silver, they're welcome to it, she always says.

"Jumping Jesus." Tess moves off the porch. Once again struggles to fit her feet into the foot-deep prints that lead back through the hard snow to the road. Her mother's footprints? The walk not shoveled for a long time. Something's gone kawacky for sure. Her sneakers soaked, the bottoms of her jeans icy, her fingers ready to fall off. She left Austin for this? Drove two thousand miles practically night and day, leaking oil and water, so her mom won't have to be alone on Christmas—for this?

She gets back behind the wheel and slams the door. Almost out of gas and the heater doesn't work for shit anyway. She pulls the blanket she appropriated from the last Super 8 around her legs and chest. When is she going to learn? What had she been expecting? Sugarplum fairies, stockings hung by the fire? "Yeah, right."

She contemplates the sky about to dump a blizzard, contemplates her options as Del Merrick used to say. Del Merrick. Maybe there's enough gas to get to Del's if she coasts down Fyler Hill. But who knows if Mark or Aaron or Del, any of them, are still around. Del and her mother on the outs even before she ran off to Texas a year ago. Her mother says it's because Del went and got all uptight about everything. Her mother—always good at coming up with rationales that leave her blameless.

Tess wiggles her frozen toes. Have to do something très pronto before they turn black and start to rot. She scoots out and reaches behind the seat for her keyboard and her backpack. Struggling under the weight of the keyboard case and pack and dragging the blanket, she teeters back through the footsteps that are just enough off her normal stretch that every plunk down threatens to send her sprawling.

If she can get the cracked pane out, maybe she can reach in far enough to take hold of the bolt. She begins to pull on the frayed edges of the duct tape that's been plastered to the broken pane for as long as she can remember. Evidence of the night your father slammed out of here, her mother says. Exhibit A for when I get rosy-eyed, start missing married life. One look at that tape and my vision clears. Tess has heard it all a hundred times. A hundred times.

Her fingers are so stiff it's hard to get them to pick away enough of the tape's corners to yank the whole mess off. Plus she has to pee and the thought of squatting out in the snow clears *her* vision. She lifts her backpack and rams it into the glass, pokes the edges until all the shards drop away, then shoves her arm through, gropes around, gropes until her fingers find the freezing metal. She grips the bolt. "Come on you, you ..." The bolt slides free and she practically falls into the hall. Home. She jams the blanket into the window hole to keep out the wind. Cold as the arctic, but she's home.

Her wet clothes piled in the tub, the little bathroom heater blasting warmth over her red feet, under her flannel nightgown, she crosses her fingers and presses *Talk*. There's the reassuring buzz of a dial tone instead of what she was expecting—silence, due to non-payment. Ring, ring, ring. Marion's voice on the machine. Bullshit you aren't there. "Dad, it's me, Tess. Pick up. I'm at Mamo's."

"Tess?" Marion's sleepy voice. "Just a minute."

It's the middle of the morning for gods sake. A muffle of words. Marion's hand over the receiver. What's she saying? Probably: It's your daughter calling for money again. Season's greetings to you too, Marion.

"Tess. Tess, darlin', where are you, baby?"

"I'm sitting on the floor of mom's bathroom, my toes practically falling off from frostbite. Plus the pipes are frozen. Where's Mamo?"

"How'd you get here? Are you okay?"

Yammer, yammer from Marion in the background.

"I'm okay. But where's Mamo?"

"I think she was going to the hospital to have some surgery on her wrist and then …"

"Alone? Why didn't you go with her?"

"Minor surgery and then …"

"And then what?"

"Tess, I offered, but your mother got herself in such an uproar of accusations, everything I'd done wrong for the eighteen years we were married, everything since then, well, I could see I wasn't going to be a comfort."

"You should've gone anyway."

"I should've done a lot of things. How about if I come over now and thaw the pipes. Bring you back here to spend the holidays with us."

Another barrage from Marion.

"What hospital?"

"Probably Memorial. But Tess, your mother's going to have to stay for a few days. Some other complications."

"What?"

"Well, I'm going to let her fill you in on that."

"Papo."

"Baby, I'll be there in forty-five minutes."

"I don't have enough gas to get to the hospital."

"Forty-five minutes. Stay right where you are."

The phonebook is under a pile of junk mail. The house, a mess. More evidence of things gone awry. *Hospitals. Memorial.* Her finger aches, burns, when she pushes the numbers. "Could you please tell me if Carla Morletti is a patient? This is her daughter."

Come on, come on.

"Yes. Mrs. Morletti has been admitted."

"Is she okay? What room is she in? Does she have a phone?"

"I'm sorry that's all the information available at this time."

"Really? How come? It's practically Christmas."

"Sorry, no more information is available."

The trouble with a portable phone is you can't slam it down.

Richard goes into his son's room where Del draws when Andrew's at college. Del's white nightgown, the one with all the little pearl buttons, is in the drawer she's set aside for her weekends at his house.

What he sometimes calls her conjugal visits. Richard smiles at the gown's perfect folds. He holds it up to his chin, checks the length in the closet mirror. Very fetching. One of the shorter ones, she said. So it doesn't get in the way when they change the dressing. He lifts a flannel gown out next. Not as nice, but warmer, less of it. Hard to say. Del's time in a gown is so brief. Unless she's mad at him, she drops it on the floor when she gets into bed. A concession to him, to skin on skin. But in her own place, she even wears pajamas. Pajamas.

He places the gown in a bag on the table. 11:30. Snow's coming down so fast it's already covered the driveway. Got to get going. Stop at the florist. Should he get roses or one of those little dish gardens that last forever? Take some shampoo. The first thing she wants him to do is help her wash her hair.

Try the call one last time. He lifts the receiver and rests his finger on the final crossed-off number under Aaron's name in Del's address book: Nooley Baker. Nooley? Somehow just the name sinks his hopes of getting a lead on Aaron's whereabouts. How credible will information coming from a person named Nooley be? "Hello, this is Rich Larson. Is Nooley Baker there?"

"Who?"

"Nooley Baker."

"Who are you?"

He resists hanging up the phone. "Richard Larson and I'm trying to locate Aaron Merrick."

"What for?"

Don't get reactive: A call from Aaron to Del is the main objective here. "I'm a friend of Del Merrick's and she's in the hospital and I'm trying to get hold of her son Aaron."

"Aaron." There's a long pause. "Haven't been in touch with Aaron in … well, more than a year. Last I knew he was taking down trees—working for Asplundh in northern California. Del's in the hospital? How's she doing?"

"Am I speaking to Nooley Baker?"

"That's me. Something serious?"

"She had surgery yesterday, but well, well, we don't know for sure, but yes, she's doing okay. Can you think of anyone who might know where Aaron is?"

"Tell you the truth Aaron wasn't in such good shape last time I saw him. Your best bet is Carla Morletti."

"Not in good shape. You're the second person who's told me that. What do you mean?"

"Oh, you know. How about Mark? I think he's still in the City."

"I left messages for him on a few machines. But nobody answered at Morlettis."

"Big storm. You'd think Carla'd be holed up by the stove. Give me your number. If I come up with anything, I'll call you."

"I'm on the way to the hospital. You can reach Del's room if you get a lead. She's at Memorial in Marwick. The number's 416-5000. But … Nooley … if it's bad news … well, maybe you better wait and call me here."

Wet snow blows into the hood of his sweatshirt when Mark turns to face the oncoming truck. White-out conditions. He shifts the duffle strap to his other shoulder and sticks out his thumb. One good thing—this orange glow vest his last ride insisted he wear. Hunter with a big gun hanging on his back window. Now all he needs is a little flashing sign: *Going to see my sick mother.* The headlights slow—a brand new truck, woman at the wheel. Neither one the criteria for a likely hitch. She passes after giving him a quick glance.

Snow dying down some. He continues to walk backwards well off the road. Chances of catching a ride in this weather about zero. Got to be almost forty miles to the hospital. At least he's got waterproof boots. Not his usual holey Converse All-Stars. Working his way up the food chain, though still a few links down from being behind the wheel of his own vehicle, his foot on the accelerator.

Behind him, an ear-splitting whistle. The truck has pulled onto the shoulder about fifty feet up the road, woman with a big head of dreads, hanging out the door, her fingers between her lips.

"What the fuck?" Mark lopes toward her, his duffle catching him in the rear with each jog. By the time he gets there, the woman's back in the cab, her flashers going. He dusts the snow off his bag and hops in. "I appreciate this. Not the best conditions for being out on the road," he says, settling his stuff between his legs. He avoids checking her out too closely. You have nothing to fear from me. But instead of pulling back onto the highway, he feels her looking at him.

"Don't you know who I am?" she says and turns to give him a big-mouthed grin. "I didn't recognize you until I saw you moving in the rearview."

The dark-eyed face beneath the wild black dreadlocks—a younger version of Carla. "Tess. Tess Morletti. Well, what do you know? Nice truck."

"My dad's. He's even got studs. Can't see for shit, but ..." Slowly she moves along the shoulder and then eases back onto the road, her flashers still going. "Four-wheel drive, a heater that works: makes me think about quitting the band and getting a real job. Where you headed?"

"Marwick. My mother's in the hospital."

"You're kidding. That's where I'm going. My mother's at Memorial too. An operation on her wrist."

"You're in a band?" he says, pulling the orange vest off and stuffing it in his pocket. Keep it for the hitch back to the City ... If he goes back to the City.

"Little juke joints in Texas. I do the vocals, play keyboard. You know *poor, poor pitiful me* songs." She laughs. "Kind of places when the fight breaks out, you hope you don't get hit with a bottle. But it pays the rent. Meanwhile, we're working on our own stuff."

Tess can't even be legal, can't be more than nineteen. Maybe sixteen the last time he saw her. As soon chew you up as look at you.

Plow ahead of them. But the snow has stopped. Even a bit of blue sky in the distance. Tess turns the wipers off. "Thank you, Jesus," she says.

He holds his fingers to the vent, feels the burn of the thaw.

"Want the heat on a little more?" She ups the fan. "You still playing drums?"

Sad topic number one. Hard to be out in the world. Tess always was a talker. When she was little, she used to tag along when he and Aaron and Rudy would be out in the hills checking their marijuana plants. Tess running circles around them, saying, Let's have a conversation.

"I used to love to listen to you play the drums. You and Aaron, Rudy jamming. You had a big influence on me."

He unzips his jacket to let the heat get to his chest, the tightening around his heart.

"You still have that beautiful set of drums, your red Pearls?"

"No." Red Pearls are long gone. Poor, poor pitiful me. Whole forty miles going to be one sad topic after another.

"What have you got now?"

Might have to curl into a little worm-ball. "Had to sell my drums."

"Oh," she says, then reaches over and touches his arm. "Something serious with your mother? I always liked your mother. So … steady."

He takes a long breath and eases down in the seat, checks the ashtray. Unused. A non-smoking long way to the hospital. "Richard Larson … You remember him? He left a message where I've been staying in the City, said my mother was having surgery. Cancer. Couple of days ago. Said it would be good if I could come see her."

"Cancer. That's scary."

"Yeah."

"But it's good you got the message, that you're on your way. Fuckin' by chance I found out my mother … I wouldn't even have known she was in the hospital. I drive all the way from Texas to be with her for Christmas. Rudy's off somewhere selling tie-dye. I get home and she's not there. Doesn't sound like her surgery's serious, but there's some other thing going on—'complications' my father says, complications he refuses to divulge. My family—like playing Clue, always trying to figure out who did it. Your family like that?"

Family. Word takes him by the throat. Not a word he ever uses.

Tess adjusts her side mirror and turns a little his way, looks at him hard. "You know: Secret, secret, who's got the secret?"

Who's got the secret?

"So here I am imagining one catastrophic story after another. Cryptography. Like those games—how many words can you make with the letters c-o-m-p-l-i-c-a-t-i-o-n. Oh, you know. Or maybe you don't? Maybe you and Aaron, your mom, you come right out with it."

Aaron? He doesn't even know where Aaron is. And if he did what would he say to him? Forgive me for being such a shitty brother. The blinking light on the snow plow keeps saying help, help, help.

Tess sighs, a big huff, "Oh, don't mind me. It's just I haven't talked to anyone in days."

Days? Ever.

"You know, really talked to anyone since last Thursday. I say to my dad when he gets to my mom's, 'Tell me exactly what's up with Mamo.' And he says, 'I brought Marion's hair dryer for the pipes.' Enough to send me to the nut house." She turns toward him again. Makes him look her right in the eye. "Mark …"

Here it comes.

"Seeing your dad walking along the road is my earliest memory. One of my only memories."

Breathe. Breathe. He sees he's taken out a cigarette. There it is in his shaking fingers.

"You want to smoke? Just crack the window. Otherwise I'll have to hear about it from Marion."

"You knew my dad? You're not old enough to know my dad."

"The thing is you look so much like him."

He takes the smoke in; he lets it out.

"I was three years old. I was sitting on my mother's lap. Papo was driving. Rudy was leaning over from the back. Your dad was walking along the road. Black shorts with an orange stripe on the side. Something was wrong with him. That must be why I remember his face. Your face. My dad offered him a ride, but he wouldn't take it. I've been wanting to tell you this for years."

He flicks the cigarette away, lights another. His hand able to hold the match almost steady now.

"The thing is, Mark, it had to be that night that he died. All the next day our phone ringing and ringing, the news all over town. My father kept talking about how he should have stopped, how he should've brought him to our house and talked to him, how he should've taken him to the hospital."

"Taken him to the hospital?"

"Your dad was out of his mind. My father felt so guilty. He kept sitting in the kitchen going over it and over it. So later when we got to know you and Aaron, I always thought, if my dad, who didn't even know your father, felt like that, well … what it must have been for you, for Aaron, for your mother."

She hands him a paper towel. He takes it. She hands him another.

He wishes he had his hood up. He keeps it all quiet. He wads the paper into balls, stuffs them in his pocket.

"The thing is," he hears his voice saying, "for years, I thought I was the only one who knew … who knew he was crazy. Delusional. And I never told anybody—not Aaron, not my mother." His throat is so tight it's hard to swallow. "If I'd told somebody, they might've stopped him."

"That's hard," her voice so low he can barely hear her, "that's hard to live with."

"Yeah, to live with," he says. "I was thirteen. Just before we moved to town, I snuck up to the tent he was living in on the bluff. He had this cross, something he'd carved, standing on a box by his sleeping bag, a candle burned way down attached to it. My dad never went to church, never talked about God."

Tess turns the fan down. Quiet.

"You're the first person I ever told this." He rubs his throat, tries to relax the muscles. "I knew he'd have a notebook, that it might tell me, well, like you say, the secret, what was going on. He was always writing. Had his typewriter up on another box, a blank piece of paper in it. His notebook was in his duffle bag, this bag." He runs both hands along the rough canvas, feels the bulge of most of his worldly goods, feels his drum sticks, hard in the side pouch.

He's expecting her to lead him on, but she's quiet, just keeps a steady pace behind the plow, lets the plow lead the way, a mound of snow piles neatly on the edge as the big blade skins along, the highway before them almost bare.

"He was hearing voices. He was hearing voices all the time and they were telling him he didn't have long to live. And they were right."

She reaches over and grips his arm, grips it hard. For a while they move forward through the silence, through the white.

Marwick 2 miles. A blue hospital sign.

"You know that one song your brother wrote? The one about the sky? I love that song. I always thought it must have been about your dad." And she begins to hum. Low, husky, she sings, "Mystic mathematicians dodging all the tolls, following behind, between to fix the hole." Her voice swells now to fill the empty quiet, "Hole in the sky …"

He begins to drum softly on the duffle: *Lee Cobb Merrick US*

66643122, his father's square black print across its side.

"… hole in the sky, hole in the sky; a whole lot of this world has already died. I hope you know this; I hope you know why."

Beyond the pain machine and the IV stand—white light, white hills, trees deep in snow. The first time she's felt well enough to see that far from her body, all the tubes bringing things in, taking things out. Down the hall the sounds of children caroling. Brownies or maybe a Sunday school class going room to room. Surely they won't come in this room, her all hooked up, their round mouths singing *Away in the Manger*. She couldn't bear it. Even Mark and Aaron's little boy pictures she's had to place on the peripheries. Head on, they make her weep. Where is Aaron? *Address unknown* her returned letter said. No response from Mark. She needs a sign for her door: No children with their cowlicks, their reedy necks, their bony shoulder blades— no singing children allowed.

They've fastened her together with staples. Each one gives off a small signal every time her heart beats. When they changed the dressing this morning, she turned her head and closed her eyes tight. Some people look and some people don't, the tall nurse said—a sure nurse, a nurse like a wall. Ms. Wilamena Gras, RN, her identity card said. A nurse in an honest-to-god starched uniform. Kind of uniform her mother used to wear. Kind of nurse you want when you're stapled together from your pubic bone to several inches above your navel.

It's all a blur: Richard kissed her, then they sped her away in the wheelchair. The operating room was cold. She got as far as 8 in her count backwards and then at the point in time where number 7 should have been, she was being rolled to the recovery room, with her doctor squeezing her foot, saying, Terrific.

Terrific. What an odd word to choose. A word that doesn't hedge any bets. Surely it meant: We got it all. That had been her main thought the days and days and days before the surgery, Go in there and get it all. Right from the beginning, after the doctor had read the lab report, he'd said, If you're going to have cancer, uterine is the one to have. It's all contained in a vessel. You have a hysterectomy, we remove the vessel. Complete recovery likely. She wasn't a person who looked, but she was a person who believed. She kept having to reassure Richard. He wouldn't believe until the pathology on the lymph nodes came back. But all along she'd hung onto those words—*complete recovery likely.*

She should ease herself up in the bed, to look around a little, but any movement beyond shallow breaths causes the signals to turn threatening. As if on cue, the nurse appears. She gives Del a long look and raises the bed while she hums *Silent night, Holy Night* along with the carolers. Del does not ask to have the children barred. Wilamena would not approve.

The nurse hands Del a gizmo that looks a little like a miniature set of gas pumps: a platform housing two clear cylinders containing several small balls, from which dangles a baby blue hose. "Place this tube in your mouth and blow gently, steadily." Del blows a little. She feels a rising urge to cough. The balls struggle up. Maybe an inch. "Before too long, you'll be able to get them up to the top. You need to do this exercise five times an hour for the next few days."

Five times an hour? Half a blow and she's exhausted already. Del tries again. The balls rise several inches this time and then drop back to the bottom with a nasty click. A spasm grips her chest. Del presses her arms across her belly and lets out small controlled croaks. Each one pulls painfully on the incision. She squeezes the bulb that controls the morphine. An icy flow streams up her arm. It feels green. Another spasm of coughing erupts.

The nurse hands her a pillow. "Hug that when you feel it coming. Really cough now. Those little yips aren't going to get you anywhere."

Fine for this woman whose intestines are packed in like the trunk of a tree. Del grips the pillow hard and lets out a few more small barks. "It feels like I'm going to split open."

"You won't." And with that the nurse departs.

Del gives the balls another try. That can count as number three.

Over the foot of the bed, Del sees movement in the doorway. For a moment she's afraid it's the carolers, their leader about to gush in on a wave of yuletide cheer. But no it's a woman, with a bandaged wrist.

The person stops just inside the door, knocks. "Del," the voice calls above the singing, "you feel up for a little company?"

The cylinders drop from her hand and clatter on the floor below the bed. Carla Morletti. No she does not feel up for a little company: Carla's like-it-never-happened soliloquies. Carla advances to the side of the bed, everything about her turned down. Her gaze somewhere off to left. Fine, she doesn't want any large-eyed looks of concern. No need to be directly rude. Just give her a *Good of you to drop by.* Carla will get it and back her sweet self out the door.

Still not looking at her, Carla holds onto the side rail with her good hand while she pokes beneath the bed with her foot. "Nope, too far under. Want me to get someone?" She turns, checks the corners. "If there was a broom or something."

There are dark blotches beneath Carla's eyes, her big mouth's line-thin. And out it comes, the thing she was not going to do. "My god, Carla," Del says, "you look awful. What happened to your wrist?"

Carla sinks into the chair close to the bed. "I'm not as bad as I look."

Carla, in a baggy brown sweater, rather than her usual bright flash; Carla, a cigarette tucked behind one ear It's going to be a long, long soliloquy. "Actually at the moment I'm A.W.O.L."

Del settles in. Here they are. Carla's made her entrance. "A.W.O.L?" Del says. Too late for *so long it's been good to know you.*

"Trying to decide if I want to submit," Carla, still off in the middle distance somewhere, "submit to the second stage of treatment." She holds up her bandages for inspection. "They gave me a local: snip, snip. I had no idea my muscles were that color." She takes out a pack of Juicy Fruit and extends it toward Del. Finally gives Del a quick top to bottom scan before she veers off again, starts to chew with gusto. "Of course, I know what you'd advise. The usual."

"And what usual might that be?" Finally the large-eyed look and it feels good to eye Carla right back.

"Lois told me you were here. She said it was something pretty bad. How are you?"

"I'm going to be all right." Del pats the pillow. "If you feel up to it, try poking your foot under there again. I'm supposed to blow into that thing five times an hour."

Carla scoots low in the chair, her bandaged arm held high as though she's waving to Del over the rail. Del thinks of the puppet Lambchop, imagines Carla's thumb and index finger with a big lipstick mouth splitting open to say, I missed you.

From below, Carla says instead, "You're afraid of that big nurse, aren't you?"

"I am."

There's the sound of plastic dragging across the linoleum, Carla's grunting efforts. Inch by inch the bandaged arm sinks and Carla is once again upright in the chair. She hands the cylinders to Del. "Go," she says.

Del blows. The balls rise halfway. "That's four. What further treatments are you evading? What's going on with your wrist?"

"Carpal tunnel syndrome. I got it from my job."

"Bartending? Opening bottles?"

"No, driving one of those big rollers on a road crew."

The carolers are right outside now. "'O little town of Bethlehem, how still we see thee lie …'"

Del raises her palm like she's about to stop traffic. "Carla, I want you to go the door and tell those kids to scram."

Carla brightens. She gets up, pulls herself straight, and picks up speed. Del sees the white flash of her bandage, of her arms lifting as though she may fly. Carla, the wounded angel to the rescue. She fills the door. The singing stops as though Carla has placed her finger on their lips. In a stage whisper she says, "The nice lady inside has just gone to sleep."

Del snaps her eyes shut.

"The best Christmas present you can give her is to tiptoe down the hall. Santa's checking you out. That's right—tiptoe, tiptoe."

Carla returns. "Eight little girls in brown beanie hats. I didn't know they were still making children like that."

Children. A dangerous topic. Del breathes. Rudy and Tess. Mark and Aaron. What to let in, what to keep out?

The nurse's voice in the hall. Del lifts the cylinders and gives a good heave of breath. The balls shoot up to the top. "You are my witness," Del says.

"Lord help you."

Ms. Wilamena's coming. Carla sits up a bit, pulls her sweater sleeve down over her wrist. Carla on the run.

When the nurse rounds the corner, she takes them both in.

Del gestures with the cylinders still in her hand. "This is ... Carla Morletti." Her mouth can't quite do *my friend*.

The nurse nods and smiles. "Maybe you can help me take Ms. Merrick for a little jog."

Del clutches the pillow. "Oh, I don't think I'm ready for that. I can barely get the balls to the top." Surely it's too soon to stand and put one foot in front of the other.

Carla looks anxious.

"Just moral support," the nurse says. "I'll be right there too. But first it's time to DC the pain machine." With a deft pull she removes the needle and swings the machine away from the bed, rolls it to the door. "We're going to get you up for a little trip along the light fantastic."

And before Del can protest further, she's gone, only the squeak of the machine fading in the distance.

"The light fantastic?" Carla leans forward. "Maybe your nurse is in cahoots with the horoscope person." She goes to the window, rests her forehead against the glass. "I wouldn't mind a zap from that machine myself."

"Are you in pain?"

Del shifts to see past Carla, to see how the snow on the roof across the way sparkles. The sun on the snow, the glints of blue and red, how she's always loved that.

The nurse returns, a hospital gown and a package of slipper-socks at the ready. She slides back the blanket. Del's legs are suddenly there, on their own, white and weak and not looking up to the job. The nurse lowers the bed, the side rails. Del feels her anxiety rising with each maneuver, feels it wedge rock-hard under her sternum.

The nurse leans over Del. "Now I want you take hold of my shoulders with both hands."

Del raises her arms, "Are you sure ..."

"I am. Good. Let's slide your legs over the side. Great."

Del's toes are now resting on the cool linoleum. The middle section of her body, a sack of sand.

"All right, now let's get another gown on to fasten down the front. How are you doing?" She makes bows of several of the ties.

"I've felt better," Del says.

"Now for your slippers. Rubber strips to keep you from skating off."

They are green. The same color as the diamonds in the gown, the same color as the morphine. All tones of nausea.

"Perhaps your friend … Ms. … "

"Carla. Carla Morletti." Carla moves so she's standing behind Del.

"Could you just put your hand on her back. Just a steadying influence."

Before Del can caution Carla against the use of her wrist, Carla's hand rests solidly between her shoulder blades. The socks add the final touch of infirmity. They are warm and comforting. With that, the nurse lifts Del to standing, Carla's hand pushing from behind.

But Del can't straighten up. "They didn't leave enough in the middle," she says.

The nurse pulls the IV stand over so it's directly in front of Del. "Every day you'll be able to stretch out a little more." She curls Del's hand around the pole. "Ms. Morletti, I'd like you to come and take hold of her right elbow."

Carla grips Del's underarm, "Like this?" she says.

"Perfect." Ms. Wilamena supports Del on the other side. "Now we're a regular little brigade. Here we go. First the IV stand forward, then a step. Good. The stand again, another step."

Bent over, the staples pulling some, Del watches her green feet inch into the hall, feels the warm pressure of each woman flanking her. A few steps at a time they move toward the sunroom at the end.

In the room to the right, there's a scream, the call light flashing. The nurse takes her hand away, checks how stable Del looks. "You're holding steady," she says, "so I'm going to duck in here for a second, see what's going on. You two feel up for that?"

"Jim Dandy," Carla says.

Richard finds a clear space at the end of the hospital gift counter. He smiles at the drawing on the front of the card: a beautiful potato sitting in a slant of light. He opens the flap and writes in large script across the double white space: *O penny, brown penny, brown penny, I'm looped in the loops of your hair.* Wyeth, Yeats, and roses—the right sort of backup for the occasion. He wishes he could tell her he'd gotten hold of Aaron and Mark, that they're okay.

A dark head of messy twists of hair bobs by the display window. Why would someone make such a nest of tangles and stick a piece of metal in her nose? Something about her is so familiar. Beside her a tall, skinny—man or boy?—it's hard to say with his hood up. And then he knows who they are: Mark Merrick and one of Carla Morletti's progeny. Mark presses the elevator button. Richard watches them pause, watches them disappear behind the closing doors.

He settles on one of the hospital benches. No hurry. He can wait.

Conjugal visits. Still, when she gets out of the hospital, she says she's going to stretch out on his couch the whole six weeks. Convalesce, reread all her favorite novels, starting with *Middlemarch*. Have him bring her tea with lots of honey.

They move to the back of the elevator to make room for the wheelchair and an old man, his knobby bald head sunk onto his bony chest.

They look at each other, then squint their eyes, lean against the rail. Mark puts his hood down. Tess yanks at her hair.

Del Merrick's in room 320, they've been told, but Carla Morletti? Carla Morletti? That's funny. She's doesn't seem to have a room number, but well ... Check back in a while...

The plan: Tess will go with Mark to say hello to his mother, lower the intensity of his sudden appearance, then she'll roam, see if she can track down Mamo. Even in the hospital, it's like playing fucking Clue.

The French doors of the sunroom seem to be receding, tunneling away. Her left side sags without the nurse's grip.

"How about if we execute a U just past the water fountain?" Del says. "We'll tell her we've had enough."

They come to a complete halt.

"Ready," Carla says.

They begin to make the slow turn. The IV stand is so much heavier now.

Third floor. The elevator opens and they step out. Tess, first, Mark, close behind. *302, 304, 306.*

Just the thought of his mother, a reminder of all the things he should have been doing all along. No question it'd be better to be smoking a joint out in the truck.

They pass the nurse's station. That's when they see them. Making a slow turn in the distance. One woman bent over, scuffling forward in green socks, her hand on a pole from which dangles a plastic bag; the other woman in an old lady sweater, holding the bent one up.

Their mothers. Sort of.

Tess opens her mouth to yell.

"Wait." Mark catches the edge of her coat. "Let them maneuver the turn. The shock of seeing us might knock them over."

Tess falls back, takes hold of Mark's sleeve. "Sweet Jesus," she says. "Sweet Jesus," she says again. "What I mean is …" she points to her mother and Del, "they're not nearly as big as I remember."

Del keeps her eyes on her feet. Her green steps blur. Almost around the bend. She stops to rest. "You know what …" The dark sides of a blackout close in. Suddenly she lurches into Carla. "The thing is … the edge is so much closer than I thought."

Carla yells, "Nurse." She throws her bandaged arm across Del's chest. "No, the thing is … the thing is: Don't look down."

Epilogue

5

Or:

They realize they're in the same tempest, grab a chunk of debris, hang on, spell each other, miraculously survive, are eternally grateful, and mutually generous.

Del Merrick

Women and Men:

Rope and Bone.
Sunday and Saturday.
That and This.

He said, "It was our finest hour."
She wept.

Speaking in tongues
untranslatable,
they move in experimental spacesuits,
uneasy in the other's gravity.
(To say nothing of the difficulty of dancing.)

He can do anything:
come down the steepest place
from the top,
pull an engine,
take her there;
but he has a hard time balancing
with one hand on his jugular
and the other over his balls
while walking on diverging wires.

She's an X-cheerleader
with the possibilities of becoming
a Harpy
or Ma Joad
depending...

Scenario:

They meet on the Midway.
His arms leave her breathless.
He hits the ball to the top,
rings the bell,
and gives her the Kewpie Doll.

She's got nice tits
which she gives to him
along with "the best years of her life."

They marry:

After a brief honeymoon, they move to the edge.
While she stands washing diapers and thinks, "Is this it?"
he works at a job he does not like, afraid
he's missed the last train to the Elysian Fields,
but maybe not if he hurries. Then he won't be able
to get the car started and it'll All be her fault.

Alternate Endings:

She smokes, becomes thin, and drinks from a bitter cup,
pouring the dregs out day after day to someone similar.

He drinks and takes his comforts where he can.

Or/And:

She gathers the children together,
(whom the sins of both shall be visited upon later)
throws the stained mattress
up over the old Pontiac,
and heads out for godknowswhere.

Alternate Trips:

They marry in the Amherst Chapel,
build a ranch in Delmar,
take the kids to the orthodontist,
have sex every other Saturday,
make a will,
and wait.

Or:

They realize they're in the same tempest, grab a piece of debris,
hang on, spell each other, miraculously survive, are eternally
grateful, and mutually generous.

Acknowledgments

Always I am grateful for the comments of my West Kortright Centre and Cedar Key writing groups and the opportunity to read excerpts of this novel during the open mic sessions at Word Thursdays in Treadwell, New York. My thanks for the gift of time without interruption granted to me by the MacDowell Colony, the Saltonstall Foundation, Blue Mountain Center, Ucross, and Hedgebrook. Much appreciation goes to other writers who have critiqued the work along the way: Wayne Somers, Rose Mackiewicz, Michael Blaine, Forrest Bachman, Kim Ilowit, KK Dewart, Maggie Schramm, and Sue Spivack. And finally kudos to Jane Higgins, the book designer, and Teresa Winchester, for copy editing.

Ginnah Howard's stories have appeared in *Water-Stone Review*, *Permafrost*, *Portland Review*, *Descant 145*, *Eleven Eleven Journal*, *Stone Canoe*, and elsewhere. Several have been nominated for a Pushcart Prize. Her novel, *Night Navigation* (Houghton Mifflin Harcourt 2009), was a *New York Times Book Review* Editors' Choice. *Doing Time Outside*, Howard's second novel, was published by Standing Stone Books in 2013. The National Alliance on Mental Illness of New York State gave Howard their Media Award for work on behalf of those with mental illness and their families. For more information visit: **www.GinnahHoward.com**

CPSIA information can be obtained at www.ICGtesting.com
Printed in the USA
LVOW10s1546030315

429104LV00006B/817/P